A TAILOR-MADE *Bride*

A TAILOR-MADE Bride

KAREN WITEMEYER

BETHANYHOUSE

MINNEAPOLIS, MINNESOTA

Published by Bethany House Publishers
11400 Hampshire Avenue South
Bloomington, Minnesota 55438

Bethany House Publishers is a division of
Baker Publishing Group, Grand Rapids, Michigan.

Printed in the United States of America

ISBN-13: 978-1-61664-519-9

To Wes:

God could not have blessed me
with a more tailor-made husband.
Your love makes life a joy.

*Favour is deceitful, and beauty is vain:
but a woman that feareth the Lord, she shall be praised.*

....

Proverbs 31:30

$\mathcal{P}$ROLOGUE

San Antonio, Texas—March 1881

"Red? Have you no shame, Auntie Vic? You can't be buried in a scarlet gown."

"It's *cerise*, Nan."

Hannah Richards bit back a laugh as Victoria Ashmont effectively put her grandnephew's wife in her place with three little words. Trying hard to appear as if she wasn't listening to her client's conversation, Hannah pulled the last pin from between her lips and slid it into the hem of the controversial fabric.

"Must you flout convention to the very end?" Nan's whine heightened to a near screech as she stomped toward the door. A delicate sniff followed by a tiny hiccup foreshadowed the coming of tears. "Sherman and I will be the ones to pay the price. You'll make us a laughingstock among our friends. But then, you've never cared for anyone except yourself, have you?"

Miss Victoria pivoted with impressive speed, the cane she used for balance nearly clobbering Hannah in the head as she spun.

"You may have my nephew wrapped around your little finger, but don't think you can manipulate me with your theatrics." Like an angry goddess from the Greek myths, Victoria Ashmont held her chin at a regal angle and pointed her aged hand toward the woman who dared challenge her. Hannah almost expected a lightning bolt to shoot from her finger to disintegrate Nan where she stood.

"You've been circling like a vulture since the day Dr. Bowman declared my heart to be failing, taking over the running of my household and plotting how to spend Sherman's inheritance. Well, you won't be controlling me, missy. I'll wear what I choose, when I choose, whether or not you approve. And if your friends have nothing better to do at a funeral than snicker about your great-aunt's attire, perhaps you'd do well to find some companions with a little more depth of character."

Nan's affronted gasp echoed through the room like the crack of a mule skinner's whip.

"Don't worry, dear," Miss Victoria called out as her niece yanked open the bedchamber door. "You'll have my money to console you. I'm sure you'll recover from any embarrassment I cause in the blink of an eye."

The door slammed shut, and the resulting bang appeared to knock the starch right out of Miss Victoria. She wobbled, and Hannah lurched to her feet to steady the elderly lady.

"Here, ma'am. Why don't you rest for a minute?" Hannah gripped her client's arm and led her to the fainting couch at the foot of the large four-poster bed that dominated the room. "Would you like me to ring for some tea?"

"Don't be ridiculous, girl. I'm not so infirm that a verbal skirmish leaves me in want of fortification. I just need to catch my breath."

Hannah nodded, not about to argue. She gathered her sewing box instead, collecting her shears, pins, and needle case from where they lay upon the thick tapestry carpet.

She had sewn for Miss Victoria for the last eighteen months, and it disturbed her to see the woman reduced to tremors and pallor so easily. The eccentric spinster never shied from a fight and always kept her razor-sharp tongue at the ready.

Hannah had felt the lash of that tongue herself on several occasions, but she'd developed a thick skin over the years. A woman making her own way in the world had to toughen up quickly or get squashed. Perhaps that was why she respected Victoria Ashmont enough to brave her scathing comments time after time. The woman had been living life on her own terms for years and had done well for herself in the process. True, she'd had money and the power of the Ashmont name to lend her support, but from all public reports—and a few overheard conversations—it was clear Victoria Ashmont's fortune had steadily grown during her tenure as head of the family, not dwindled, which was more than many men could say. Hannah liked to think that, given half a chance, she'd be able to duplicate the woman's success. At least to a modest degree.

"How long have you worked for Mrs. Granbury, Miss Richards?"

Hannah jumped at the barked question and scurried back to Miss Victoria's side, her sewing box tucked under her arm. "Nearly two years, ma'am."

"Hmmph." The woman's cane rapped three staccato beats against the leg of the couch before she continued. "I nagged that woman for years to hire some girls with gumption. I was pleased when she finally took my advice. Your predecessors failed to last more than a month or two with me. Either I didn't approve of their workmanship, or they couldn't stand up to my plain speaking. It's a dratted nuisance having to explain my preferences over and over to new girls every time I need something made up. I've not missed that chore."

"Yes, ma'am." Hannah's forehead scrunched. She couldn't be

sure, but she thought Victoria Ashmont might have just paid her a compliment.

"Have you ever thought of opening your own shop?"

Hannah's gaze flew to her client's face. Miss Victoria's slate gray eyes assessed her, probing, drilling into her core, as if she meant to rip the truth from her with or without her consent.

Ducking away from the penetrating stare, Hannah fiddled with the sewing box. "Mrs. Granbury has been good to me, and I've been fortunate enough to set some of my earnings aside. It will be several years yet, but one day I do hope to set up my own establishment."

"Good. Now help me get out of this dress."

Dizzy from the abrupt starts, stops, and turns of the strange conversation, Hannah kept her mouth closed and assisted Miss Victoria. She unfastened the brightly colored silk, careful not to snag the pins on either the delicate material of the gown or on Miss Victoria's stockings. Once the dress had been safely removed, she set it aside and helped the woman don a loose-fitting wrapper.

"I'm anxious to have these details put in order," Miss Victoria said as she took a seat at the ladies' writing desk along the east wall. "I will pay you a bonus if you will stay here and finish the garment for me before you leave. You may use the chair in the corner." She gestured toward a small upholstered rocker that sat angled toward the desk.

Hannah's throat constricted. Her mind scrambled for a polite refusal, yet she found no excuse valid enough to withstand Miss Victoria's scrutiny. Left with no choice, she swallowed her misgivings and forced the appropriate reply past her lips.

"As you wish."

Masking her disappointment, Hannah set her box of supplies on the floor near the chair Miss Victoria had indicated and turned to fetch the dress.

She disliked sewing in front of clients. Though her tiny boarding-house room was dim and lacked the comforts afforded in Miss Victoria's mansion, the solitude saved her from suffering endless questions and suggestions while she worked.

Hannah drew in a deep breath. *I might as well make the best of it.* No use dwelling on what couldn't be changed. It was just a hem and a few darts to compensate for her client's recent weight loss. She could finish the task in less than an hour.

Miss Victoria proved gracious. She busied herself with papers of some kind at her desk and didn't interfere with Hannah's work. She did keep up a healthy stream of chatter, though.

"You probably think me morbid for finalizing my funeral details in advance." Miss Victoria lifted the lid of a small silver case and extracted a pair of eyeglasses. She wedged them onto her nose and began leafing through a stack of documents in a large oak box.

Hannah turned back to her stitching. "Not morbid, ma'am. Just . . . efficient."

"Hmmph. Truth is, I know I'm dying, and I'd rather go out in a memorable fashion than slip away quietly, never to be thought of again."

"I'm sure your nephew will remember you." Hannah glanced up as she twisted the dress to allow her better access to the next section of hem.

"Sherman? Bah! That boy would forget his own name if given half a chance." Miss Victoria pulled a document out of the box. She set it in front of her, then dragged her inkstand close and unscrewed the cap. "I've got half a mind to donate my estate to charity instead of letting it sift through my nephew's fingers. He and that flighty wife of his will surely do nothing of value with it." A heavy sigh escaped her. "But they are family, after all, and I suppose I'll no longer care about how the money is spent after I'm gone."

Hannah poked her needle up and back through the red silk in rapid succession, focused on making each stitch even and straight. It wasn't her place to offer advice, but it burned on her tongue nonetheless. Any church or charitable organization in the city could do a great amount of good with even a fraction of the Ashmont estate. Miss Victoria could make several small donations without her nephew ever knowing the difference. Hannah pressed her lips together and continued weaving her needle in and out, keeping her unsolicited opinion to herself.

She was relieved when a soft tapping at the door saved her from having to come up with an appropriate response.

A young maid entered and bobbed a curtsy. "The post has arrived, ma'am."

"Thank you, Millie." Miss Victoria accepted the envelope. "You may go."

The sound of paper ripping echoed in the quiet room as Miss Victoria slid her letter opener through the upper edge of the flap.

"Well, I must give the gentleman credit for persistence," the older woman murmured. "This is the third letter he's sent in two months."

Hannah turned the dress again and bent her head a little closer to her task, hoping to escape Miss Victoria's notice. It was not to be. The woman's voice only grew louder and more pointed as she continued.

"He wants to buy one of my railroad properties."

Hannah made the mistake of looking up. Miss Victoria's eyes, magnified by the lenses she wore, demanded a response. Yet how did a working-class seamstress participate in a conversation of a personal nature with one so far above her station? She didn't want to offend by appearing uninterested. However, showing *too* keen an interest might come across as presumptuous. Hannah floundered to find a suitably innocuous response and finally settled on, "Oh?"

It seemed to be enough, and Miss Victoria turned back to her correspondence as she continued her ramblings.

"When the Gulf, Colorado and Santa Fe Railway out of Galveston started up construction again last year, I invested in a handful of properties along the proposed route, in towns that were already established.

I've made a tidy profit on most, but for some reason, I find myself reluctant to part with this one."

An expectant pause hung in the air. Keeping her eyes on her work, Hannah voiced the first thought that came to mind.

"Does the gentleman not make a fair offer?"

"No, Mr. Tucker proposes a respectable price." Miss Victoria tapped the handle of the letter opener against the desktop in a rhythmic pattern, then seemed to become aware of what she was doing and set it aside. "Perhaps I am reluctant because I do not know the man personally. He is in good standing with the bank in Coventry and by all accounts is respected in the community, yet in the past I've made my decision to sell after meeting with the buyer in person. Unfortunately, my health precludes that now."

"Coventry?" Hannah seized upon the less personal topic. "I'm not familiar with that town."

"That's because it's about two hundred miles north of here—and it is quite small. The surveyors tell me it's in a pretty little spot along the North Bosque River. I had hoped to visit, but it looks as if I won't be afforded that opportunity."

Hannah tied off her thread and snipped the tail. She reached for her spool and unwound another long section, thankful that the discussion had finally moved in a more neutral direction. She clipped the end of the thread and held the needle up to gauge the position of the eye.

"What do you think, Miss Richards? Should I sell it to him?"

The needle slipped out of her hand.

"You're asking me?"

"Is there another Miss Richards in the room? Of course I'm asking you." She clicked her tongue in disappointment. "Goodness, girl. I've always thought you to be an intelligent sort. Have I been wrong all this time?"

That rankled. Hannah sat a little straighter and lifted her chin. "No, ma'am."

"Good." Miss Victoria slapped her palm against the desk. "Now, tell me what you think."

If the woman was determined to have her speak her mind, Hannah would oblige. This was the last project she'd ever sew for the woman anyway. It couldn't hurt. The only problem was, she'd worked so hard *not* to form an opinion during this exchange, that now that she was asked for one, she had none to give. Trying not to let the silence rush her into saying something that would indeed prove her lacking in intellect, she scrambled to gather her thoughts while she searched for the dropped needle.

"It seems to me," she said, uncovering the needle along with a speck of insight, "you need to decide if you would rather have the property go to a man you know only by reputation or to the nephew you know through experience." Hannah lifted her gaze to meet Miss Victoria's and held firm, not allowing the woman's critical stare to cow her. "Which scenario gives you the greatest likelihood of leaving behind the legacy you desire?"

Victoria Ashmont considered her for several moments, her eyes piercing Hannah and bringing to mind the staring contests the schoolboys used to challenge her to when she was still in braids. The memory triggered her competitive nature, and a stubborn determination to win rose within her.

At last, Miss Victoria nodded and turned away. "Thank you, Miss Richards. I think I have my answer."

Exultation flashed through her for a brief second at her victory, but self-recrimination soon followed. This wasn't a schoolyard game. It was an aging woman's search to create meaning in her death.

"Forgive my boldness, ma'am."

Her client turned back and wagged a bony finger at Hannah. "Boldness is exactly what you need to run your own business, girl. Boldness, skill, and a lot of hard work. When you get that shop of yours, hardships are sure to find their way to your doorstep. Confidence is the only way to combat them—confidence in yourself and in the God who equips you to overcome. Never forget that."

"Yes, ma'am."

Feeling chastised and oddly encouraged at the same time, Hannah threaded her needle and returned to work. The scratching of pen against paper replaced the chatter of Miss Victoria's voice as the woman gave her full attention to the documents spread across her desk. Time passed swiftly, and soon the alterations were complete.

After trying the gown on a second time to assure a proper fit and examining every seam for quality and durability, as was her custom, Victoria Ashmont ushered Hannah down to the front hall.

"My man will see you home, Miss Richards."

"Thank you, ma'am." Hannah collected her bonnet from the butler and tied the ribbons beneath her chin.

"I will settle my account with Mrs. Granbury by the end of the week, but here is the bonus I promised you." She held out a plain white envelope.

Hannah accepted it and placed it carefully in her reticule. She dipped her head and made a quick curtsy. "Thank you. I have enjoyed the privilege of working for you, ma'am, and I pray that your health improves so that I might do so again."

A strange light came into Miss Victoria's eyes, a secretive gleam, as if she could see into the future. "You have better things to do than make outlandish red dresses for old women, Miss Richards. Don't waste your energy worrying over my health. I'll go when it's my time and not a moment before."

Hannah smiled as she stepped out the door, sure that not even the angels could drag Miss Victoria away until she was ready to go. Yet underneath the woman's tough exterior beat a kind heart. Although Hannah didn't fully understand how kind until she arrived home and opened her bonus envelope.

Instead of the two or three greenbacks she had assumed were

tucked inside, she found a gift that stole her breath and her balance. She slumped against the boardinghouse wall and slid down its blue-papered length into a trembling heap on the floor. She blinked several times, but the writing on the paper didn't change, only blurred as tears welled and distorted her vision.

She held in her hand the deed to her new dress shop in Coventry, Texas.

CHAPTER 1

COVENTRY, TEXAS—SEPTEMBER 1881

"J.T.! J.T.! I got a customer for ya." Tom Packard lumbered down the street with his distinctive uneven gait, waving his arm in the air.

Jericho "J.T." Tucker stepped out of the livery's office with a sigh and waited for his right-hand man to jog past the blacksmith and bootmaker shops. He'd lost count of how many times he'd reminded Tom not to yell out his business for everyone to hear, but social niceties tended to slip the boy's notice when he got excited.

It wasn't his fault, though. At eighteen, Tom had the body of a man, but his mind hadn't developed quite as far. He couldn't read a lick and could barely pen his own name, but he had a gentle way with horses, so J.T. let him hang around the stable and paid him to help out with the chores. In gratitude, the boy did everything in his power to prove himself worthy, including trying to drum up clientele from among the railroad passengers who unloaded at the station a mile south of town. After weeks without so much as a nibble, it seemed the kid had finally managed to hook himself a fish.

J.T. leaned a shoulder against the doorframe and slid a toothpick out of his shirt pocket. He clamped the wooden sliver between his teeth and kept his face void of expression save for a single raised brow as Tom stumbled to a halt in front of him. The kid grasped his knees and gulped air for a moment, then unfolded to his full height, which was nearly as tall as his employer. His cheeks, flushed from his exertions, darkened further when he met J.T.'s eye.

"I done forgot about the yelling again, huh? Sorry." Tom slumped, his chin bending toward his chest.

J.T. gripped the kid's shoulder, straightened him up, and slapped him on the back. "You'll remember next time. Now, what's this about a customer?"

Tom brightened in an instant. "I gots us a good one. She's right purty and has more boxes and gewgaws than I ever did see. I 'spect there's enough to fill up the General."

"The General, huh?" J.T. rubbed his jaw and used the motion to cover his grin.

Tom had names for all the wagons. Fancy Pants was the fringed surrey J.T. kept on hand for family outings or courting couples; the buggy's name was Doc after the man who rented it out most frequently; the buckboard was just plain Buck; and his freight wagon was affectionately dubbed the General. The kid's monikers inspired a heap of good-natured ribbing amongst the men who gathered at the livery to swap stories and escape their womenfolk, but over time the names stuck. Just last week, Alistair Smythe plopped down a silver dollar and demanded he be allowed to take Fancy Pants out for a drive. Hearing the pretentious bank clerk use Tom's nickname for the surrey left the fellas guffawing for days.

J.T. thrust the memory from his mind and crossed his arms over his chest, using his tongue to shift the toothpick to the other side of his mouth. "The buckboard is easier to get to. I reckon it'd do the job just as well."

"I dunno." Tom mimicked J.T.'s posture, crossing his own arms and leaning against the livery wall. "She said her stuff was mighty heavy and she'd pay extra to have it unloaded at her shop."

"Shop?" J.T.'s good humor shriveled. His arms fell to his sides as his gaze slid past Tom to the vacant building across the street. The only unoccupied shop in Coventry stood adjacent to Louisa James's laundry—the shop he'd tried, and failed, to purchase. J.T.'s jaw clenched so tight the toothpick started to splinter. Forcing himself to relax, he straightened away from the doorpost.

"I think she's a dressmaker," Tom said. "There were a bunch of them dummies with no heads or arms with her on the platform. Looked right peculiar, them all standin' around her like they's gonna start a quiltin' bee or something." The kid chuckled at his own joke, but J.T. didn't join in his amusement.

A dressmaker? A woman who made her living by exploiting the vanity of her customers? *That's* who was moving into his shop?

A sick sensation oozed like molasses through his gut as memories clawed over the wall he'd erected to keep them contained.

"So we gonna get the General, J.T.?"

Tom's question jerked him back to the present and allowed him to stuff the unpleasant thoughts back down where they belonged. He loosened his fingers from the fist he didn't remember making and adjusted his hat to sit lower on his forehead, covering his eyes. It wouldn't do for the kid to see the anger that surely lurked there. He'd probably go and make some fool assumption that he'd done something wrong. Or worse, he'd ask questions J.T. didn't want to answer.

He cleared his throat and clasped the kid's shoulder. "If you think we need the freight wagon, then we'll get the freight wagon. Why don't you harness up the grays then come help me wrangle the General?"

"Yes, sir!" Tom bounded off to the corral to gather the horses, his chest so inflated with pride J.T. was amazed he could see where he was going.

Ducking back inside the livery, J.T. closed up his office and strode past the stalls to the oversized double doors that opened his wagon shed up to the street. He grasped the handle of the first and rolled it backward, using his body weight as leverage. As his muscles strained against the heavy wooden door, his mind struggled to control his rising frustration.

He'd finally accepted the fact that the owner of the shop across the street refused to sell to him. J.T. believed in Providence, that the Lord would direct his steps. He didn't like it, but he'd worked his way to peace with the decision. Until a few minutes ago. The idea that God would allow it to go to a dressmaker really stuck in his craw.

It wasn't as if he wanted the shop for selfish reasons. He saw it as a chance to help out a widow and her orphans. Isn't that what the Bible defined as "pure religion"? What could be nobler than that? Louisa James supported three kids with her laundry business and barely eked out an existence. The building she worked in was crumbling around her ears even though the majority of her income went to pay the rent. He'd planned to buy the adjacent shop and rent it to her at half the price she was currently paying in exchange for storing some of his tack in the large back room.

J.T. squinted against the afternoon sunlight that streamed into the dim stable and strode to the opposite side of the entrance, his indignation growing with every step. Ignoring the handle, he slammed his shoulder into the second door and ground his teeth as he dug his boots into the packed dirt floor, forcing the wood to yield to his will.

How could a bunch of fripperies and ruffles do more to serve the community than a new roof for a family in need? Most of the women in and around Coventry sewed their own clothes, and those that didn't bought ready-made duds through the dry-goods store or mail order. Sensible clothes, durable clothes, not fashion-plate items that stroked their vanity or elicited covetous desires in their hearts for things they couldn't afford. A dressmaker had no place in Coventry.

This can't be God's will. The world and its schemers had brought her to town, not God.

Horse hooves thudded and harnesses jangled as Tom led the grays toward the front of the livery.

J.T. blew out a breath and rubbed a hand along his jaw. No matter what had brought her to Coventry, the dressmaker was still a woman, and his father had drummed into him that all women were to be treated with courtesy and respect. So he'd smile and doff his hat and make polite conversation. Shoot, he'd even lug her heavy junk around for her and unload all her folderol. But once she was out of his wagon, he'd have nothing more to do with her.

❧❧❧

Hannah sat atop one of her five trunks, waiting for young Tom to return. Most of the other passengers had left the depot already, making their way on foot or in wagons with family members who'd come to meet them. Hannah wasn't about to let her belongings out of her sight, though—or trust them to a porter she didn't know. So she waited.

Thanks to Victoria Ashmont's generosity, she'd been able to use the money she'd saved for a shop to buy fabric and supplies. Not knowing what would be available in the small town of Coventry, she'd brought everything she needed with her. Including her prized possession—a Singer Improved Family Model 15 treadle machine with five-drawer walnut cabinet and extension leaf. The monster weighed nearly as much as the locomotive that brought her here, but it was a thing of beauty, and she intended to make certain it arrived at the shop without incident.

Her toes tapped against the wooden platform. Only a mile of dusty road stood between her and her dream. Yet the final minutes of waiting felt longer than the hours, even years, that preceded them. Could she really run her own business, or would Miss Ashmont's belief in her prove misplaced? A tingle of apprehension tiptoed over Hannah's spine. What if the women of Coventry had no need of a dressmaker? What if they didn't like her designs? What if . . .

Hannah surged to her feet and began to pace. Miss Ashmont had directed her to be bold. Bold and self-confident. Oh, and confident in God. Hannah paused. Her gaze slid to the bushy hills rising around her like ocean swells. *"I will lift up mine eyes unto the hills, from whence cometh my help. My help cometh from the Lord, which made heaven and earth."* The psalm seeped into her soul, bringing a measure of assurance with it. God had led her here. He would provide.

She resumed her pacing, anticipation building as fear receded. On her sixth lap around her mound of luggage, the creak of wagon wheels brought her to a halt.

A conveyance drew near, and Hannah's pulse vaulted into a new pace. Young Tom wasn't driving. Another man with a worn brown felt hat pulled low over his eyes sat on the bench. It must be that J.T. person Tom had rambled on about. Well, it didn't matter who was driving, as long as he had the strength to maneuver her sewing machine without dropping it.

A figure in the back of the wagon waved a cheerful greeting, and the movement caught Hannah's eye. She waved back, glad to see Tom had returned, as well. Two men working together would have a much easier time of it.

The liveryman pulled the horses to a halt and set the brake. Masculine grace exuded from him as he climbed down and made his way to the platform. His long stride projected confidence, a vivid contrast to Tom's childish gamboling behind him. Judging by the breadth of his shoulders and the way the blue cotton of his shirt stretched across the expanse of his chest and arms, this man would have no trouble moving her sewing cabinet.

Tom dashed ahead of the newcomer and swiped the gray slouch hat from his head. Tufts of his dark blond hair stuck out at odd angles, but his eyes sparkled with warmth. "I got the General, ma'am, We'll get you fixed up in a jiffy." Not wasting a minute, he slapped his hat back on and moved past her.

Hannah's gaze roamed to the man waiting a few steps away. He didn't look much like a general. No military uniform. Instead he sported scuffed boots and denims that were wearing thin at the knees. The tip of a toothpick protruded from his lips, wiggling a little as he gnawed on it. Perhaps General was a nickname of sorts. He hadn't spoken a word, yet there was something about his carriage and posture that gave him an air of authority.

She straightened her shoulders in response and closed the distance between them. Still giddy about starting up her shop, she couldn't resist the urge to tease the stoic man who held himself apart.

"Thank you for assisting me today, General." She smiled up at him as she drew near, finally able to see more than just his jaw. He had lovely amber eyes, although they were a bit cold. "Should I salute or something?"

His right brow arced upward. Then a tiny twitch at the corner of his mouth told her he'd caught on.

"I'm afraid I'm a civilian through and through, ma'am." He tilted his head in the direction of the wagon. "That's the General. Tom likes to name things."

Hannah gave a little laugh. "I see. Well, I'm glad to have you both lending me a hand. I'm Hannah Richards."

The man tweaked the brim of his hat. "J.T. Tucker."

"Pleased to meet you, Mr. Tucker."

He dipped his chin in a small nod. Not a very demonstrative fellow. Nor very talkative.

"Lay those things down, Tom," he called out as he stepped away. "We don't want them to tip over the side if we hit a rut."

"Oh. Wait just a minute, please." There was no telling what foul things had been carted around in that wagon bed before today. It didn't matter so much for her trunks and sewing cabinet, but the linen covering her mannequins would be easily soiled.

"I have an old quilt that I wrapped around them in the railroad freight car. Let me fetch it."

Hannah sensed more than heard Mr. Tucker's sigh as she hurried to collect the quilt from the trunk she had been sitting on. Well, he could sigh all he liked. Her display dummies were going to be covered. She had one chance to make a first impression on the ladies of Coventry, and she vowed it would be a pristine one.

Making a point not to look at the liveryman as she scurried by, Hannah clutched the quilt to her chest and headed for the wagon. She draped it over the side, then climbed the spokes and hopped into the back, just as she had done as a child. Then she laid out the quilt along the back wall and gently piled the six dummies horizontally atop it, alternating the placement of the tripod pedestals to allow them to fit together in a more compact fashion. As she flipped the remaining fabric of the quilt over the pile, a loud thud sounded from behind, and the wagon jostled her. She gasped and teetered to the side. Glancing over her shoulder, she caught sight of Mr. Tucker as he shoved the first of her trunks into the wagon bed, its iron bottom scraping against the wooden floor.

The man could have warned her of his presence instead of scaring the wits out of her like that. But taking him to task would only make her look like a shrew, so she ignored him. When Tom arrived with the second trunk, she was ready. After he set it down, she moved to the end of the wagon.

"Would you help me down, please?"

He grinned up at her. "Sure thing."

Hannah set her hands on his shoulders as he clasped her waist and lifted her down. A tiny voice of regret chided her for not asking the favor of the rugged Mr. Tucker, but she squelched it. Tom was a safer choice. Besides, his affable manner put her at ease—unlike his companion, who from one minute to the next alternated between sparking her interest and her ire.

She bit back her admonishments to take care as the men hefted her sewing machine. Thankfully, they managed to accomplish the task without her guidance. With the large cabinet secured in the wagon bed, it didn't take long for them to load the rest of her belongings. Once they finished, Tom handed her up to the bench seat and scrambled into the back, leaving her alone with Mr. Tucker.

A cool autumn breeze caressed her cheeks and tugged lightly on her bonnet as the wagon rolled forward. She smoothed her skirts, not sure what to say to the reticent man beside her. However, he surprised her by starting the conversation on his own.

"What made you choose Coventry, Miss Richards?"

She twisted on the seat to look at him, but his eyes remained focused on the road.

"I guess you could say it chose me."

"How so?"

"It was really a most extraordinary sequence of events. I do not doubt that the Lord's Providence brought me here."

That got a reaction. His chin swiveled toward her, and beneath his hat, his intense gaze speared her for a handful of seconds before he blinked and turned away.

She swallowed the moisture that had accumulated under her tongue as he stared at her, then continued.

"Two years ago, I was hired by Mrs. Granbury of San Antonio to sew for her most particular clientele. One of these clients was an elderly spinster with a reputation for being impossible to work with. Well, I needed the job too badly to allow her to scare me away and was too stubborn to let her get the best of me, so I stuck it out and eventually the two of us found a way to coexist and even respect each other.

"Before she died, she called me in to make a final gown for her, and we fell to talking about her legacy. She had invested in several railroad properties, and had only one left that had not sold. In an act of generosity that I still find hard to believe, she gave me the deed as a gift, knowing that I had always dreamed of opening my own shop."

"What kept her from selling it before then?" His deep voice rumbled with something more pointed than simple curiosity.

A prickle of unease wiggled down Hannah's neck, but she couldn't quite pinpoint the cause.

"She told me that she preferred to meet the buyers in person, to assess their character before selling off her properties. Unfortunately, her health had begun to decline, and she was unable to travel. There had been a gentleman of good reputation from this area who made an offer several times. A Mr. Tuck . . ."

A hard lump of dread formed in the back of Hannah's throat.

"Oh dear. Don't tell me you're *that* Mr. Tucker?"

CHAPTER 2

J.T. slanted a look at the woman beside him. She was dressed as he'd expected, in some kind of fancy traveling suit that had enough extra material gathered along the back side that she probably could have made another whole dress if she'd had an eye for frugality instead of extravagance. Yet he'd be lying if he were to say he hadn't noticed the way the cornflower blue fabric matched her eyes or how the buttoned jacket accentuated her tiny waist. And when she bent over to arrange those dummies in his wagon, he found himself rather thankful for all those flounces and ruffles hiding the shape of what was beneath.

As he watched her bite her lip and try to figure out what to say to him after discovering his connection to her shop, he had to admit that his expectations had only proven true for her clothing. Most beautiful women he'd known over the course of his twenty-seven years possessed an innate skill for manipulation. A seductive smile, pout, or subtle hint woven into the fiber of an ordinary conversation and she would have a man stumbling over himself to please her.

Miss Hannah Richards, on the other hand, didn't seem to subscribe to such artifice. Her yellow hair, trim figure, and pleasant features worked together to form a very handsome woman. Yet when something needed doing, she jumped in and did it herself instead of making sheep's eyes at him or Tom to get one of them to do it for her.

Of course, he had just met her. It was doubtful she'd continue as the exception to the rule over longer acquaintance.

"Forgive me for rambling on like that, Mr. Tucker. I had no idea . . ."

J.T. kept his head straight and his mouth shut, but he watched her out of the corner of his eye.

"All that talk about God's Providence must have been a slap in the face to you. I'm so sorry. It seems unfair that my blessing turned out to be your disappointment." She exhaled a long breath, then bounced in the seat and swung her knees toward him. "I know! I'll give you a discounted rate on any mending or tailoring you need done."

He chomped down on his toothpick. "No thanks. My sister, Cordelia, does all my mending."

"Oh."

Her cheery smile wilted, and he felt as if he'd just crushed a flower. He steeled himself against the regret that threatened to soften him, though. He didn't want any favors from her. Besides, she was only offering in order to make herself feel better.

"Well," she continued, having regained a measure of her previous enthusiasm, "perhaps I could give your sister a discount on a new dress. I've brought a wonderful selection of—"

"No." The last thing he needed was for Delia to get caught up in a bunch of fashion rigmarole. She was too sensible to fall into that trap, but he didn't plan on leaving her exposed to unnecessary temptation.

Miss Richards made no further overtures. In fact, she made no further efforts at conversation of any kind. By the time the first buildings of Coventry came into view, J.T.'s conscience was pressing down on his shoulders like a fifty-pound sack of grain.

"Look, I didn't mean to be rude." He shoved his heel against the wagon's footrest and shifted his hips against the hard wooden bench. "I appreciate you making those offers. But there's no reason for them. You own the shop fair and square. You don't have to mollify me. I can deal with it."

He grabbed the crown of his hat and resituated it on his head so he could see her better as he stole another glance her way. She didn't look at him, but the smile that curved her lips as she stared at her lap made him glad he'd spoken.

"Thank you for your understanding, Mr. Tucker. I hope there will be no hard feelings between us over this matter."

J.T. grunted a response. He couldn't very well tell her that his hard feelings had started before he'd ever met her. That would make him sound narrow-minded. Which he wasn't. Not really. He didn't have any problem with Miss Richards as a person. She seemed likable enough. But her profession was another matter altogether.

He'd seen firsthand what damage such temptation could do to a woman, to a family. Females fawned over Parisian designs until they were no longer content with their lot in life. They looked down on their menfolk for not being able to provide for them in the manner in which they believed they were entitled. And those that did have the funds for such opulence lorded it over those who didn't.

Why, he'd been to some big town church services where the women seemed to be in some kind of fashion competition. Who had the biggest hat? Whose dress was modeled after the latest style? Who wore the most expensive fabric? Wearing one's Sunday best was all fine and dandy, but these ladies acted as if they had dressed to impress their fellow congregants more than the Lord.

Narrow-minded? Not likely. Was it narrow-minded to disapprove of saloons and bawdy houses? They supplied temptations that led people astray. Fancy dress goods did the same thing, only in a more socially acceptable way.

His jaw clenched, and the softened toothpick trapped between his teeth bent in two. J.T. turned to the side and spit out the offending sliver of wood. He wiped his mouth with the back of his gloved hand and rolled his neck in an effort to rid himself of the tension that had built there. Getting all worked up wasn't going to help matters.

Besides, all her talk about God's Providence made him wonder if the Lord really did bring her to Coventry. He supposed if the Almighty could use a woman like Rahab to bring about victory for his people, it wasn't outside the realm of possibilities that he could use a dressmaker for some good purpose, as well. Doubtful, but possible.

Still struggling to believe that she'd finally arrived at her new home, Hannah drank in her first glimpse of Coventry as the wagon rolled by the various storefronts. Two well-dressed men looked up from their conversation in front of a tall limestone building to the right. They nodded a greeting. Hannah smiled back.

"We just finished that hotel a couple months back," Mr. Tucker said as he dipped his chin to the men.

Hope stirred in her. Though Coventry was much smaller than San Antonio, it was growing. A railroad, a new hotel, businessmen coming to town. Businessmen who had wives. Wives who would want fine-tailored dress goods. Yes, there were definitely possibilities here.

Farther down the street, her optimism waned a bit. As Mr. Tucker dutifully pointed out the locations of the telegraph office, bank, and drugstore, Hannah paid little attention, her interest focused on the ladies who strolled down the boardwalk with shopping baskets on their arms. Their dresses were simple, plain. Did they not care for fashion? Or worse, did they not have funds for dress goods? She was pretty sure her designs would draw them in, but if they had no money to spend . . .

Hannah's fingernails jabbed into the skin of her palms. No. She'd not get lost in a pile of *what ifs* again. God brought her to Coventry for a reason. It didn't matter if the town was small or if its citizens were ordinary folk. She'd planned for that, adapting patterns ahead of time to reflect more practical styles and selecting fabric suitable to small-town life. Besides, it would be a lovely change to sew for people of her own social standing, women she could befriend and chat with as equals. Maybe even Mr. Tucker's sister.

Hannah glanced at the grim man driving the rig. He didn't seem all that friendly, but that didn't mean his sister would share his reticence. Then again, she'd probably be grumpy, too, if she'd just found out the shop she wanted had been given to someone else.

The horses slowed to a stop, and all at once, her concerns blew away on the wind. They had arrived.

Stomach fluttering, Hannah gazed upon the simple clapboard structure that represented her future. It had a lovely false front and windows facing the street. Ideas blossomed as she considered where she should position the mannequins to best be seen by passersby and which dresses she would use to entice them into her shop. Perhaps the lavender morning dress or the olive polonaise costume she made up last month. Both reflected the latest styles and techniques while not inhibiting everyday duties. No sheaths that wrapped so snugly around the knees that a woman had to take mincing steps. No flowing trains to collect dirt and mud from the unpaved roads and country lanes. Minimal use of silks and velvets or any fabric that wouldn't hold up to normal wear in a western town.

"Do you want a hand down or not?"

Hannah jumped at the growling voice, caught up as she was in the intricate web of her business strategies.

"Oh! Of course." Heat warmed her cheeks. She stood and set a foot atop the raised side of the wagon, then reached out to the irascible Mr. Tucker. Her hands pressed against the corded muscles of his shoulders at the same time his encircled her waist. A frisson of awareness coursed through her as she sunk slowly to the ground, secure in his capable grip.

This close, she could smell a bit of horse on him mixed with harness oil. Masculine scents.

"Thank you." She avoided his penetrating gaze and fumbled with the ball clasp on her handbag. "I'll just get the key and unlock the front door."

Hannah extracted a nickel-plated key from the pocket in the lining of her purse and stepped onto the boardwalk. She paused outside the door and pressed a trembling hand to her abdomen. Taking a deep breath, she fit the key into the lock and twisted. A satisfying click sounded, and the door swung open.

Looking past the dirt and grime that had accumulated while the store stood vacant, Hannah crossed the threshold, her artistic mind awhirl with possibilities. A counter jutted out into the room from the left wall about halfway back. It would make a lovely display for her pattern catalogs and fashion magazines. She could put in some shelves along the right wall to showcase her fabrics, stacking complementary bolts together to help her customers visualize the final effects she could achieve for them by blending patterns and colors. The coatrack and wardrobe hangers for her pre-made dresses could be mounted on the left wall, leaving plenty of room for ladies to wander about.

Hannah's boot heels thumped against the bare floor as she made her way behind the counter. She was pleased to discover cubbyholes that could be used to store her till, ledger, and fabric swatches. It appeared there'd be sufficient room for her sewing machine back here, as well, which meant she wouldn't have to hide in the back room. She could save that space for fittings and project storage.

Yes, this little shop would accommodate her quite well.

A shuffle sounded behind her. She turned to see Tom and Mr. Tucker standing inside the doorway, each with a trunk balanced on one shoulder.

"If you're done woolgathering, you might show us where you want this stuff," the liveryman groused.

She supposed he had a right to be testy. With all the excitement of the new shop, she'd completely forgotten about the men. She was thankful she had thought to label the trunks. Colored ribbons tied to the handles indicated which ones contained dress shop items and which held her personal belongings.

"Let's see." She approached the men and fingered the thin strip of grosgrain silk that hung near Mr. Tucker's hand, careful not to touch the man himself. "The ones with blue ribbons can be left down here behind the counter. The ones with pink ribbons need to go upstairs in my personal quarters."

Hannah lifted her chin to meet his gaze and suddenly found it difficult to breathe.

"What color's mine, J.T.? I can't see it."

Mr. Tucker looked away and Hannah drew in a deep breath, willing her stomach to stop its silly fluttering. The man was as prickly as a cactus. Just because he had eyes the color of melting honey didn't mean she had to go all soft over him.

The man gestured with a jerk of his head for Tom to move past them. "Yours is blue. Go put it over yonder and then head back to the wagon and look for any others with blue ribbons. I'll haul this one upstairs." He raised a brow at Hannah. "Whenever Miss Richards decides she's ready."

Riled at his insinuation that she was some kind of lollygagger, Hannah thrust out her chin and marched out the door. "If you'll follow me, Mr. Tucker?"

The nerve of that man. Hannah fumed as she rounded the corner of the building to reach the exterior stairs on the north side. She hoped he was carrying one of the heavier trunks. It'd serve him right if he ended up with a permanent crease in his collar and a crick in his neck. Any person seeing their home or place of business for the first time was bound to need a minute or two to soak it all in. Why, she'd bet a dollar of profits that when he walked into his livery stable for the first time, he gawked like a boy in a gun shop.

Irritation fueling her steps, Hannah slammed her foot onto each stair as she made her way to the top. She clutched the key in her left hand, disregarding the handrail. Pausing before the second to last step, she peeked over her shoulder to gauge Mr. Tucker's progress. He'd had to switch the trunk to the opposite shoulder in order to grip the railing, and was still near the bottom.

"Are you coming?" she taunted in a sugar-sweet voice.

The brim of his hat lifted, allowing her to see his scowl. Satisfaction surged through her as her foot pounded down on the next step.

A crack shouted like thunder in her ear as the board beneath her gave way, and with a surprised squeak, she plummeted feet-first through the yawning hole.

CHAPTER 3

J.T. didn't take time to think. In a single motion, he dropped the trunk and vaulted over the railing. His boots crashed into the earth with a jolt that surged through his bent knees and into his thighs.

Springing out of his crouch, he ran forward, praying that Miss Richards wasn't hurt too badly. But instead of coming upon a pile of crushed blue fluff as he expected, he found himself eye level with a pair of delicate ankles pumping madly through a froth of white petticoats.

Her skirt hung unevenly, hiked up somewhat on the side closest to him. Her black stockings stood out against the white petticoats like coal on snow. The ribbed lines that started above the top of her shoe drew his gaze over the gentle curve of her calf before disappearing into the flurry of white cotton that surrounded them.

J.T. turned away, a cough rising in his throat. The woman was dangling from a second-story staircase, and he was ogling her legs. What kind of a lecher was he? J.T. tugged his hat down and cleared his throat, wishing he could clear his mind as easily.

She must have heard him, for the kicking stilled.

"Mr. Tucker?"

Her voice sounded breathless. Taking firm control of his wayward thoughts, he stepped aside to better assess her predicament. She must have managed to grab hold of the top step as she fell, for her head, shoulders, and arms were blocked from his view.

"I'm here, Miss Richards." He cleared his throat again, despite the fact that his mouth had gone bone dry.

"I seem to have dropped my key."

A quiet chuckle escaped him before he could stuff it back inside. He shook his head, unable to tame the smile that lingered on his lips.

"Yes, ma'am. I believe you have. Looks like you might have dropped one or two other things, as well."

"I'm afraid so."

He chanced another look up, careful to steer his gaze along appropriate paths. Was it his imagination, or was she hanging a bit lower than she had been a minute ago?

"Um . . . Mr. Tucker?" His name came out pinched, and he thought he heard a grunt as she shifted.

"Yes, ma'am?"

"I know it wasn't part of our original agreement . . ." A second noise interrupted. Definitely a grunt. And he swore he could see the edge of her collar peeking out beneath the wooden slats now. She was slipping. His heart rammed against his ribs.

"But might you be willing to catch me? I don't think I can—"

He dove back under her, her quiet gasp ringing in his ears as loud as any scream. Bracing himself against the impact, he scooped her legs into the crook of his left arm before they hit the ground and caught her upper body with his right. He clasped her close to his chest as he fought to stay on his feet. Once his boots were firmly planted, he looked down into her face, concerned to find her eyes squeezed shut.

"Are you all right?"

The lines around her eyelids softened, and her lashes fluttered upward. The twilight blue of her eyes held him captive.

"I . . . I'm fine, I think. Thank you, Mr. Tucker."

She blinked and dipped her chin, breaking the connection. As he lowered her feet to the ground, his chin knocked against her already-askew bonnet. The thing sat lopsided on her head, and one of the flowers from around the crown had abandoned its place to drape drunkenly over her forehead. He reached for it and tried to stick it back where it belonged, but the stubborn stem refused to cooperate. Fed up, he plucked the ornery bloom straight off of its mooring and shoved it at its owner.

"Here."

A hint of a smile played over Miss Richards's lips as she accepted it from him. "Thank you."

She must think him an idiot. And why not? He was one. Trying to fix a stupid flower. What had come over him? Looking around for an escape of any kind, he spied her small purse in the shadow of the building.

"I'll . . . uh . . . look for your key."

She didn't say anything, but he could hear the swish of her skirts as she no doubt set about repairing her appearance. He bent over to collect the purse and searched the area around it for the key.

"Perhaps I should have heeded the wisdom of Proverbs before I allowed my pride to send me stomping up those steps in a huff." Her self-deprecating chuckle drew his attention away from the weed-strewn ground and back toward her. "You know . . . a haughty spirit goeth before a fall."

Her saucy taunts as she'd rushed up the stairs had surely irritated him, but truth be told, he probably shared the blame because of his impatience in the shop. No one had ever accused him of having a silver tongue.

"I don't know about the haughty spirit," he said with a shrug, "but you certainly fell."

Full-blown feminine laughter rang out, and the sound lifted his mood.

"That I did." She started walking his way, a free-spirited smile bedecking her face.

J.T. cleared his throat again and returned to his perusal of the ground beneath the staircase. After a moment, he caught a glimmer of reflected light. The key lay beside the broken pieces of what had once been a secure step. He shoved the purse under his arm and picked up the key, along with one of the defective hunks of wood. The thing was rotted through. He frowned. How many other steps had deteriorated?

Miss Richards slipped up beside him and retrieved the purse and key. "Thank you again, Mr. Tucker. If it weren't for your quick actions, I would likely have suffered a serious injury."

He felt her withdrawal, but he had already started inspecting the other steps and didn't pay her much mind.

"I know you're anxious to return to the livery," she said, "so I'll get the door unlocked in a trice."

She was halfway to the top when her meaning finally sank into his distracted brain.

"Get down from there, woman, before you take another tumble!" His words came out sharper than he'd intended, but fear for her safety had ignited his temper. That and the fact that when he raised his head from his stooped position under the stairs to call out to her, he got another eyeful of stockings and petticoats.

"Don't worry, Mr. Tucker. I'm not stomping this time, and I've a firm grip on the railing. I'll be fine."

Gritting his teeth, J.T. strode out from under the steps and glared up at the stubborn woman whom he had earlier mistaken for intelligent.

"The wood from that broken step is rotten. There might be others ready to give way, as well."

Her eyes narrowed and the skin around her lips drew taut. "Thank you for your concern, but if they held me the first time, there's no reason to believe they won't do so now."

"What if you weakened them the first time?" He crossed his arms and raised a brow in challenge. Just because the steps he had checked so far had turned out to be sound didn't mean the remaining ones wouldn't cause a problem.

The woman deliberately took another step before answering him, her chin angled toward the sky. "You need not treat me like a child, sir. I am perfectly capable of navigating this staircase on my own."

He snorted.

Her nostrils flared. "I promise not to ask you to catch me again, all right? Now stop scowling."

Of course he did no such thing.

Those deep blue eyes of hers shot sparks at him, and he had to work to keep his expression stern. The woman was a firecracker.

"Tell you what," she huffed, "if I fall, you have my permission to gloat as much as you like. How about that?"

Without waiting for his answer, she spun around and marched the remainder of the distance to the top, stretching her stride to span the gulf over the missing stair. He followed her from below as a precaution and didn't relax until she disappeared into the room that would serve as her personal quarters.

Fool woman. She'd rather risk her neck than admit she might not be able to manage something on her own. He jumped up and grabbed hold of one of the higher steps, testing its strength against his dangling weight. It held. The top step, too, remained firmly in place even after all of Miss Richards's clinging and scraping. Apparently, the only unstable lumber was the step she fell through. Didn't matter, though. She still should have waited until he checked it out before trudging up the stairs like Joan of Arc on some kind of crusade.

J.T. pulled another toothpick out of his shirt pocket and wedged it between his molars. His tongue fiddled with it as he stared up through the hole in the staircase. He had to give her credit. Miss Richards knew how to handle herself in a crisis. Not only did she have the presence of mind to latch onto another step to keep from crashing to the ground, but there'd been no screaming, no hysteria, just calm conversation and a polite request to *please catch her*. Any other woman, his sister included, would have shrieked like a hog at butchering time.

Shaking his head, J.T. headed back to where he had left the dress-maker's trunk. The box had tumbled to the bottom of the stairs and now lay upside down. He flipped it over just as Tom came around the corner with the other pink-ribboned trunk hefted on his shoulder.

"I done finished the blue ones, J.T., so I thought I'd bring this 'un to ya. How come you're so slow? I expected you'd be done afore me."

"Miss Richards had a mishap on the stairs."

Tom's eyes widened in glazed panic.

"She's all right," J.T. hurried to assure him. "She's up in her room."

"W-what happened?"

J.T. hauled the trunk off Tom's shoulder and set it down next to his. "One of the steps broke and she fell, but she's fine."

"If she's fine, how come I can't see her anywheres?"

The boy's breathing came in quick shallow gasps, and his head flew from side to side.

J.T. squeezed his arm to get him to focus on him. "You know how womenfolk are, Tom. She's probably up there figuring out what kind of curtains she should hang in the windows and where to put all her knickknacks. She'll be down in a bit."

The boy glanced up at the open door. "You sure?"

"I'm sure." J.T. stepped behind him and started steering him across the street. "Now, what we menfolk oughta do is fetch a new plank from the lumber pile in back of the livery and fix that step for her so she doesn't have to worry about any more mishaps. You think you can find me a good board while I dig up a hammer and nails?"

Tom's head bobbed up and down. "Yes, sir."

"Good." J.T. thumped him on the back and moved into place beside him. They walked several yards in silence, but when they reached the livery doors, Tom turned back to look at the building across the street.

"You know, J.T., since Miss Richards ain't got no regular menfolk, it'd probably be a good idea for us to look after her. You reckon that's why God brought her to us? So's we could take care of her?"

J.T. chomped down on his toothpick and clenched his jaw. He didn't want to think about the Lord purposefully bringing the dressmaker into his life. He had enough responsibility looking after Cordelia and widows like Louisa James. He didn't want to be bothered with an opinionated, stubborn piece of baggage like Miss Hannah Richards, even if she did fit in his arms like a pistol in a custom-made holster. No, sir. After he fixed her step and finished unloading her paraphernalia, she'd be on her own.

CHAPTER 4

Hannah hid out in her living quarters until the muted male voices below faded away. She peeked out the doorway to make sure they were gone, then flopped into the single wooden chair that resided in her room. It tilted to the side and nearly threw her to the floor before she caught her balance with her boot heel. A frustrated scream welled up inside her, held at bay by the barest thread of self-control. Even the furniture plotted to steal her equilibrium.

A scrap of kindling shoved beneath the too-short leg would fix the chair, but what was she to do about Mr. Tucker? One minute he was a gallant knight, rescuing her from a mess of her own making, teasing and charming her, and holding her with arms that made her feel cherished and safe. The next he was an arrogant, overbearing lout who chastised her as if she were a child and ordered her about on her own property. She didn't know if she should kiss his cheek or kick his shin.

Right now, the shin kick was winning.

She sighed and tossed her purse onto the worn oak table beside her, the movement highlighting the ache beneath her arms. More concerned with the state of her clothing than any scrapes or bruises resulting from her fall, Hannah raised each arm in turn and examined the fabric and seams. She found a small tear on the left where the side seam met the sleeve—easily repaired with a few strokes of her needle. The snags on the fabric would be harder to fix, but at least they were in an inconspicuous area. The front of the dress had been spared, and she hadn't lost a single button. Of course, she always double stitched hers, so she'd expected nothing less.

Having assured herself that the damage to her traveling suit had been kept to a minimum, Hannah broadened her inspection to include the room. A cookstove stood on the left wall flanked by small windows on either side. A primitive-looking bedstead and mattress dominated the back corner. A few hooks protruded from the wall for hanging clothes, but no bureau or washstand could be found. A table and the lop-sided chair she sat on completed the tally of furniture. Pretty spare. And it would be more so after she hauled the table and chair downstairs.

Her shop demanded top priority. She needed a work surface for cutting patterns and piecing them together, and a chair was essential for using her treadle sewing machine. Not knowing how long it would take her to build up a steady income, Hannah planned to save whatever money she could.

Once her business was turning a decent profit, she would order furnishings for her apartment. Until then, she'd make do with the trunks she'd brought. She could use them for storage as well as make-shift benches. If she stacked two, they might be tall enough to give her a counter of sorts. An oilcloth cover and her large breadboard would give her a surface for food preparation. That should suffice. She'd have to keep meals simple anyway, with all the time spent in her shop.

Hannah pulled a small tablet out of her purse and began jotting down a list of the items she would need to purchase at the mercantile. Halfway through the word *potatoes* a thought occurred to her. If the store owner boxed up her purchases, she could use the crates for stools and even a washstand. She smiled and nibbled on the end of her pencil. With a little ingenuity, she'd have all the comforts of home in no time. Of course, she'd have to find someone to supply her with fresh milk. She wouldn't last a day without her morning cocoa.

A sudden pounding outside made her jump. Grabbing up her handbag and list, Hannah rushed to the door. Three steps down, Mr. Tucker stood bent over the gaping hole in her stairway, legs straddled, arms swinging as he nailed a new stair into place. As he reached for a second nail, he caught sight of her. He gave her a brief nod and then hammered the nail in with a tap followed by a single sure stroke.

"Tom and I moved your sewing cabinet inside," he said without looking at her. "He's taking the rig back."

Another nail slammed into place. "As soon as I get this step finished, I'll bring up your trunks and leave you in peace."

Still grumpy, Hannah thought, but sweet nonetheless.

"Thank you for fixing the step. I'll gladly pay you for your time."

Mr. Tucker glared up at her as if she had just impugned his honor. "I don't charge for being neighborly, ma'am."

"So I guess I shouldn't offer to compensate you for your heroic rescue of me, either, then." She grinned, hoping to get some kind of reaction out of him, but he never looked up.

"Nope." He accented his refusal with a final swing of the hammer and jumped with both feet onto the new stair.

His craftsmanship held.

"There." He tipped his hat back and finally met her eyes. "That should stand up to any amount of stomping you feel the need to dish out."

His lips stretched, and for a moment she thought he might smile, but his mouth never actually curved. Hannah shifted against the railing, unsure if he had spoken in jest or censure.

"Yes, well, thank you. I never know when the urge to stomp might next come over me." Although she imagined if it did recur, the man before her would somehow be responsible.

He flicked the brim of his hat in salute and turned to go, but she remembered the table and called out to stop him.

"Mr. Tucker? On your way down, would you help me carry this old table to the shop? It's too large for me to manage on my own."

He shrugged and followed her inside. "What's wrong with it? Planning on ordering a roomful of new furniture or something?"

The playfulness she thought she'd detected in his voice earlier had vanished, leaving nothing but frost in its wake. Well, she needed his muscles more than his cheer, so as long as he was willing to help, he could grouch to his heart's content.

"It's a perfectly fine table. The only problem is that I need it downstairs." She set her purse on the seat of the rickety chair and moved around to the far end of the table. Grabbing hold of the edge facing her, she waited for Mr. Tucker to pick up his end. He chose to stare at her instead, with a look that raised her hackles.

Hannah eyed his shins and aimed the point of her toe in his direction. Lucky for him a hefty piece of furniture stood in her way.

"I don't plan to entertain many guests up here," she said, "so I can make do without a table. But I can't very well cut out patterns for my customers on the floor of the shop, now can I?"

He just stared at her, a clouded expression on his face. She was about to shoo him away, determined to move the table without his help, when he stepped up and clasped his side of the tabletop.

"It . . . uh . . . wouldn't be nothing fancy . . ." He stopped and cleared his throat. "But if you want, I could loan you a couple of sawhorses and some spare planks I got piled out back. It'd serve until you could buy a real table."

The heat of her temper mellowed into a warm pool of gratitude. "You would do that for me?"

He nodded, finally meeting her gaze. His mouth held fast to its rigid line, but the hard glitter had left his eyes, giving him an oddly vulnerable appearance despite the steely strength that radiated from the rest of him.

"Thank you, Mr. Tucker." A soft smile curved her lips. "I must warn you, though, that I don't plan to order any furniture until I've successfully established my business, so it could be months before I am able to return the borrowed items."

"Keep 'em as long as you need. I can always make more."

"Really?" The seed of an idea sprouted in her mind.

"Sure. I got a heap of scrap lumber left from when I tore out the dividing wall in the wagon shed last year."

"Enough to spare me four boards that I could use for shelving in my shop? I'd pay you for them, of course."

He leaned over the table toward her. "Now, don't you go insulting me again."

"No, sir," she rushed to assure him, even though there was no heat behind his words. "But I don't want to take advantage of your generosity, either. Are you sure I can't mend a shirt or darn a sock for you in trade? Anything?"

"You can quit your yammerin' and carry this table downstairs so I can get back to minding my own business instead of messing around in yours."

His sudden rudeness set her back on her heels, but as he ducked his head to hide behind the brim of his hat, an internal light dawned. This tough cowboy didn't know how to deal with gratitude. He could repair a step and catch a falling damsel, but try to thank the fellow, and he got all surly. Maybe if she could remember that, he wouldn't rile her so easily.

If he could just remember that she was a dressmaker, maybe his gut wouldn't end up in knots whenever she looked at him like that. It was enough to give a man indigestion.

J.T. bit back a groan and flipped the table onto its side before she could distract him further. Miss Richards grabbed the leg and helped him maneuver the table through the doorway. She anticipated his movements and worked well with him as they eased down the steps, never once complaining about the weight or asking to take a break.

They carried the table through the back door and set it up in the workroom. He then returned to finish with the trunks while she carried her only chair down to the shop, as well. Something about needing it for her sewing machine and using her trunks for benches. Maybe he could check into finding her some real chairs.

After he deposited the last trunk, she locked up her room and followed him down the stairs.

"How much do I owe you?"

J.T. glanced off toward the livery, dodging her gaze. "A dollar for the wagon, and two bits for the unloading."

She handed him a one-dollar note and a silver twenty-five-cent piece. He tucked them into his pants pocket and nodded his thanks.

"Was the dry-goods store down this way?" She bit her lip and pointed toward the south, her blue gaze losing some of the assurance that had blazed there since she'd arrived. "I need to stock up on some supplies before they close this afternoon."

An offer to escort her rose to his lips, but he quickly suppressed it. It was bad enough that he would have to see her tomorrow when he delivered the sawhorses and shelves he'd foolishly promised when the urge to make amends for his hasty judgments temporarily overrode his good sense.

"Yep," he said, choosing the safer option. "It's two doors down. Just on the other side of Mrs. James's laundry."

"Thank you." She smiled in that way of hers, the one that made him feel like he had swallowed his toothpick. He frowned back.

Miss Richards turned away and started down the boardwalk, her skirts swaying in a subtle rhythm. Left. Right. L—

"Oh, Mr. Tucker?" She spun around, and J.T. jerked his focus back to her face. A cough that nearly strangled him lodged in his throat.

"Do you happen to know of someone in town who might be willing to sell me a jar of milk in the morning?"

The Harris family had a small dairy operation on the edge of town, where they sold milk, butter, and cheese to the locals. Will Harris, the eldest boy, usually made deliveries to the folks in town who didn't keep their own cow, but J.T. hesitated to mention him. He was a big, strapping lad with an eye for the ladies. A woman on her own didn't need a man like that coming around to her personal quarters in the early morning hours. Will was an honorable, churchgoing fella, yet the idea of him sniffing around Miss Richards set J.T.'s teeth on edge.

"I'll have my sister bring you some."

She snapped open the clasp on her purse and started swishing those hips toward him again. "Can I pay ahead for a week? I'll give you—"

"You and Delia can settle on a price tomorrow." He waved her off and stepped down into the street. "I've gotta get back to the livery."

"Thank you for all your help, Mr. Tucker," she called out to his back. "You truly have been a godsend."

He waved a hand in acknowledgment but didn't turn around. Clenching his jaw, J.T. pulverized as many dirt clods under his boots as possible while he crossed the road. First he tangled himself up with the dressmaker for another day by promising to make her a table, and now he'd dragged Cordelia into it, too. Exactly what he'd been trying to avoid.

J.T. stormed into his office and shut the door. He pounded the wall with his fist as his rebellious eyes sought Hannah Richards through the window and followed her until she disappeared into the mercantile. With a growl, he spun around and pressed his back into the wall, banging his head against the wood.

A godsend?

J.T. tipped his chin toward the ceiling. "If it's all the same to you, the next time she needs help, send someone else."

CHAPTER 5

By the time all trace of pink had faded from the sky the next morning, Hannah had already completed her calisthenic regimen, arranged her trunks and crates about the room, and organized her food supplies and personal belongings. A mountain of work still awaited her downstairs, but that knowledge did nothing to dim the excitement skittering across her nerves. If all went according to plan, she'd have her shop in basic working order by the end of the day and be open for business on the morrow. The very thought sent her into a pirouette. The shortened skirt of her loose-fitting gymnastic costume belled out around her.

Now, if only Miss Tucker would arrive with her milk, the day would be off to a grand start. Fighting off a spurt of impatience, Hannah decided to start in on her devotional time without her breakfast cocoa. Whenever possible, she began the day by sipping chocolate and reading from her Bible, but she couldn't afford to wait on the cocoa with all that had yet to be accomplished.

She had utilized every scrap of yesterday's daylight to knock down cobwebs from the rafters and corners of her living quarters, clean out ashes from the stove, scrub the floor, and curtain off her bedroom area. When the early darkness of the autumn evening had finally forced her to stop, she collapsed onto her lumpy mattress like a dervish that had run out of whirl and slept unmoving until a nearby rooster let out his predawn squawk. Spun back into action by the sound, she'd been swirling about in a frenzy ever since. She was more than ready for a little quiet time.

Hannah pushed the curtain aside, trying to ignore the unattractive fabric as she collected her Bible from the crate next to her bed. When Floyd Hawkins, the dry-goods store owner, heard she was a seamstress, he had dug out a bolt of dusty calico that had apparently been languishing untouched for over a year in his cloth bin and demanded she take it off his hands at the wholesale price. Hannah certainly understood why no one had purchased the appalling fabric. She would swallow a bug before fashioning the orange-dotted cloth into a dress. But knowing she could put it to use, her practical side wouldn't let her pass up the bargain. Tacked up in pleated folds along a ceiling beam, it offered privacy, if not great aesthetic value. Perhaps she could drape an eye-pleasing swag across the top and add a ribbon to the hem to dress it up a bit when things settled down.

Bible in hand, Hannah took a seat on the trunk bench she had positioned beneath the window to the left of the stove. She tugged the red satin ribbon that held her place and opened to Proverbs 16, the passage she had been meditating on for the last month as she made preparations for this day. Morning sunlight illuminated the wisdom on the page. Verse three promised that if she committed her work to the Lord, her thoughts would be established. Yet verse eight cautioned that having little while being righteous was better than great revenues without right. Finally, verse nine, the verse of balance, brought her hopes and fears together in a call to trust.

" 'A man's heart deviseth his way,' " she whispered, " 'but the Lord directeth his steps.' "

Hannah read the familiar words one more time before sliding her eyes shut. "Father, you know how badly I long for my thoughts and plans to be established. I have dreamed of this dress shop since my first apprenticeship. You have opened doors for me, doors I could not open on my own, and I thank you.

"At the same time, I confess to wanting success. I want customers to find satisfaction in my designs." Hannah's forehead crinkled as honesty warred with her desire not to appear overly ambitious or greedy before her Lord. "All right, more than satisfaction," she admitted. "I want them to be amazed at my skill. Help me to battle my pride and remember that it is by your grace alone that I have this opportunity.

"As I embark on this endeavor, remind me to cling to righteousness, not to revenue; to look for ways to serve and glorify you, not myself; and to follow where you lead, even if you direct my steps on a path that deviates from the way I have charted. Thank y—"

A quiet knock thumped against the door, cutting off her prayer and accelerating her heartbeat. Hannah shoved her Bible aside and jumped to her feet. She sent a silent amen heavenward and rushed to the door.

She opened the portal to find a softer, rounder, and more feminine version of Mr. Tucker standing on her stoop. The woman's brown hair was pulled into a nondescript knot beneath a plain straw bonnet that seemed more appropriate for a young girl than a grown woman. No frills adorned her brown dress, either. Yet the shy smile on her face erased any semblance of severity, and the aroma of fresh-baked bread that wafted from the basket she held filled Hannah with a sense of comfort and put her instantly at ease.

"You must be Miss Tucker. Please come in. I've been looking forward to meeting you."

The woman's cheeks flushed and her gaze fell to the floor, but her smile widened as she crossed the threshold. "Thank you, Miss Richards.

I have the milk you asked J.T. about and brought some of my apple muffins as a welcome gift."

"How thoughtful. They smell delicious. I hope it wasn't too much trouble." Hannah took the offered fruit jar of milk and set it on the arm of the stove while Miss Tucker extracted a napkin-wrapped bundle from the large basket hanging from the bend of her elbow. Hannah spied several loaves of bread and additional muffins before the cloth cover was tucked back into place.

"I supply baked goods to Mr. Hawkins's store, and it was a simple matter to stop here on the way. No trouble."

"A fellow businesswoman." Hannah accepted the muffins and held the offering up to her nose. "And if these taste as good as they smell, you no doubt turn a tidy profit."

Miss Tucker shook her head. "I'm not a *real* businesswoman. Not like you, with your own shop and everything." The blush was back, painting her cheeks a dusty pink.

Hannah examined the woman more closely. She truly possessed some lovely features. Long dark lashes, a dainty nose, full lips. She might be considered a tad plump by some, but Hannah could easily minimize that with the right cut and color of fabric. If she could just get her out of that drab brown and put her into a deep rose or peacock blue. . . .

"I enjoy baking, that's all." Miss Tucker broke into her thoughts, and Hannah refocused on the conversation. "J.T. provides a good living for us, but after all he's done for me, I'm glad to make whatever contribution I can."

"I know what you mean. I still send funds to my mother when I get the chance. She lives with my younger sister and her husband back east and is always worried about being a burden to them. Which, of course, she's not. Emily's the nurturer of the family and loves having Mama around, especially now that a child is on the way."

"Your family's back east?" Miss Tucker eyed her curiously. "How did you come to be in Texas, then?"

Hannah smiled as she moved her Bible to the windowsill and motioned for her guest to be seated on the trunk bench. She gently extricated the oversized basket from Miss Tucker's arm and set it on the floor.

"When I was sixteen, my mother arranged for me to apprentice with an established dressmaker in Boston, not far from our home in Dorchester. After three years, I had worked my way up to first assistant when my employer married the brother of one of her clients. It was quite a scandal, although all of us girls thought it terribly romantic."

"Did she move her business west after the wedding?"

Hannah shook her head as she dumped a bunch of potatoes out of a crate and into an empty dishpan. Turning the crate upside down, she drew the short seat across from Miss Tucker and sat down, folding her crossed ankles off to the side.

"No. Her new husband wouldn't hear of her continuing to work, so she closed her shop. Unfortunately, that left many of us without employment. I could have hired on as an apprentice-level seamstress with one of the other dressmakers in Boston, but the pay would have been a pittance, and my mother and sister depended on the funds I sent them. So when my employer's aunt, also a seamstress, came to town for the wedding and offered me a full-pay position if I was willing to return to San Antonio with her, I decided seeing the great American West was an adventure I couldn't refuse.

"I spent the last two years with Mrs. Granbury, and I must say, I've developed quite a taste for Texas."

"Surely it's hard to be so far away from your family, though."

"Yes." Hannah thought of Christmases missed and how she wouldn't be around for the birth of the niece or nephew who was due in a couple of months. Loneliness permeated, and her posture sagged until she caught herself and stiffened her spine. "But it's not so bad. I've had the opportunity to develop my business out here much more quickly than would have been possible back in Boston. And if I'm blessed enough to make a few good friends in Coventry, my life will be rich."

As she glanced at the quiet girl who was listening so intently, a feeling of kinship rose up in Hannah. Perhaps the Lord was already paving the road for a lasting friendship.

Thinking to offer her guest some refreshment, Hannah rose and stepped over to the stove. She pried open the fruit jar lid and poured the milk into a saucepan. Then she reached to the top shelf and pulled down her five-pound canister of Baker's Breakfast Cocoa, turning it so Miss Tucker could see the trademark Chocolate Lady with her apron and tray. "When Emily and I were girls, Mama took a job at the Baker Chocolate mill to support us after Papa died. She scraped and saved until she managed to buy that first apprenticeship for me. I owe her everything."

"She sounds like a wonderful woman." Miss Tucker smiled, but her eyes held a sad, wistful look.

"Mama's also the one responsible for my chocolate craving." Hannah winked, and steered the discussion in a lighter direction. "Every week, she'd come home with another can of powder, so we drank cocoa religiously every morning. That's the reason I needed the milk. I can't get through the day without my cup of breakfast cocoa. Would you stay and share some with me? It will only take a couple of minutes to warm the milk."

"I wish I could, but Mr. Hawkins likes me to deliver my goods before the store opens." Miss Tucker pushed to her feet and collected her basket. "Perhaps another time."

"We'll definitely find a time." Hannah smiled as she replaced the cocoa canister. "Now, what do I owe you for the milk, Miss Tucker? I would like to pay ahead for the entire week, if that would be acceptable."

"I'll only charge you twenty cents since I skimmed off the cream and kept it for my baking. And please, call me Cordelia."

"Gladly, and I'm Hannah." She handed over the coins and walked

Cordelia to the door. "Thank you again for the muffins. Your brother was such a help to me yesterday, and this morning you have made me feel welcome. I am blessed to know you both and would be honored to count you as friends."

"I would like that immensely," Cordelia said, her eyes alight with sincerity. "Oh . . . J.T. asked me to tell you that he wouldn't be able to bring the wood by until later this afternoon. I hope that will be all right."

"Goodness, yes. I'll be up to my armpits in soapsuds and vinegar water all morning, I'm sure. This afternoon will be fine."

As Hannah waved good-bye to Cordelia, her gaze roamed across the street to the livery. An annoying tingle of anticipation wiggled through her stomach at the thought of seeing Mr. Tucker again. Traitorous stomach. The man could seesaw her emotions fast enough to make her dizzy. She didn't need that kind of distraction today. Nevertheless, the insolent tingle remained.

J.T. lumbered toward the dreaded dress shop with the crosspieces of two sawhorses under one arm and six stacked planks under the other. Making two trips would have been easier, but he wanted to get this good deed over and done.

Miss Richards was standing on the boardwalk, rubbing a rag in circles against a pane of glass in her window. When her motions elicited a series of squeaks, she dipped her rag back into the bucket at her feet and moved on to the next pane. J.T. dropped the ends of the boards onto the walkway beside her, making no effort to keep them quiet. Why should he when it was so much fun to watch her jump and squeak at the same pitch as her clean windows?

Splat!

Ah. That's why.

Pungent vinegar fumes scratched his throat and would have made his eyes water if they weren't already wet from the rag that had just slapped across his face. The rag slid down the length of his face in a cold, slimy trail, rolled down his chest, and plopped onto the ground. Blindly, he angled the boards toward the wall and leaned them against the frame of the building, then bent his knees and set the sawhorses down on the opposite side. They clattered and probably tumbled off the boardwalk, but he didn't care. As he straightened, with deliberate slowness, he drew a handkerchief from his trouser pocket and wiped the moisture from his face while the esteemed dressmaker unsuccessfully stifled her giggles. Once he deemed it safe to open his eyes, he glared at her.

"I'm so sorry, Mr. Tucker." She covered her mouth with her hand for a moment, probably trying to stuff the rest of her laughter back inside so as not to spoil the effect of her pretty apology. When her hand fell away, she was biting her lip, but even her teeth could not contain her smile. "You really oughtn't sneak up on a person like that. You startled me and the rag flew right out of my hand." She demonstrated the action as if he hadn't been right there to witness it firsthand.

"Maybe you should pay more heed to your surroundings."

"I'll try to do that. I have a tendency to get absorbed in my thoughts at times, especially when I'm debating strategies." She tipped her head sideways and gave him a thoroughly coquettish glance over her shoulder. "What do *you* think, Mr. Tucker? Would a lavender morning dress be too pale for a window display, or would the demure cut be more likely to attract clientele than a flashy party gown?"

He rolled his eyes, and her laughter showered over him.

"Never mind. I won't draw you into my dilemma. I'm sure you have more manly tasks to pursue."

Unfortunately, he couldn't recall a single one of those tasks as he watched joy flow out of her like a stream of sweet-tasting water.

She stooped to pick up the fallen rag, and he realized she had tied a remarkably similar one over her hair. Some ugly tan thing with orange blotches all over it. One would think such a sight would be enough to make him look away, but even combined with her stained, shapeless work dress, it wasn't enough to deter his gaze.

Hadn't his past taught him anything? Beautiful women were nothing but trouble—shallow, empty husks that would blow away the minute life got a little uncomfortable. J.T. had vowed never to allow feminine beauty to overrule good sense. He wouldn't fall into that trap. If he ever married, it would be to a woman of spiritual depth who selflessly served others. A helpmeet, someone to encourage him and stand by his side as stalwartly in hard times as in easy. Not a pretty piece of fluff who would tangle herself around his neck and drag him down like a millstone.

"One day I'm going to catch you in the grips of a full-blown grin, Mr. Tucker," she said, wagging a finger at him, "and when I do, watch out because I'm going to crow in victory."

"We all need goals in life, Miss Richards." J.T. swung two boards up onto his shoulder and peered down at her. "Mine's to get this stuff delivered before the first snow falls. You think I got a chance at making that happen?"

CHAPTER 6

Hannah shook her head and tiptoed up the stairs, determined not to let Mr. Tucker catch her stomping again. He might have crawled under her skin and set her temper to itching, but she didn't have to scratch it.

He set the boards down inside the door and without a word headed back down for the sawhorses. Once he returned, it only took a minute or two to erect the makeshift table. She dipped a cupful of water while he worked and had it ready for him when he finished.

Frowning, as usual, he reluctantly accepted the cup. The competitor within her whooped over the small victory. Mr. J.T. Tucker might tilt her off balance, but from now on, she refused to let him take her feet out from under her. She'd prove her mettle to him, and maybe in the process, she'd finally witness that elusive grin.

"Thanks." He thrust the cup into her hands and turned for the door. "I'll move those shelves inside the shop for you, then be on my way."

Gulping down a quick drink of her own, Hannah tossed the cup into the dishpan on the floor and scurried after him. By the time she locked up and ran down the stairs, he was already inside. She leaned against the door and reached for the handle to follow him, but it fell away from her grasp as he wrenched it open from within. Hannah tumbled through the doorway, her head colliding with Mr. Tucker's chest.

Strong, yet surprisingly gentle hands clasped her arms and steadied her. Heat flooded her face. Hadn't she just resolved not to let this man knock her feet out from under her? The fact that her resolution had been figurative, not literal, gave her no comfort. Twice in as many days she had fallen onto the poor fellow. No wonder he was in such a hurry to escape her.

Not quite able to look him in the eye, she focused on his chin. "I'm sorry to keep throwing myself at you like this, Mr. Tucker. It truly wasn't my intention."

The Adam's apple beneath his jaw rose and fell in a slow movement Hannah found strangely fascinating. Then before she could blink, he cleared his throat and released her so suddenly, she nearly fell into him again.

"I . . . uh . . . need to go." He sidestepped and tried to squeeze past her through the doorway.

Thankfully, Hannah regained her senses and her memory a second before he made it around her. She needed one more thing from him in order to finish the preparations on her shop.

"May I ask one last favor of you, Mr. Tucker?"

He stopped, and she swore she could hear heavy breaths coming from him, as if he were a green-broke stallion fixing to buck his way out of a saddle. "I wouldn't ask except you're the only man I really know in town."

He didn't say a word, just stood there breathing through flared nostrils, making her nervous. Taking a deep breath of her own, she spat out the rest of her request.

"I was hoping I could borrow a couple of tools from you. A level and a screwdriver? I'd return them by the end of the day, or tomorrow morning at the latest. I'd like to get my shelves in place and my display rack mounted before nightfall so I can open the shop tomorrow."

Hannah stared at his profile to gauge his reaction. He stretched his chin out a bit and a muscle ticked in his jaw before he finally spoke.

"Sorry," he said, his voice clipped. "I've got my own business to run. I can't play handyman for you, hanging shelves and things all afternoon. You'll have to ask someone else."

Despite her earlier resolve, Hannah's temper flared. She moved closer to the arrogant, assumption-spewing Mr. Tucker and planted her feet. "Did I *ask* you to play handyman for me? No. I simply asked a neighbor if I might borrow his tools. If you had listened to my words instead of focusing on your own preconceived notions, you might have actually understood that. I am perfectly capable of hanging a few brackets without a man commandeering the task, so you're off the hook. I'm sure Mr. Hawkins will sell me the items I need. I won't bother you again."

She stepped aside to give him his freedom, but he just stood there, so she marched over to her window-washing bucket, slapped the sopping rag against the center pane, and started scrubbing. The entire window had already been cleaned, but she couldn't push past the liveryman statue blocking her doorway to closet herself up in her shop, so she had to settle for ignoring him.

The shop door clicked shut. She refused to turn. His boot heels pounded against the wooden boardwalk, then thudded as they hit the dirt of the road, but she didn't look his way. He'd offered no apology, no parting words.

Grabbing her bucket, she strode into the shop, uncaring that water was sloshing onto her shoes as she went. She held her head high just in case he was watching, but the moment she closed the door, she deflated. Indignation could only fuel her for so long before regret crept in, and her affront had quieted enough to let the voice of conscience through. And the lecture it wrote on her heart shamed her.

She had no right to harangue the man just because he didn't want to help her. After all, she'd done nothing but impose on him since arriving in town. He clearly wasn't the cheerful sort, and while he shouldn't have jumped to such uncomplimentary conclusions about her, he didn't deserve her wrath. He had rescued her from a potentially harmful fall, arranged for his sister to supply her with milk, made her a table without being asked, and even gave her free wood to use as shelving in her shop.

Hannah ran a hand along the edge of one of the boards he had set against the wall just inside the door. Not wanting to get a splinter, she traced it lightly until she realized that the surface was smooth. She took a closer look, handling each plank in turn. All of them had been sanded from stem to stern and cut to a uniform length. Spare wood from a scrap lumber pile wouldn't be this ready for use without someone taking the time to cut and sand each one.

Now she felt even worse.

Why did the man have to be such a contradiction? His actions exuded kindness and consideration, going well beyond the neighborly help she had requested of him. Yet his surly demeanor riled her like a tangled bobbin thread that refused to unknot. Which side of his character was she to believe?

A muted thump sounded on the other side of her door. She probably wouldn't have heard it if she hadn't been standing so close. Hannah pivoted toward the sound and caught sight of a familiar male form passing by her window. Taking a deep breath, she scrambled to find words for a proper apology, then opened the door. She stepped outside to call to him but tripped over something in her path. Lurching forward, she sucked in a pain-filled breath as she caught her balance. By the time she steadied herself, Mr. Tucker was entering the laundry next door.

Toe throbbing and heart equally sore over her missed opportunity to make amends, Hannah turned around and limped the few steps back to the door. Glancing down to see what she had tripped over, she bit her lip, her toe forgotten.

There, in front of her door, lay a level and screwdriver.

She gathered the tools in her arms, her gaze trailing the path Mr. Tucker had taken to the laundry. She might never figure him out, but something told her she had just received an apology, one that spoke with an eloquence that outshone any words he could have offered.

A barrage of steamy heat accosted J.T. as he pushed through the laundry house door. He tugged his hat from his head and closed the door behind him, wishing he could leave it open to create a breeze, but Louisa would scold him good if he let dust blow in to soil her clean wash.

"Pickin' up or droppin' off?" a harried voice called from the back room.

"It's me, Louisa." J.T. frowned as he surveyed the warped floorboards and chinks in the wall. The roof probably leaked, too. If he couldn't move her into a different building, he'd have to find a way to repair this one, which was tricky since the laundress's pride prickled faster than a cactus pear.

"Come on back, J.T."

After consumption took her husband two years ago and left her with three kids to feed, Louisa James had sold her farm and rented this space in town. She'd barely had anything left after paying off the mortgage, but she managed to eke out a living washing trousers and starching shirts for the townsfolk. He admired her grit, yet it was that same toughness that made her reject anything that smelled of charity.

He wound his way past tables stacked with cleaned and pressed items awaiting their owners, empty washtubs, and folded drying racks that could be set up inside when the weather turned rainy. Stepping through the doorway, he found Louisa bent over her ironing table, sadiron in hand, smoothing wrinkles from the sleeve of a man's white cotton shirt. With a practiced motion, she set her iron on the stove, clicked the handle off, and snapped it onto a hotter one while six-year-old Mollie handed the finished shirt to big sister, Tessa, then pulled another garment from the oversized basket on the floor and laid it in place for her mother. Tessa, the middle child at age eight and the most outgoing of the bunch, looked up at him and smiled.

"Hi, Mr. Tucker. Danny's waiting for you out back. He separated out all the small pieces, just like you asked, and saved the big ones for you."

How the child managed to converse and fold at the same time was a marvel, yet the shirt lay in a tidy rectangle by the time she came up for air.

"Thanks, squirt." He winked at her and she giggled.

He tweaked Mollie's nose as he passed her by and nodded a greeting to Louisa. The woman was thin and worn, her hands reddened and creased from her constant labor. Strands of ash brown hair clung to her face, wet with perspiration, yet he'd never heard her complain. Now that harvest was nearly done, she'd be losing her help as the kids headed back to school for the winter term. Many in her position would keep the children home, especially the girls, but Louisa always had them spit-shined and ready before the teacher rang the bell. J.T. figured she didn't want Tessa and Mollie to end up doing other people's laundry for the rest of their lives, and he respected her for that. He just wished she'd accept a little help from folks from time to time.

"I need to speak with you, J.T., before you start in on the wood." Louisa rubbed the underside of her chin with the back of her hand and tipped her head toward the rear door.

"All right." He followed her outside and welcomed the cool breeze that fluttered across the yard as he slipped his hat back on.

"I met the new seamstress this morning," Louisa said. "Ran into her at the water pump at first light."

J.T. nodded as his mind shifted to Miss Richards. He hadn't expected her to be an early riser. The woman was as unpredictable as a Texas cyclone.

"Offered to pay my boy a dollar a week to keep her woodbox full. Said she didn't need much, cookin' for just herself, and she'll gather her own kindlin' during her daily *constitutional*, whatever that is." Louisa crossed her arms over her chest and braced her legs as if preparing for a fight. "I know I ought to've checked with you first, seeing as how you're the one that chops it all, but I accepted her terms, and I don't aim to go back on the agreement."

J.T. reached into his shirt pocket and drew out a toothpick. He took his time moving it to his mouth, and only after it was clamped securely between his molars did he address the widow James, hoping she'd relaxed a bit in the interim.

"I reckon you can do whatever you want with it, Louisa. It's your wood, bought and paid for every time Daniel mucks out a stall at the livery. I pay Tom a wage for the same work."

"The boy's only ten. He works twice as long to do half the work Tom does, and you know it."

"Maybe. But he does the work I ask him to. I don't hold with slavery, ma'am, so if you don't consider my chopping wood for you once a month true payment, I guess I can leave off the wood and start paying the boy in cash money. Which do you prefer?" He switched the toothpick to the opposite side of his mouth and angled a hard look at her.

"You know I ain't got time to chop the wood myself, and the last thing I need is for Danny to try to take over the job and chop his foot off." He watched pride battle with practicality as she gazed at young Daniel dragging large logs over to the chopping stump. J.T. had only asked Daniel to work at the livery so he'd have an excuse to keep her in wood, and Louisa was too smart not to know that. But with all the water she heated for washing and the stove that had to be kept hot all day for the ironing, she ran through her fuel supply faster than she could replenish it.

Practicality won out, but pride put in a fair showing.

"Well, I just wanted to make sure you weren't offended or nothing. I knew we owned the wood all right and proper." She sniffed and, with a twirl of her faded skirts, returned to her work inside the house.

Lord, save me from proud, stubborn women. They seemed to be swarming him lately.

Thankful to be left alone with the only male in the general vicinity, J.T. ducked under a row of clothes still drying on the line and joined Daniel. The kid was a quiet one, which suited J.T. just fine. After tousling the boy's hair and thumping him on the back, he picked up the ax and started swinging. The two worked side by side—J.T. split the logs; Daniel arranged them on the pile. Simple. No ruffled feathers, no pecking accusations, just a couple of men working together without a lot of gab.

Unfortunately, all he managed to think about while he worked were the ruffled feathers and pecking accusations from one hen in particular. Miss Hannah Richards.

J.T. slammed the ax blade into the log below him with a crack that failed to banish the picture of her from his mind.

He swung again, and the log spit unevenly. J.T. scowled.

Now that he'd had time to think on the matter, he realized her protests didn't necessarily mean she hadn't been hinting for him to come help her. She probably just didn't want to admit it. After all, most women didn't know one end of a screwdriver from the other, and she looked pretty beat from her day of cleaning. She'd be too tired to lift those boards high enough to place shelves. He still needed to take care of some business at the bank, but afterward he could stop by her shop to save himself from having to deal with her on the morrow.

An hour and a half later, after he'd split all the logs in the yard, J.T. washed up at the pump, shook hands with the little man who had helped him, and headed for the bank. Louisa might not willingly accept charity, but J.T. had a plan to get around that. She couldn't refuse his help if she was unaware of it, now, could she?

CHAPTER 7

J.T. entered the bank just as the clerk set the *Closed* sign in the window. The fellow nodded a greeting to him before scurrying back to his teller's cage. The proprietress of the local boardinghouse stood at the counter impatiently tapping her foot, apparently displeased by the interruption of her transaction.

"Is Paxton in?" J.T. asked.

The clerk disappeared behind the counter, then opened the gate of his window and met J.T.'s eye around a bent plume in the lady's bonnet. "He's with a customer at the moment, but you can take a seat on the bench outside his office. He should be finished shortly."

"Thanks."

J.T. fingered his hat and nodded to the woman, who glared at him over her shoulder before swinging her accusing eyes back to the unfortunate clerk. After sharing a commiserating look with the two cowhands standing in line, all three males grateful to be on the customer side of the counter, J.T. took his cue and meandered over to the bench.

Too restless to sit, he propped a foot on the seat of the bench and braced one elbow on his thigh. He didn't like sneaking around behind Louisa's back, but the woman didn't leave him much choice. The Good Book taught that a man should give without his left hand knowing what his right was doing. Louisa was just playing the role of the left hand. Still, the secrecy grated on him, made him feel as if he were doing something disreputable.

The quiet swish of a well-oiled door opening drew J.T.'s attention. He dropped his foot to the floor and straightened his stance.

Floyd Hawkins and his son, Warren, emerged from Elliott Paxton's office. The elder Hawkins chatted amiably with the banker while his son separated himself from the conversation.

Warren pushed his overlong hair out of his face and caught sight of J.T. His eyes widened a bit, and his neck stretched as if his collar had suddenly grown too tight.

The kid was always nervous around him. Never used to be. But lately, Warren had been acting different, like he was trying to impress him or something.

Not that his efforts had been paying off. The kid had a chip on his shoulder the size of Gibraltar's Rock. He wasn't a bad egg, just irritating with his sullen looks and woeful attitude. Seemed to think the world owed him something because he was born with a mark on his face. J.T. could sympathize with the embarrassment and frustration that went along with schoolyard teasing, but Warren wasn't a boy any longer. Time to stop the pouting and start acting like a man. Respect wouldn't come any other way.

As if Warren had heard his thoughts, he straightened his shoulders and approached.

"J.T."

J.T. cocked his head. Either his ears needed a good scrubbing or Warren had just lowered the timbre of his voice a couple of levels below normal. J.T. fought the urge to roll his eyes.

"Warren."

The kid tugged on his coat lapels and pushed up on his toes. "Dad and I are considering an expansion of the business. Mr. Paxton is helping us plan the finances."

"That so?" J.T. really had no particular interest in the Hawkins family's business endeavors, but Warren seemed to expect some kind of reply.

"I . . . ah . . . thought your sister might like to join us for dinner one evening to discuss the expansion. Since the change will affect her. . . . I mean, because we sell her baked goods and all."

J.T. arched his brows and shot Warren a look that must have communicated how senseless he thought that comment was, for the kid dropped his gaze and scuffed his toe against the wooden floorboards.

Why would Delia care about them opening another store somewhere? It wasn't like she was going to bake anything for it. Hers was strictly a local operation.

Still, Delia considered Warren a friend, and she wouldn't want J.T. giving the kid a hard time—no matter how much he deserved it. So he cleared his throat and came as close to an apology as he could manage.

"I'm sure Delia would enjoy hearing about your plans one of these days."

Warren's head shot up, and a grin split his face. Seeing his response, J.T.'s conscience flared up. Maybe he should cut the kid a break. He was still young. A little more life experience and he might grow out from under that oversized attitude of his. He'd never really had to fend for himself, what with his father's store always being there for him. And from what J.T. understood, Warren had started taking over more responsibilities—keeping the books, making deliveries, overseeing the inventory. Maybe he should make more of an effort to be tolerant.

"I'll be sure to tell her about it, then," Warren said, swagger restored.

"She'd probably enjoy sharing a meal with a man who didn't smell like manure for a change."

Then again, maybe he should just expedite the kid's real-world education and stuff his tongue down his throat.

J.T. stared at him without moving so much as a finger, channeling all his affront into his expression. The snorting laugh blowing out of Warren's nose at his careless jest morphed into a cough and, finally, silence. Even after Warren ducked his head, J.T. did not relent. He wanted to bore his glare into the boy's skull until it stirred up some common sense.

Fortunately for Warren, his father concluded his chat with the banker and came to join them. J.T. lifted his gaze. "Afternoon, Hawkins."

"Tucker." He held out his hand to J.T. and shook it with a solid grip. The man's smile and genuine warmth went a long way to soothe J.T.'s temper. "Sorry for monopolizing Mr. Paxton's time. I didn't realize you were waiting."

"That's all right. I haven't been here long."

Warren edged toward the entrance. "Let's go, Dad. You know how Mother hates to watch the store when she's trying to get supper on the stove."

"You're right." Hawkins offered a little wave as he moved past J.T. "Give Cordelia our best."

"I will."

The two disappeared onto the street, and J.T. barely had time to remind himself why he had come before Elliott Paxton descended upon him.

"Mr. Tucker!" The banker stretched his arms wide in welcome, his nature so ebullient, J.T. would have cringed had it been anyone else. But that was just Paxton's way. After five years, he had gotten used to the banker's fulsome ways. Had the man greeted him with a solemn nod, J.T. would have ordered the clerk to fetch the doctor.

"Come in, young man. Come in." Paxton held the door wide until J.T. entered the office and took a seat. "What can I do for you today, sir?" he asked as he clicked the door closed.

"I want to find out if the owner of the property where Louisa James runs her laundry might be talked into selling."

The banker sat in the chair behind his desk and rapped his finger against its surface. "I could make some inquiries, I suppose. If I remember correctly, the man in question runs a land company over in Waco. Wouldn't be hard to send a few wires to the account manager. I can't say as I'd recommend that building as an investment, though. The place has been in ill repair for years."

"I know." J.T. rubbed his chin. "I'd planned to buy the shop next door, but the owner rejected my offer."

"Ah, yes. It's to be a dress shop, I believe. I spied the new seamstress washing her windows earlier. Lovely woman."

"Yes . . . well . . . I had hoped to be able to offer Mrs. James a more suitable location for her laundry business—one with four decent walls and a roof that doesn't leak. But that opportunity is no longer available. So I figured I could buy the place she's in, lower her rent, and be a proper landlord. You know, fix the roof, keep the pump in working order—that kind of thing."

"I see." Elliott Paxton tapped a finger to his mouth and contemplated him with an intensity that made J.T.'s throat ache.

"That's a commendable plan, son," the banker said. "I'm impressed."

J.T. shifted in his seat and glared at the worn spot on his trouser knee. He hated it when people made too much of things. It wasn't like he was building Louisa a mansion or anything. He just wanted an excuse to help her out from time to time without raising her hackles. That's all. Nothing to be impressed about.

"It's a rare man who would spend his hard-earned money on

a worthless piece of property in order to benefit a widow woman unrelated to him. Why, most would scoff at the idea."

Paxton's commendation waxed on and on, extolling his nonexistent virtues until J.T. could bear it no longer.

Jumping out of his chair as if the cushion had suddenly grown teeth, J.T. retreated. He strode to the door in two steps and gripped the knob.

"So, you'll look into it for me?"

Paxton nodded, brows arching in puzzlement. He started to rise. "Of course, but—"

"Thanks." J.T. waved him off and fled the banker's office. But the tightness in his chest didn't loosen until he exited the bank.

He knew Paxton would be discreet. The man had built a reputation on being trustworthy. Still, it would have been easier if Hannah Richards hadn't stolen his building. Then there would have been no need to involve the banker in the first place, no awkward conversation, no sneaking around behind Louisa's back.

A pang of honesty poked at him. Okay, so Miss Richards hadn't exactly *stolen* his building. Nevertheless, the woman was proving inconvenient. Not only did she throw a wrench in his plans for helping Louisa, but thanks to their earlier run-in, he now felt obligated to hang her shelves.

J.T.'s boots clomped over the boardwalk planks as he made his way to the shop situated at the end of the street. He paused outside the door and drew in a deep breath, probing his shirt pocket for a pick. Placing it between his teeth, he clamped down and reminded himself to keep his mouth shut as much as possible. It wouldn't do for him to snap at Miss Richards again. She'd been working hard all day and was probably exhausted. Frustrated, too.

He winced at the image the thought produced. The gal must have had a rough time of it the last couple of hours. If she stuck with it, that is. J.T. stole a glance through the window, curious to see if she had abandoned her project or if she lay buried beneath it. What he found so startled him, he tipped his hat back and looked a second time for verification.

A rack of hooks had been mounted on the north wall, perfectly level and apparently secure, for three dresses hung on display. Eight brackets paired in staggered positions jutted out from the south wall with three shelves already in place. Colorful fabric adorned the shelves, and even his untrained eye could tell they were artfully matched. Several of her dummies, not yet clothed, stood in the corner observing their mistress as she fussed with the way the material draped from the corner of the third shelf.

As his jaw slackened, J.T.'s toothpick dangled unanchored across his bottom lip. Miss Richards's capability had been no idle boast, and her request *hadn't* been a manipulation. But that made no sense. Why would a woman of integrity run a shop that glorified superficial beauty?

CHAPTER 8

Hannah awoke to a day full of promise. The sun had not yet crested the horizon, but a soft glow lightened the predawn sky as she dipped water from the stove reservoir to wash her face.

Wednesday—not the usual day to open a new business, but she was too excited to postpone. She'd spent yesterday evening painting pasteboard signs. One carried the words *Open* and *Closed* on opposite sides, and a second one listed her services. *Dressmaking and Fine Tailoring* took top billing in large block letters with *Alterations and Mending* mentioned in smaller script along the bottom. One placard for each window. She would order a larger sign for the front of the building later today. Mr. Hawkins mentioned that the blacksmith also cut and stenciled signs. She could visit with him after she returned Mr. Tucker's tools.

Pushing her thoughts quickly from the annoying livery owner, Hannah returned to her sleeping area and removed her nightgown. Skirts of any kind hindered the extension of her lower limbs during her calisthenic routine, so she preferred to conduct the exercises in her drawers and shift when privacy allowed. Kneeling down, she pulled a small crate full of exercise equipment from under the bed. She selected the two-pound polished maple dumbbells and positioned herself with the heels of her bare feet together and her toes pointed outward.

It took thirty minutes to work through the repetitions. Straight arm lifts to the side, overhead, and forward. Then again with bent arms curling up and punching down, up, or out in keeping with the various positions. She continued with backward leans and leg lunges, all with the dumbbells in hand. Next came the floor sweep, where she stretched to her toes, weights overhead, then bent her knees and crouched, touching the dumbbells to the floor. She repeated each motion twenty times before advancing to the next exercise, and by the time the routine ended, her muscles had been well stretched and carried a satisfying ache.

Hannah sponged the light sheen of perspiration from her body with the wet rag she had used on her face earlier and dressed in her gymnastic costume. She replaced the soiled apron with a fresh one and laced up her low-heeled walking shoes. Since she didn't know the surrounding area well, she planned to walk along the road to keep her bearings. On the way back, she'd venture farther afield to collect sticks and dry twigs for kindling. She looped the strap of a large canvas bag over her head and shoulder and placed the pouch behind her, where it wouldn't interfere with her brisk pace. Then she set out on her first Coventry constitutional.

Not expecting to see anyone out and about in the early morning hours, Hannah nearly tripped when J.T. Tucker appeared along a crossroad that bordered the livery. She swallowed her surprised gasp and kept moving, offering him only a smile and a tiny wave in greeting as she headed north out of town. He returned her gesture with a raised brow that could have stemmed from either shock or disapproval. It was impossible to tell.

Hannah lifted her chin and increased her pace to a near jog, her arms swinging at her sides with gusto. Mr. Tucker didn't intimidate her.

He could think what he liked. Vigorous physical exercise was good for a body. Why, it had probably saved her life.

As the distance between her and Coventry lengthened, Hannah's steps slowed to their usual pace, quick but not frenzied. The beauty of the morning calmed her with birdsong and sunshine. A cool breeze ruffled wispy strands of hair from her braid, and she lifted a hand to secure them behind her ear.

Mr. Tucker's response was no different than that of most people. The lady who ran the boardinghouse she'd stayed at back in San Antonio had pointed out often enough that Hannah had to be out of her mind to waste so much energy walking nowhere.

She supposed it did seem a bit strange. Most Westerners labored from sunup to sundown in physically demanding tasks. They had no need for calisthenics and constitutionals. But for a sickly girl growing up in a crowded city, Professor Lewis's system of gymnastic exercise had been a salvation.

Hannah strode up a hill and passed the Coventry schoolhouse. Judging by the cross that jutted up from the belfry, it served as a place of worship, as well. A small footpath veered off to the right behind the building, and Hannah decided to follow it. The grassland turned woodsy the farther she went, and she spied several large pecan trees that promised to provide kindling for her. Not wanting to lose her momentum, though, she trudged on until she came upon a creek and an arched wooden bridge that spanned its width.

Enchanted, Hannah scurried to the center of the bridge and leaned her ribs against the railing. She gazed upriver, drinking in the sunlight sparkling on the slow-moving water, breathing in the smell of moist earth and tree bark, and swaying to the whispering melody of leaves rustling in the wind as sung by the river birch and cottonwood trees that lined the banks.

Lord, how marvelous you are. The beauty of your creation humbles me. If I can imitate even a hint of your artistry with my needle, I will be content. May my craftsmanship reflect your glory and bring you pleasure.

Hannah inhaled long and slow, allowing the loveliness of the moment to infuse her spirit with peace. Never did she feel closer to the Lord than when she was in nature. The busyness of town life distracted and misdirected her, but the Lord sought her out with gifts of beauty. Sometimes she was blessed with an experience like this where she was surrounded by his majesty, unable to do anything but praise him. Other times, he presented her with smaller reminders of his presence and his love. A full moon shining white in a black sky; a wildflower springing up through a crack in the boardwalk; a crimson oak leaf falling from an autumn branch, beautiful in death.

That final thought made her think of Victoria Ashmont and her scandalous red burial gown. A sad smile curled her lips, and she mouthed a prayer for the departed woman's soul. A single act of kindness on her part had changed Hannah's life forever, and Hannah was determined to prove that the old woman's confidence in her had not been misplaced.

Hannah made good time on her way back to town, the weight of the full kindling bag adding to her exertion but not slowing her speed. Coming off the hill by the schoolhouse, she spotted an old man and a mule not far in front of her. The man's stooped shoulders and plodding steps made him the tortoise to her hare, and she overtook them in a matter of minutes. Compassion slowed Hannah's steps as she approached, but then the wind shifted and something altogether different came over her—a suffocating stench that grabbed her by the throat and triggered a powerful urge to retch.

Thankful to have not yet broken her fast, Hannah concentrated on breathing through her mouth instead of her nose and forced a smile of greeting as the man turned.

"Good day to you, sir. It's a lovely morning to be out for a stroll." Her lungs begged to cough, but she wrestled them into submission.

"That it is, young lady. That it is." He smiled in return, or at least she thought he did. It was hard to tell what shape his mouth formed beneath all the whiskers.

His gray, matted beard hung halfway to his belt, an inch or two longer than the stringy hair that draped down his back from under a hat so caked with dust she couldn't determine its original color. The only thing not filthy about him was the tall walking stick clasped in his left hand. She'd never seen one like it. Fashioned from a twisted branch that had been stripped of its bark and varnished to a high gloss, it stood proudly beside its owner, as tall as the man himself. The wood's rich cinnamon color blended with lighter yellow streaks to create a stunning contrast that sent Hannah's creative mind whirling with ideas of how to mimic the effect with fabric.

"What a beautiful staff. Is it made from mesquite?"

"The very same. It shines up right purdy, don't it?" His tone was friendly, but his faded blue eyes groaned with sadness. "I sell 'em down at the depot along with my other carvings."

Hannah examined the mule's load more carefully. What she had initially assumed to be firewood was actually a cluster of handcrafted walking sticks. The animal also packed two large sacks that undoubtedly held the other items he mentioned.

As they neared the edge of town, Hannah discreetly turned her head to the side and gulped in two quick breaths of less potent air.

"If any ladies debarking the trains ask about dressmakers," she said, "send them my way. Today is the grand opening of my new shop here in Coventry. I'm Hannah Richards," she said with a nod.

"Pleased to meet ya, Miz Richards. Ezra Culpepper at your service." He dipped his head and doffed his hat with the walking-stick hand. "You can call me Ezra."

"And you must call me Hannah," she said, charmed despite the unwashed odor wafting from the crusty fellow. Maybe it was his red flannel shirt or the gray hair or the loneliness he radiated, but for some reason, he reminded her of Miss Victoria. The woman would no doubt be horrified by the comparison, but Hannah couldn't escape the feeling of similarity, and her heart softened toward him.

"I'm afraid I don't get the chance to speak to many of them there ladies, Miz Hannah. They tend to give me a wide berth."

She could certainly understand why.

"But I could inform the stationmaster, so's he can pass the word to any females what need new duds."

"I'd be much obliged. Thank you, Ezra."

They passed the livery, where a hay wagon stood out front, a heaping load ready to be delivered, but there was no sign of Mr. Tucker. Unsure if she was disappointed or pleased by that fact, Hannah turned her attention away from the livery and toward her shop.

Pride surged in her breast as she gazed through the clean windows to the well-dressed display dummies. She itched to place the *Open* sign in her window and see who came through the door first. Mr. Hawkins had promised to post a notice in his store to advertise the shop, although she knew she'd be foolish to expect much, having only been in town two days. A seamstress had to build up a reputation before her business could flourish. That required time, satisfied customers, and word of mouth. Nevertheless, little bursts of excitement rebounded through her like popping corn.

"This your place?"

Hannah beamed at the old man beside her. "Yes, sir. What do you think?"

Ezra halted and scratched a spot behind his ear. "Looks nice, I reckon. Don't know much about such things, a course, but if my Alice were still around, I'm sure she'd be knocking on your door." His eyes glistened with moisture as he gazed at the shop window. "Alice was a simple woman, but she always wore a pretty ribbon in her hair. I think she woulda liked having a place like this to visit."

Sensing his grief, Hannah tentatively touched his shoulder. "If you can spare a few minutes, I would love to have you join me for a cup of cocoa." She'd seen Cordelia's milk delivery at the top of the stairs. "I could have it ready in minutes."

"You don't have to do that, Miz Hannah." Ezra dipped his chin, but not before she caught the longing in his eyes. "I know I ain't fitting company for a gal like you."

"Nonsense." Hannah patted his shoulder. A delicate tickle crawled along the back of her hand, sending shivers shooting through her like heat lightning. Keeping her smile bright and praying he didn't notice, she dropped her hand away and shook it vigorously behind her. She wanted to befriend the poor man, but offering hospitality to any vermin he might have been carrying was out of the question. "It would be doing me a favor," she cajoled. "I'm a little nervous about opening the shop today, and having someone to talk to over a cup of cocoa would take my mind off of things. Please?"

"Well . . . if you insist." His eyes brightened a shade as he wagged a dirt-encrusted finger at her, the nail black around the edges. "But I ain't gonna risk your reputation by coming inside. Jackson and I will wait for ya right here." He jabbed his finger toward the boardwalk steps and lowered himself to a seat with a groan.

Ezra Culpepper was a lot more astute than his appearance suggested. Hannah got the distinct impression that he had recognized her gift to him and had responded with one in return.

"Wonderful," she said. "I'll be back in a trice."

She rushed up the stairs, collected the fruit jar of milk Cordelia had placed on her doorstep, and let herself into her room. Using some of the kindling she had brought back with her, she stoked up the fire in the cookstove and pulled out a pair of small pots. She measured two cups of milk into the first and two cups of water into the second. While she waited for them to boil, she rolled up her sleeves and scrubbed her hands with her strongest lye soap—just in case any unwelcome guests had crawled or hopped onto her without her noticing.

The water pot began to bubble, so Hannah grabbed a small bowl and mixed two tablespoons of cocoa powder with two of sugar, added a couple grains of salt, and then stirred in half a cup of boiling water, making a nice paste. She scooped the mixture into the rest of the boiling water for a brief time until she smelled the milk scald. She added the cocoa water to the milk, removed it from the heat, and blended it with an egg beater for two minutes. The aroma of the chocolate made her mouth water, and her stomach let out a hungry gurgle. There was just enough milk left to mix up some biscuits, but she would have to do that later. Ezra was waiting on her.

By the time she returned downstairs, the breakfast cocoa had cooled sufficiently to be drunk without burning their tongues. Hannah handed a cup to Ezra and took a seat beside him on the edge of the boardwalk.

"Ya know, I was thinking while you were gone...." Ezra paused to lift his cup to his nose. He sniffed at it as if unsure what is was. Then he shrugged and gulped down a hearty swig. His eyes lit up and he smacked his lips. "Say, this here's good stuff. Didn't 'spect to like it, seein' as how it ain't coffee, but it's not too bad." He tipped the cup to his mouth again. "Just don't tell the other fellers around town. Wouldn't want them thinking I've gone all soft, drinkin' such a girly concoction."

Hannah set her cup down, placed her right hand over her heart, and raised her left. "I vow not to tell a soul."

Ezra winked at her. "Good. Now what was I saying...? Oh yeah. A bench."

"A bench?" Hannah scrunched her brows.

"Yeah. I was thinking that a man might have cause to wait on his woman a good long time if she were in your shop gawkin' at all those fancy getups. A bench outside might come in real handy."

Warmth seeped through the porcelain cup and into Hannah's hands as she mulled over his words.

"Back at the house I got one that I put together last spring."

"A bench?"

"Yep. Oak. Sturdy legs. It don't wobble none."

Hannah blew a ripple across her cocoa as she weighed his offer. A bench *would* be welcoming to passersby and practical for those needing a place to wait, but she didn't have money for more than necessities right now. Even if the bench were as lovely as the walking sticks. But if she didn't have to part with any ready cash . . .

"Would you consider a trade?"

Ezra nodded and downed the rest of his chocolate in a single gulp.

Hannah examined his tattered ensemble. "I could make you a new shirt, a fine one with fancy stitching. And I'll mend any existing clothes you have." She'd have to boil them first, but she wouldn't mention the laundering for fear of offending him.

"Shucks, Miz Hannah. I don't need all that. I'd give it to you in exchange for sharing a cup of this here cocoa with you every morning." The light that had brightened his eyes suddenly dimmed. "Unless, a course, having a grizzled feller like me outside your shop would be bad for business."

"If we meet early, like we did today, I don't think any harm would come of it." Hannah smiled and reached for his empty cup. "But I am going to make you that shirt. It's the least I can do." Trying not to think too much about what she was doing, Hannah held out her hand to him. "Deal?"

Ezra hesitated. Then he wiped his palm on his trouser leg, which was probably even dirtier than his hand, and clasped hers in a firm shake. The dull eyes that had made her heart ache upon first seeing him sparkled with new life, and she prayed that their morning meetings over chocolate would help keep it there.

"See ya tomorrow, Miz Hannah." Ezra tipped his hat.

"Bring an extra shirt with you when you come," Hannah said. "I can mend any rips there may be or replace buttons, but I can also use it as a pattern for your new shirt. You'll be my first customer."

"I like the sounda that." He picked up his walking stick and used its support to lever himself up. "Gives me braggin' rights, now, don't it?"

Hannah laughed. "I guess it does."

He waved to her, then ambled off down the road toward the railroad station, his mule, Jackson, at his side. Ezra Culpepper was not exactly the type of client she had envisioned for her shop, but somehow she thought Miss Victoria would approve.

An hour later, Hannah emerged from her upstairs room a changed woman. Gone were the loose-fitting exercise clothes and the single braid that had hung down her back. She had set aside her cocoon to stretch her butterfly wings in a smart day dress in deep mauve, button-up heeled shoes, and a tasteful straw bonnet with matching ribbon. Her hair was twisted into an elegant chignon designed to impress but not outshine the women who might visit her shop.

When she reached the bottom of the stairs, she took a deep breath. The idea of opening her shop wracked her nerves, but even more unsettling was the other task she'd have to complete before placing the *Open* sign in her window. She still owed Mr. Tucker an apology for snapping at him yesterday.

Over her arm hung a basket containing his tools along with a peace offering that she hoped would please him. Hannah worried that, with a sister like Cordelia who could bake muffins that melted in a person's mouth, Mr. Tucker would find the biscuits and jam she offered lacking. But they were fluffy and warm, without a single burnt bottom, and the jam she'd bought at the store was sweet. Since he didn't want anything to do with her needlework, food was the best she had to give.

Exhaling a shaky breath, she straightened her shoulders and

marched across the street. Better to get the daunting task over with now so she could concentrate on running her dress shop.

She found Mr. Tucker outside the livery, standing in the bed of the hay wagon. Hannah stopped short. The man was slinging giant forkfuls of hay above his head into the loft door as if they weighed no more than feathers. The fabric of his cotton shirt pulled snugly against his muscular shoulders as he scooped the fork forward. . . .

Mr. Tucker certainly has no need of a daily constitutional.

At the same time that thought ran through her head, J.T. Tucker's gaze locked with hers, lighting fire to her cheeks.

CHAPTER 9

J.T. caught the rosy blush that colored Miss Richards's cheeks and flexed his muscles. The roses deepened before she turned her head, and something instinctual within him cheered. Just in case she looked his way again, he pitched another two loads of hay, each larger than the last. Remembering the challenge she'd issued of catching him smiling, he schooled his smug grin into an annoyed line, hoping she would think him irritated at the interruption. He wanted to tease her something fierce, but that wouldn't serve his purposes. He was supposed to be putting distance between them, not instigating a flirtation.

That reminder put an edge to his words as he addressed her. "What do you need, Miss Richards? I'm a little busy."

"Yes, I . . . I see that."

Her stammer only bolstered his ego. He guessed it was rather childish of him to enjoy her discomfiture, but for the first time since he met her, he was the one with the advantage, and it felt awfully good.

She tipped her chin up to him, and he swore he could see her spine stiffening. There went his advantage. He stifled a sigh and leaned on the handle of his pitchfork.

"I came to return your tools." She raised her arm, lifting a basket that he supposed contained the level and screwdriver he'd dropped off at her shop yesterday afternoon.

He nodded toward the small door off to his right. "Just put them on the desk in my office."

J.T. tried to dismiss her by turning his back and shoving the fork into the hay, but she didn't take the hint.

"I have something else for you, too, Mr. Tucker. A peace offering."

Of all the harebrained female ideas. The last thing he needed was peace between them. If she started being nice to him . . . well, it would be that much harder to fight his growing attraction.

"I owe you an apology for the way I spoke to you yesterday." Her soft voice sounded much closer. He speared the pitchfork into the dwindling pile of hay and spun around to find her less than a foot away from the wagon.

Her brows arched at his abrupt movement, and he scowled. Why did her eyes have to shine up at him like deep reflections of the mill pond on a spring evening?

"You don't owe me anything, Miss Richards. We both spoke out of turn. Now move along and let me get back to work."

She stiffened and set her jaw. He couldn't help but wonder how hard she was biting her tongue to keep from lambasting him.

"By all means, continue your work, Mr. Tucker. Don't let my olive branch stop you."

J.T. took her advice and grabbed his pitchfork again, half expecting her to find a real branch and start thrashing him with it.

"I came here to apologize, and I aim to do just that. Whether or not you listen is up to you."

Her apology sounded more like a scolding, but he had to respect her for not letting him deter her.

"I had no right to lecture you on being neighborly. You have shown me much kindness since I arrived. Except, of course, for the arrogant, ill-tempered manner with which you seem determined to goad me, for reasons only the Lord above could possibly comprehend." She mumbled that last part, but not so quietly that he couldn't make out the words. "At any rate, I should not have imposed on that kindness, and I am sorry."

He grunted as he pitched a load, cuing her to leave. She took the hint. Out of the corner of his eye, he saw her moving toward his office.

"I brought you some biscuits and jam," she called out to him. "Feel free to give them to Tom or feed them to your horses if you don't want to sully your hands with something I've touched. With as much as you dislike me, they'd probably give you indigestion anyhow."

Were those tears he heard beneath her anger? His conscience roared at him. Keeping distance between them was one thing, but actually hurting her was inexcusable.

He peered through the office window. She emptied her basket, leaving not only his tools, but a generous-sized mound of biscuits wrapped in a bread cloth. Then she swiped a finger under her eye. Twice.

Blast. I did hurt her.

A verse ran through his head, unsummoned: "*. . . neither cast ye your pearls before swine.*" Miss Richards had the pearls, and he was definitely the swine. Not a flattering comparison. He stretched his neck, cracking the first few vertebrae.

All right, Lord. I get the message. I crossed the line and need to put things right.

J.T. dropped the pitchfork. He braced his hand against the side of the wagon and leapt over it to the ground. Miss Richards hadn't emerged from his office yet. She was probably trying to compose herself. A woman as strong-spirited as she wouldn't want to show weakness in front of the enemy. J.T. pounded his leg with his fist as he covered the distance to the open door. He might not want to strike up an intimate friendship with the seamstress, but that didn't mean he wanted her to consider him an enemy.

He burst into the office just as she tried to exit. A tiny gasp escaped her lips as she lurched away from him. She wobbled to the side, her head coming dangerously close to the sharp corner of his tack shelf. He latched on to her elbow to steady her. What was it about them and doorways?

She gently tugged her arm free and ducked her chin. He tried to meet her eyes, but all he could see was the top of her hat.

"I'm sorry. Again," she said, still not looking at him.

He cleared his throat. "I'm . . . ah . . . sorry, too. And not just for nearly running you down. I was rude to you out there." He paused. "Forgive me."

Slowly, the hat tilted back and her lovely face peered up at him. She had freckles across the bridge of her nose, and her lashes were damp. Those blue eyes of hers spoke of her confusion and pain even though her mouth remained silent. But it was the hint of hope shimmering in their moist depths that penetrated his heart. All at once, he could think of nothing save kissing her. His gaze fell to her lips, and he felt himself sway forward.

What am I doing? J.T. jerked back and locked his neck firmly in an upright position.

Clearing his throat, he stepped around her to the desk. "Uh . . . thanks for the biscuits. It was thoughtful of you."

J.T. made a point to unwrap the bundle and take a bite of one of the golden brown halves. The crust flaked, the soft center still warm. The strawberry preserves tempted him to take another bite and relish the sweetness, but the sour feeling in the pit of his stomach told him he was not done with his apology.

"You're a fine cook, ma'am."

She still didn't smile. Two delicate frown lines veed between her brows. "Why do you dislike me so, Mr. Tucker?"

Had he been a cursing man, he would have done so just then. Instead he choked on the bite of biscuit that lodged itself in his throat at her question.

"I don't dislike you, Miss Richards."

She stared up at him, no doubt waiting for an explanation. He stuffed another bite of biscuit into his mouth.

What exactly could he say? That she frightened him and his rudeness was an act of self-preservation? Yeah, that would go over well.

"How's the table working out?" He sat on the corner of his desk, which brought his face level with hers. A mistake. Her gaze bored into him with an intensity that made him squirm. He shoved back up to his feet and strode to the door. She blinked but didn't stand in his way.

"The table's a blessing. Thank you."

He'd forgotten he'd asked the question until he heard her answer. Escape was too close to stop now, though, so he kept moving through the doorway. "Good," he called over his shoulder. "Glad to hear it. I . . . ah . . . need to get back to work. Thanks for bringing the tools back . . . and for the biscuits."

J.T. scrambled up into the wagon as if the ground were suddenly crawling with snakes. He snatched up the pitchfork and starting throwing hay with a vengeance.

"Good day, Mr. Tucker."

He heard her voice but pretended he didn't. After three more pitches up to the loft, he risked a glance behind him. Head high, she was walking down the street toward the blacksmith shop. She looked so prim and professional dressed in her fancy pink dress and bonnet, but when he'd seen her in her plain, loose-fitting work dress, he'd found her no less appealing.

And then she'd waltzed into town with Ezra Culpepper and sat in front of her shop with the man drinking coffee or tea or whatever it was women like her drank in the morning. Which only confused him further. Ezra hadn't bathed since his wife died last spring, probably hadn't changed his clothes, either, just added layers as the temperature cooled. He stunk to high heaven. Even if the woman had no sense of smell, one look at the fellow should have been all it took to turn her away in disgust at his unkempt state. Yet she hadn't turned away. In fact she'd reached out to him.

What seamstress in her right mind would encourage a connection with a dirty, smelly old man? It couldn't possibly be good for business.

Turning back to the task at hand, J.T. gripped the pitchfork and shoved it into the hay. He doubted he'd ever understand Miss Hannah Richards. Trying only made his head hurt.

CHAPTER 10

Hannah bit into the bacon sandwich she'd made from her breakfast leftovers, trying not to let discouragement steal her good humor. She'd swept the shop floor, straightened her collection of fashion plates and pattern books at least six times, and repositioned her display dummies twice. Still, no one came. The idleness was about to make her daft.

Didn't word of mouth travel at high speeds in small towns? Surely the women in Coventry knew her shop was open for business. Why didn't they come?

Hannah set aside her half-eaten sandwich. How was she supposed to entice customers? True, it was only the first day, but curiosity if nothing else should have brought potential patrons to her door. Was something wrong with her display? Had she committed some unforgivable social blunder? Was the fact that she was an outsider keeping people away?

Her stomach twisted and a dull throb crept behind her eyes. Hannah moaned and rubbed at her temples. What did she know about running a business? All her professional life, she'd sewn for someone else—someone with an established clientele. She'd had no need to drum up customers. They'd simply been handed to her. Apparently, her assumption that a notice in the general store and an *Open* sign in her window would be enough to bring the women of Coventry flocking to her door had been a tad naïve. So now what should she do?

Not having a good answer to that question, she crammed the rest of her bacon biscuit into her mouth. And of course, that was the precise moment her shop door opened. Mortified, Hannah spun around, cheeks bulging as she tried to swallow the lump of food rapidly expanding in her mouth. She grabbed her water glass and sipped small drinks until she managed to get the bite down, then turned to greet her customer.

"Good afternoon," she gushed.

Louisa James stood in the center of the shop with a daughter clinging to each hand. After meeting the laundress yesterday morning, Hannah had not expected the hardworking woman to be her first customer, but then again, there was no law against a laundress looking her best when the occasion called for it.

Hannah stepped around the counter to greet the threesome. "What can I do for you ladies?"

"We come by to welcome you to town, official-like—and introduce you to my daughters." Louisa's no-nonsense voice echoed loudly in the quiet room. "You done met my boy, Danny. This here's Tessa," she said, lifting the clasped hand of the taller girl, "and this 'un's Mollie."

"What a pleasure to meet such lovely young ladies. Thank you for stopping by my shop." Hannah kept her smile firmly in place even while her optimism crumbled. Louisa had not come to purchase dress goods.

However, she *had* taken time from her own business to pay a call, Hannah pointedly reminded herself, and such a gift deserved appreciation, not disappointment.

"Welcome to Coventry, Miss Richards!" the taller girl enthused.

She dropped her mother's hand and bounced forward to wrap her arms around Hannah's waist.

Surprised yet delighted, Hannah staggered back to catch her balance, a giggle rising up in her throat.

"Tessa!" her mother scolded. "Don't bowl the woman over."

Hannah met Louisa's eye over Tessa's head and smiled. "It's no bother. A hug is exactly what I needed today."

The other woman nodded, understanding glowing in her gaze. "The first couple weeks are the hardest. But business will pick up."

Tessa released her grip on Hannah's waist, and Hannah focused on the young girl. "Thanks for the warm welcome, Miss Tessa. You brightened my day."

"Sure." The youngster smiled with a grin so infectious it was impossible for Hannah to keep hold of her doldrums. Tessa tilted her head toward her sister and whispered in a confidential rasp, "Mollie woulda hugged you, too, but she's kinda shy."

"That's all right." Hannah hunkered down in front of the smaller girl. "I'm glad to know you, Miss Mollie."

Slowly, the quiet child lifted her chin.

"Would you like to see my scrap box?" Hannah asked, an idea blooming. "I have almost every color of the rainbow in there. In fact, if you find a piece of fabric you particularly like, I can make it into a doll for you. Would you like that?"

Mollie had barely begun her nod when Tessa bounded up to interrupt.

"Can I have one, too, Miss Richards? Can I?"

"Of course." Hannah led the girls behind the counter to one of her trunks. She opened the lid and pulled out the top inlaid divider full of ribbons and other notions to reveal the scraps in the bottom. "You can look through these as long as you keep them folded so they don't get wrinkled. Can you do that for me?"

"Yes, ma'am."

Louisa stepped up beside her. "You don't have to do that."

"I know, but it will give me something to do, and hopefully the girls will like them."

"I'm sure they will. Thank you."

Hannah gave Louisa a thoughtful look, the woman's earlier comment about her business picking up returning to mind.

"Did you experience trouble when you first started the laundry?"

Louisa followed Hannah a short distance away from the girls. "Yep. Had a lean couple o' months before I figured out a thing or two. Folks around here are slow to take to change. They like to wait till the shine wears off a bit afore they're ready to try something new. You just gotta convince one or two people to rub off some of your newcomer polish. Then the rest will follow."

"How do I do that?"

The laundress shrugged. "I don't know what'll work for you, but I can tell you what I did. I washed shirts for free."

Hannah's forehead scrunched. "Free? Didn't you lose money that way?"

"Nah. I only washed one free shirt per family. It got people to come in, even if they only brought one thing. I gave those shirts my best effort, and let the quality speak for itself. It took a while to build up a reputation, but now I nearly got more business than I can handle."

Giving things away for free. It seemed so backward, yet Hannah couldn't argue with Louisa's success. But how could she use the same strategy? She couldn't give away free dresses. That would be too costly. She couldn't piecemeal out parts of her service the way Louisa had. A single free seam would do no one any good.

Hannah blew out a breath as she brushed her biscuit crumbs off the worktable and into her hand before dumping them into the wastebasket. She shook out the napkin she had wrapped her lunch in, as well, and idly wove it through her fingers.

"What about making up some of those?" Louisa flicked the dangling corner of the lunch cloth. "You got a bunch of scraps, right?"

Bread cloths. Hannah brightened, her previously infertile mind suddenly sprouting a garden of ideas. "Louisa, that's brilliant! A practical gift the ladies can use, and every time they cover their dinner rolls or wrap up a sandwich, they will think of my shop." Hannah hustled over to where the girls were making their selections and grabbed a sky-blue piece they had discarded. She shook out the folds and held it out before her, tilting it this way and that.

"I could scallop the edges to dress them up a bit and use a wide assortment of colors and fabrics so the women could choose one that fits their tastes." Her gaze found Louisa's. "Do you think it will work?"

"It couldn't hurt." Louisa patted her shoulder and moved past to collect the girls. Mollie had a pink gingham piece in her hand, but Tessa's lap still held three options. "Time to go, Tessa. Hurry and pick one. I got a pile o' pressing waiting back at the laundry."

After a final deliberation, Tessa settled on a saffron yellow calico spotted with tiny green sprigs. She handed her selection to Hannah.

"Thank you for making dolls for us, Miss Richards."

"You are most welcome."

They said their good-byes and Hannah returned to her scrap box. With new energy vibrating through her, she dug through the trunk, pulling out solid-colored broadcloth in earthy hues like tan, rust, and orange. Perfect for the harvest season. Then she found a host of cotton plaids in shades of blue, green, and yellow. Cheerful and fun. Finally she selected half a dozen floral print calicoes for clients who preferred a more feminine design for their baskets.

She spread the pile of fabric across her worktable and cut a folded piece of brown broadcloth into two large, wavy squares. She would sew up one, and if it turned out well, she'd use the second for a pattern. Twenty minutes and one scalloped hem later, she had a fine-looking bread cloth.

Taking up her shears, Hannah began cutting the rest of the fabric into similar patterns. She could keep extra bread cloths on hand in the shop and give them to any new customer who came through her door. That way no one would feel left out. The women from the outlying farms and ranches deserved the same treatment as the ones in town.

Halfway through cut number sixteen, the shop door opened. A customer?

"Good afternoon," she said as she raised her head. "How can I help you?"

Cordelia Tucker crossed into the room. "Oh, Hannah. It's all so lovely."

"Cordelia!" Hannah scurried around the half wall that separated her work area from the rest of the shop. "I'm so glad you came by. Things have been dreadfully quiet."

"I'm sure you'll have more traffic in the coming days. How could you not with such beautiful merchandise?" She fingered a green silk gown that hung on the coatrack, undeniable longing in her eyes.

"Louisa James and her girls are the only ones who've stopped by today. I was growing quite discouraged until she helped me come up with an idea to entice people into the shop." Hannah explained about the bread cloths, relieved when Cordelia showed enthusiasm for the plan.

"And since you are the first one to visit my shop, you get first choice." Hannah steered her friend toward the worktable. "Pick a fabric and I will sew it up while you look around. I have several pattern books you can browse."

Cordelia hesitated. "Oh, but I'm not here to buy anything. I just stopped in to see how you were getting along."

Hannah wrapped her arms around Cordelia's shoulders and gently urged her closer to the table. "You don't have to order anything. Everyone who comes in gets a bread cloth, regardless of whether or not they make a purchase."

The dark blue wool dress Cordelia wore complemented her complexion and figure only slightly better than the dull brown one she'd worn yesterday. Hannah itched to get her into some colors that would bring life to her face.

Cordelia chose green plaid for her gift. She seemed to have a preference for that color. Hannah mentally cataloged the material she had in stock. A sage or hunter shade would be lovely on the young woman.

"You don't have to buy anything," Hannah reiterated. "Just have fun looking. We can talk while I sew."

"J.T. would say it's dangerous to look at things one can't afford." Cordelia made this comment as she tentatively thumbed through the Butterick fall catalog. "It opens the door for temptation."

Hannah gritted her teeth as she sat down at her machine. "I suppose that could be true. But there's no harm in appreciating beauty and letting your imagination run down a brighter path for a little while. It's like playing pretend. Girls have fun dreaming that their mud pies are chocolate cakes, but they have sense enough not to eat them. The joy is in the pretending."

Cordelia looked up from the fashion book and grinned, her eyes twinkling. "I loved playing with mud pies." She glanced over her shoulder as if worried someone would hear what she had to say, then turned back. "I respect my brother a great deal, but J.T. *can* be a bit too strait-laced at times."

"That's stating it mildly," Hannah mumbled.

Cordelia quirked her brow in question. The mannerism must be a family trait. However, it was far less hostile and annoying when Cordelia did it.

"Your brother has been exceptionally helpful to me since I arrived, Cordelia, but he drives me to distraction at the same time with his overbearing attitudes. Is he disagreeable with everyone, or is it just me?"

Hannah pumped her treadle hard and fast, alleviating her frustration while she sewed.

Cordelia giggled, and only then did Hannah realize how her words could have offended. "He can seem a little harsh to those who don't know him well. J.T.'s not exactly what I would call affable, but he has a good heart."

Hannah sighed and her foot slowed. The whir of the machine quieted to a dim hum. "I know he does, and I shouldn't have spoken ill of him. His actions toward me have been nothing but kind. It's his words and demeanor that fire my temper. Perhaps if I could find a way to get the upper hand during one of our verbal skirmishes, I wouldn't feel at such a disadvantage."

With a final turn of the fabric, Hannah finished the hem of Cordelia's bread cloth. She pulled the material free and clipped the loose threads.

"All done." Hannah stood and handed Cordelia her gift. "Here you go. One new bread cloth for the woman who bakes the finest bread in Coventry."

"Thank you." Cordelia smiled and looked over the workmanship. "You did that so quickly. It would have easily taken me an hour to complete this, and it would not have turned out half as nice."

"Swift, quality service. That's my specialty."

A thoughtful look crossed Cordelia's features as she fingered the cloth. Then a downright mischievous sparkle lit her eyes. "You've given me a gift today, Hannah—more than the bread cloth. You reminded me that it is permissible to dream and pretend and think on 'whatsoever things are lovely,' as Scripture says. I want to give you something in return."

She stepped closer and dropped her voice. "J.T. has been extra surly since you came to town. I can only conclude that you are getting under his skin as much as he is getting under yours. And as a female who knows what it's like to live with him when he gets ornery, I would be happy to tip the scales a bit in your favor the next time the two of you spar."

Hannah held her breath.

"Everyone in Coventry knows not to call J.T. by his given name. He absolutely abhors it. From the time he entered school, he refused to answer to anything except J.T. or Tucker, even with Mother and Father. So the next time you feel the need for an advantage, try calling him *Jericho.* I don't know if it will help or simply escalate matters, but it is sure to get his goat one way or the other."

Cordelia's grin was the essence of sisterly devilment. "I only hope I'm there to see his reaction."

"Jericho, hmm?" Hannah felt an answering grin curve her lips. "I suddenly feel a great fondness for that name."

The two women giggled like young girls scheming behind the schoolhouse. Jericho Tucker had no idea what was coming his way.

CHAPTER 11

Cordelia introduced Hannah around town on Thursday, and together they handed out close to two dozen of the colorful bread cloths. Word spread, and a steady trickle of visitors came through the shop. Unfortunately, that's all they were—visitors, not customers.

At closing time on Saturday, Hannah flipped her sign so the word *Closed* faced the window, then leaned her shoulder against the door. Not one order. Her mind told her to be patient, that the women who wandered through the shop would return and make purchases in the future. But logic couldn't keep her heart from sinking. Words like *failure* and *mistake* and *disaster* circled through her mind, making faces and taunting her as they spun. Hannah sagged further into the door until she began to slip. She snapped up. In a bid for control, she shook out her skirts and imagined herself brushing off the negativity that clung to her.

"Land sakes, Hannah," she lectured herself, "it's only been four days. Have a little faith."

She marched across the floor and collected the brown-paper-wrapped parcel that waited on the corner of her worktable. Ezra's shirt. He would soon be stopping by to pick it up on his way home from the depot. Hannah fiddled with the string bow that held the package closed, making sure both loops were even and the knot tight. Her first and only customer. Yet he'd paid handsomely. The bench outside her shop gleamed, and more than one visitor had commented on it.

Ezra still insisted on sitting on the edge of the boardwalk while they had their morning cocoa, but she was thankful to have a more comfortable option. The bench was smooth and sturdy and wide enough for three adults. She'd often seen the James children steal a seat there for a minute or two when they were able to get away from the laundry—and whether they were quietly sharing a snack or pestering each other with pokes and pushes, she always enjoyed their antics.

Now the bench sat empty. The weather was pleasant, though, so she decided to make use of it herself while she waited for Ezra. She locked the shop and slid onto the bench, leaning into the crosspieces at her back. Exhaling a long breath, she closed her eyes for a moment and simply breathed. When she opened them again, their focus relaxed. No longer consumed with fabrics and threads, needles and patterns, Hannah let her gaze drift over her surroundings, seeking bits of unexpected beauty. She fancied the search as something of an expedition to uncover God's hidden messages of love. Whenever she found one, she received it as a gift and savored the serenity it brought.

A monarch butterfly fluttered past and landed on the hitching post. Hannah leaned forward for a better view. The orange wings rimmed and veined in black—like stained glass in a church window—winked at her. It lingered only an instant before taking flight once again. Hannah followed its erratic movements until she spotted an interesting knothole in one of the boards near her feet. Golden streaks spiraled inward against a dark brown backdrop, revealing the place a branch once grew. This made her think of trees and how the leaves would soon be changing, covering the area hills in a patchwork of green, gold, and red. Lifting her eyes to examine the outlying hills beyond the town, a particularly fluffy cloud captured her attention. She was in the midst of deciding whether it looked more like an armadillo or a handlebar mustache when a loud bang followed by high-pitched voices jolted her out of her reverie.

"Did not!"

"Did so."

"I'm telling Ma."

"Go ahead. It's your fault we lost it."

Hannah craned her neck in time to see Mollie James stomp back inside the laundry house, apparently intent on carrying out her threat to tattle. Tessa uttered a closed-mouth cry that surely would have been a full scream had her lips parted. Then she spun toward Hannah in a fit of obvious pique and ran blindly for the bench. She pulled up short when she realized the seat was already occupied. Tears pooled in her eyes but didn't fall as she looked at Hannah. Before the child could run away, Hannah patted a spot on the bench beside her.

"I'll share."

Tessa hesitated. Then, with a shrug, she sat down and scooted back until her feet swung freely above the ground. She crossed her arms over her chest and settled into an impressive pout.

Hannah sighed in dramatic fashion and crossed her own arms. "Little sisters can be such a trial. I have one, too, you know."

Tessa's arms loosened a little. "You do?"

"Mm-hmm."

"She ever get you in trouble for something that wasn't your fault?"

"Oh yes, on several occasions." Hannah kept her expression sober even though she wanted to laugh. "I remember the first time Mother let me attend one of her quilting bees. Usually Emily and I had to stay in our room on quilting nights so that we didn't bother the ladies, but this time Mother had deemed my stitching good enough to join the adults. I was so excited and proud. Emily, however, felt left out. She begged Mother to let her help, too, and finally Mother agreed to let her snip threads with a small pair of embroidery scissors.

"The problem, though, was that Mother sewed with a long thread that didn't need to be snipped often. So Emily took it upon herself to snip my threads, too. Only I didn't want her to. I asked politely for her to let me use the scissors, but she insisted it was her job to snip the thread ends. I insisted that I would snip my own threads. Thankfully, the rest of the women's chatter kept them from noticing our argument. Had Emily just given me the scissors, all would have been well, but she refused." Hannah wagged her head at the injustice of sibling interference. "I tried to grab them from her, and we tugged back and forth until I finally won. But that win quickly turned into a defeat."

Tessa wiggled closer to Hannah, her pout replaced by a look of avid curiosity. "What happened?"

"I yanked on the scissors so hard that when they popped free of Emily's hand, I couldn't hang on to them. They sailed through the air and clanked against Myrtle Butler's teacup. She squealed and dropped the cup and saucer, spilling tea all over her dress, and worse, the quilt."

Tessa gasped.

Hannah nodded, a residual shame creeping over her at the memory. "I'd never seen Mother so angry. She yelled at me in front of the Ladies Auxiliary and sent both Emily and me to our room. I wasn't allowed to join the quilting group again for two years, until Emily was old enough to join, as well."

"That's not fair!"

"I didn't think so, either, at the time." Hannah patted Tessa's knee. "But now I understand it better. Emily might have been guilty of instigating the trouble, but my reaction to her is what caused the situation to escalate out of control. If I had simply let her snip the thread, everything would have worked out fine."

Tessa's face scrunched in thought.

"Is that similar to what happened with you and Mollie?" Hannah asked.

"Sort of. Except me losing the button was all Mollie's fault. She bumped into me when I was just sitting there. The button dropped out of my hand and fell through a crack in the floor. Now Mr. Smythe will prob'ly refuse to pay again. He don't pay if anything's wrong with his clothes. And he looks real hard to find something wrong every time. Ma's gonna tan my hide good for this."

Tessa pulled her knees up to her chest and wrapped her arms around them, burying her face in the faded calico material of her skirt. Hannah laid a hand on the girl's rounded back.

"Did the button come off during the washing?"

Tessa nodded against her knees without raising her head. "Uh-huh. I'm the one in charge of sewing them back on. But now I don't have a button, and Mr. Smythe is bound to notice." Her voice hitched, and Hannah feared tears were close to the surface again.

"I've got an idea." Hannah waited for Tessa to lift her face a couple of inches before continuing. "Do you think you can sneak back into the laundry and get Mr. Smythe's shirt?"

"Yeah . . ."

"I've got a whole Mason jar full of buttons in my workroom. I bet we can find something to match."

Tessa straightened, and her legs plopped back to a normal sitting position. Looking at Hannah as if she were a fairy godmother, she blinked away the moisture that had collected in her eyes. "You think so?"

"It's worth a try, wouldn't you say?"

"Yes, ma'am!"

Before Hannah could say another word, Tessa bounded away to retrieve the shirt. She returned in less than a minute. The linen garment had already been washed, starched, and dried but had not yet been pressed. Hannah collected Ezra's package and ushered Tessa into her shop, where she pulled out her jar of buttons. Tessa eyed it with open-mouthed amazement.

"There must be more than a thousand in there," she stated, her gaze glued to the abundant mix of styles, shapes, and sizes.

Laughter bubbled up in Hannah. "Probably closer to two hundred, but I've never actually counted."

She unscrewed the lid and poured nearly half the contents onto the table, spreading them into a thin layer. Black, white, brass, pearl, engraved, plain, two holes, four holes, no holes—the choices were extensive.

"It was a white one," Tessa said. "See?" She laid the shirt on the table and pointed to one of the buttons still in place.

Hannah squinted down at it. "Looks like pearl, or pearl agate. Start searching through the pile, and when you think you've found a match, hold it up to this one to see if it's the same pattern and size. Look for one with a fluted edge that resembles a sun."

"All right."

The two set to work. Several buttons were similar, but something was always off. They were too large, too small, too translucent, or too plain. Hannah started congregating a different set of pearl shirt buttons off to the side as she came across them. If they couldn't find a match to the existing buttons, they could replace all of them with a new set. Most men didn't pay attention to little details like the design of a shirt button, so she doubted Mr. Smythe would notice the difference. But deception was never a good policy, so she would send Tessa back with all the original buttons so her mother could explain to the gentleman what happened and how they had remedied the situation. Hopefully, he would be impressed with their service and not only pay the promised amount, but leave a tip, as well.

"I found it!" Tessa declared.

"You did?"

Relief swept through Hannah. An identical button would make

things a great deal easier. She leaned forward to examine it more closely. The button was indeed a match.

"Great job, Tessa! Let me get you a needle and some thread."

Hannah opened the spool drawer on her sewing cabinet and grabbed a reel of white thread. She cut off a strand and handed it to Tessa along with a needle. The girl moistened the end of the thread with her tongue and jabbed it through the tiny eye like an experienced seamstress. Impressed, Hannah grew thoughtful as she watched Tessa knot the end and sew the button into place with precision.

"Most girls your age have trouble threading their own needle, but you seem quite adept. Do you sew more than buttons?"

Tessa tied off the thread and held it out for Hannah to cut.

"Ma keeps saying she'll teach me one of these days, but she's too busy."

"Maybe after my business is better established," Hannah said, thinking aloud, "I can give you a few lessons. If your mother approves, of course."

"Could you teach me to make fancy dresses? Like the ones hanging in your window?"

Hannah smiled as she scraped the leftover buttons back into the jar. The tinkling sound they made as they bounced against the glass mirrored the eager excitement ringing in Tessa's voice.

"We would start with something simpler, like an apron." Tessa pulled a face and Hannah stifled a giggle. "However," she continued, "if you work hard and practice long, by the time you are out of short skirts, you might be ready to make your very own party dress for all those church socials the boys will be asking you to." Hannah winked and Tessa grinned.

The sound of someone calling Tessa's name quickly evaporated their vision of the future.

Tessa jumped. "That's Ma. I gotta go."

She grabbed up the shirt and dashed for the door. Halfway there she stopped and turned around. "Thanks, Miss Richards."

"You're welcome, Tessa."

The girl dashed off, and an unexpected longing rose up within Hannah, catching her by surprise. A longing for a child and a family of her own. Most women her age already had a husband and children, but she had chosen a different path—the path of a seamstress and now a businesswoman. Did that mean she would have to forfeit the chance to share a home and hearth with someone special? She'd never really thought much about it before. After all, she'd known practically all her life that she would be a seamstress, and she'd dedicated herself to making the most of her talent. Now, for the first time, she wondered if it would be enough.

Hannah stepped to her project basket and picked up the cloth doll she'd been working on for Tessa. Mollie's slept peacefully in the basket, complete and ready for adoption. Tessa's lacked a bonnet and a ribbon to cover the bleached-linen head. Hannah cradled the doll to her chest and patted the tiny back. Emily's last letter had been filled with details about the cradle they had purchased and the booties she'd been knitting. Mother had already pieced together two baby quilts in anticipation of the blessed event. Hannah gently lowered the faceless doll back into the basket. Unable to resist the motherly compulsion, she covered the rag creation and her sister with a piece of muslin, tucking them in for the night. Would this be as close as she ever came to motherhood?

Thankfully, Ezra arrived at that moment and distracted her from the dangerous question.

"That young'un nearly ran me down," he said with a chuckle as he stepped up to the door that gaped open after Tessa's hasty departure. He didn't cross the threshold, though. The same invisible barrier that kept him from sitting on the bench with her kept him from entering her shop.

She wanted to believe that it was just his overzealous sense of propriety, but deep down she knew he was self-conscious about his physical state. So why didn't the man simply wash up? He obviously hungered for companionship, yet he pushed everyone away with his lack of basic hygiene. Had the loss of his wife made him reluctant to let anyone else get close? If so, why did he continue coming to her shop every morning to visit and drink cocoa?

No answers were forthcoming, so she smiled and held out the brown paper package as she walked toward him. "I have your shirt ready."

He licked his lips but showed no other sign of eagerness. "I ain't had a new shirt in years, Miz Hannah. I don't rightly know what to do with it."

"Well, I have an idea."

He accepted the package from her, then stepped aside as she exited the shop and closed the door behind her. The strong odor she had come to associate with him assaulted her with its usual pungency, but it seemed she had built up a resistance to it over the last few days, for she managed to breathe without her throat closing up. Definite progress.

Slipping the key into the lock, she secured the building and smiled up at him. "I was hoping you would escort me to church tomorrow. Being new in town, I would feel much more comfortable with someone I know by my side."

His face fell. "Me, Miz Hannah?" He shook his head slowly from side to side, then faster and faster as if to accentuate his denial. "You don't want me to take you."

"Of course I do."

"But I'm . . ."

"I know you know where it is, you rascal," she interrupted, shaking a playful finger at him while inwardly praying that she wasn't making a mistake by pressing him. "We walk by there every morning."

Ezra's shoulders drooped and he hung his head. His fingers dug into the brown paper encasing his new shirt, making it crinkle and pop.

"The truth is, Miz Hannah, I ain't been to church since my Alice died. I don't belong there no more."

She ached for him, this dear old man who had allowed his grief to drive him away from everyone, including God.

"It doesn't matter how long you've been away, Ezra. God is always ready to welcome a child of his back into his house."

He snorted and looked sideways at her. "God might welcome me back, but I doubt the rest o' the town will be glad to have me there, smellin' up the place."

This was the first time she could recall him verbally acknowledging his uncleanness. However, the underlying scorn in his tone made it seem he was repeating a phrase he'd heard others use, not his own opinion. Hannah bristled at the thought of people being unkind to Ezra. So what if he didn't conform to the accepted social norms of personal cleanliness? That didn't give people the right to be cruel.

She tapped her foot and thrust out her jaw. "Well, we can just sit in the back, then. If they don't like it, they're welcome to worship elsewhere."

Ezra met her gaze, his jaw gaping just a hair. Then he blinked the surprise away so that mirth could take over. "You're a regular she-bear when you get riled, ain'tcha?" He shook his head again, but this time the movement had a lightness to it that spoke of suppressed laughter instead of sadness. A corresponding lightness buoyed Hannah's spirit.

"All right," he conceded. "I'll take you to church in the morning, and I'll even wear the shirt you made me. Anything else you wanna wring outta me while you're at it?"

"Just one thing."

He rolled his eyes. "What?"

Hannah took a deep breath before making the final plunge. "Since your shirt is the first made-to-order item I've sewn for anyone in this town, could you do me a small favor?"

Bracing his feet apart on the walk, he nodded once. "Name it."

"Before you take it out of the paper, could you please wash your hands?"

A booming laugh like she'd never heard erupted from Ezra and nearly knocked her over. He hobbled down the stairs and carefully wedged the shirt under one of the ropes that crisscrossed Jackson's back. "You're a hoot, Miz Hannah. Wash my hands. Ha!"

He led Jackson down the road, leaving her with a wave and an unsettled feeling. Was he teasing, or would her first Coventry sale be displayed in church tomorrow as a grubby mess? A dull pain began to throb at the base of her skull.

CHAPTER 12

J.T. stood among the horses and wagons in the churchyard as he always did come Sundays. The good Lord hadn't given him the gift of words like the preacher, or music like the fellow who led the hymn singing, or even patience for listening to all the yammering that went on before and after the service. But he had been blessed with a gift for managing horses, so that's what he gave back to God.

He made sure all the wagons and buggies were spaced out enough to prevent tangles and jams when it came time to leave and saw to it that each animal had plenty of grazing space. When he could, he met folks at the church steps and volunteered to take charge of the reins so a husband could enter with his wife. The rich townsmen seemed to expect it as their due and rarely expressed any gratitude, but the farming families and elderly folks always smiled in genuine appreciation, making him feel as if his simple offering was a true ministry.

"Mornin', J.T.," young Daniel James called from several yards away. The boy abandoned his mother and sisters and angled a path toward him.

"Don't you go pesterin' Mr. Tucker, now. You hear me, Danny?" Louisa admonished.

"I won't, Ma." Exasperation dripped from each syllable.

J.T. couldn't blame him. The kid was stuck in a house with nothing but womenfolk all day. He hungered for male attention, and J.T. preferred he got it from him rather than one of the older boys in town who considered rabble-rousing a noble pursuit.

As Danny jogged up the slope toward him, J.T. stroked the dull brown coat of Warren Hawkins's mare. The shopkeeper's son had ridden the old gal up and down this hill since his school days. Cordelia had been a couple of years behind Warren in school, and J.T. remembered her packing bits of carrot or apple in her lunch tin for the pitiful creature. The horse had been old even then.

J.T.'s jaw tightened. The faithful animal deserved to retire. Yet he knew it would never happen. Owning a horse, even a broken-down nag like this one, gave Warren status over the poorer folk who had to walk to church. Cordelia excused his behavior by saying that Warren had never felt accepted by others due to the large birthmark on his face and was only trying to fit in as best he could. But J.T. found it impossible to summon sympathy for a man who treated his animals with callous disregard.

"What's got ya so glum?"

J.T. looked down to find Danny gazing up at him with wide eyes. Clearing his throat, J.T. decided he best start steering his thoughts in a direction more suited for a day of worship.

"I was just thinking." J.T. tapped Danny's forehead and then, with a quick motion, pinned the boy against his body and rubbed the knuckles of his free hand into his hair. Danny moaned and flailed around in halfhearted protest until J.T. finally let go.

The kid scowled up at him in a fairly good imitation of one of his own dark looks, and J.T.'s mood lightened.

"What'd you go and do that for?" Danny whined. "Ma ain't gonna be happy if I show up all mussed."

"Well, we can't have that, can we?" J.T. finger-combed the boy's hair back into place. "There you go, partner. Good as new."

"Thanks," the kid mumbled.

The distant jangle of harness and creaky wheels brought J.T.'s head around. Everyone from town who either owned a buggy or rented one of his was already inside. In fact, the only person he hadn't seen yet was Miss Richards, and he knew she didn't have one. Besides, the woman hoofed out to the river and back every morning, so she surely wouldn't mind the shorter hike to the church. Not that he'd been paying particular attention to her comings and goings. Anyone out and about in the early morning would have noticed. She was hard to miss, after all, with her free-swinging arms and purposeful strides.

"I wonder where Miss Richards is," he mused aloud. He'd expected her to be there by now. The service was fixing to start.

"I reckon that's her coming up in the rig." Danny pointed down the hill. "I saw it sittin' out front o' her shop when we passed it this morning. Some slicked-up old feller was climbin' up the stairs to fetch her."

Jealousy walloped J.T. in the gut and nearly knocked the breath out of him. He strained forward with narrowed eyes, trying to make out the faces of the man and woman in the approaching coal-box buggy. Miss Richards had been in town less than a week, for pity's sake. When'd she find time to snag a beau? The fact that the driver had snowy white hair didn't make him feel any better. Plenty of women married older, more established men. His mother had. Older meant more security and wealth. Pretty women, *fashionable* women, liked that sort of thing. Although he had a hard time picturing the fiercely independent Hannah Richards bending that stubborn streak of hers enough to pander to the whims of a man she didn't respect. Yet if that man offered her the life she wanted without having to work in a shop six days a week . . .

A sharp ache speared through his temples. J.T. forced himself to unclench his molars, but the tension refused to leave. It simply ran down from his head into his neck and shoulders.

"Ma's calling me, J.T. I gotta go."

"What? Oh, yeah. Go ahead, kid. I'll be there in a minute." He chucked Danny under the chin and sent him off. "I just need to get this last buggy settled." Along with his curiosity.

J.T. hung back as the buggy drew near. His tongue would probably get him in trouble again, if he gave it a chance. It always did around the pretty dressmaker. Probably the reason the Lord gave him horse duty.

Miss Richards was wearing a smile brighter than a summer sky and patted the arm of the old man beside her in a familiar way. Too familiar. The spry codger scrambled down to help her alight, then scampered back as she moved up the church steps. The fool was grinning like a giddy young buck. J.T. met him at the edge of the churchyard, legs braced.

As the buggy came closer, it lost some of its luster. The decrepit thing wasn't exactly the stylish gig one usually employed to impress a gal. Oh, the fellow had given it a spit shine, but thick dust remained in the crevices of the folded-down top, and the faded blue stripe on the side combined with the missing spokes in the wheels gave the thing an air of disrepair. It had probably been around since the War Between the States.

"Whoa there, Jackson."

The mule pulling the rig came to a stop, and J.T. grabbed hold of his harness. Something about the beast jiggled a memory, but he was more concerned with taking the man's measure than that of his animal.

"Beautiful day, ain't it?" The old geezer made no effort to tame his irritating grin as he hopped to the ground. "A good day for turning over a new leaf. Yep, Miz Hannah and me is bound to cause something of a stir this morning."

Hannah? Her given name flew off the fellow's lips like it was accustomed to nesting there. And what kind of stir was he talking about? J.T. ground his teeth. If he hurt or embarrassed her in any way . . .

"Best not stay out here too long. You'll miss the fun."

The man winked at him. Winked!

But then something about his voice registered. J.T. pushed his hat back to examine the man more closely. His white hair had been hacked in a ragged line above his shoulders and was held in place by a faded black bowler hat. A tightly trimmed beard clung to his face, matching the well-groomed mustache higher up. The white shirt he wore looked new under a jacket that might have fit him a decade earlier, and his pants had so many crease lines, J.T. imagined him pulling them out of the bottom of a forgotten trunk moments before leaving the house. He smelled like soap and liniment with a touch of mule. 'Course it might just be the mule that smelled like mule. Either way, the fellow had no business courting a woman like Miss Richards. He was old enough to be her grandfather.

That grandfather whacked him on the back and chuckled. "Come on, Tucker. I 'spected Miz Hannah not to recognize me since she didn't know me when Alice was alive, but not you."

All at once the wool fell away from J.T.'s eyes, and shock supplanted the agitation that had blinded him. "Ezra?" he croaked.

"Yep."

How could he have been so stupid? Of course it was Ezra. Just because he hadn't seen the man look this good in a month of Sundays didn't mean he shouldn't have recognized him.

"It's . . . ah . . . good to see you. We've missed you at services."

The man's grin sobered. "Alice always put great store in church-goin' and I know she'd be disappointed in me lettin' it slip, but I just couldn't stomach sitting in there without her by my side. So's when Miz Hannah done made me this purty new shirt and asked me to escort her this morning, I figured it was God's way of telling me it was time to come back."

Ezra stuck out his chest and ran his beefy hands over the fancy stitching that formed a V around the buttoned area of his shirt, then leaned forward toward J.T.'s ear.

"You know, that gal fully expected me to show up looking as I have the last several months and was ready to sit beside me anyhow. She's something else, all right. Why, if Alice didn't still hold sway over my heart, I'd seriously think on giving you young fellers a run for your money in courtin' the lady."

J.T. shook his head. He had no intention of competing with the old man or anyone else for the fair Miss Hannah. God would lead him to the right woman one day. He just had to be patient and not get distracted by a complicated piece of muslin who frustrated and confused him at every turn.

Hannah slid onto a bench at the back of the church just as the singing began. She still couldn't get over the change in Ezra. He must have soaked and scrubbed for hours to make such a transformation. If Jackson hadn't been hitched to the buggy in front of her shop, she'd never have believed that the tidy gentleman who came to her door was Ezra Culpepper. His change probably had more to do with entering God's house than with her request to wash his hands, but she didn't care what motivated it. Ezra had made an effort to rejoin the living, and she planned to delight in watching the living accept him back.

Adding her soprano to the congregation as they moved into the second verse of "How Sweet, How Heavenly," Hannah found herself praying that the idea of love and unity the hymn expressed would penetrate the hearts of the people gathered so that they would look past their prejudices and welcome Ezra back into the fold with warmth and joy.

" 'When each can feel his brother's sigh, and with him bear a part,' " she sang, her voice growing stronger as the lyrics resonated in her soul. " 'When sorrow flows from eye to eye, and joy from heart to heart.' "

A gravelly voice joined hers as Ezra sat on her left, away from the aisle. His fingers gave away his nervousness as they worried the brim of the hat now in his lap. " 'When, free from envy, scorn and pride, our wishes all above,' " he intoned slightly off-key. " 'Each can his brother's failings hide, and show a brother's love.' "

Boot heels thudded softly against the floor, and suddenly Hannah's wishes were no longer all above. Jericho Tucker strode past her to sit with his sister—across the aisle, two rows up. Memorized words from the hymn continued to flow from Hannah's mouth, but her mind wandered elsewhere—two rows forward, to be precise.

He folded his lean frame into a space that seemed much too small for him. The backless benches that served for pews were better suited for the children who used the building as a schoolroom than for a man of his height. In order to avoid the ample hips of the woman seated in front of him, he had to jut his left leg out into the aisle. Apparently accustomed to such an awkward position, he hung his hat on his bent knee as if it were a fence post and then glanced over his shoulder.

Hannah's heart swelled painfully in her chest. He'd likely intended to look at Ezra, since her seatmate was the one who had drastically altered his appearance, but Jericho's gaze collided with hers instead and lingered. Her singing trailed off midstanza as she tried to interpret his look. He didn't smile. Yet neither did he frown. He just stared at her as if the answer to some incredibly vital question lay in the lines of her face.

If he found any answers there, they must not have pleased him much, for his mouth thinned and he turned away.

Dragging her focus away from the back of his head, she looked down to her lap, at the Bible lying there—reminding her where she was. She lifted her chin and faced forward, determined to return her concentration to the God they were praising instead of the man across the aisle. She inhaled a deep breath and launched into the final verse of the opening hymn.

" 'Love is the golden chain that binds the happy souls above.' "

She tried to imagine those happy souls linked in heaven. She really did. But another image popped into her mind that was frightfully hard to dislodge. The image of a golden chain of love binding her to Jericho Tucker.

Mercy. She couldn't possibly fall in love with Jericho Tucker. The man never smiled. And judging by the number of scowls he sent her way, he probably didn't even like her much. And nearly every time he opened his mouth, he riled her temper. Yet his acts of kindness, despite their disagreements, melted her ire and proved him a man of character.

Those strong shoulders and muscled arms didn't hurt, either.

Ugh. The back and forth was making her head spin.

Hannah straightened and ordered herself to stop analyzing Mr. Tucker. Romance at this juncture would only complicate things. She had a business to run and a reputation to build. She couldn't afford distractions. God would let her know when the time was right to start thinking about a man, and it certainly wouldn't be in the middle of worship.

Jericho Tucker could just keep those consuming glances to himself. She didn't need him complicating things. What she needed was . . . was . . .

"Let us pray." The preacher's voice resonated from the front of the room, and her heart echoed the sentiment.

Yes, Lord. Thank you for the reminder. That is exactly what I need to do.

Hannah bowed her head, but the minute she closed her eyes, all she could see was the man across the aisle.

CHAPTER 13

Around noon the following day, Hannah sat at her sewing machine stitching persimmon fabric into a swag. Since she'd finished the dolls for the James girls and had no orders to work on, she'd decided to do something to disguise the unattractive curtains hanging around her sleeping area. She smoothed out the wrinkles from where the material had bunched up in her lap and grimaced slightly at the way the color turned her skin sallow. Did it have to be orange?

Hannah sighed but set her foot back in motion on the treadle. Mrs. Granbury used to remind her girls that an ordinary seamstress could make a beautiful woman look exceptional, but only an exceptional seamstress could make an ordinary woman look beautiful. If the same held true for fabric, this exercise would be a true test of her skills. Thankfully, she wouldn't be wearing the creation, so she didn't need to worry about its effect on her complexion. Hannah finished the seam and tied off her threads. Trying to set her prejudice aside, she moved away from the sewing cabinet and held the cloth up at arm's length, letting it drape over her arms as she eyed it with as much objectivity as possible.

Many people found orange to be warm and cheerful. Of course, most of them didn't look bilious under its influence, but that was neither here nor there. God had painted many things in his creation this color—butterflies, sunsets, and the tiny wildflowers that grew along the path to the river. If the Lord saw beauty in such a color, she could, too. It certainly fit with the time of year, bringing to mind autumn leaves, pumpkins, and the creamy mashed winter squash her mother used to make on cold evenings. The cozy memory made her smile and opened a crack in her heart. Perhaps orange wasn't so bad after all.

Her arms began to tire, so she dropped the swag onto the worktable and folded it into a tidy rectangle. She supposed in the right light it could be considered cheerful. And she needed all the cheer she could get to help her deal with the fact that she had no customers.

Yet.

Hannah pressed her fingers into the sore muscles of her lower back.

No customers, *yet*. That would change in time. It had to. She had spent most of her savings purchasing fabric and supplies. If she didn't start generating some income, she'd be penniless by Christmas.

She had hoped that Ezra's new shirt would pique a bit of interest, but people were more impressed by his physical transformation than the craftsmanship of his garment. Which was only right. Ezra deserved to bask in the welcome of his community after being on the outside for so long. She was happy for him. Truly.

If only she could contract that first custom order. She just needed one woman brave enough to sample her skills. After others saw the flattering effects her fine tailoring had on one of their own, surely they would flock to her door.

Needing to do something other than sit at her empty machine, Hannah grabbed a feather duster and ambled around the shop, swishing the feathers over windowsills, cloth bolts, and anything too slow to get out of her way. As she brushed invisible lint from the shoulders of her display dummies, she caught sight of Cordelia standing across the street, her face etched with yearning as she stared at the olive gown in the window. She fingered the fabric of her plain navy gored skirt and drooped like a flower starved for rain. Then she snapped her wilted posture to attention and marched toward the shop.

Hannah's heart jumped, and she scurried across the room to stash the duster behind the counter. Taking a deep breath, she flattened the pleats of her shirtwaist with a trembling hand and quickly patted her hair before turning to greet her friend and possible first female customer.

Cordelia walked into the shop and closed the door behind her. She scanned the room with a sweeping glance, then turned to Hannah. "I need you to make me beautiful."

The tears that glistened in Cordelia's eyes banished the smile from Hannah's face. Responding to her friend's obvious pain, Hannah rushed forward and wrapped an arm around the other woman's shoulders.

"What happened?"

"He doesn't see me." She hiccuped as a sob tried to break free.

"Who?" Hannah asked. "Who doesn't see you?"

Cordelia buried her face in her hands. The empty basket slung over her arm creaked as her movement squashed it into her side. She might have said a name, but it was too muffled to make out. Hannah extracted a handkerchief from her sleeve and dangled it against the back of Cordelia's hands until she took it.

"Let me close up the shop. Then you can tell me all about it."

When Hannah twisted the key in the lock, the click reverberated in her ear. What if another customer came by? Closing the shop could cost her a sale. Dread churned in her stomach and acid burned the back of her throat. She couldn't afford to lock out a customer. But then one of the verses from Proverbs that she'd been meditating on during her morning devotions floated across her mind.

"Better is a little with righteousness than great revenues without right."

Hannah swallowed the bitter taste in her mouth and flipped over the *Closed* sign without further regret.

By the time Hannah finished with the door, Cordelia had composed herself somewhat. The dear girl was obviously still in a fragile state, however, so Hannah ushered her behind the counter and into her work area. She pulled the chair away from the sewing cabinet and up to the table and gently pushed Cordelia into it.

"Now," she said, dragging her fabric trunk away from the wall and seating herself upon it. "Who is this man with the atrocious eyesight that has you so upset?"

"Only the most wonderful man in all of Coventry."

Hannah could hear the heartbreak in the girl's voice, and her own heart ached in sympathy. "If he's so wonderful, why are you crying?"

"Because he doesn't see me! Not as a woman, anyway. To him I'm just J.T.'s little sister." She wrung the handkerchief between her fists. "I've loved him for ages, and the dim-witted man has no idea."

Hannah smiled. "Dim-witted, huh?"

Cordelia looked up sharply. "Oh, no. I didn't mean that. Not really. He's actually very intelligent. He operates the telegraph and post office down by the bank. You might have met him at church yesterday. Ike Franklin?"

Hannah tried to fish out a visage matching that name from the sea of faces that swam through her memory. Finally one clicked—a thin man in a well-cut gray wool sack suit. Dark mustache. Kind eyes. "Was he the one who led the hymns?"

"Yes." A dreamy look came over Cordelia's face. "Doesn't he have the most luscious voice? It's like chocolate icing, smooth and rich. I could listen to him all day."

"You're making me hungry."

Cordelia giggled. "Sorry."

Hannah reached out and covered Cordelia's hand with one of her own. She didn't want to add to the girl's pain, but she didn't want it prolonged, either. It would be better to face the truth now than to wallow in the misery of unrequited love. Hannah gave Cordelia's hand a gentle squeeze.

"I don't want to dash your hopes, Cordelia, but what if he simply thinks the two of you don't suit and is trying to spare your feelings by pretending not to notice your femininity? It might be better to set your sights on someone else."

"There is no one else! Not for me." She yanked her hand away from Hannah and balled the hankie into her fist. Her knuckles began to whiten, but then she exhaled a long breath and relaxed her grip. "I know you're trying to help, and believe it or not, I've asked myself that same question. But I don't think it's true. The two of us get along famously. We share many of the same interests—books, music, food . . ." She blushed. "He loves my cooking."

What man wouldn't? The woman could bake like an angel.

"About six months ago he hired me to bring him lunch every day, since he's not allowed to leave his post, even for meals. He has to man the wire at all times during his shift." She paused, then her lips curved into a shy smile. "He claims I'm the best cook in the county."

"Well, that proves he's not completely dim-witted, then. He may not be a lost cause after all."

"Oh, Hannah. Do you think so? Do you think I might still have a chance?" Cordelia bounced to the edge of her chair and leaned so far forward that if the table hadn't been supporting her, she would have toppled to the floor. "This isn't just a schoolgirl infatuation. I honestly believe Ike and I would suit. I've come to treasure the friendship that has sprung up between us over the last few months. If the line is quiet when I arrive with his lunch, he sometimes invites me to sit and visit with him while he eats. We talk about books we've read, or he'll tell me funny stories about the scrapes he got into as a boy. He's even taught me how to tap my name in Morse code."

Hannah nodded thoughtfully. Lasting relationships had been built on less.

"If you could fashion me a dress that would somehow make me at least passably pretty, he might finally notice me as a woman and decide to come courting. And if he doesn't . . . Well, at least I would know where I stood and could pack my hopes away quietly."

Hannah could hear the pain and insecurity embedded in Cordelia's words, and they tugged at her heart. There was no question about whether she would help. She'd known she would the minute she flipped the *Closed* sign in the window. The question that plagued her was how. They had only one chance to make a new first impression—an impression so striking that Cordelia's gentleman friend, myopic though he might be, couldn't help but see the beautiful woman in front of him.

The seed of an idea burrowed into her brain and began to take root. This called for more than just a new dress. This called for an Ezra-esque transformation.

Hannah got up and started pacing. "Are there any upcoming community festivities, like a harvest celebration or box social or something of that nature?"

Cordelia's face scrunched up in confusion. "There's the Founders' Day picnic in a little over a month, but what does that have to do with—"

"That's where you will make your debut." Hannah clapped her hands and grinned, but Cordelia failed to catch the excitement.

"It will take you six weeks to make me a new dress? I didn't expect to have to wait that long."

Hannah plopped back down on the trunk and took Cordelia's hands in hers. "I don't need six weeks to sew a dress. I don't need six days. But if you are patient and willing to work hard, I have a plan that will make it impossible for your Mr. Franklin to see you as anything but a desirable woman."

Finally a spark of interest lit her eyes. "Really? You can make me desirable?"

"You've already got all the makings of a beauty. Thick, shiny hair; lovely complexion; dark lashes."

"But I'm fat."

"No you're not. You're just . . ."

Cordelia shook her head. "Don't try to spare my feelings. I see the truth every time I look in the mirror. If I were thin like you, I—"

"You can be." Hannah released her friend's hands to clasp her shoulders. "You can be. I'll teach you my calisthenic routine, and you can join me on my morning walks. Dr. Lewis asserts that if a woman wants to be thinner, she has only to eat less and exercise more."

"Who's Dr. Lewis?"

"Dio Lewis. He's a great proponent of physical education for women and children. He developed a whole new system of gymnastics that can be used by anyone to great result. If you're willing to try, I promise you will see a marked difference. The exercises will improve your health and give you increased energy and strength with the added benefit of trimming your figure. Then, as the day for the picnic draws closer, I can fashion the perfect party dress for you, one in vivid colors and flattering lines that will make it impossible for Mr. Franklin to take his eyes off of you. You'll make as big a splash as Ezra did at church yesterday."

Hannah stood and pulled Cordelia to her feet. "It will mean sacrifice and hard work: changing your morning routine, eating less of those delicious baked goods of yours, and living with some aches and stiffness as your muscles adjust to their new activities. Are you willing to try?"

"Yes! Oh yes. Can we start today?"

Hannah laughed and embraced her friend. "Let's start with the

fun stuff. Patterns and fabric. We can start the exercise tomorrow."
She flopped her collection of swatches onto the counter and drew
Cordelia over to the latest issues of *Harper's Bazar*, *The Delineator*, and
Peterson's Magazine as well as the Butterick catalog she had brought with
her from San Antonio.

An hour later, they were still huddled over the counter oohing and
aahing at the fashion plates of elegant ball gowns and sophisticated day
costumes neither of them were ever likely to wear, yet both women
found great pleasure in admiring the designs.

At last, Cordelia released a sigh of regret and closed the last magazine. "I should probably go. I have to put supper on for J.T., and I've
monopolized too much of your time."

"Nonsense," Hannah said. "I can't remember when I've spent a
more enjoyable afternoon." She straightened the pile of books and
put the fabric swatches back under the counter. "And I look forward
to starting our new regimen tomorrow morning. We'll be able to talk
more."

"As long as I can still breathe." Cordelia grinned. "J.T.'s told me
how fast you walk out to the river."

A little thrill shot through Hannah at the thought that Jericho
had noticed. Of course, she had no way to determine whether he
found her athleticism appealing or not. Many men seemed to prefer
their women soft and fully dependent on the man's greater strength.
Would Jericho appreciate a strong woman, or was that just another
mark against her?

"I guess I'll have to tell him about my plans to join you on your
constitutionals during supper tonight," Cordelia said as she retrieved
the basket that lay forgotten on the worktable. "He'll probably take that
news better than when he learns I intend to order a new dress. That
little discovery will probably send him over the edge."

Hannah frowned. "He would begrudge you a new dress even when you have your own income to cover the cost?" The man could certainly be a grouch at times, but he'd never struck her as harsh.

Cordelia waved off her concern. "No, not if I needed one. But this will be a purely frivolous purchase, the kind he believes leads to vanity. You have to understand . . . J.T. was only sixteen when our pa died, and he'd been running the farm on his own long before that. For years he scraped and saved just to put food on the table. Even now, when he has a successful business and a surplus of money in the bank, he'll only buy himself a new pair of boots when he's worn the soles clear off his old ones. Practicality has been burned into his nature by necessity. He can be incredibly generous to those in need, but he has little tolerance for frivolous spending by those who could be putting their money to better use."

A stone the size of a bread loaf sank into Hannah's stomach. No wonder the man was always so touchy around her. He saw dressmaking as a promotion of vanity and wasteful spending. She'd been foolish to think for even a minute that he might find her attractive.

She understood his point of view. Practicality was certainly a virtue, but so was beauty. The Lord himself wove it into the very fabric of his creation, making it visible to anyone with eyes to see. Why couldn't Jericho perceive the value in that? Just because he was right didn't mean she was wrong. Yes, a love of beautiful things could be taken too far, leading to greed and vanity, but so could practicality. She'd known plenty of embittered misers who sucked the joy out of the lives around them by harping about every little thing that failed to be useful.

Why, if Jericho Tucker were there right now, she'd tell him a thing or two about—

The door rattled. Pounding followed. "Delia? Are you in there?"

A dark shape pressed itself against the window glass trying to peer inside.

Hannah swallowed.

Jericho Tucker *was* there.

CHAPTER 14

J.T. stepped back from the window unable to see much past the display. Where *was* that girl? Hawkins had come by the livery twenty minutes ago looking for her. Something about his bread order. The man said he'd already tried the house and she wasn't there. J.T. had promised to pass the message along, thinking it would be an easy task. Cordelia usually went only three places on her own: the mercantile, the telegraph office, or the drugstore, if she got a hankering for a peppermint stick. Since Hawkins was looking for her, that narrowed the options down to two.

Yet she hadn't been either place. Ike said she left his office at half past noon, and it was nearly two o'clock. J.T. had checked their home in case she'd returned, but he couldn't find any evidence that she'd been back since her noon outing. The stove had even grown cold. That's when he started to worry. Delia never let the stove go cold.

He'd been about ready to mount up and start searching along the road when Tom mentioned that he'd seen her go into Miss Richards's shop. But here he stood, and the door was locked, the shop closed.

Were the two females together? Were they in trouble? His pulse sped from a trot to a canter.

"Delia!" He pounded the door again. Harder.

Finally, the latch clicked and the door swung open.

"Goodness, J.T. The whole town can hear you yelling," Delia scolded as she grabbed his arm and dragged him inside. "Do hush."

He glowered at her, his relief turning quickly to ire. "Where the devil have you been? I've been looking all over for you."

She gave him one of her looks that questioned his intelligence. "I was here, obviously."

"Doing what?" he snapped.

"Visiting with Hannah and . . ." She glanced away and fiddled with the buttons at her waist. "And ordering a new dress for the Founders' Day picnic next month."

Everything inside him went deathly still. "What?"

"You heard me. I'm ordering a dress. A pretty dress." Cordelia lifted her chin, then dropped it as if drawing an exclamation mark. "I know your feelings on the matter, and I don't mean to hurt you by my actions, but I'm a grown woman and have the right to decide how I spend my money. I've made more than enough with my baking this year to cover the cost."

An invisible vice tightened around his lungs, making it hard to breathe. This couldn't be happening. Not to Delia. She'd been young, but she knew what their mother had become, how her love for fine fashions and the trappings of wealth had surpassed her love for husband and children.

His gaze moved past the women as he sought control. Unfortunately, it landed on the counter, where fashion magazines and pattern books lay strewn. Memories cut free of their bonds and leapt for his throat. He pictured his mother pouring over *Peterson's Magazine* as if it were the only thing in the room, ignoring his questions as he struggled to make sense of his homework. And he could hear the scorn that spewed from her as she upbraided his father for choosing to spend the money he scratched out of the farm on luxury items like flour and coffee instead of the bonnet she craved or the length of lace she would die without.

He fought to break memory's hold, but when he turned back to Delia, for a moment the face he saw was his mother's.

"It's just one dress, J.T." Delia swept by him on the way to the door, but as she passed his side she leaned in to whisper a final argument. "I'm not her."

Before he could manage to respond, she left. He hadn't even given her Hawkins's message.

He couldn't seem to move as thoughts spun round and round his brain. It might only be one dress, but it was a beginning. One dress could lead to another and another and another, until nothing satisfied her any longer.

"What does she want with some fancy getup, anyhow?" he mumbled.

"What any woman wants," a quiet voice said behind him. "To feel pretty."

J.T. pivoted. Miss Richards stood by her counter, probably counting Delia's money in her mind. He jerked a toothpick out of his pocket and jabbed it into his mouth. Clenching it between his teeth, he glared at the dressmaker. He'd known she'd be trouble the first time he clapped eyes on her. Delia never would have gotten this idea in her head if Miss Richards hadn't come to town with all her ribbons and lace and independent ways.

"I'm not going to let you change her." J.T. took a menacing step toward her, his finger pointing at her chest in accusation. His nostrils flared like those of a bull fixing to charge, but instead of shrinking from him, she leapt forward to meet him in battle.

"What are you afraid of, Mr. Tucker? Afraid you'll lose your devoted housekeeper if Cordelia finally catches the eye of the gentleman she favors?"

What gentleman? Cordelia didn't have eyes for any fellow that he knew about. He opened his mouth to say so but never got the chance. The she-cat wasn't done hissing at him yet.

"Is that the real reason you dress her in drab colors and unflattering styles? Because you're too selfish to let her have a life of her own?"

The finger he pointed at her curled into his fist. He squeezed it tight, barely containing the urge to slam it into the nearest wall. "That shows how little you know," he gritted out through clenched teeth. "I would die for my sister."

Clearly too riled to be wary, Miss Richards advanced another step until she was so close to him, he could make out individual sparks glittering in her eyes. "That may be true," she said, biting off each word, "but would you trust her enough to make her own choices?"

The question hit him like an unexpected punch to the gut. For the last decade, he'd appointed himself Delia's protector and provider, making sure she had food to eat, clothes to wear, a place to sleep. He saw to it she finished her schooling even when he'd had to drop out to look for work. She was his responsibility, and he'd shouldered the load without complaint because they were family. All they had was each other. But now that she was out of pigtails, could his protection be smothering her?

J.T.'s frown deepened at the disturbing thought. *Did* he trust Cordelia to make her own decisions?

He shifted the toothpick to the other side of his mouth and narrowed his eyes at his opponent. He had no answer to give, so he opted for silence.

After a tense moment, she banked the fires in her eyes and softened her stance. "I apologize, Mr. Tucker. I may have been a bit overzealous in Cordelia's defense." She took a step back and reached for the counter as if she needed it for support. "I'm not trying to change your sister.

She came here in tears this afternoon, begging for my help. That's all I'm trying to do. Help."

"And you think a new dress will solve all her problems." He spat the accusation at her.

"Of course not. Nor does Cordelia. But right now she feels invisible and unattractive. She despairs of ever securing the affections of the man she admires."

"What man?" J.T. shook his head. Why did she keep talking about this nonexistent man? "Cordelia has no beau."

"Not yet." Miss Richards smiled the smile of one holding a secret. "But we hope to change that situation soon."

Cordelia and a man? He'd strangle the guy.

"Did you think she would stay your little sister forever?" Her soft voice held more compassion than censure, but it grated on him nonetheless as he tried to deny what she was telling him. "Cordelia's a grown woman who loves her brother," she said. "But she also longs to step out of his shadow and live her own life. To marry a man who finds her beautiful."

J.T. gazed around him at the fancy dresses hanging on display, symbols of the hollow values he so despised. "Cordelia is already beautiful. She doesn't need your finery. Beauty doesn't come from outward adornment, Scripture says, but from a godly spirit."

"First Peter 3. I know it well. And I agree. However, if you will be honest with yourself, I think you'll realize that on a practical level, men rarely take the time to discover a woman's inner beauty if they are not first attracted to the outer person. How many times have you asked a pock-faced girl to join you on a buggy ride or invited an overly plump one on a picnic?"

J.T. rubbed the edge of his tongue back and forth across the end of his toothpick, the wood abrading his tongue almost as much as her question abraded his conscience. He'd taught himself to look past a handsome woman's face to determine the depth of her character, but he'd never thought much about doing the same for an uncomely gal. And to his shame, he doubted even now he'd be much inclined to try.

Was that what was happening to Delia?

He suddenly wanted to round up all the single men in Coventry and pound some sense into them.

J.T. pulled the toothpick from his mouth and snapped it in two with his thumb, wishing he could do more to expend the frustration roiling around inside him. He shoved the pieces into his vest pocket and glanced up to meet the eyes of the woman who was watching his every move. Upset as he was, he was still drawn to her. Which only heightened his agitation.

"You say you know the Scriptures," he said, "and yet your choice of occupation flies in the face of all they stand for. Clothes are meant to protect the body from the elements and preserve a woman's modesty, not to entice men or put on airs." He flung his arms wide and gestured to the dresses draped so decadently around the room, making no effort to filter the scorn from his voice. "All these items are designed specifically to draw attention to the wearer, to stroke her pride, and to elevate her above others. You may see a room full of harmless fashions, but if you open your eyes, you'll find that, in truth, it is filled with the temptation to indulge in sinful vanity."

Miss Richards pushed away from the counter and planted her hands on her hips, her arms shaking with the force of her affront. "You think *my* eyes are closed? I've never heard such narrow-minded drivel in all my born days."

Her arms fell to her sides, and she marched forward until she stood toe-to-toe with him. J.T. raised an eyebrow but held his ground. If the she-cat wanted to sharpen her claws on him, she was welcome to try. He wasn't backing down. She could hiss and scratch all she wanted. He was on the side of right, and he wasn't budging.

"I'll have you know, there's not a single immodest gown to be found in my collection, nor would I ever consent to sew one. If you would climb down off that high horse of yours for a minute, Mr. Liveryman, you'd see that the only difference between my dresses and the ones you favor from the mercantile is that mine are actually made well, custom-fit to each client.

"There is nothing wrong with bright colors and beautiful lines. If God had wanted the world to be a somber, colorless place, he would have made everything in black and gray. But he didn't. He filled his creation with color and beauty. Why do you think he instructed Moses to call all the skilled artisans to adorn his tabernacle with items of gold, bronze, and silver and with weavings done in blue, purple, and scarlet? Because our Lord appreciates beauty and chose to surround himself with it. I am an artisan, Mr. Tucker, the same as those skilled workmen in the days of Moses. God has given me a talent, and as his Son taught, it would be sinful of me to bury this talent and refuse to utilize it. So I use my gift to bring loveliness into the world."

She waltzed over to the rack that held several gowns and lifted a rosy pink one off its hook. Holding it up to her, she balanced the sleeves upon her arms and caressed the fabric with her fingers. "When a woman puts on one of my dresses and feels better about herself," she said, a faraway look in her eyes, "or smiles in pure enjoyment of the colors and style I've brought together, that's when I know I've created something beautiful, something the Lord could be proud of."

Miss Richards looked at him, and under his unrelenting stare the idealism faded from her eyes. Good. Maybe a dose of reality would wake her up to the truth.

Turning her back to him, she replaced the dress on the rack. "If a pretty dress can bring a woman pleasure, where's the harm in that?"

She really had no idea, did she?

"The harm, Miss Richards, comes when a woman relies on the temporary happiness that a new dress or hat or piece of jewelry can bring her instead of trusting the deeper, abiding joy that can be found in faith and family." J.T. stepped toward her, his slow, deliberate footfalls echoing in the still room.

Hannah Richards stood firm, her chin lifting with every step he took. "You have a poor opinion of women, indeed, sir, if you think we cannot tell the difference between the two."

"My mother couldn't." The words slipped out before he could call them back.

"Excuse me?"

A flood of anger, resentment, and pain rose up in him so quickly he couldn't contain it. "My mother craved the *harmless* pleasure of fashionable dresses, new bonnets, and pretty baubles to such a degree that she abandoned her husband and children in favor of playing mistress to a wealthy railroad surveyor. Delia was only four. Four! Just a baby. And our mother left her with a broken-down man and an eleven-year-old, wet-behind-the-ears kid who didn't know the first thing about taking care of a little girl."

Miss Richards's eyes widened, and the frown lines across her forehead eased, but he didn't want her pity. He wanted her to understand the truth about what her shop represented.

"You might think there's nothing wrong with offering the women of Coventry a taste of fashion and beauty, and for a select few of our citizens, you would probably be right. However, for the majority, what you offer is not beauty but temptation. They will lust after things they cannot afford. They will envy those who can. And they will grow discontent with their current circumstances."

She opened her mouth—to argue with him, no doubt, but he was in no mood to listen any longer. He shook his head and pinned her with a stare that she must have understood, for she clamped her lips tightly together.

"I know that most women would never abandon their families like my mother did, but discontent and selfishness can spread their poison, too, doing just as much damage. The Lord might see value in beauty, but he cares more about a person's heart than the beautiful shell that houses it.

"You asked me to be honest with myself, and now I ask the same of you. Of all the clients you have sewn for in the past, how many do you think derived pleasure simply from the style and color of your design, compared to how many used the beauty of that design to feed their vanity?"

Uncertainty played across her features, and her previously steady gaze wavered. He reached for another toothpick and slipped it into his mouth as he turned away and headed for the door. "Maybe not Delia, but many of the women who walk into your shop will not be strong enough to withstand the temptation you offer. Do you really want to be responsible for putting a stumbling block in their path?"

His fingers closed around the knob, and he glanced back one final time. Stricken eyes in a pale face filled his vision and twisted his gut. J.T. yanked the door open and stomped outside. As the door slammed behind him, he tried to convince himself that hurting her had been necessary, that she would grow from the experience and come to a fuller knowledge of the truth. But as he walked into the livery, her wounded expression haunted him.

Ignoring Tom's chatter, he saddled his best gelding and mounted up without a word. Once beyond the boundaries of town, he urged his horse into a gallop, pushing himself and his animal to the limit. Yet he couldn't outrun the memory of her face or the regret that gnawed on his insides more fiercely than a starving man's hunger.

CHAPTER 15

Glad her *Closed* sign was already in place, Hannah tidied up her sewing cabinet and fastened her bonnet strings with numb fingers. She exited the shop, locking it behind her, and climbed the steps to her room, no longer concerned about the loss of potential customers.

Once upstairs, she tore off her bonnet and crumpled onto the makeshift bench by the window. She had left her Bible on the seat that morning after her devotions, and it beckoned to her like a lighthouse signaling a ship lost in the storm. And, oh, how she needed guidance. She picked up the leather-bound book and clasped it to her chest, praying for the Lord to anchor her once again.

"Do you really want to be responsible for putting a stumbling block in their path?" Jericho's parting words crashed against her heart and bruised her spirit.

Was that what she was doing?

She couldn't deny that the majority of the wealthy clients she had sewn for in San Antonio had a selfish bent. Some saw fashion as a way to set themselves apart from the lower rungs of society. Others used it as a means to impress. Most pouted and complained through the fittings, finding fault with everything save themselves.

Yet there were exceptions, too. Women like Victoria Ashmont, who utilized color and style to express her personality while moving in the elite circles necessary to conduct her business. And the awkward young society daughters, fearful of embarrassing their families, whose gasps of genuine delight and relief at the sight of their reflection were anything but vanity.

"Lord, I'm so confused."

For so many years she'd thought she was honoring God by developing the talent he had given her and putting it to use by creating things of beauty. Had she deceived herself? Was she truly a stumbling block?

Searching more for comfort than answers, Hannah bent back the cover of her Bible and flipped to the book of Acts. She needed to reread the stories of her mentors, women of the cloth, like her, who served the Lord faithfully.

She read of Dorcas, a woman well loved by her community because of her ministry to widows, a ministry of sewing coats and other garments. Perhaps God wanted her to be more like this faithful disciple, sewing for the poor and needy instead of those who could pay for her services. Her needlework would truly be a ministry then, not a catalyst for pretentiousness.

But how could she afford to do so? She would run through her savings before winter and then be left unable to provide for anyone, including herself.

Hannah pushed a few more pages aside, the thin paper crinkling in the quiet room. Her finger ran down the length of one column until she came to the passage she sought.

Lydia. What of her example? She was a businesswoman, a merchant, and yet faithful to God's call. She sold purple cloth, the finest, most costly fabric of her time. Her customers had to have been affluent, the social and political elite of Philippi. Yet no one condemned her for selling her finery. In fact, her success in business allowed her to have a home large enough to provide a place for the new Philippian church to meet. And surely funds from her sales made up a substantial portion of the contribution that church later sent to Paul to aid his missionary journeys.

Justification poured over her like a salve on her wounded heart. She'd been right all along. Her dress shop offered a service to the people of Coventry, not temptation and iniquity. Jericho Tucker was simply a bitter man who let the pain of his childhood color his judgment.

So why did that gentle tug on her soul keep nagging her? And why could she not forget the anguish hiding behind the anger in Jericho's face?

Hannah knew the grief of losing a parent, but she couldn't imagine how much worse it must have been for Jericho, having his mother leave of her own accord instead of falling prey to illness, as had been the case with Hannah's father. What else could he conclude but that a closet full of pretty clothes and a handful of trinkets meant more to his mother than her own flesh and blood? No wonder he despised fine clothes.

But was he wrong? She shifted in her seat to press her back more firmly against the wall from whence she had slipped. It would be easy to wrap herself in indignation and toss out his arguments, yet there had been too much truth in them to be discarded.

Balance. She needed balance. Perhaps the Lord wanted her to be both Dorcas and Lydia. Like Lydia, she could run a successful business while at the same time reaching out to the poor and needy as Dorcas did. And now that she was more conscious of the genuine threat of becoming a stumbling block to some, maybe she could make an effort to encourage godly values in her customers. She had no idea how to accomplish that, but she'd pray for wisdom. Of course, she'd need to actually have customers before she could exert any influence. That was in the Lord's hands, too.

Father, I have no desire to be a stumbling block to any of your children. Teach me how to conduct my business in a way that honors you. And if . . .

A physical pang stabbed through her stomach. Hannah squeezed her eyes tight and curled her body down over the still-open Bible in her lap. She didn't want to pray the next words. Her mind resisted where her soul led. However, she knew submission was the only road to faithfulness. With the edge of her Bible digging into her middle, she forced her mind to shape the words that could kill her dream.

If I will do more harm than good by having a shop here, then keep all the customers away and let me fail. But if you can use me—

A thump against her door caused Hannah to jerk upright and suck in a startled breath. It came again, sounding more like a shoe banging upon the wood than a set of knuckles.

"Miss Richards? It's Danny. I brung your wood."

Hannah jumped to her feet and ran a hand over her hair as she hurried to the door. "Hello, Danny. How did you know I was home?"

Arms full of split logs, Danny sauntered in and dropped them into the box by the stove. "Ma saw you come up the stairs while she was bringin' in the wash from the lines. Said to ask if you would come down a minute so's she could ask you something." He dusted off the front of his shirt and then his hands. "If you weren't feelin' poorly or nothin', that is."

"No . . . I–I'm fine. I'd be happy to visit with your mother."

"Great! I'll tell her you're comin'." Danny dodged around her and bounded down the stairs. The echo of his clunky steps worked to pull Hannah out of her haze. She blinked several times, then followed at a more sedate pace.

Mrs. James met her on the back porch, a large basket of sun-bleached petticoats beneath her arm. She passed the basket on to Danny, who nearly disappeared behind the massive mound. "Take these in to Tessa, and add some wood to the stove. Those sadirons need to be plenty hot by the time I get in there."

"Yes'm." Danny wavered under the weight and ungainliness of the basket but made it inside without mishap.

An image of an eleven-year-old Jericho rose in Hannah's mind, unbidden. Only a year older than Danny, would he have been the one to tend to the laundry and cooking after his mother left? She could almost see the determination carved into his young face as he strove to conquer each task. Those determined lines were still evident in his manly profile, likely having been permanently etched into his being.

"Thanks for coming down." Louisa James's voice cut into her thoughts.

Hannah turned toward the hardworking woman and mustered a smile. "Of course."

"I . . . ah . . . never thanked you proper for the dolls you made my girls. They tote them things around everywhere."

Hannah's heart warmed at learning that something she made had brought the girls pleasure. No stumbling block in that. "I'm so glad they are enjoying them. It's been too long since I put my needle to something besides clothing. It was a fun change."

"Well, I also needed to thank you for helping Tessa." Louisa met Hannah's eye. "She told me about the button."

"Oh, yes. She and I had quite a time of it, searching for the perfect match. Did the owner make any complaint?"

"Nope, and that was a first for him." Louisa's mouth tipped up at one corner, bringing a flash of youth back into her haggard features for a moment.

"I was glad to be of help," Hannah assured her. "Tessa is a lovely girl and is a good hand with a needle."

The tiny smile on Louisa's face melted away. She rubbed a spot of perspiration off her temple with the back of her chapped hand and shifted her gaze to the ground.

"That's what I wanted to talk to you about. Tessa told me how you offered to teach her to sew more than buttons." Louisa leaned against a support post and shuffled her foot back and forth several times before she finally glanced back up at Hannah. "I told her you probably said that just to be polite, that you were too busy to be handin' out lessons to little girls. But she keeps pesterin' me about it. Goes on and on about how you meant it and begging me to let her go over there some afternoon."

Hannah heard the question behind Louisa's words and took pity on the proud woman who couldn't quite manage to ask it. "The offer was sincere, Louisa. I would be happy to instruct Tessa when you can spare her."

The other woman's chin began to wobble, but she clamped her jaw shut and stifled the emotional display. "I don't want my girls to end up like me," she said in a hushed voice. "They need a skill so's they can make their own way in this world if their men up and die on them. I done what I had to, and I see no shame in hard work, but they deserve better than raw hands . . . and backs that never stop aching."

Something tingled at the corner of Hannah's eye. She blinked it away as Louisa drew in a shaky breath.

"I can't afford to pay much for the lessons," she said, "but I could do your washin' and Tessa could clean up around your shop. She's good with a broom."

Hannah didn't have the heart to tell her that there was nothing to clean. With no customers to wait on, it took very little effort to keep the place spotless. However, it did give her an idea. One that had less to do with disguising charity and more to do with keeping the doors of her shop open.

"Louisa, there's something I need more than laundering, and I'd be glad to trade sewing lessons for it."

Wary hope flickered in the woman's eyes. "What is it?"

Hannah smiled. "Advertising."

"Advertising?" Louisa huffed out a breath and gestured around her as if Hannah were a simpleton who could not see the obvious.

"I'm stuck here from sunup to sundown. I scarcely find time to run to the mercantile when our foodstuffs run low. I can't traipse around town—"

"I don't expect you to," Hannah said. "Cordelia Tucker and I have already gone around town with the bread cloths you suggested, and I've had a few visitors to the shop since then, but I need some way to catch their interest when they have a need. I hadn't thought of it until just this moment, but perhaps I should stop emphasizing my larger services and focus instead on the mending and alterations I can do. Ease people in, like you were talking about."

Louisa's eyes narrowed. "How do you expect me to help with that?"

Hannah grinned, a new enthusiasm building within her. "If you find a tear or worn area in an item that you wash, mention to your customer that the dressmaker next door can mend it for a fair price. Stressed seams or skirt hems that are excessively dirty might mean an alteration would be welcome. I also remake old dresses into more current styles for those ladies who are interested in updating their wardrobe without having to purchase new items."

Hannah stepped close to Louisa and laid her hand on her neighbor's arm. "To be frank," she murmured in a low tone, "I can use all the patrons you can send me. I have yet to make a cash sale."

Louisa patted Hannah's hand and nodded. "I had wondered how you were faring. I'll do what I can to help."

"Thank you." Hannah squeezed Louisa's arm before stepping back, gratitude bringing that moist tingle back to her eye.

It must be true that God knew what his children needed before they asked, for she had barely begun to pray when he interrupted her with an answer. Far from closing down her shop, he had provided her with an opportunity to be both a Dorcas and a Lydia through one simple conversation, and blessed her with a deeper relationship with her neighbor in the process.

Hannah returned home, her stomach calm and her step light. As she reached the landing at the top of the stairs, though, she cast a glance across the road to the livery. A reminder that the path before her still held obstacles.

If the Lord would just work on convincing Jericho Tucker that she wasn't a false prophet sent to lure the fashion-minded women of Coventry down a lacy path to perdition, all would be well.

CHAPTER 16

Standing in one of the livery's box stalls, J.T. ran a hand down the right
front hock and fetlock of his favorite gray gelding. It'd been two weeks
since he'd ridden the animal away from town like an outlaw on the run.
Two weeks since he'd spoken to Miss Richards.

Not only had he injured a gal's feelings that day, he'd injured his
horse. Eager to gallop, the gray had responded to J.T.'s urgency with
energetic strides, but he'd pushed too far. The hard ride over the hilly
countryside took its toll. By the following morning, the animal favored
his right front leg, and a warm, swollen area emerged above the fetlock.
J.T.'s guilt doubled. Unintentionally hurting a woman's feelings was
bad enough. At least he could take comfort in the fact that he'd been
trying to open her eyes to the truth. But his horse? He'd punished his
mount with a heedless, bone-jarring run that left the animal nearly
lame. Horses were his livelihood, for pity's sake. He knew better.

His treatment of cold compresses and bandages had restored the
gelding's soundness, though. J.T. found no evidence of swelling this
morning, only smooth bone and cool skin beneath the gray coat. He

turned the gelding out into the corral and lifted his chin to the sky. A cold mist spat in his face. Fitting.

He might've been able to fix things with his horse, but mending things with Miss Richards was a different matter entirely. He wasn't even sure he should. After all, what could he do? He had no intention of taking back anything he'd said; he only regretted that she'd been hurt by it.

Not knowing how to proceed, he'd opted for the easy way around the predicament. He was avoiding her.

At first, he'd harbored hope that their confrontation would discourage her from working with Delia. But it didn't. He'd barely had time to duck behind the chicken coop the next morning when Miss Richards arrived to collect his sister for their walk. Every morning since, he'd made a point to get out of bed thirty minutes early to ensure he was safely inside the livery walls before she emerged from her place across the street.

Not that he didn't still keep tabs on her. He had Delia to consider, after all. And it was amazingly easy to stay abreast of Miss Richards's activities, thanks to Danny. According to the kid, she'd started giving Tessa sewing lessons. At first, J.T. hadn't been too thrilled about the arrangement. The last thing Coventry needed was another fancy seamstress. But then he figured the girl needed to learn how to sew if she planned to take care of a family of her own one day, and as much as he hated to admit it, Miss Richards knew a thing or two about pushing a needle through cloth. If Louisa didn't have the time or energy to train the child, Miss Richards was a logical second choice.

So now, whenever Danny showed up to muck stalls, J.T. engaged him in conversation. He'd learned all kinds of fascinating tidbits. For instance, the mystery beverage that Miss Richards drank every morning with Ezra Culpepper was cocoa. She apparently had a strong hankering for the stuff. Then there was the small matter of her still not having chairs. She did have her new sign, though, and to hear

Danny tell the tale, she'd climbed out her upstairs window to hold the thing steady while the blacksmith nailed it to the support boards on her roof. Fool, stubborn woman. Didn't she know prancing around on a roof two stories above the ground was a good way to break her pretty neck? Though he didn't want her to operate her business in this town, he didn't want her dying here, either.

Between his own observations and what he could glean from both Danny and Delia, J.T. was as confused as ever about Hannah Richards. The woman designed gowns for a wealthy clientele while at the same time taking a poor laundress's daughter under her wing. She even found a way to get around Louisa's pride. Two days ago at church, Tessa and Mollie showed up in new dresses cleverly pieced together from smaller scraps of material, like a patchwork quilt. Tessa bragged to everyone who would listen that she had made them herself, which explained why Louisa didn't consider them charity. Tessa's tiny foot might have pumped the pedal, but J.T. had no doubt whose expert hands had guided the fabric through the machine.

J.T. stamped his feet to knock the mud off his boots before trudging through the wagon shed to his office. Judging by her profession, Miss Richards should be a vain, shallow creature, and therefore easy for him to dismiss. Unfortunately, all evidence indicated she was kind, hardworking, and compassionate. He didn't know what to do with that. Especially since she obviously intended to keep her shop open. A woman of true spiritual integrity would never knowingly offer temptation to others. So what did that make her? Sinner or saint?

A shadow bounced across his desk. "Mornin', J.T."

Tom flapped his arm in a greeting much too energetic for this early in the morning. And his lopsided grin only made J.T. grit his teeth.

"I saw Miss Richards and Cordelia playing with some more of those funny toys when I passed your place. You think she'd let me try them things if I asked 'er?"

J.T. ran a hand over his face, weary of the battle raging inside him. "I don't know, Tom. I don't really talk to Miss Richards much these days."

"Why's that? She's nice."

Biting back a groan, J.T. got up and clapped Tom on the shoulder as he wedged past him, needing to escape the kid's black-and-white simplicity. Things were either fun or work. People were either nice or mean. No need to look deeper, to bust a blood vessel trying to guess motives or predict spiritual repercussions.

A quizzical frown stretched Tom's mouth back at one corner as he turned to follow J.T. "I thought we was supposed to be lookin' out for her since she don't have no menfolk. Ain't that kinda hard to do if ya don't talk to her?"

J.T. pulled his hat down over his eyes as he made his way to the livery door, wishing he could shut out the kid's words as easily. "Miss Richards seems to manage just fine without us. She's a capable woman." And beautiful, and fiery, and good-hearted—and a dressmaker. Why did she have to be a dressmaker? J.T. shoved a toothpick between his teeth and bit down until his jaw ached.

"Don't worry about her, kid. I'm keeping an eye on her even if I'm not jawin' with her constantly. She's getting along all right."

But was she? All he really knew was that she showed up for work every day. Work and her morning walks with Delia. And what exactly were those *toys* Tom was talking about? Maybe it was time to stop avoiding the contradictory Miss Richards. After all, the only way to understand something was to study it, and he aimed to figure this woman out.

"The stock is out in the corral," he called to Tom as he strode toward the street. "Start mucking the stalls. I'll be back in a bit." He rounded the corner toward home, determination fueling his steps.

J.T. found the dressmaker with his sister under the large oak tree behind his house. The morning mist had dampened the women's hair flat to their heads, but neither seemed to mind. Their cheeks, rosy from their exertions in the cool air, lent them a healthy glow, and he grudgingly admitted that he hadn't seen Delia look so exuberant since her days of playing tag around the schoolhouse.

"You're doing great, Cordelia. Keep going. Ten more. You can do it."

Something akin to elongated wooden pears hung from Miss Richards's hands. She swung the clubs in a giant *L* shape. The right arm rose straight in the air above her head and the left pitched out to the side at a perpendicular angle. Then the positions reversed. She alternated arms back and forth as she counted off the repetitions. Miss Richards held her arms stiff and strong. Delia's bent a bit at the elbows and didn't quite reach the same height. Her breaths came in heavy puffs as she followed Miss Richards's example, but she didn't quit, and even though she looked ridiculous, J.T. couldn't help but be proud of her tenacity.

"Good. Now lower the clubs to your sides and do the lower pendulums."

Delia moaned. "My arms are burning."

Miss Richards would not be deterred. "That's good. Your muscles are working. We'll do ten of these and then take a break."

"All right."

This time instead of making the *L* above their heads, they formed it in front. The right arm lifted sideways at the shoulder while the left poked straight out in front. Then the alternations began again. They looked like a pair of trainmen flagging down a locomotive.

". . . seven . . . eight . . . nine . . . ten. You did it!" Miss Richards exclaimed. "Go ahead and rest for a minute and then bring the rings over. We'll finish up with those today."

Delia dragged herself up onto the back porch and collapsed into the rocker that sat under the eaves. Her arms draped over the sides, dangling toward the floor. J.T. bit back a grin. The girl was exhausted. Miss Richards, on the other hand, looked as fresh as a yearling colt, antsy and ready to go. While Delia rested, she continued on with a more complicated routine. Lunging with her legs, she twirled the clubs in large, full-bodied circles. The graceful arcs accentuated her flexibility and athleticism, holding J.T.'s gaze captive. Her plain blue dress, dampened by the moist air, clung to her form as she stretched. J.T. tried to swallow, but his mouth had gone dry.

Tearing his attention away from her shape, he focused instead on the silly clubs she was flinging around. He cleared his throat and stepped out of the shade of the house.

"Are you going to start juggling those things next?" Frustrated by his physical reaction to the woman who caused him no end of mental angst, his voice came out with more derision than he'd intended. The little lady jumped and emitted a quiet squeak, much like she had the day she'd fallen through the rotted staircase and into his arms.

That was not a memory he needed at the moment.

He was having a hard enough time clearing his mind of inappropriate thoughts without remembering how good she'd felt bundled up against his chest.

"Goodness, J.T. You scared me half to death sneaking up on us like that," Delia said from her now fully upright position in the rocker. "What are you doing here? You never come home before noon."

"I decided to see for myself what kind of secret activities the two of you engage in every morning." J.T. spared a brief glance for his sister before striding toward the tree and the bristling woman beneath its branches. "Had I known you were entertaining the notion of joining a circus act, Miss Richards, I would have offered to wire P.T. Barnum on your behalf."

"Circus act?" Her lips thinned into a straight line, and she waved the wooden clubs at him.

J.T. halted a few steps away. Perhaps he shouldn't have provoked her while she was still gripping the clubs. They looked less like juggling toys and more like weapons the closer he came.

"I'll have you know, all the implements I use are scientifically researched and proven effective for improving flexibility and strength. Dr. Dio Lewis and Simon Kehoe both published books extolling the benefits of proper and repeated use of the Indian club. In fact, in Mr. Kehoe's volume, he included sketches of several gentlemen who work daily with such clubs. I can tell you their muscular physique would outmatch any man."

The annoying woman made a point to glance at his chest and then roll her eyes away, as if she found him lacking. *Him*. No dandy from New York who passed time swinging some feeble little clubs in a gymnasium somewhere could compete with a man who worked hard for a living. Not on any day of the week. He'd like to see one of those fellows fork hay into a loft for an hour or plow a field of tough Texas soil under the hot sun from dawn till dusk.

And just what was she doing gawking at pictures of men's physiques, anyhow? J.T. shrugged his shoulders and flexed his muscles under his coat.

"You really shouldn't criticize something you know so little about . . . Jericho."

He blinked and narrowed his gaze. No one had dared call him by that name in years. Not since his mother had left. His pa's belt had kept him from back-talking when his mama insisted on using the name despite his protests, and he'd even borne up under his teacher using it. But not one of his peers dared go against his wishes. He'd pummeled the last fellow who'd tried—a twelve-year-old kid who didn't think a nine-year-old could thrash him. The smart aleck hadn't reckoned on how much J.T. hated the name. What boy wanted to be named after a city that crumbled when a bunch of nomads walked around it? Not exactly an image of strength or fortitude.

Besides, *she* liked it. If Mama could abandon him, he could sure as shooting abandon the name she tried to saddle him with.

J.T. silently worked his jaw back and forth. There was only one person who would've dared tell this woman his given name, and she was stifling giggles on the porch behind him. Choosing to ignore his sister for now, J.T. faced the impudent woman whose eyes issued challenges his pride could not ignore.

He prowled forward, jaw clenched so hard his facial muscles ticked. "The name's J.T."

"No," she said, tapping her chin as if pondering some great mystery. "Those are initials. Your *name* is Jericho."

Wiggling his fingers to keep them from curling into fists, J.T. reminded himself that she was a woman. He couldn't deal with her the same way he had the boy in the schoolyard.

"Are you purposely trying to rile me?" His voice rumbled with menace, warning her against such a dangerous path.

An all-too-innocent smile stretched across her face. "Why, yes. Yes, I am. Is it working?"

CHAPTER 17

Hannah struggled to keep her expression bland. The incredulous look on Jericho's face nearly made her laugh out loud. He stood stock-still ... and blinked five times. She counted.

Then his lips twitched. A smile? Surely not. He quickly covered the bottom half of his face with his hand, ostensibly to rub his jaw, but Hannah believed he was hiding something. Perhaps she had finally managed to make a crack in that wall of stoic arrogance he used as a shield. She could hope.

"Care to try them for yourself?" Hannah held out her clubs to him. "Give me thirty minutes, and I bet I can change your opinion of their worth."

"You're on." He rolled up the sleeves of his shirt past his elbows, exposing muscular forearms, and then took the clubs from her. Arms wide, he reached back in a stretch that drew his shirt tight across his chest.

The men pictured in Mr. Kehoe's book suddenly seemed less impressive.

Jericho continued to stretch and Hannah continued to watch until she happened to meet his eye. The look on his face clearly said he'd noticed her noticing. She jerked her attention away and bent to retrieve Cordelia's clubs.

"Usually men use longer and slightly heavier Indian clubs," she said, trying to cover her embarrassment by beginning her instruction, "but you'll have to make do with mine. I'll demonstrate with these."

Hannah showed him the proper way to grip the handles and summarized the different positions. "Now, in order to make this a fair trial, you must put true effort into the exercises. Keep your arms straight, and make your movements fast and strong."

"I'll give you a fair test . . . Hannah."

An absurd thrill shot through her at the sound of her given name on his lips. The mockery in his tone only hurt a little. But she'd brought that on herself. What she had to do now was prove him wrong. And who knew—maybe if he realized he could be wrong about the value of exercise equipment, he might be willing to consider that his view on her profession could benefit from a slight adjustment. Why not wish for the whole pie instead of only a slice?

"All right, Jericho, follow my lead."

He scowled at her use of his name, which only made her want to use it as often as possible. She was done tiptoeing around him. He never smiled anyway, at least not at her, so pandering to his ego would serve no purpose. Perhaps he was one of those misguided creatures who actually preferred vinegar to honey. Well, let someone else try to sweeten him up. She'd take a different tack. Jericho Tucker stood in the way of her finding full acceptance in this community, and she planned to fight her way past him. Starting now.

Hannah swung her clubs into first position, skipping the beginner exercises she'd been using with Cordelia. Jericho needed a more exacting routine. He would expect it to be easy, and it would probably seem so at first, but she planned to double the number of repetitions and increase the level of difficulty without giving him the breaks she allowed Cordelia. It didn't matter that she'd already completed most of her own routine before he arrived. She'd outlast him. Her muscles were used to the movements; his weren't. The determined set of his jaw assured her he'd not quit, but if she could get him to sweat, even a little, that would be victory enough.

After completing all the perpendicular sets, Hannah moved on to arm presses and lunging circles. Jericho stayed right with her. The scoundrel wasn't even breathing hard.

Her arms began to tremble slightly. She locked her elbows into place to hide the tremors and pushed harder, unwilling to let him best her.

"This next move is complicated," Hannah told him, careful to regulate her exhalations so as not to huff at all. "Think you can handle it?"

"I can handle anything you want to throw at me, sweetheart." He cocked a brow at her.

Hannah cocked one right back. He'd not fluster her with his swagger and mock endearments.

"You'll like this one, Jericho," she said. "It's named the Moulinet, or broadsword exercise. Very manly."

"Stop calling me that."

Hannah couldn't hide her grin this time. "What . . . manly?"

His scowl darkened.

"Oh, you mean Jericho." She shook her head. "No, I don't think so. I like it too much. Jericho—a city so sure of itself and its strength that it couldn't acknowledge the possibility that someone else might succeed with methods that appeared foolish and wrong in its eyes. Fits you rather well."

Before he could comment, she began the next movement. It required concentration and a loose wrist to twirl the clubs before tucking in the elbows and circling the arms around in a large arc. Jericho seemed to have a little more difficulty mastering the precision of this one, and Hannah inwardly gloated.

"It's been thirty minutes," Cordelia called out from her vantage point on the back porch. "Why don't you work the rings with him before the two of you quit?"

Hannah winced. She'd been so caught up in proving her point to Jericho, she'd completely forgotten about Cordelia. Her friend didn't seem to mind, though. She leaned forward in her chair, as if she had a front-row seat at an outdoor theatrical.

"Your brother only agreed to thirty minutes," Hannah called back as she brought her spinning clubs to rest. "I wouldn't want to tire him so much that he can't perform his duties at the livery today."

"No chance of that," Jericho grumbled.

Hannah wasn't sure that working the rings with him was a good idea. The apparatus required that two people grip them at the same time, often bringing the exercisers into close proximity. Being near this man tended to have an addling effect on her brain, and she needed all her wits about her to battle him successfully.

"I won't ask you to do the rings," she said, dropping her clubs into the box of equipment at the base of the tree. "You've sacrificed enough time already. I'm sure you'll agree, though, that these instruments are not mere toys."

He came up behind her, reached over her shoulder, and dropped his own clubs in the box. Was that faint musky odor . . . perspiration? Triumph welled in her. Then his arm brushed against hers. Triumph fled, replaced by a wobbly-kneed feeling that rattled her nerves. She stiffened and demanded that her body cease its traitorous behavior, but her pulse ignored her and continued with its giddy little dance.

"I haven't made up my mind yet about your methods," he said, still standing much too close. "I better try these ring things, too. I should make sure they're safe for Delia."

"Of course they're safe," she snapped. "Children use them." She tried to move away, but his piercing eyes kept her feet planted.

"Afraid your contraption will prove ineffective?"

"No." What she feared was that Jericho's nearness would render *her* ineffective. But she'd never been one to back down from a challenge, so she hobbled her high-stepping pulse and looked Jericho square in the eye. "Very well, I'll show you the rings."

He nodded and stepped back, finally allowing her to draw a full breath. She crouched down by the box and dug out the two cherrywood rings that always found their way to the bottom. Holding one in each hand, she straightened and faced the large man in front of her.

"Those are the rings?" he scoffed. "They can't be more than six inches across. What are you supposed to do with them? Play horseshoes?"

Hannah speared him with a look. "I prefer braining pompous livery owners with them. Should I show you the technique?"

He raised his hands in surrender and mumbled a halfhearted apology. Though his lips didn't twitch this time, the skin around his eyes crinkled. If she could just get the two actions together, she might have the makings of a genuine Jericho Tucker smile. Discarding that thought as too distracting, she focused on the fundamentals of her lesson and thrust her arms out toward him.

"Grab hold of the rings."

The moment he complied, an unwelcome heat surged through her. His broad hands encompassed such a large portion of each ring.

"These were designed to be used by two people of similar height and strength for maximum efficiency." She tilted her chin up to look him in the face. "Since you are taller and stronger than I am, the exercise will not be as beneficial to you, but I think I can present enough of a challenge to give you an idea of how it works."

"We'll see."

Hannah's ire sparked. Hesitation fell away as the spirit of competition took over.

"Match my strength and keep up if you can . . . Jericho."

They began with a series of push-and-pull exercises that mimicked the motion of a piston pumping back and forth. Their left feet stood together in the center while their right legs supported them from behind. At first, he offered her little resistance as she dragged his arm forward and back, but he soon adjusted, and her muscles strained to keep up.

Next, they stood back-to-back and did opposing side lunges with their still-connected arms overhead. Her skirts swished against his legs several times. He gave no indication that he'd noticed, so she affected the same undisturbed mien.

"You should be able to feel a stretch along the outside of your arm," she said. "These routines are excellent for improving flexibility."

Jericho grunted in answer.

They did the same position again, only this time they faced each other. Hannah made certain to lean back as they lunged to avoid coming into contact with Jericho's chest. However, the effects of her extended workout combined with the fact that she was within a hairsbreadth of touching the man whose nearness invited her pulse to polka left her struggling for air.

Which had to be the reason she progressed to the next section of the ring routine without first considering the consequences.

Their right feet together, she and Jericho faced each other and leaned backward as far as possible, using one another's weight as a counterbalance. Then, she explained, on the second count, they would press their arms forcefully outward, bringing their heads and shoulders together. Like a good student, Jericho followed her instructions not to bend his elbows. Unfortunately, she failed to take into account his much longer arms. As he pulled wide, she was helpless to stop her forward momentum and thumped directly into his chest. His well-braced leg kept them from tumbling onto the ground, but nothing could keep them from pressing so closely together that she could feel his heart beating against hers. For an endless moment, he stared down at her, surprise and something much warmer flaring in his eyes. Then common sense prevailed. He released the rings, held her about the waist, and set her on her feet.

"I think I've got the general idea now." Jericho cleared his throat and backed away until he reached the back fence. "I'm heading to the livery, Delia," he called to his sister, never once glancing back at Hannah. "I'll see you at lunch."

Then he left, his long-legged stride eating up the turf at a near run.

Hannah leaned into the tree for support as she watched him go, a sinking feeling settling into the pit of her stomach. She had no idea if she'd proved anything to Jericho with her exercises, but she'd proven something to herself. Something disastrous. She was falling in love with a man who could never return her affections.

CHAPTER 18

J.T. took the shortcut home for lunch, through the corral and across the strip of land behind his house. As he passed the big oak, he kneaded his upper arm. He hated to admit it, but flinging around those silly clubs had made him a bit sore.

And the rings? He should have taken Hannah up on her offer to forgo the blasted things. She'd been so close to him, he could smell the mist in her hair, see the sky in her eyes. And when she moved, her skirt brushed against his legs like sandpaper scoring a match.

Until she fell and accidentally ignited the flame. It had taken a wagonload of self-control to set her away from him.

He'd spent the bulk of the morning recounting the reasons she was unsuitable for him and asking God for strength to resist her wiles. Only, deep down, he knew they weren't wiles. Hannah Richards might try to foist her fashionable wares on the people of Coventry, but she'd never foist herself. He'd seen her efforts to maintain a discreet distance between them while they worked through the ring routine, a Herculean task considering they were connected at the fingertips. No, she was just a lovely, misguided woman who tugged at his heart and tempted his body. With God's help, he could resist. He had to. He'd not repeat his father's mistakes.

J.T. thought back to the day his father had taken him aside to tell him the woman they had both loved was gone for good. His face haggard, his eyes dull, he clapped J.T. on the shoulder with one hand while pulling down the wedding photograph from the mantel with his other. Color slowly drained from his knuckles as he tightened his grip on the thin metal frame until his thumb pressed the glass so hard it cracked.

"Don't follow in my footsteps, son."

That was all he said, but it was enough.

J.T. remembered the excuses his father had made when his mother closed herself in her room in one of her huffs, leaving him to finish dinner or soothe a crying baby Delia. He'd said that she was just high-strung, as if that explained anything. Then, more often than not, he had passed the stirring spoon or baby over to J.T. and disappeared behind the closed door to mollify his child bride. It didn't take much imagination to figure out their history.

When his father met his mother, he must have been so taken by her fine looks and youthful exuberance that he willingly closed his eyes to her faults. She'd been fourteen years younger than he, and J.T. supposed his father had been flattered by her attentions, sure that once she matured and settled down, her pretty pouts and artful manipulations would disappear. But they didn't. They intensified. J.T. had seen it firsthand. She birthed him two children and complained all the while about the loss of her figure. She demanded expensive clothes and trinkets until her husband's savings were depleted, threatened to leave him if he tried to tell her no. J.T. couldn't remember her ever sacrificing something for another person strictly out of kindness—not even for him or Delia.

The day they laid his father to rest, J.T. stood at the grave and vowed to take his father's advice to heart. And he had. Until Hannah.

Something about that woman weakened his defenses, and he needed to figure out what it was. Soon.

Reaching the house, J.T. paused on the back porch. He shoved thoughts of his parents back into their pigeonholes and threw a mental blanket over Hannah before pushing through the door. The safety of routine restored the last fragments of his control as he stepped into the kitchen and hung his hat on its hook. "What's for lunch, sis?"

"Roasted chicken and parsnips, with apple dumplings for dessert."

Delia opened the warming oven and a blend of savory and sweet aromas filled the kitchen. J.T.'s stomach gurgled in anticipation. He washed up at the kitchen pump and took his place at the table.

Concentrating so hard on keeping everything normal, he was halfway through his meal before he realized his sister was staring at him. Glaring at her over his chicken leg, he swallowed the hunk of meat he'd been chewing.

"What?"

Elbow propped on the table, she braced her chin on her hand. "I think she's right."

"Who?"

"You don't smile. Strange that I hadn't noticed it before." After imparting that keen observation, she turned her attention to her plate and stabbed a roasted parsnip with her fork.

J.T. had no doubt to whom his sister referred. Not wanting to encourage conversation in that direction, he said the first thing that came to mind. "The gray's all healed up."

Of course, thinking of the injured gelding did nothing to stem the flow of thoughts regarding Miss Richards.

"That's good." Delia took a dainty bite of chicken, and only then did J.T. notice that her plate held a much smaller portion than usual.

"You feeling all right?"

She nodded. "I'm fine."

With a shrug, he cut into his dumpling. Baked apple and cinnamon wafted up to him as he slid a healthy portion onto his fork. He lifted the bite to his mouth, already tasting the juicy goodness when he caught Delia grinning at him with a gleam in her eye. The fork clanked down onto his plate.

"Now what?"

"You and Hannah had a lively time this morning. What'd you think of those exercises?"

Swallowing a groan when he would much rather be swallowing his dumpling, J.T. leaned back in his chair. "I think I would've been laughed out of town if anyone had seen me swinging those ridiculous clubs. If you and Miss Richards want to embarrass yourselves with that stuff, be my guest, but don't expect me to touch one of those things ever again."

"But did they work?"

Not yet willing to concede that point, he merely grunted. In response, she reached across the tabletop and snagged his fork. Before he could stop her, she slid the fruity tidbit off the tines and into her mouth.

"Hey!" He made a grab for her arm but missed as she flopped back into her seat.

She smiled in triumph, her lips as wide as they could be while still concealing their prize.

"Imp. Get your own dumpling." He sawed off a second section and crammed it into his mouth before she could steal it.

"I only wanted a bite," she said as she dabbed her lips with her napkin. "I'm taking the others to Mr. Franklin at the telegraph office."

"You didn't make yourself one?" That wasn't like her. Delia loved sweets.

"Not today." She got up to refill his coffee cup, and J.T. considered her more closely. Her brown dress was hanging a bit looser around her middle. She was losing weight.

"You sure you're not sick?"

Delia set the coffeepot back on the stove and began packing a man-sized portion of food into her delivery basket to take to Ike. "I'm fine, J.T. Really. Stop your fussing."

He lifted his coffee to his lips and sipped the hot brew. "Maybe you should cut back on all that walking and calisthenic nonsense. You're getting thin."

"Do you think so?" She looked downright pleased by the idea.

J.T. frowned. "If you're feeling poorly, you should rest, not wear yourself out with crackbrained exercises."

"Actually, feeling poorly is exactly why Hannah got involved with Dr. Lewis's gymnastic system in the first place." Delia collected his empty plate and set it in the dishpan.

He told himself not to ask, but an irresistible curiosity drove him to it anyway. "She was ill?"

"As a child, yes. From what Hannah told me, she nearly drowned the summer she was ten, swimming in a pond near her home. She developed pneumonia, and her lungs weakened to the point that the doctors believed she'd be an invalid the rest of her life."

J.T. drew a toothpick from his pocket to clean his teeth and tried to picture a young Hannah lying in bed with nothing to occupy her beyond a needle and thread. The image didn't fit the woman he knew. It was much easier to envision her as a rambunctious girl bounding over hills and dales in pursuit of rainbows, butterflies, and armloads of wildflowers.

"She's certainly no invalid now."

Delia chuckled as she covered the food basket with a clean napkin. "No, she's certainly not. Apparently her mother ran across a book by Dr. Lewis that emphasized the stimulating effects of sunshine and exercise on curing weak lungs and recommended the use of apparatus such as Indian clubs and lightweight dumbbells. She started Hannah on a simple regimen and built on it little by little until her health was fully restored. Hannah never gave up the habit."

"Gotta go," J.T. mumbled. He pushed away from the table and got up, eager to escape the conversation about Miss Richards. The last thing he needed was another reason to admire the woman. Lots of children faced and overcame adversity. It didn't make her special.

"I'm going to stop by the dress shop on my way home." Delia's giddy grin captured his attention. She gripped the sides of her basket as if trying to keep her hands from clapping together in glee. "We're going to do some preliminary measurements and select fabric."

J.T. scowled at his sister. "I'd hoped you'd abandoned that notion."

She released the basket and blew out a breath. "Land sakes, J.T. It's just one dress. I'm not going to turn into some vainglorious peacock who constantly obsesses about her wardrobe. You raised me better than that. I simply want to wear something nice to the Founders' Day picnic this year. That's all."

He crossed his arms over his chest and broadened his stance. "I'm starting to think that maybe you're spending too much time with Miss Richards. She's a bad influence on you."

Delia gasped. "How can you say that? She's my dearest friend, and she's done nothing wrong—to you or anyone else in this town."

"She operates a shop filled with temptation," J.T. declared, thrusting his finger in the direction of the offensive place. "Her designs aren't simple dresses created to keep a person protected from the elements. No, every last one of them has been specifically crafted to draw attention to the figure of the woman who buys it, stroking the customer's vanity, and giving her reason to snub those less wealthy or attractive than she. And what of those who can't afford the luxury of such clothing? They are left to lust over ruffles and lace, coveting what is out of their reach when they should be content with what they have."

"Which am I?"

J.T. chomped down on his toothpick, tension spearing through his jaw. Delia stood before him with her hands on her hips, daring him to place her in one of those objectionable categories.

"I have the means for the dress, saved from my own earnings," she said, "so that must mean that I'm a status-seeking snob. Is that what you're saying?"

"Of course not. You're different."

"I'm different? Really? Because a moment ago it all sounded very black and white coming from you."

"Delia . . ." She was twisting things around.

"So you're willing to concede that it's possible for a woman, like me, to purchase one of Hannah's creations without plunging into moral decay."

"Yes," he said through clenched teeth, "but she should be more responsible toward those who are weaker. A true Christian wouldn't lay out a stumbling block for others to trip over."

"Jericho Riley Tucker. When did you get so sanctimonious?" Her lips pursed in distaste. "A true Christian, indeed. I guess a true Christian couldn't own a gun shop, then. Too much temptation for those with murderous impulses. Or a bank. Greed leads to all kinds of dissipation, you know. Better not open a restaurant, either. Why, the poor soul who is prone to gluttony would be tempted to order mounds of food each time he entered the establishment."

"Enough! You've made your point." J.T. grabbed his forehead and massaged his temples.

Delia's arms fell to her sides and she sighed. "If Hannah filled her shop with scanty gowns that incited men to lust and promoted an immoral agenda, I would be the first to help you close her down. But she's an honorable woman who makes her living sewing high-quality, modest dresses that glow with the colors and beauty God inspires within her. There is nothing shameful in that.

"You are letting what our mother did cloud your judgment, J.T. She was a selfish woman who craved beautiful things, but that doesn't mean that people who make beautiful things are wrong to do so."

Arguments swirled in J.T.'s mind, setting him adrift. What Delia said made sense, but he feared her logic was another test of his conviction. He *wanted* to believe that Hannah was innocent of any wrong. If she were, there would be no reason to continue fighting his attraction for her. Waves of doubt tossed him to and fro until the verse from First Peter about beauty coming from within and not from outward adornment sprang to the surface like a life preserver. He latched on to it.

"She might not be promoting immodesty, but she is promoting false ideas about beauty that could lead others astray."

"Is that all you can see? Can you not see all the good that she's done in the short time she's been here?" Delia came up to him and touched his arm. He flinched and stepped away from her.

"Do you not see her ministering to Tessa James, teaching the girl to sew and using that opportunity to meet the child's need for new clothes at the same time? Do you not see the happiness her friendship has brought me?" She inched close to him again. J.T. fought the urge to retreat.

"You know I've always struggled to fit in. Between the scandal with Mother and my own shyness, friends have been a rare commodity for me. Yet the first day I brought Hannah a jar of milk, genuine affection sprung up between us."

J.T. frowned. He'd been so busy as a young man trying to keep a roof over his sister's head, he hadn't paid much attention to how she fared with other kids. Had she been lonely all this time?

"And what of Mr. Culpepper?" Delia continued. "How many months did the people of Coventry, you and me included, let that man wander around in the stench of his grief doing nothing about it? Hannah took him under her wing and in less than a week managed not only to get him to bathe but, more importantly, to return to church.

"If anyone can be an influence for good in a shop filled with fancy dresses, Hannah Richards can. She already has."

The life preserver was slipping from his hands, and he didn't know how to reestablish his grip. The truth embedded in his sister's words swirled around him in a current that pulled him in a direction he didn't want to go. Why couldn't he just cling to his simple understanding of what God wanted from his people? It had served him well in the past. But Hannah had muddied the waters with her contradictions. She didn't fit into his clean, simple way of thinking.

J.T. ran a hand through his hair and tugged at the roots. He hissed under his breath at the self-inflicted pain. Then Delia reached out and gently tugged his arm free. Surrounding his large hand with her two smaller ones, she peered up at him.

"You're afraid, J.T. Afraid to believe that someone who values beauty and is so beautiful herself can also be good." She squeezed his fingers, and a small smile lifted the corners of her mouth. "I saw how you looked at Hannah this morning. You're developing feelings for her, aren't you? Despite your rigid rules. Don't let Mother's choices poison yours. Just because *she* broke your heart doesn't mean that Hannah will, too. Beauty in and of itself is not wrong."

Without conscious thought, a verse he'd quoted often while Delia was growing up tumbled from his lips. " 'Favour is deceitful, and beauty is vain: but a woman that feareth the Lord, she shall be praised.' Proverbs 31:30."

His sister shook her head, her smile fading. "No one's arguing that a woman should pursue beauty above a relationship with her Lord. Maybe it's time you went back and reread that chapter in Proverbs. Look again at the woman who is praised as a godly example of virtuous femininity. The wife whose value is above rubies. I dare you, J.T. Look for yourself. What type of clothing does *she* wear? How does she earn *her* living? Then maybe we can have this discussion again."

CHAPTER 19

J.T. trudged back to the livery, a Bible tucked under his arm. He'd never thought of himself as a coward, but he'd been extremely tempted to toss his conversation with Delia to the wind and ignore her challenge. What if he dug deeper into the Word as she suggested and discovered he needed to adjust his beliefs? Could he do that? They'd been his rock for so long. Guiding him. Shaping him. If they turned out to be shifting sand . . .

Tom waved at him as he approached the office. "Doc came by to rent the buggy. Said Mrs. Walsh was due to have her next young'un any day, and he wanted to pay a call on her. I hitched up the roan. Hope that's all right." He crammed his hands into his pockets and rocked up and back on the balls of his feet.

J.T. slapped him on the arm. "You did fine. I'll add it to his account."

A grin exploded across Tom's face.

The Bible under his arm poked J.T.'s ribs as he moved past the young man and reached for the knob on the office door. A similar jab from within made him hesitate. He glanced over his shoulder.

"Uh, Tom?"

The boy spun around and trotted back to J.T.'s side like an eager puppy. "Yeah?"

"Would you mind sticking around for an extra hour or so? I've got some things to work on, and I'd rather not be disturbed."

"Sure." Tom eyed the black leather protruding from beneath J.T.'s bicep. "If them things need a Bible to figure out, I reckon they must be mighty important. No one'll bother you unless there's an emergency. I'll see to it."

"Thanks." J.T. pulled the book from under his arm and lifted it to the brim of his hat in salute. Then he entered his office and closed the door.

A tangle of harness leather cluttered the top of his desk. With one hand, he scooped it up and tossed it onto a barrel in the corner as he circled the table and lowered himself into his cane-backed chair. He set the Bible on the desktop in front of him, then pushed it over to a corner. The scrape of leather on wood echoed loudly in the small room, but J.T. ignored it. He swiveled away to collect a different book.

He extracted the account ledger from the drawer to his left and flipped to the page that held the current entries. With a nub of pencil, he added a dollar to the doctor's balance and totaled the sum since the man's last payment.

Black leather tugged at his peripheral vision. He scratched an itchy spot on his jaw and turned back to the ledger. Might as well total up all the accounts. It'd make the end-of-month tally much easier. J.T. welcomed the mathematical diversion, his focus only occasionally drifting over to the Bible that sat patiently on the corner. Until the numbers ran out. With no sums to keep his conscience at bay, the black book loomed large, creeping into his line of sight.

He scanned the room for something else to do. The harness still needed work. And he'd been meaning to fix that rickety shelf since last month. The pipe on his potbellied stove was dented. The windowsill needed dusting.

Dusting?

J.T. braced his arms on the desk and pressed his forehead into the heels of his hands. As he exhaled, a self-castigating chuckle vibrated against the wall of his chest. He *was* a coward if he'd rather dust a windowsill than read a passage of Scripture. This was a livery office, for pity's sake, not a fancy parlor. Dust was part of the decor.

With a small groan, he pushed the ledger aside and drew the Bible toward him.

Lord, I don't know what you're aiming to teach me, but I pray for enough wisdom to recognize it when I see it.

Standing the book on its spine, J.T. thumbed the pages back until he found Proverbs. He turned to the last chapter and began to read. Nothing momentous caught his attention in the beginning, except the warning to Lemuel against giving his strength to women. J.T. had been a believer in that philosophy for ages. However, his assurance started dissolving around verse nineteen with the mention of the noble wife's spindle. And at verse twenty-one, it deteriorated completely.

" 'She is not afraid of the snow for her household: for all her household are clothed with scarlet. She maketh herself coverings of tapestry; her clothing is silk and purple.' "

Silk and purple? Her household clothed in scarlet? Wouldn't a modest woman wear plain clothes like wool dyed brown or dark blue? Yet God's Word clearly stated that this virtuous woman wore purple silk.

And it got worse the further he read.

" 'She maketh fine linen, and selleth it; and delivereth girdles unto the merchant. Strength and honour are her clothing; and she shall rejoice in time to come.' "

Not only did she wear the fancy clothes, she sold them to others.

Just like Hannah. And the Bible declared it honorable and worthy of rejoicing.

There was more to the virtuous woman than her occupation and dressing habits, of course. Proverbs painted her as trustworthy, kind, diligent. Strong, productive, and wise. She practiced good stewardship, reached out to those in need, and feared the Lord. All qualities Miss Richards demonstrated, as well.

How could he condemn Hannah for selling fine clothing when the virtuous woman did the same? In the biblical example, her husband and children praised her and called her blessed. For Hannah, all he'd done was tear her down and call her a stumbling block. Not exactly the kind of thing to recommend a fellow as husband material.

J.T. closed the Bible and leaned back in his chair, rubbing his hands over his face. He still believed true beauty came from a woman's spirit, not her physical shape or choice of garment. Yet God seemed to be telling him through this passage in Proverbs that it was possible for a woman to have both. Not only that, but it implied a smart man would claim such a female and count his blessings. J.T. glanced out the window to the shop across the street. *Apparently, I'm an idiot.*

As he stared, his vision blurred with images of what could have been. Thankfully, a dilapidated freight wagon came to his rescue. It rolled to a stop in front of his window and blocked his view. Giving himself a mental shake, J.T. stood and walked to the door. He never missed one of Harley's visits.

The county junkman had befriended J.T. during the dark time after his mother left, a time when his father had been too consumed with grief to worry about where food or other necessities would come from. J.T. had snuck off to town one evening a week and dug through people's garbage, searching for anything that might interest the old man. Cracked mirrors, tuneless music boxes, wheels without spokes—these acquisitions provided shoes for him and Delia, secondhand winter coats, and occasionally a ribbon or some other small pretty to surprise his sister with at Christmas.

Harley never admitted it, but J.T. long suspected that the man set things aside specifically for him and Delia and accepted whatever J.T. could offer in payment, no matter how lopsided the trade. He'd never forget the winter after his father died, when their food stores consisted of little more than a handful of potatoes and one onion. The only thing J.T. had to barter with was a rusted pocket knife that wouldn't close. Harley had exclaimed over that knife, saying that it was a rare specimen, and that once he cleaned it up, he knew of a buyer that would pay a king's ransom for it. He then proceeded to hand over a mound of foodstuff in trade—a sack of flour he claimed had been thrown out because of weevils, a can of lard apparently too dented to sell to anyone else, tinned vegetables that had lost their labels, and a barrel of salt pork that Harley complained took up too much space in his wagon.

Without the junkman's generosity, they would not have survived that winter, and even though J.T. no longer spent his spare time salvaging items for trade, he still made a point to buy a selection of Harley's goods whenever the peddler crossed his path. And deliberately overpaid him each time.

Eager to greet his old friend, J.T. opened the door; but before he could reach the street, Tom ran out of the stable like a guard dog, barking up a storm.

"You gotta come back later, Harley. The boss is working on something real important and can't be disturbed."

J.T. came up behind the youngster and clapped him on the back. "That's all right, Tom. I'm done for now. Why don't you bring out a couple water buckets for the man's horses."

"Yessir. I'll have them out in jiffy."

Tom disappeared into the stable, and J.T. turned back to the stoop-shouldered man climbing down from the seat. He found the ground with a moan, then winked up at J.T.

"Ain't as spry as I used to be."

J.T. grinned and accompanied Harley to the back of the wagon. "I'm not exactly a kid anymore, either."

"Don't feed me that nonsense, Tucker. You're still in your prime." Harley gave him a playful jab with his elbow. "What you need is a pretty young wife to chase after. My Sarah's kept me going for near on forty years."

The grin slid from J.T.'s face as he glanced across the street. His stomach churned, but he covered it up with a forced chuckle. "Well, now, if I could find me a gal like your Sarah, I just might do that, but I reckon she's one of a kind."

"That she is, son. That she is." Harley untied the tarp that kept all his goods from escaping. Each man took a side and rolled the canvas covering back. When they reached the front of the bed, Harley wagged a gnarled finger at him. "Don't get discouraged, boy. The Lord will bring the right woman to you when he sees fit. You just got to keep an eye out for her so's you don't miss your opportunity."

J.T. stared at his boots. "I'll keep that in mind."

But what if a man's eyes didn't open until after he'd already pushed the woman away? Would God, or the lady in question, give him a second chance?

Hoping to distract Harley from his advice-giving, J.T. reached over the side of the wagon and picked up a warped eggbeater. He cranked the handle until it hummed, stirring the air. "What'd you bring today?"

The salesman in Harley overpowered the meddler. A familiar gleam sprang to life in his eyes.

"I've been saving something for you. I think you'll be pleased." He shuffled odds and ends and hefted out a large crate covered in oilcloth. With a flourish, he flipped a corner of the cloth back. "See? What did I tell you?"

Shingles. Enough to repair Louisa's roof before winter hit if he ever got things squared away with the current owner. "You remembered."

Harley drew back, affronted. "Of course I remembered. What kind of a junkman would I be if I didn't acquire what my customers are looking for?" His ready smile reappeared quickly, though, as he leaned over his prize. "They're machine-cut cypress from the sawmill in Bandera. Notice the clean, even lines." He handed one to J.T. to inspect. "Met a fellow who worked down there. He traded 'em for an ear trumpet. Guess all that mill work took a toll on his hearing."

"These will be perfect," J.T. said. "Better than any I could have picked up around here." He tossed his sample shingle back into the crate, replaced the oilcloth, and set the box against the wall of the livery.

As usual, Harley insisted on showing him a handful of other treasures, none of which caught his interest. But when the peddler removed a quilt from a three-legged side table to show him the ornate carvings, J.T. glimpsed a couple of chair backs.

"Are those chairs a matched pair?" he asked.

"Ah, you have a fine eye. They are indeed. Help me lift them out."

They cleared away a mantel clock, a chipped bowl and pitcher set, and several miscellaneous pots and pans from the seats of the chairs before J.T. could lift them out. Careful to position them between the wagon and the livery so no one from, say, across the street could see, he took stock of their condition.

"They're missing a few spindles," Harley said, "but the overall construction is sound. A little sanding, staining, and they'll be good as new."

J.T. sat in each and wiggled the framework. They held his weight fine, and except for being a bit banged up, they were decent chairs. He could shape a couple spindles and refinish them in the evenings. It'd probably only take about a week to get them done.

Once again, the shop across the street drew his gaze and prompted an ache in his chest. He'd have to make up an awful lot of ground if he hoped to win Hannah's heart. In the meantime, he would take care of her practical needs. The woman might not think she needed *him*, but she definitely needed chairs.

CHAPTER 20

"Cordelia, I'm so proud of you." Hannah marked the tape measure with her thumb and held it up for her friend to see. "You've lost an inch around both your waist and chest. Two inches from your hips. You're making marvelous progress."

A blush rose to Cordelia's cheeks. "J.T. did mention that he thought I looked thinner."

"And he was absolutely correct." At the mention of Jericho, Hannah's mind immediately jumped back to her encounter with him under the tree, but she didn't allow it to linger. Cordelia deserved her full attention.

"Do you really think this will work?" Cordelia asked as she buttoned up her dress. "I just came from the telegraph office, and Ike doesn't seem to notice any difference in me at all."

"Well, the change is subtle. The new dress will be more dramatic." Hannah idly flipped through one of her fashion magazines while Cordelia finished dressing. She'd seen the dresses a hundred times, so her eyes wandered to the bonnets and faces of the models. A pattern began to emerge, and Hannah stood a little straighter. "What do you think about adding a change that's not so subtle, one we can do now?"

Cordelia tilted her head at her reflection in the mirror, then turned sideways to examine her profile. "What kind of change?"

Hannah came up behind her and began pulling pins from her hair. Cordelia raised her brows in silent question.

"It just occurred to me," Hannah said, "that all of those stylish ladies in *Peterson's Magazine* have not only fashionable dresses but fashionable hairstyles, as well." She met Cordelia's widening gaze in the mirror. "If we're giving you a new look, we might as well revamp all of you, including your hair."

She raised a hand to her head. "My hair?"

"Sure." Hannah hugged Cordelia's shoulders as excitement ricocheted through her. "Your hair is one of your best features. It's so thick and wavy. We could cut just a little in the front to give you some bangs. Nearly all the models in the magazine have them. I bet yours will curl up on their own without you even having to crimp them. Then we can exchange your simple bun for a braided chignon. Nothing too fancy, just something different and slightly more elegant. You'll need to wear it lower on your neck so it won't be hidden by your bonnet, but I imagine it won't go unnoticed."

"I . . . I don't know."

Hannah gave Cordelia a squeeze and waited for her to decide. She didn't have to wait long. In the mirror, Cordelia's chin jutted out a bit and her lips tightened in a determined line.

"Let's do it." She turned around and faced Hannah directly. "Now. Before I change my mind."

Hannah grinned and took up her shears, and twenty minutes later Cordelia's new style was complete. Wavy bangs disguised her broad forehead, giving her a more dainty appearance. The looser chignon softened her face and drew attention to the curve of her neck. When Hannah finally let her see her reflection, Cordelia gasped.

"That's me?" She fingered her bangs and twisted her head to get a better view of the rest of her hair. "I can't believe it. I look completely different."

"Do you like it?" Hannah held her breath.

Cordelia's smile beamed the answer. "I love it!"

"We should go for a stroll and see if anyone comments." Hannah handed Cordelia her bonnet and took her own down from the wall hook.

"I don't know," Cordelia hedged. "Maybe I should get used to it first."

"Oh, no you don't. I'm not going to let you crawl back into that shell of yours." Hannah firmly set Cordelia's hat on her head for her and tied the strings. "If you hide from people, men especially, they're not going to see you. You have to carry yourself with confidence. Meet their eyes. Smile." Hannah finished with the hat and grasped Cordelia's hands. "Are you ready?"

"No." Cordelia shot her a wry glance. "But I'll give it a try anyway."

"Good. Let's go."

When they reached the mercantile, a thin young man was out front sweeping the walk. His ash-blond hair hung long over his right cheek, but Hannah made out a large reddish birthmark through the camouflage.

"Hello, Warren," Cordelia said, her head erect, her voice cheery, and her smile warm. Pride surged in Hannah's breast. Her protégée was doing an admirable job.

The man's wary eyes drilled into Hannah with uncomfortable force, but then darted away. When they lit on Cordelia's face, however, they softened. "Hey." He stopped sweeping and propped his palms on the end of the broomstick. "Dad ordered some new muffin and cake tins yesterday. They should be in next week. I thought you might like first pick."

"Thank you for telling me. I'll be sure to look them over when they arrive." Cordelia, still smiling, moved toward the store entrance, but Warren stopped her with his next comment.

"What'd you do to your hair?"

Hannah could feel Cordelia tense beside her at the man's abrasive tone. Warren was obviously not the most sensitive male of the species. She stepped closer to her friend, tempted to take her hand or pat her arm in a show of support even though she knew Cordelia needed to handle things on her own.

"I decided to try a new style. Hannah cut it for me." Cordelia turned to include Hannah in the conversation and perhaps in the blame should he not like the change. Hannah didn't mind. In fact, she welcomed it. Cordelia would never fish for a compliment, but now Hannah could throw out a line on her behalf.

"Do you like it, Mr. Hawkins? I think it becomes her quite well."

Pink dusted Cordelia's cheeks, and her gaze fell to the ground for a moment before she gathered her courage and looked back up at the shopkeeper's son.

"She looks fine," Warren said, directing his comment to Hannah, "but she looked fine the old way, too. She doesn't need you changing her." Hot accusation burned in his eyes.

Hannah flushed under the scalding look and was grateful when Cordelia linked their arms and led her toward the store entrance.

"Have a nice afternoon, Warren." Cordelia's bright inflection sounded a trifle counterfeit, but Hannah wasn't about to complain. "And thanks again for the information about the baking tins."

"Sure." His scowl melted into a wan smile as he shifted his attention back to Cordelia. "I'll ask Father to let you see them before he sets them on the shelves."

Cordelia waved but didn't speak again until she and Hannah were safely inside the mercantile.

"I'm sorry about Warren," she whispered. "His disposition has always been a little on the sour side."

"That's all right. He seemed more protective than sour. I think he's sweet on you." Hannah winked, feeling more herself now that she was out from under Warren's censure.

"He's only a friend." Cordelia sputtered as if the idea had lodged in her throat like a piece of beef that didn't want to go down.

"It doesn't matter." Hannah batted away her friend's protest with a flick of her wrist. "What he said is true. You *were* just as lovely before we cut your hair as after." Hannah slipped her arm free from Cordelia's, thankful her friend hadn't been disheartened by the events outside. Of course, the young man hadn't aimed any animosity at her. He'd saved that for Hannah.

Cordelia smiled and led Hannah past a pair of gray-haired women debating the merits of leather handbags over the tapestry variety. "You're sweet to say so, but I consider the change an improvement, regardless of what Warren said. I'm glad we did it."

Hannah breathed easier, the knot of uncertainty loosening within her. "Me too."

They browsed through the soaps and feminine toilette items near the rear of the store. The rose and lilac scents of the French milled bars tickled Hannah's nose and soothed her spirit. Cordelia passed them by in favor of a ribbon display.

"Maybe I should change the trim on my bonnet before I visit Ike tomorrow."

"That's a good idea," Hannah said, matching Cordelia's hushed volume. "Make it as easy as possible on the poor man. If he still doesn't notice, maybe you can send him a telegram."

Giggles burst from Cordelia, and she quickly covered her mouth in an effort to stifle the sound.

"Oh, let the little bells free, Miss Tucker. Laughter makes the world a better place."

Cordelia jumped, her eyebrows disappearing into her newly cut bangs. "Mr. Paxton! You startled me."

The middle-aged man swept off his hat and bowed over her hand. "Forgive me, my dear. I thought only to rescue the delightful chimes I overheard clamoring for escape. You really shouldn't imprison such a joyful melody. Music is meant to be shared."

Hannah recognized the banker from her transactions in his establishment. The man was a consummate charmer, yet it seemed he was also a devoted husband who doted on his wife and daughters. The first time she had met with him to set up her account, she'd thought him quite the rogue until she noted the way his eyes caressed the framed photograph of his family that sat on his desk. And since the men of the town treated him with cordiality and respect, she'd concluded that his silver-tongued ways must pose no real threat to the women of Coventry.

As Cordelia blushed and struggled to meet the banker's eye, Hannah glanced between the two, her mind spinning. This could be the perfect opportunity for Cordelia to practice her confidence. Unlike Warren, Mr. Paxton would never say a word to injure a lady's feelings, and though his compliments were smooth, they were never false.

"Miss Tucker is contemplating a new ribbon for her bonnet. Which color would you recommend, sir?" Hannah smiled at the man, hoping he would pick up on her hint.

"Why, Miss Richards," he said. "What an honor to be asked for my opinion, especially by a woman as knowledgeable on the topic of fashion as yourself." His brows lifted ever so slightly, and she gave an almost imperceptible nod in return. "My wife rarely seeks my advice before making a purchase, but I would be happy to offer my meager services if you believe they would be helpful."

"We would be grateful for your assistance."

Cordelia looked as if she wanted to muzzle her with the bonnet in question. Hannah just smiled.

"Let me see . . ." Mr. Paxton leaned back to survey Cordelia. "A brown ribbon would match your dress, but if you are anything like my wife, you'd find that dreadfully dull. Hmm . . . Maybe something bright and cheerful to match that lovely laugh of y—" He stopped midthought and tapped the side of his jaw.

"Mr. Paxton?" Cordelia shot Hannah a nervous glance.

"There's something different about you, but I can't put my finger on it." He stepped to the left and then to the right, studying her. Poor Cordelia looked as if she wanted to make a run for the door.

"I've got it. You changed your hair. Is that it?"

Cordelia patted the tresses that stretched over her temple. "Yes. I thought to try something new."

"Well, the style is most attractive on you, my dear." Finished with his scrutiny, his jovial manner returned. "Most attractive. I think I might recommend a similar fashion to my daughter Eleanor."

"Truly?" A radiant smile broke free across Cordelia's face, and she made no effort to hide it behind her hand.

"Truly. Now, I'm off in search of some tooth powder. Have fun with your ribbons, my dear."

"I will. Thank you." Happy roses blooming in her cheeks, Cordelia wiggled her fingers in a tiny wave as the banker meandered over to the next aisle.

It was amazing how the right words spoken by a man could soothe insecurities. And if things continued progressing as they were, Hannah had no doubt that Cordelia would soon be hearing those words from the *right* man. Unfortunately, the right man for Hannah didn't know the first thing about finding the right words. Although, seeing as how she was so wrong for him, he probably hadn't put much effort into the search.

Oh well. Words weren't everything. Jericho's actions spoke with plenty of eloquence and had the added benefit of being subject to interpretation. If her misguided heart chose to read more into them than he intended and to harbor unwarranted hope, that was her business. She'd face the consequences when she must.

Later.

CHAPTER 21

Over the next week, Hannah and Cordelia stepped up their calisthenic program. Cordelia's improved stamina allowed them to lengthen their morning walks past the schoolhouse to include climbing a second hill instead of stopping at the river. She also graduated to more difficult club and dumbbell routines. Then, since Saturday marked the midpoint of their journey to a slimmer, more confident Cordelia, the girls celebrated by taking in the seams on two of Cordelia's best dresses—a chore they tackled with enthusiasm.

Business at the dress shop had improved, as well. Hannah contracted two alteration projects the previous week, in addition to the steady trickle of mending the town's single men brought to her door. And on Tuesday, miracle of miracles, she sold a ready-made traveling suit to one of the guests staying at the hotel.

Some might have scoffed at the notion that such a sale was a sign from God, but it resonated in her soul nonetheless, fortifying her faith. She had asked the Lord to allow her business to fail if it wasn't in his will, and though she struggled to find significant profits when she tallied her books, she chose to view the sale of one of her original designs as confirmation that she was where the Lord wanted her to be. And as long as the voice within her didn't rise up to contradict her assumption, she would forge ahead.

Or sit and wait, as the case may be.

On the bench outside her shop, Hannah curled her fingers around a cooling cup of cocoa and peered toward the edge of town. She hadn't seen Ezra since church on Sunday. At first, she assumed the rain that had dampened Coventry for the first three days of the week had kept him away, but now she wasn't so sure. The sun had emerged bright and warm yesterday afternoon and returned again today, drying puddles and firming up the roads. She and Cordelia even managed to resume their walking this morning after being confined to Cordelia's parlor half the week doing only calisthenics. There should be no reason Ezra couldn't make it to town, unless something other than the weather was responsible for his absence.

Hannah gulped down her lukewarm cocoa and collected Ezra's unclaimed cup. She climbed the stairs to her room, worry dogging her steps. Was he ill? Had Jackson gone lame? Or worse—could something have happened during one of the storms, leaving Ezra injured with no way to get help? Living alone and as far from town as he did, if an accident befell him, he could go for days or weeks before someone chanced by.

Visions of the dear man being pinned to the ground by a fallen lightning-struck tree or huddled in his sickbed so weak with fever that he couldn't get up to feed himself lent a frantic edge to her movements as she washed and dried the cups along with her dishes from breakfast.

By the time she hung up her apron, she knew what she had to do. She would drive out to Ezra's homestead and see for herself that he was all right. Immediately. Leaving the shop closed for the morning was a small price to pay.

Flinging her black wool cape over the shoulders of her primrose polonaise and fastening the hook and eye under her chin, she dashed for the door. The northern breeze blew cool, and without the exertion of walking, she'd need the hip-length cape to stay warm. She stopped briefly at the laundry to tell Tessa they would have to postpone their lessons until tomorrow, then darted out to the street, only to careen to a halt to avoid a farm wagon lumbering across her path. Too impatient to wait for it to pass, Hannah angled around behind it, skirting the worst of the dust as she crossed the street to the livery.

As she entered the dim stable, Hannah wrinkled her nose at the smell of wet straw and manure. She remembered Jericho's office from the time she'd brought him biscuits, but she was strangely reluctant to knock on his door. He'd kept his distance since their escapade with the exercise rings.

She'd found him looking at her on several occasions, though. At church, on the street—always with the same unreadable expression. And at times she was sure she sensed him staring at her through the dress shop's walls from the confines of his office. It was pure fancy on her part, of course, but it still left her a bit unnerved.

"Hello, in the stable," she called, anxious to put the awkwardness behind her and get on with her business. "Is anyone there?"

"Be right with you." The masculine voice cracked on the first word. Tom.

Relief and disappointment swept through Hannah in equal measure.

The lanky young man emerged from the shadows and grinned when he caught sight of her. "Good to see ya, Miss Richards. You looking for J.T.?"

"Not necessarily. I'm sure you can help me just as well." Hannah hid her grin as Tom's chest expanded. "I need to rent a horse and buggy."

"Where you going?"

"Out to Ezra Culpepper's place. I should have the rig back by early afternoon."

Tom sniffed and ran a hand under his nose. "I could let you take Doc, I guess. Mrs. Walsh done had her baby a few days back, so the real Doc shouldn't need it. It's smaller and easier for a lady to handle. Plus it's got a cover if the rain should start up again."

Hannah nodded to him. "It sounds like just the thing."

"You can sit over there while I fetch it for you." He pointed to a cluster of barrels standing near the wall. "It'll take a couple minutes to getcha all hitched up."

"All right."

Tom left, and Hannah surveyed her seat options. Selecting the cleanest-looking cylinder, she laid her handkerchief over the top and gingerly sat down, trying to ignore the way the raised rim dug into the back of her thighs.

"Miss Richards?"

Hannah jumped back to her feet, her stomach seesawing at the familiar voice—a deep, resonant one, devoid of boyish squeaks.

"What brings you to my side of the street?" Jericho approached not from the office, but from the rear of the stable. His shirt gaped open at the neck and his rolled sleeves revealed powerful forearms that had probably been manipulating a pitchfork moments ago. Smells of horse and hay clung to him in an inherently masculine mix.

Dragging her gaze up to his face, she forced a smile. "I'm renting a buggy. Tom's getting Doc for me."

"What for?"

Hannah frowned and blew out a breath. When Tom had asked, she assumed he was simply making conversation without realizing it was impolite to pry. But now she wondered if he wasn't imitating his employer, a man who should know better. "Do you make a habit of badgering all your customers, Jericho?"

"Nope. Just you." His mouth held its serious line, yet his eyes sparkled with suppressed laughter. She could almost imagine deep chuckles vibrating in his chest.

"Well, since you're paying me such a special courtesy, I suppose I can share my plans with you." She smiled playfully at him, but her frivolity dimmed as the seriousness of her purpose rose to the surface. Twirling the fringe of her cape around her finger, she looked at the ground.

"I'm worried about Ezra." She glanced up and caught him staring at her. His eyes locked with hers and didn't look away.

"He's a grown man."

Hannah finally broke away from his gaze and caught sight of Tom maneuvering the buggy out of the wagon shed. Deciding that was a safer place to direct her attention, she continued watching Tom even though the rest of her senses stayed shamelessly attuned to the man beside her.

"I know he is," she said. "However, he's never missed a morning visit at my shop until this week. I thought perhaps the rain had kept him home, but he didn't come today, either, and the weather is fine."

"There could be a hundred reasons why he didn't make it to town. Maybe he's busy carving up more of those sticks to sell at the depot."

"Maybe. But what if he's hurt or sick?" Needing him to understand, she turned and searched his face. "He lives out there all alone, Jericho. He'd have no way to summon help if something went wrong. I need to go out there. If for no other reason than to reassure myself that he's all right."

He stared at her long and hard. "You're a softhearted woman, Hannah Richards. Hardheaded, but softhearted." He reached out as if to touch her cheek, then dropped his hand to his side. "I'll give Tom a hand. We'll have you ready to go in two shakes."

She stood motionless as he retreated, longing for the contact that had failed to materialize. For a brief moment, the hard lines of his face had relaxed with tenderness, changing his countenance so completely her breath had caught in her throat. What would it be like to feel his hand cup her cheek? To lean into the comfort of his caress? To have him look on her with love?

"It's ready, Miss Richards." Tom waved her forward.

She gathered her wits and joined him by the buggy.

"You know how to handle the reins, right?" The stern Jericho had returned.

"Yes."

"Good. I've double-checked the harness and all the straps. The carriage is sound." He tugged on the leather and kicked at the spokes as if to verify his words. "If you get stuck in mud or have any difficulty with the buggy, just leave it where it stands, unhitch the horse, and ride him back to town. I don't want you stranded out there."

Hannah smiled at the gruffness in his voice. "Now who's worrying unnecessarily?"

She picked up her skirt and placed her foot on the step, but when she reached for the handle on the outside of the seat to pull herself in, Jericho was suddenly there, offering his hand.

She accepted, enjoying the feel of his callused skin against her palm. The contact was far too brief, but it warmed her nonetheless. Reluctantly, Hannah let go and retreated onto the seat, where she extracted a silver dollar from her purse and passed it over to him.

"Can you give me directions to Ezra's place? Except for my constitutionals with your sister, I haven't ventured far from town."

Jericho tipped his hat back and pointed to the north. "Take the main road out of town. Go about a mile past the schoolhouse, then turn right on the road that leads to the river. You'll cross a wagon bridge. Go another two miles or so until you see a post to the left with a hummingbird carved into the wood at the top. His wife loved the things. Follow the ruts that turn off by the post. They'll take you to the house."

Hannah collected the reins, and the horse stomped the ground in anticipation. "Thank you for your help, Jericho."

"Um . . ." Tom sidestepped up to the buggy, shooting leery glances at his employer as he moved. He cupped his hand around his mouth as if to tell her a secret but forgot to lower his voice. "He don't like that name, ma'am. Nobody calls him that."

"I do." Hannah grinned and flapped the reins. The roan set off down the street, leaving a stunned Tom and a scowling Jericho in its wake.

Feeling better than she had all morning, Hannah reveled in the freedom of being out in nature. Thickets of trees covered distant hills, where random specimens boasted the first red leaves of autumn. White clouds rimmed in gray blew gently across the sky, and the same breeze that propelled them pushed the loose tendrils of hair away from her face and cooled her skin. A pair of blue jays flew overhead, scolding each other as they swooped in and out of the mesquite. A lovely morning to be out for a drive.

Jericho's directions proved easy to follow, and Hannah soon found herself at the wagon bridge. Desert hackberry with its dark green oval leaves and bright orange berries combined with prickly graythorn and other shrubs to line the banks of the North Bosque River. The fragrant aromas of juniper and cedar teased her nose and induced a sneeze as she brought the buggy to a halt. The rush of the river seemed unusually loud. She edged forward until she could make out the water below. The usually narrow, slow-flowing stream had swollen with the recent rains. The trestles still cleared it by several feet, though, so she clicked to the horse and rolled from the dirt onto the bridge's planks. The roan's shod hooves thunked against the wooden boards with a hollow cadence that sent a shiver tiptoeing down her neck. Hannah tightened her grip on the reins, but she made it to the opposite side without incident.

Once back on the road, Hannah urged the horse to a trot. The river reminded her of how quickly things could change. She needed to get to Ezra.

When she finally reached his homestead, the sun stood high in the sky. As she stepped down from the buggy, a door on the weathered house creaked open. Ezra hobbled out into the yard, leaning heavily on one of his walking sticks.

"Miz Hannah? What are you doing all the way out here?"

She hurried to his side and steadied him with a hand at his elbow. "I was worried when you didn't make it to town for so many days. I wanted to make sure that everything was all right."

Ezra shook his head and let her lead him back to the house. "You should be in town sewing up some fancy piece of calico instead of checking up on an old-timer like me. I ain't worth your worry."

"Of course you are. Now, let's get you back in the house so I can make you some tea."

Before she could make tea, however, she had to find the kettle. A mound of dishes, pots, and pans littered the kitchen. All of them dirty. The poor man probably hadn't eaten off a clean plate since his wife died. It was a wonder he ate at all in this mess. A half-empty can of beans sat on the table, a spoon standing stiff in its middle. His lunch, no doubt. He hadn't even bothered to warm it up. Hanging up her cape and bonnet, Hannah vowed to make the place habitable before she left.

She located an apron, tied it about her waist, and pushed up her sleeves. Not allowing Ezra to talk her out of her mission, she dragged in the washtub from the back porch, filled it with well water, and started dropping pots and pans into its depths. The plates went into the dishpan along with the cups and flatware, and she left them to soak until she had heated enough water on the stove to clean them properly.

Ezra finally stopped trying to dissuade her and sat at the table whittling while she chattered on about the progress Cordelia was making. She told him about the lovely fern-green wool they had decided on for the main body of the dress, the jet buttons, the fern-and-burgundy-striped skirting, the way the polonaise would gather at the back for a slight bustled effect. She doubted he cared a whit about her babble, but it helped pass the time.

When the dishes and utensils were clean, Ezra insisted on helping her dry. Hannah made him do it sitting down. The way he grimaced and limped around, his pain was obvious. She didn't question him about it, though, until the work had been completed and they both sat at the table with a cup of honey-sweetened tea.

"Did you hurt yourself this week? I can send the doctor out to see you."

Ezra took a sip and shook his head. "Naw. It ain't worth the bother. He can't do nothing for these old joints." He set the cup down and rubbed his leg. "My rheumatism acts up somethin' fierce when it rains. And with the way my knee is aching, I bet we're in fer some more."

"Do you have a soup bone I can use to make stock? I could put together some beef or vegetable soup before I go, to tide you over until you're feeling better."

"No. You done too much already." He slapped his palms onto the tabletop and pushed to his feet. With a hitch in his step, he shuffled over to the window and tilted his head to view the sky. "Looks like that new storm is rolling in. There's a wall of dark clouds to the northwest. No telling how soon it'll reach us. You better head back to town."

Hannah swallowed the last of her tea and stood. "Are you sure there's nothing more I can do for you?"

"I'm sure. Now skedaddle before I have to sic Jackson on you. That mule's as ornery as I am when the weather turns sour."

"All right. I'm going." Hannah held up her hands in surrender as she moved to collect her hat and cape. "I did promise Mr. Tucker I'd have his rig back this afternoon. I wouldn't want him to think me irresponsible."

"From what I've seen, the boy's more likely to think you irresistible," Ezra mumbled with his head aimed at the floor.

A thrill passed through her at his words, but caution quickly rose to quell it. She probably hadn't heard him correctly. However, when Ezra raised his head, his eyes were dancing with roguish light, resurrecting her optimism.

When they stepped outside, the wind immediately whipped over them, tugging Hannah's cape with such ferocity it nearly choked her.

"I think you're right about that storm." She leaned into the wind and moved to inspect her rented horse. The roan lifted its head from the trough where it had been drinking, seemingly unperturbed by the gusty conditions. Jericho had trained him well.

Ezra led the horse around so the buggy faced the road, then handed Hannah up. He took something out of his pocket. Hannah recognized the wood he'd been whittling on in the kitchen. "Here, I made this for you. Alice always liked 'em."

She accepted the offering—a hummingbird, complete with feathered wings and a long, narrow beak. "Thank you, Ezra. It's beautiful." She placed it in her purse. Then, afraid the wind might blow the small bag off the seat, she tucked it deep into the crease of the cushions, leaving only the hummingbird bulge free.

Ezra handed her the reins. "Time to get going, gal. Take care on the way back."

"I will." Hannah set the roan in motion with a flick of her wrist and waved farewell to her friend.

By the time she reached the bridge, fat raindrops were plopping with great frequency against the carriage top. The sky to the north had gone nearly black. She could hear the water rushing, and as she started the buggy onto the bridge, she found the river had risen a good foot since her earlier crossing.

The horse snorted and shook its head, pawing the ground restively.

"I know it looks frightening, but the bridge is solid. We can make it." Hannah spoke to the horse, but she used the words to convince herself, as well.

The storm was still upriver. They had time.

She drove the buggy onto the bridge. Hannah focused on the horse's rump as they traversed the bridge, not trusting her courage to last if her focus wandered to the river.

They were midway across when she heard the roar.

Heart pounding, she looked upstream. A surge of water was thundering toward her, overwhelming the meager banks that fought to contain it.

Flash flood!

"Yah!" Hannah slapped the reins against the roan's back. He lurched forward. They had to get off the bridge.

Ten yards from the end, the water caught them. It crashed over the trestles and threw the horse into the rails. The roan screamed and struggled to find purchase through the torrent that swirled at its knees. The weight of the buggy kept the animal from being swept away, but soon that anchor lost its grip, as well.

The carriage tipped under the pressure of the water's barrage. Hannah released the reins and grabbed the seat handle on the upstream side. She could feel the wheels on that side lifting off the ground. The conveyance shifted and rammed the railing at an angle, splintering the wooden rods that supported the carriage top on the left side. Hannah toppled onto the floor. She clung to the handle above her with both hands as cold water soaked her skirts.

With the underside of the buggy now blocking the main thrust of the floodwater, Hannah crawled up the sloping floor and swung a leg over the side. Tilted and broken, the buggy was useless, but if she could unhitch the horse, perhaps he could get her to safety.

The roan strained against the shafts that twisted toward the river and pinned him to the bridge railing. Hannah debated whether to risk climbing down over the foot of the driver's box in order to get to the horse, but between the flailing hooves and tangled harness lines, it looked too hazardous. So instead, she plunged into the swirling pool beside the upturned buggy. The icy water stole her breath as it reached past her knees, but she slogged forward, fighting the current as she circumvented the wheel. Once at the front, she no longer benefited from the buggy acting as a dam. The water was not as deep, but it rushed faster, nearly knocking her from her feet.

Using the shafts to keep her balance, Hannah edged closer to the horse. She unclipped the driving bit and worked free the straps that anchored the horse to the right shaft. She'd have to find a way to undo the ones on the left next. Wading to the horse's head, she latched on to his bridle and tried to soothe the animal, but his terror was too great. The roan lunged for his freedom, and Hannah lost her footing. She fell to her knees, the violent flow tugging her toward the river. Still holding the bridle leather, she fought the water and managed to stand.

"No more of that. Do you hear me?" She yanked the horse's head down and yelled in his face. "I need you to get me off this bridge. I'll get you free of the carriage, then you'll get me to dry ground. Understand?" The roan jerked his head up and down, probably in a struggle to escape her hold, but she chose to take it as a sign of agreement.

She moved back to the carriage, climbed over both horse shafts, and wedged herself between the second wooden pole and the railing. She undid the first loop but couldn't squeeze her way farther up the shaft. The railing was already digging painfully into her back.

The horse must have sensed the nearness of his freedom, for he strained against the final loop that tethered him to the carriage. His wild movements opened a space for her. She stretched forward and loosened the loop. The roan did the rest. Hannah lunged for the harness saddle so he could pull her free, but she was too slow. The traitor ran for the road, leaving her behind.

"Hey!"

Hannah barely got the shout out before the wooden shaft pounded her back into the railing. The blow knocked her feet out from under her. She flung her arms around the offending pole and tried to pull herself upright as she had done before. Only this time, her legs dangled over the side of the bridge between the rail posts. There was nothing but water to push against. The current tore at her. She slid farther and farther over the side. Her strength waned. Her knees scraped over the side. Then her hips. Finally, the edge of the bridge jabbed its planks into her ribs. Water pounded her face and filled her mouth. She swiveled her head and sputtered, desperate for a breath.

Out of options, she did the only thing she could. She let go of the pole and allowed the river to take her.

CHAPTER 22

J.T. peered out the back of the livery, across the corral, and down the road that led out of town. She should have returned by now.

Dark clouds were converging from the north. The light rain that had arrived ahead of them a few minutes ago had sent him out to gather the horses. Now that they were all stabled and dry, he couldn't tear himself away from the open doorway.

Where are you, Hannah?

Surely if something had been seriously wrong with Ezra she would have driven back to town for help right away. So what was keeping her? Maybe she decided to wait out the rain at his place. Or she could have taken a wrong turn.

His gut told him there was more to it.

"Tom!" J.T. spun around and marched through the stable.

The boy stuck his head out of one of the stalls, a currycomb in his hand. "Yeah?"

"Saddle up the gray for me while I get my slicker. I'm going for a ride." Trusting that his order would be obeyed, he strode on without stopping.

"In the rain?" the boy called out after him.

"Yep."

He had just retrieved the oiled raincoat from the nail on his office wall when the pounding of hoofbeats set his heart to racing. He dashed out to the street. The roan ran past him, straight into the livery.

Hannah.

J.T. shoved his sleeves into the arms of his slicker but didn't bother with the buttons as he sprinted toward the gray's stall. "Tom! I need that horse. Now!"

"I got him. I just need to cinch him up."

J.T. ran a calming hand over the roan's heaving sides. "It's all right, boy," he murmured. "You're safe. But where's Hannah, huh? You didn't throw her, did you?" Tension crept back into his voice at the thought of Hannah injured or lost out on the road somewhere. The horse side-stepped, and J.T. backed away.

"Tom," he gritted out through clenched teeth.

"Here, J.T. He's ready."

The second Tom emerged from the stall, J.T. grabbed the reins and swung into the saddle. "Take care of the roan."

Tom eyed the animal, then turned a panicked look on J.T. "B-b-but where's Miss Richards and the buggy?"

"That's what I'm going to find out." Not taking the time to offer any more explanation, J.T. nudged the gray forward and sped out of town.

He held the gelding to a moderate pace so he could scan the brush for signs of Hannah. But as each consecutive section he passed yielded no sign of her, the tension in his gut wound tighter. J.T. rounded the bend that preceded the bridge, a thicket of pecan trees blocking his view of the river. Through the branches, however, he caught a glimpse of a large black object. He reined in his mount and approached with caution.

When his view cleared, his heart dropped to his knees. It was the buggy, all right, but it lay broken and tipped against the railing. Debris cluttered the bridge, and J.T. knew at once that the dripping planks had been drenched by something more sinister than the drizzling rain that fell now.

"Hannah!"

He jumped off his horse, grabbed the lariat from the back of his saddle, and ran onto the bridge. His boots slid on the damp wood, but he didn't slow his pace. Praying that the only reason he didn't see her was because she was huddled inside the carriage, J.T. climbed between the lopsided horse shafts and thrust his head into the buggy's interior.

Nothing.

He punched a fist into the side of the carriage.

Lifting his head, he searched the banks, the water, the brush. No sign of the pretty pink outfit she'd been wearing that morning. Where was she?

Lord, help me find her. Alive. Please, alive.

J.T. scanned the carriage for any clue it could offer. He spotted her purse jammed into the seat cushion and jerked it free. Opening the front of his slicker, he tucked it inside his vest. Something stiff and hard poked him in the chest, but he welcomed the discomfort if it meant having a piece of her close.

He looked back at the empty rigging. The roan would never have been able to free himself without her aid. Therefore, she must have survived the flash flood. At least initially. But he hadn't passed her on the road or seen footprints in the muddy earth. That didn't bode well. Surely she wouldn't have walked back to Ezra's place. Not when the buggy was closer to the town side of the bridge. So where was she?

Cupping his hands around his mouth, he shouted her name loud and long. "Hannnnahhh!"

He waited, straining to hear some kind of response. Anything. But all he heard was the rush of the angry river.

She must have been washed over the side. J.T. ground his teeth. Hannah was strong—stronger than any woman he'd ever known. Physically. Mentally. The buggy had collapsed near the bank. Despite the fast currents, she might have made it to shore. That's where he'd start the search.

He angled his arm through the coil of rope and shoved the lariat up to his shoulder. Leaving the bridge behind, he sunk into the mud lining the west bank. He wove around trees and brush, grabbing limbs and roots to maintain his balance as his boots continually slid out from under him. Twice, he nearly ended up in the river himself.

About a quarter mile from the bridge, he spotted a snippet of color in the distance. There, where the river dipped slightly to the right, a fallen tree stretched out over the edge of the water. Something pink lay in its arms. Pink!

Heedless of the risk, J.T. rushed toward the log. Thornbushes scratched his face and hands. His downhill leg throbbed with the effort of keeping him upright. Mud sucked at his boots and dragged him down, but he charged on.

When he reached the uprooted tree, he lodged himself behind the circular base and unwound his rope. A small cedar stood nearby. J.T. looped the end of the rope around the cedar's trunk and knotted it. He shrugged out of his slicker, folded it up to keep the inside dry, and then tied the free end of the rope around his waist. Taking a deep breath, and petitioning God for an extra measure of strength and agility, he climbed onto the log and began making his way to Hannah.

The log narrowed the farther J.T. went. Not trusting his footing, he lowered himself to his belly and crawled.

He could see her now. Pale hands lying outstretched and limp, alarmingly white against the dark, wet wood. Her face down. Yellow hair strewn every which way, tangled with twigs and soggy leaves. She wasn't moving.

Please be alive. Please.

He inched closer, the river now licking his knees. Nearly there. He could almost touch her. Then the rope snagged, halting his progress. With a growl, he grabbed the cord and yanked. A stub of a broken branch held the rope captive. He yanked again, harder. "Come on!" Finally the branch snapped. J.T. turned back to his goal.

"Hannah?"

She was less than a foot away, but she gave no sign that she heard him.

"Hang in there, darlin'. I'm coming."

The log split into a V with Hannah wedged in the middle. J.T. reached for her hand and clasped it. The coldness of her fingers chilled his heart. He folded her hand inside his palm and squeezed. His eyes closed on a wordless prayer, then burst open as determination gripped him. He would compel the river to relinquish its prize. Hannah was not dead. Only unconscious. She could still be revived.

Clinging to that bit of faith, he released her fingers and latched on to her wrist. Once he found a grip on both of her arms, he dug his heels into the side of the tree and pulled. A groan tore from his throat as his muscles strained against the river's hold. Hannah's lower half was still submerged, her skirts weighing her down. He managed to lift her only a short distance before he had to stop and rest.

He needed more power.

Slowly, without releasing his grip on her arms, J.T. scooted his hips forward until he was sitting upright. His balance teetered, but the grip of his legs kept him from falling. Once secure, he unclenched his knees, lifted his bent legs forward, and locked the heels of his boots onto the branches on either side of Hannah.

J.T. kicked at the wood to make sure it would hold, then with a mental count to three, he leaned back and pushed with all his might.

His legs straightened little by little as Hannah came to him. He dragged her higher until he could tuck her lolling head onto his shoulder and wrap his arms around her middle. With a final thrust of his legs, she was free.

He wiggled out from under her and drew her backward until he could reach an arm around her knees. Carefully, so as not to throw them both into the river, he lifted and twisted her position until she sat sidesaddle across the log in front of him. He cradled her to his heaving chest and, with a shaky hand, combed the hair out of her face.

"Hannah? Can you hear me? Open your eyes."

He felt along her throat for a pulse. A weak vibration tickled his fingertips. Hot moisture pooled in his eyes. He blinked it away and gathered her close, rocking her back and forth, for his own comfort as much as hers.

"Thank you, Lord."

Turning her body so her back lay flush against his chest, he wrapped an arm around her middle and started shuffling back toward the base of the tree. Once there, he laid her along the length of the log, collected and recoiled his rope, then tried one more time to rouse her. He pillowed her head with his arm and lightly slapped her cheeks.

"Hannah, wake up," he demanded. Too frightened to cajole, he ordered her to comply. "This is no time to be stubborn, woman. Open your eyes."

Her lashes fluttered, and his breath caught in his chest. Then they stilled. He gave her a shake. "Look at me!"

Blue eyes peeked through tiny slits beneath her lids.

"That's it. Come on, Hannah. Look at me."

She blinked and her lashes parted a little more. "J-Jericho?"

He decided in that moment that he loved the sound of his given name. "I'm here, Hannah." He pressed a kiss to her forehead. "You're safe."

"I'm c-c-c-cold." Her eyelids drifted closed again.

J.T. frowned. She needed a hot bath, dry clothes, and a doctor before she came down with some kind of lung fever. Hadn't Cordelia told him she'd had weak lungs as a child? What if she had a relapse?

He wrung as much water from her skirts and petticoats as he could while still preserving her modesty, then retrieved his slicker and wrapped it around her. He doubted it held any residual warmth from his body, but it would block the wind. After buttoning her in, he took her in his arms and started the muddy trek back up to the road.

By the time he made it to his horse, it had stopped raining. J.T. eased his precious burden down to the ground to give him a minute to regain his strength. He knelt behind her so she could lean against him. To keep her head from flopping forward, he cupped her jaw in his hand. His thumb stroked her cheek.

"You're not going to like this next part, darlin', but it can't be helped." J.T. plucked a twig from her hair. "I'm hoping you won't remember it. If you do, I promise to let you upbraid me as much as you like. I won't even frown while you do it. Okay?"

Being as gentle as he could manage, he hoisted her onto his shoulder and pushed to his feet. Then, with a whispered apology, he slung her facedown across the saddle, climbed up behind her, and headed toward town.

CHAPTER 23

"Delia! Open up!"

J.T. kicked at the front door, his arms full of a still-unconscious Hannah. It was probably for the best that she hadn't awakened during the bumpy ride back to town, but he would've felt a lot better if she had.

As soon as Delia unlatched the door, J.T. pushed his way in.

"What on earth are . . . ?" The question died on her lips, a horrified gasp taking its place. "Hannah?"

J.T. didn't stop to offer explanations. He strode into his bedroom, ignoring the caked mud that clung to both him and his charge, and set Hannah down on his bed. Delia dogged his steps.

"What happened, J.T.? Where'd you find her? Is she alive?"

"Yes," he snapped. "She's alive. I'll tell you what I know later, but right now we need to get her warm and dry." He opened the chest at the foot of his bed and started tossing every blanket he owned onto the floor. "Get one of your flannel nightgowns for her to wear and heat some water for tea in case she wakes and can drink something. I'll fetch the doctor, and while I'm gone, I want you to strip every piece of wet clothing off of her. Everything. Understand?" He waited for Delia to nod. "Good. Dry her with a towel, and tuck her into my bed. If she stays overnight, I can sleep on the cot at the livery."

Delia scrambled from the room to do his bidding, and J.T. stole a few seconds to just look at Hannah. In his bed. Wrapped in a man's bulky coat, her skin smeared with mud, her hair matted and dripping river water on his pillow, she wasn't exactly a picture of feminine entice-ment. Nevertheless, his heart ached with tenderness.

He hunkered down beside the bed and clasped her hand. "You will not sicken, Hannah Richards. Do you hear me?" His throat clogged as he spoke. Then, before his sister could return, he pressed a kiss into Hannah's palm and returned her arm to her side.

Delia met him in the doorway carrying a steaming basin of water, a nightdress, and two towels slung over her shoulder. The shock that had dulled her eyes when he first arrived had sharpened to a gleaming fortitude. Hannah would be in good hands.

"Take good care of her, sis."

"I will, J.T. Now go get the doctor."

After one last glance at the delicate woman in his bed, he did just that.

Hannah came awake slowly. Flashes of remembered sounds and touches penetrated the fog of her mind. Delia's concern and gentle hand as she combed out Hannah's snarled hair. A man's no-nonsense voice and blunt fingers prodding her ribs. Jericho's arrogant demand to get well and a mysterious softness in her hand. They were no more than vague impressions, yet they lingered with a sense of reality no dream could instill.

The overwhelming weariness that had ruled her lifted. Awareness of her surroundings seeped in little by little. She noticed the quiet first.

The angry roar was gone. But so were the voices she remembered. Was she alone? She didn't want to be alone.

Hannah tried to move, but her body wouldn't cooperate. If she could just open her eyes and see where she was . . .

Her lashes parted enough to reveal a flat ceiling, not the sloping roof that sheltered her bed above the dress shop. Panic gripped her, and a whimper vibrated in her throat.

"Hannah?" A masculine voice echoed near her ear. A familiar voice, one that reached beyond the fear and calmed her. "It's all right. You're in my house. Delia cleaned you up, and she's in the kitchen heating some broth. Doc said nothing was broken. You should be fine after a day or two of rest."

She struggled to follow the stream of words. Willing her eyes to focus, she blinked and pried her lashes farther apart. A dark blur materialized above her. Then he touched her. The backs of his knuckles whispered against her cheek, and she turned into his caress. When the features of his face finally converged into a recognizable image, she started to wonder if this wasn't a dream after all.

"Jericho? You're smiling."

"Am I?" He stroked her cheek again. Warm tingles coursed through her, and instinctively, she followed his touch a second time. His smile widened. "I must be happy."

The change in him was quite startling. His amber eyes glowed with an inner light she'd not seen before, and the worry lines that creased his face faded into the background. He looked younger, more vibrant, more . . . everything.

"You're quite handsome when you're happy."

Jericho trailed the back of one finger under her chin. "I'll make note of your preference."

Heat rose to her face as she realized she had spoken the thought aloud. She'd better get a grasp on her faculties before she completely humiliated herself in front of him. Hannah turned her head away in a pointless attempt to hide her embarrassment and heard him scrape a chair closer to the bedside. Only then did she recall the words he had said earlier.

She was in his house.

In a *bed*, in his house.

Her eyes darted about the room. A shaving mug and razor sat next to the ewer and bowl on the bureau. A pair of men's boots lay discarded in a muddy heap by the door. A battered brown hat hung on the bedpost.

She was in *his* bed, in his house.

"I shouldn't be here." Hannah clutched the blankets to her chest and bolted upright. Pain ripped through her head. She moaned and squeezed her eyes shut, releasing the covers to press her fingers against her temples.

"Easy now," Jericho said. "You've got a pretty good knot on the side of your head. If you move slower it won't hurt so much." He wrapped his arm around her shoulders and gently laid her back on the pillow.

The soreness retreated under his tender ministration, and she opened her eyes again. Just in time to see that she was in a nightdress. Before she could do more than gasp, Jericho covered her back up to her chin.

"J.T.?" Footsteps sounded in the hall. "Is Hannah awake? I thought I heard her voice." Cordelia entered the room, carrying a cup full of something that smelled of herbs and beef. "I brought some broth, if you think she can manage a few sips."

Jericho rose from his chair. "Here, take my seat. I'll get some more pillows to prop her up."

Hannah relaxed her grip on the blankets. Having Cordelia in the room restored the propriety of the situation, and the irrational panic that speared through Hannah upon waking in Jericho's bed diminished. There was sure to be a sensible explanation for why she was in their home. She simply couldn't remember what it was at the moment.

Jericho returned with an armload of cushions. He laid them on the foot of the bed and came around to the far side. "I'm going to help you sit up, but we're going to do it slowly this time."

He supported her head and shoulders, lifting her with exaggerated care. Cordelia plumped the pillows and arranged them behind Hannah's back. Jericho eased her down, and she sank gratefully into the cushioned softness.

"Here you go." Cordelia placed the broth cup in her hand. "I let it cool some, so it's not too hot."

Hannah let the warmth seep into her fingers for several seconds before taking a drink. The well-seasoned stock flowed over her tongue and enlivened her sluggish senses. Her nostrils flared to take in more of the aroma and to inhale the heat of the steam.

"Mmmm. It's delicious. Thank you."

She finished most of the broth before her stomach began to churn. Deciding to extend Jericho's advice to eating as well as moving, Hannah didn't push herself to drink the rest. Lowering her arms to her lap, she looked from sister to brother. "What happened to me?"

"You don't remember?" Cordelia reached forward to claim the cup.

Hannah scrunched her forehead. "I'm not sure. Things are jumbled in my mind."

She looked to Jericho for a clue. He'd put distance between them again, leaning against the wall near the doorway, seemingly content to let his sister take over her care. His smile had retreated, too, although warmth still radiated from his eyes. Hannah loved Cordelia dearly, but she missed the unguarded man who had stroked her face and hovered over her with such tenderness moments ago. Would he ever come to her again?

"J.T.," Cordelia said. "Tell her what you know. Maybe it will spark a memory."

One side of his mouth quirked upward. "You went for a swim, and I had to fish you out of the river."

The river.

Images shuffled in her brain, some sharper than others. The storm. The bridge. The flood. An unseen hand pulled mental pictures out of the scrambled deck that was her brain and set them before her in an order that finally made sense. The carriage tipping. The horse running off. The river sweeping her away.

Water everywhere. Over. Under. Currents dragged and flipped her. Which way was up? Her lungs threatened to burst. Flailing her arms, she finally broke through the surface and gulped a breath. She glimpsed the bank. *Swim!* She stroked with all her might but made little progress. Her legs tangled in her skirt. Debris from the flood crashed into her, bruising her body and jarring her off course. *I'll never make it.* Exhaustion sapped her strength. Her muscles rebelled. Unable to do more, she submitted to the river's will. Her shoulders, then neck, then chin sank beneath the surface. As she begged the Lord to take her swiftly, the arms of a fallen tree stretched out to catch her.

"It's coming back to you, isn't it?" Cordelia's soft voice brought Hannah back to the present.

"Yes." The word scratched against her fear-swollen throat.

"J.T. told me you were caught in a flash flood."

Hannah nodded and glanced at Jericho. He watched her with an intent expression yet remained silent in the background. She returned her gaze to Cordelia and drew in a deep breath. She was safe. The river was gone.

"I . . . ah . . . was on the bridge when I realized what was happening." Hannah squirmed beneath the covers. "It was too late to go back. We tried to outrun it, but it crashed into us before we could reach the other side. I managed to get the horse unfastened and tried to hold on to his harness so he could pull me free of the carriage poles, but he was too fast. Then the river knocked the shaft into me. I lost my balance.

I tried to hang on, but there was too much water. I couldn't breathe. The next thing I knew, I was hurtling down the river."

"How frightful! It's a wonder you survived." Cordelia clasped her hand. "Surely, God sent his angels to protect you."

Hannah smiled. "Yes, he did. Two as a matter of fact. One that resembled a tree with long arms, and one who looked an awful lot like your brother." Hannah turned her smile on Jericho, who frowned and pushed away from the wall. He'd shuttered his face, withdrawing from her. Why?

"Thank you for pulling me out of the river," she said, trying to scale the wall he was reconstructing. "I'm sure my story would have ended much differently had you not come looking for me."

"I figure you would have found a way to crawl out eventually," Jericho grumbled. "You're too stubborn to let a little thing like a flash flood best you."

Hannah's smile faded at his surly tone. Though he'd played the gallant hero for her, it seemed his attitude hadn't changed much regarding her character. Then she recalled the busted carriage. If someone had borrowed her sewing machine and broken it, even unintentionally, she'd be grumpy, too. Perhaps her accounting of the afternoon's events had reminded him of his financial loss. She'd rather believe that to be the cause of his sudden irritability than a continued disapproval of her as a person, even if it meant shouldering the blame for the buggy's destruction. Besides, it *was* her fault. She never should've driven onto that bridge.

"Jericho, I'm so sorry about the carriage." She spoke before he could escape from the room. "As soon as I'm able, I'll make payments to cover the repairs."

He spun around and glared at her. "Do you think I care about a stupid buggy when you nearly lost your life today? The thing can sit on that bridge and rot as far as I'm concerned." He stormed out of the room, mumbling something to his sister about a cot at the livery.

Hannah just sat and stared, more confused than ever. "I didn't mean to make him angry."

"Don't mind him," Cordelia said. "J. T.'s never been one to accept gratitude from others with much grace. I think your comparing him to an angel got him flustered. As for the rest . . . ?" She stood and fussed with the blankets, smoothing out wrinkles and tugging the edges flat. "You gave him quite a scare today. I don't think he's completely recovered yet. He's just a little testy from all the excitement."

Cordelia helped Hannah lie down, taking out the extra pillows. "Rest now," she said. "You'll feel better in the morning."

Hannah complied, and when she drifted into slumber, she dreamed of Jericho—smiling.

CHAPTER 24

Hannah moved back to her own quarters the following afternoon, and by Saturday she was ready to resume her routine. She'd urged Cordelia to exercise without her yesterday, but the girl refused to leave her side. Now that she'd had two full nights of sleep and more rest than she could stand during the day, Hannah planned to eradicate Cordelia's excuse for abandoning her calisthenics. She was still a bit sore and prone to headaches, but Hannah couldn't let her friend down. Founders' Day was only two weeks away. They couldn't stop now.

She stepped into her loose-fitting gymnastic costume and laced up her low-heeled boots. Glancing at her reflection in the small mirror above the crate that held her pitcher and basin, she frowned. Her sleeping braid hung down her back, and frizzy wisps of hair stood out around her head. Most mornings, she flattened the worst of the fluff with a lick to her fingers and a tuck behind her ears before heading out for her constitutional, but today that didn't seem sufficient. What if she ran into Jericho?

Her heart stuttered as she remembered his smile and the husky

quality of his voice as he spoke to her when she first awakened. She
hadn't seen much of him yesterday, but he had come home for the
noon meal and sat with her while Cordelia made her lunch delivery
to the telegraph office.

He told her about how he and Tom had gotten the buggy back on
its wheels and dragged it to the wagon shed. She told him about Ezra's
rheumatism and the whittled hummingbird. Teasing her about the way
that bird had stabbed him repeatedly in the chest, Jericho returned her
purse. Then he sheepishly admitted to slinging her over his saddle like
a bounty hunter's prize and laughed over the justice the hummingbird
had doled out on her behalf.

It had been the most delightful hour she'd ever spent in his company. They hadn't argued once.

Hannah undid her braid, dampened the flyaway ends around
her face, and brushed the wavy tresses until they shone. Not wanting
Cordelia to suspect she had put any extra effort into her appearance,
she refashioned her hair into the normal braid that hung just short of
her waist. Only this one was tidier.

With a giddy flutter in her stomach at the thought of possibly seeing
Jericho, Hannah opened her door . . . and gasped. Two large shadows
loomed on her landing. It took her startled brain several seconds to
recognize that the shapes resembled furniture more than crouching
villains. Sagging against the doorframe in relief, she tried to puzzle out
how a pair of oak dining chairs had come to be on her staircase.

"You planning on turning that landing into a sittin' porch?"

Hannah stretched her head over the side rail to see Louisa walking
to the water pump between their buildings.

"Seems a bit tight for gettin' in an out o' your door, if you ask me."
The laundress winked as she set her bucket under the spout.

"Did you see who left these here? I've no idea where they came
from."

Louisa abandoned her bucket and moved closer to the staircase, examining the chairs through an upturned squint. "They look decent. Maybe a friend left 'em. Someone who knows you're a little short on furniture."

Hannah glanced back into her room, blushing a little at the humble trunk benches and makeshift table that adorned her home. She really could use some chairs, but who would know that?

"So you didn't see who it was?" Hannah wedged herself between the chairs and the railing, cupping her hand around the top of the slender rod that formed the outer edge of the seat back closest to her.

"Nope," Louisa answered, retracing her steps to the pump. She offered no further clues as she turned her attention to working the handle.

Hannah sighed. Not knowing the giver's identity was going to drive her batty. She scoured her mind for names of people who could possibly know of her need for chairs. Jericho and Tom had helped her move in. Cordelia, of course. Danny came in whenever he delivered her wood. Neither Jericho nor Cordelia would've said anything to anyone, but Tom or Danny, in their innocence, could have jabbered about it. It was possible that she mentioned something about her accommodations to Ezra during one of their morning chats, but she didn't remember anything specific. With his woodworking skills and soft heart, he would be a logical benefactor, but living so far from town would make it nearly impossible to deliver goods in the middle of the night, especially with his rheumatism.

She searched the empty street below for anyone who might be watching, but as usual, no one was about so early in the morning. At least no one she could see. Unable to solve the riddle, she relegated it to the back of her mind and carried the chairs inside.

They really were quite lovely. A floral pattern was carved into the back of each one and five thin spindles connected that piece to the slat at the back of the cane seat. The legs stood secure against the floor. No wobbles. She placed the chairs at different spots around her plank table until finally deciding to position them kitty-corner, facing the windows.

It looked cozy. Intimate. An image of Jericho sitting there rose to greet her. Him holding her hand or sharing a piece of pie off her plate. That deep voice whispering private messages in her ear. A brush of his lips across hers.

A tardy rooster crowed outside, shattering Hannah's daydream. She jumped and scurried out the door. Cordelia would worry about her if she didn't show up soon.

As she passed the livery, a movement in the office window caught her eye. Jericho was already there. Hannah tamped down her disappointment. It wasn't as if this visit would be her only chance to see him. He'd be at church tomorrow. And maybe she could make him another batch of biscuits or something—a thank-you-for-fishing-me-out-of-the-river gift. A groan vibrated in her throat at the idiotic idea.

Why was it she could give Cordelia advice on securing a man when she didn't have the first idea how to manage the task for herself? Maybe she should just concentrate on being a seamstress and making her shop a success. That had always been her dream.

Yet her dream was shifting. She could feel it. Jericho was weaving his way into its very fabric, and she feared that without him, the whole thing would tear to shreds.

Hannah shook off the dismal thought as she approached the Tucker home. Cordelia rose from her seat in a front porch rocker.

"I wasn't sure if you'd be coming today," she said. "Have you recovered enough?"

"I'm ready to find out." Hannah grinned and motioned Cordelia forward. She hiked past the house without stopping, forcing Cordelia to trot to catch up. "I'll waste away if I spend any more time abed. It feels good to be up and moving again."

"I'm glad you're feeling better," Cordelia said as she came abreast of Hannah.

"Me too."

They strode together in comfortable silence as they made their way toward the schoolhouse. Hannah usually enjoyed the quiet companionship of their walks, but today questions about her mysterious gift kept bobbing to the surface and irritating her like a host of mosquito bites that begged to be scratched.

"Do you happen to know anything about a pair of dining chairs that appeared on my landing this morning?"

Cordelia turned a startled face to her. "Someone put chairs on your landing?"

"Yes." Hannah leaned forward as the road began to steepen. "And what I can't figure out is how this mystery person discovered that I needed them." She looked sideways at her friend. "You didn't tell anyone, did you?"

Cordelia shook her head. "Of course not."

Disappointed not to have learned anything new, Hannah let the conversation lull as they climbed the hill. Then, as they arrived at the top of the hill a moment later, they stopped to catch their breath.

Cordelia bent forward and braced her hands above her knees. She tilted her head and ventured into a new topic. "I had a novel experience at Hawkins's store after I left you yesterday afternoon."

"Oh?"

"A man offered to tote my basket for me," Cordelia said, her eyes glowing with coquettish glee. She straightened and Hannah gestured for them to resume their walk.

"Who was it?" Hannah asked, accelerating the pace now that they were back on flat ground.

"I have no idea." She giggled. "He must have been a rail passenger or some other traveler. But he made such a fuss over me. I've never experienced the like. He followed me around the store, asking question after question," she said between winded exhalations. "He prattled on about the weather, the town, whatever merchandise happened to be near. It was quite endearing. Although I can't imagine why he didn't tire of me immediately. I was so surprised by his attentions, I could barely string two words together."

"A genuine flirtation! How marvelous." Hannah patted Cordelia's shoulder briefly and returned to her arm-pumping rhythm. "Men are noticing you. That's very encouraging."

"Well, it might have been even better, except Warren scared the poor fellow off."

That young man was becoming a thorn in their sides. Cordelia claimed him as a friend, yet he seemed to go out of his way to discourage her from improving herself. First, he made disparaging comments about her hair. Then, aware of her weakness for sweets, he plied her with free penny candy whenever she went in the store, even when she tried to refuse. And each time Hannah encountered him, he glared at her with such animosity, her skin crawled.

Hannah suppressed a shiver. "What did he do?" she asked as she steered them back toward town.

"He swooped in like some kind of avenger and told the man to stop bothering me. Then he glowered at him until he left. It was humiliating." She speared Hannah with a look that clearly communicated her irritation over yesterday's events. "J.T.'s bad enough. I don't need another man playing big brother for me."

Hannah doubted Warren would take kindly to the brother comparison. His actions better fit those of a jealous suitor than a protective sibling. But she kept that observation to herself.

"Did you say anything to him about it?"

"I sure did." Cordelia set off down the hill, her boots slamming into the earth with increasing aggravation. "As soon as the gentleman left, I took Warren to task for his rude behavior."

"I hope he apologized."

"No. Just the opposite." Cordelia marched on like a soldier who couldn't wait to tear into the enemy. "He started lecturing me on decorum! Can you believe it?"

Hannah didn't reply.

"He warned me not to encourage such men's attentions and said he disliked the changes I was making to my appearance and manner. He made some ridiculous accusation about you being a bad influence on me and predicted that if I continued following your advice, I would end up with a man who only cared about my looks, not one who appreciated me as a person. Made me so mad, I left without collecting my bread money."

Hannah's own ire piqued at the man's audacity. How dare he call her a bad influence? She wanted nothing more than Cordelia's happiness.

Yet a niggling truth poked at her beneath the cloak of her affront.

"As much as I hate to admit it," Hannah said, "there is a bit of wisdom in what he said."

Cordelia stopped in the middle of the road. "What?"

Hannah clasped her friend's elbow and urged her forward. "Keep walking." Once Cordelia was matching her stride again, Hannah continued. "There are many men in this world whose affections never run any deeper than physical attraction. I can't tell you how many society wives I've sewed for who were desperate to recapture their youth because their husbands had lost interest in them. A lasting relationship requires an abiding friendship, godly commitment, and an unselfish love that truly makes a couple one."

"But you know I've already given my heart to Ike."

"I know. And I'm sure he's not the sort of man to care only about a pretty face. However, we *are* hoping to turn his head by altering your physical appearance. If we are successful, you must pray for discernment to determine whether or not his interest develops into something that penetrates that surface we created. Because if it doesn't, he is not the man for you."

Cordelia said nothing, and Hannah walked several yards in silence. "Your brother said the same thing to me, and he was right about that part of it," she finally said. "Beauty *is* superficial, and a relationship built on such a shallow foundation cannot last."

Hannah peered at her friend, but Cordelia's eyes remained focused on the ground in front of her. Judging it best to let her think without interruption, Hannah said nothing further. However, in the resulting quiet, her own mind drifted . . . to Jericho.

Where Cordelia longed to have Ike notice her as a woman, Hannah longed for Jericho to appreciate her inner qualities. He was already physically attracted to her. She'd seen that. As well as the fact that he fought his attraction more vigorously than a cattleman fighting a prairie fire. If only he would trust her enough to allow one of those sparks to ignite his heart, she'd prove her faithfulness, remaining loyal to him all her days. She'd love him passionately and be the mother to his children that he'd never had for himself. She'd tease him and fill his days with laughter until that elusive smile became a permanent fixture on his face. If he ever gave her the chance.

Deep in thought, both women trudged on until they reached the house. There, out of habit more than conscious choice, they went inside and quenched their thirst.

Sitting in the kitchen, Cordelia refilled Hannah's glass from a ceramic water pitcher in the center of the table, then turned and met her gaze. "I want to continue with our plan."

Hannah waited.

"I'm in love with him. I can't give up." Cordelia stood and spun away to stare out the window. After a moment, she pivoted, her hands gripping the back of the chair. "I won't settle for superficial. If that's all he can offer me, I'll let him go. But what if there could be more?" She clenched her fist and pounded it against her breast. "What if he does notice me, and that leads to an attraction, and that attraction leads to love? I can't forfeit the chance. I have to try."

Cordelia's passion enlivened the hope that had been flagging in Hannah's heart. Eyes moist, Hannah rose and circled the table. She wrapped an arm around her friend and hugged her close.

"We'll keep pressing on, then." Hannah rested her head against Cordelia's temple and silently vowed to do everything in her power to help the young woman gain her dream. And if the Lord proved merciful, perhaps she'd realize her own in the process.

CHAPTER 25

J.T. raised his gaze to the roof of the meetinghouse and clenched his jaw. He appreciated a good sermon as much as the next fellow, but as a nondrinking man, today's treatise on the evils of drunkenness had grown tedious after five minutes. J.T. changed positions in his seat, twisting slightly toward the center.

He could almost see her out of the corner of his eye. Two rows back, across the aisle. Sitting next to Ezra.

She'd worn that pretty blue dress, the same one she'd had on the day he'd met her at the depot, the one that made her eyes look like moonlit ponds. Crossing his arms over his chest, he ran his hand across the pocket of his shirt. The crinkle of paper as he brushed past afforded him a momentary satisfaction. Hannah had slipped him the note when he'd helped her out of Ezra's buggy prior to services. Her gaze had sought his, and he'd known that whatever was written on the note was important to her and that she trusted him with it. He'd nodded to her, giving wordless assurance that he would take care of it. Whatever it was.

A self-deprecating smirk tugged at his cheek. If she had asked him to chop down a forest to make her a meadow, he probably would have gone home to fetch an ax. But, of course, she hadn't. She demanded no grand gesture of devotion from him. Just a simple act of kindness springing from her compassionate nature—a nature he had once thought shallow and frivolous. What idiocy.

He'd remained outside with the horses, wanting to ensure his privacy before opening the note. Once all the latecomers were safely inside, he ducked behind a wagon and unfolded the half sheet of paper, heart pounding. Her tidy script looped and curled in lovely patterns, fitting for one so enamored with creating beautiful things. Yet as he read, an odd disappointment filled him. The words were friendly but less personal than he had hoped. Which was absurd. Why should he expect the note to contain an impassioned declaration of her feelings when he'd never given her any reason to develop such affection? Nevertheless, he reread the thing a half dozen times, just because she'd written it.

> Jericho,
>
> Please don't mention my mishap at the river to Ezra. I fear he will blame himself for my predicament when it was my own lapse in judgment that caused the problem. I'm sure questions about the damaged carriage will arise, and I will gladly accept responsibility for wrecking the vehicle. All I ask is that when you tell the tale, please minimize the danger of the situation so that Ezra doesn't fret.
>
> Thank you,
> Hannah

Now, sitting on the hard bench built more for a school-age child than a grown man, J.T. considered her request. It wouldn't be hard to grant. He hadn't said much to Tom about what had happened beyond letting him know that Hannah was all right, so no one besides Delia should be privy to the events surrounding the buggy accident. He didn't figure it was anyone else's business anyway.

The sermon finally ended, and J.T. gladly rose to his feet to sing the closing song. Ike Franklin led them in three verses of "For the Beauty of the Earth." The hymn's lyrics floated through his heart and fell from his lips with newfound freedom. For the first time, he felt comfortable praising God not only for the beauty of the earth and skies, but for the beauty of the people around him, a certain dressmaker in particular. Like any other heavenly gift, beauty could be corrupted. He'd witnessed ample evidence to that effect in his lifetime. However, Hannah had proven that such a fate wasn't inevitable. Her inner character exuded as much loveliness as her physical features—a combination that succeeded in reflecting the glory of her Creator much like a field of bluebonnets or a host of gleaming stars in the night sky.

But what did she see when she looked at him? A grouchy old bear, most likely. J.T. bit down on the edge of his tongue, wishing he had a toothpick to grind. He had no right to hope that Hannah could care for him. Every time he opened his mouth around her, he managed to insult either her or her business.

If she needed him, she might be willing to overlook his bullhead-edness, but the woman was as independent and capable as any man. Running her own business. Hanging her own shelves. She even managed to rescue herself from a flash flood. All he'd done was drag her out of the water. Hannah didn't need his money, his strength, or his skills. All he could offer her was his heart. But would that be enough? It hadn't been for his mother. And even though Hannah shared as much in common with his mother as a dove did with a rattlesnake, he couldn't quite banish the doubt that gnawed on his gut.

J.T. added his amen to that of the congregation even though he hadn't heard a word of the prayer the preacher had pontificated. He silently begged God's pardon for his inattention as the hum of conversation escalated around him. Ike Franklin approached and shook his hand.

"Good to see you, J.T."

"Ike."

The fellow darted a glance at Delia and stammered an inane greeting. Delia smiled and stepped closer, which set the man rocking back on his heels.

"I enjoyed the songs you led this morning," Delia said.

"Th-thank you, Miss Tucker." His face reddened, and he stretched his neck as if trying to escape a snug collar. "I . . . uh . . . remembered you mentioning that 'Father of Mercies' was one of your favorites."

Since when did Ike get nervous around Delia? He saw her every day, for pity's sake.

"Indeed it is. The others you selected were uplifting, as well. I especially liked 'Sweet By and By.' The lilting melody put me in mind of a boat of believers sailing for heaven and singing of the joy that awaited them on that beautiful shore."

"I've never thought of it that way, but you're quite right."

J.T. frowned as he shifted his gaze from Ike to Cordelia and back again. Normal people talked about the weather, crops, or their sick aunt Myrtle after services, not poetic song lyrics. What was going on with these two? Poor Ike was probably wishing he'd never opened his mouth. J.T. cleared his throat to gain the man's attention and was about to offer a comment on the recent rains when someone slipped up beside him and touched his arm.

"Excuse me, Mr. Tucker." Hannah smiled up at him, and J.T. promptly forgot about his noble intentions to rescue Ike. "I find myself in need of your assistance. Would you mind stepping outside with me for just a moment?"

"Of course." Ike could fend for himself.

"I hope it's not something too serious, Miss Richards," Ike said.

"Not at all, but thank you for your concern. I'm sure Mr. Tucker will set everything to rights for me in no time."

Feeling like he'd just grown two inches taller, J.T. followed her as she made her way down the aisle. She didn't stop at the steps or even the yard, but strode directly to Ezra's buggy. Did she want him to fix something on the old man's rig? He crammed his hat onto his head and caught up to her, confident he could take care of whatever she needed.

He stripped out of his good Sunday coat and hung it over Ezra's worn leather seat. "What needs fixing?"

Hannah leaned back against the coal-box body of the carriage and drew a line in the dirt with the toe of her shoe. "Oh, I think you've already taken care of it."

J.T. squinted at her. "I don't understand."

She smiled. "I know."

What was she up to? He stared at her until she finally looked away.

A sick suspicion that she'd just manipulated him churned his stomach. A pretty smile, a touch on his arm, and he'd followed her like a pup on a leash. "So you lied to me?" he growled. He was no better than his father after all. "You don't need me." He jerked his coat off the seat and stomped off. *Women!* He should have known better than to let his defenses down.

"Wait, Jericho. I didn't lie." Hannah ran up behind him and latched on to his arm.

He shook off her hold.

"I *did* need you to come outside, Jericho, but that was all. Just come outside."

He spun to glare at her. "What kind of riddle is that?"

The sparkle that lit her eyes a moment ago disappeared. "You were going to interrupt them. They needed more time. Without your interference."

None of this was making any sense. He slapped his fist against his thigh and jerked his shoulders up in question. "Who?" he demanded. "Who needed more time?"

"Cordelia and Ike."

"Delia and . . ." All at once, the scales fell from his eyes, followed by an infusion of sweet relief. She hadn't been manipulating him. Well, maybe a little, but it had only been a harmless ploy to aid his sister, not some feminine machination to twist him to her will. She was simply playing matchmaker.

With his sister.

His ire sparked back to life.

"Delia and Ike? Ike is the man you hinted at all those weeks ago? The man Delia's pining after?"

Hannah glanced around the yard. "Hush. Someone will hear you."

J.T. didn't care about the volume of his voice. His sister was in there flirting with a man. A man whom she visited every day. Alone. With no one to chaperone.

"If he's stepped out of line with her, so help me, I'll—"

Hannah grabbed the ends of his black string necktie to restrain him. He glared down at her in disbelief. She glared right back. "Cool your heels, cowboy. Nothing improper has happened and nothing's going to happen. They're in a church with dozens of other people, for heaven's sake. Stop and think for a minute."

J.T. flared his nostrils and drew in several deep breaths.

"Cordelia's not a girl anymore, Jericho. She's a woman of marriageable age. An intelligent, loving, giving woman who longs to share her life with someone."

He ground his teeth. His mind recognized the truth in her words, but his heart fought against it. Delia was his baby sister, his responsibility, his family.

"Ike Franklin is a decent man, a godly man," Hannah insisted. "He'd make a good husband. Unless you know of some blot on his character that Cordelia is unaware of?"

He'd considered the man a friend for years. Respected him, too. He had no reason to change his opinion just because he'd decided to take an interest in his sister. But Delia married? It seemed too soon. Even if most girls already had husbands and even a kid or two by the time they were nineteen. Not Delia. She'd kept house for him and quietly gone about her duties, never hinting that she was anything but content. And he'd never bothered to ask.

"Jericho?"

He blinked and refocused on the woman in front of him. Exhaling, he unclenched his fists and laid a palm over Hannah's hand, the one still clutching his necktie.

"You're right," he said. Her grip loosened, and he shifted his fingers until she released his tie strings in favor of his hand. It felt awfully good holding her arm against his chest. Delia deserved to feel this way, too. "If I had to pick a husband for her, Ike would be a likely candidate. I guess I just have a hard time picturing Delia under another man's protection."

"She'll always be your family, Jericho. Those bonds won't be severed. But there are some spaces in a woman's heart that a brother's love cannot fill."

He peered into her eyes. A warmth glowed in their depths, daring him to believe that she was speaking as much for herself as for Delia. He covered the length of her arm with his and tugged her close. She came to him, her body only a whisper away. The pink of her lips beckoned to him, promising softness and delight. He wrapped his left arm about her waist. He dipped his chin.

Then the distant drone of voices hit a marked crescendo as the congregation filed out of the building and began swarming toward the wagons.

This was not the time, nor the place.

But as he stepped away from Hannah and released her hand, J.T. vowed to himself that there would be a time and a place. Soon.

CHAPTER 26

During the noon hour the next day, J.T. kept one eye on the street as he oiled a pile of spare harness leather in his office. Delia had passed by thirty minutes ago with Ike's lunch in hand and hadn't yet returned. As soon as she did, he planned to have a little talk with the telegraph operator.

Two bridles and a pair of reins later, she finally moseyed by, all smiley and dreamy-eyed. J.T. spat out his toothpick so hard it arced over his desk. His fingers curled into fists, tangling in the breast strap he'd been working on. Breathing deeply, he unclenched his hands and gently set the leather aside.

He trusted Delia. Shoot. He even trusted Ike. But there was something about the two of them together that stuck in his craw. Probably because he wasn't quite ready to admit that his baby sister had grown up. It had been just the two of them for so long—even before Pop died, truth be known—and J.T. had a hard time bending his mind around the idea of turning her care over to another man. Yet she deserved happiness, a family of her own, children.

J.T. pushed to his feet and started for the door. He wouldn't keep her from her dreams, but heaven help him, he'd make sure no one hurt her along the way, either. If Ike didn't have good answers to the questions he was fixin' to get asked, the man could kiss his homemade lunches good-bye.

After telling Tom where he was headed, J.T. marched down the street toward the edge of town, where the telegraph office sat across from the hotel. He chose the dirt instead of the boardwalk to avoid the people milling about. In no mood to chat, he lifted a hand if someone called out a greeting but otherwise kept his mouth shut and his gaze locked on the telegraph office.

"J.T. Tucker! Just the man I'm looking for." Elliott Paxton dashed down the walk on the opposite side of the street.

J.T. tried the wave-and-ignore method, but Paxton had never been one for subtlety. He scurried directly into J.T.'s path and clapped him on the shoulder as if completely unaware of his efforts to avoid him. Then again, the fellow probably *was* unaware. Elliott Paxton had a tendency to see what he wanted to see.

"Hold up a minute, Tucker. I've got some news you'll want to hear."

J.T. kept walking.

"About a certain property . . ." Paxton let his words dangle like a worm on a hook, and J.T. bit back a sigh. No wonder the man always caught the biggest catfish in the county. His bait was irresistible. J.T. slowed.

"You made contact with the owner?"

Paxton gave a quick nod and slid his focus meaningfully around the street. "Come to my office, and I'll tell you about it."

It took J.T. several seconds to drag his eyes away from the telegraph office, but he knew Ike wasn't going anywhere. Not till his shift ended, anyway. Louisa's roof needed those new shingles. The sooner he got things settled with the owner, the better.

"All right. But I've only got a minute."

The banker's eyes twinkled much as J.T. imagined they did when he reeled in a defeated fish. "It won't take long. I promise."

Anxious to get the chore done, J.T. ate up the ground with his long stride and forced the banker to stutter-step to keep pace. Once in the office, he cut to the heart of the matter.

"So, will he sell?"

Paxton shook his head. "No. At least not for the price you offered."

"I can't afford more," J.T. admitted as he dropped into a chair. "Besides, the place ain't even worth what I did offer."

"I know. The fellow claims that he can't get out of his rental agreement with Mrs. James. If he sold to you, he'd have no way to guarantee that you wouldn't turn the woman out."

J.T. slammed his palm against the polished wood of Paxton's desk. "I'd never do that! The whole reason I want to buy the place is to *help* Louisa."

"Yes, I explained that to him, but he refused to relent." Paxton shrugged as he leafed through a stack of papers, setting one aside. "I have no way of knowing if he sincerely cares about Mrs. James's welfare or if he's just using that as an excuse to not sell. Either way, it doesn't bode well for your interests."

"No, it doesn't." J.T. flopped backward into a slouch. Covering the lower half of his face with his hand, he pushed out a long breath.

Slowly, Paxton slid a paper from in front of him over to J.T.'s edge of the desk and rotated it 180 degrees.

J.T. sat forward. "What's this?"

"I still have a few negotiating tricks up my sleeve."

Glancing over the words, J.T. frowned. "This is a contract naming me property manager." He shot a glare across the desk. "I'm no man's lackey, Paxton."

"Of course not, but think about it for a minute. Though the owner's not willing to sell, when I happened to mention the dilapidated state of the structure and how the people of Coventry held him in such low esteem because of his poor oversight, he warmed up to my counter-proposal. He agreed to hire a man, on my recommendation, for a small monthly stipend to make repairs and keep the building in good working order. All expenditures will have to be submitted for preapproval, of course, but basically, he would give the manager free reign."

J.T. rubbed his chin, the corner of his mouth tilting up at one corner as he mentally took Paxton's plan a step further. "And if said manager chose to deposit his stipend into Louisa's account . . ."

The banker grinned, and for the first time J.T. recognized the shrewdness in the man's eyes. Paxton continued, "We could honestly tell the widow James that we worked out a deal with the owner to lower her monthly rent in exchange for property maintenance."

"Maintenance I'd be willing to do for her in exchange for . . . say . . . laundry service, since Cordelia is so busy with her baking business these days."

Paxton nodded, and the two men shared a conspirator's chuckle as J.T. signed his name to the contract.

"You brokered me a good deal, Paxton," J.T. said as he thrust out his hand. The banker clasped it firmly.

"Always willing to aid a noble cause."

Leaving in a considerably better mood than when he'd arrived, J.T. bid the banker a good day and crossed the road to the small square building that housed the Western Union office. A bell jangled as he pushed through the door, and Ike emerged from the back room to meet him at the counter.

"Afternoon, J.T. Need to send a wire?"

"Nope. Need to visit with you. About Delia."

The man's face paled and then turned an entertaining shade of red before finally settling on a dull pink. He coughed a bit but then lifted his chin and faced J.T. squarely. "Come around the counter. We can talk in back."

J.T. mentally ticked one mark in Ike's column as he stepped through the doorway that led to a simple room that held only a table with a telegraph machine and a couple of chairs. The room was cozy. Too cozy. He scratched out Ike's mark.

"So what's on your mind, J.T.?" Ike asked, offering him a seat with a gesture of his hand.

"I've noticed that Delia takes longer to deliver your lunches these days than she used to. Makes me wonder what's changed. Especially after the two of you acted different at church yesterday. Friendlier . . . if you get my meaning."

Ike's face darkened a bit, but he held J.T.'s gaze. "I get your meaning. And you're right. Something has changed. At least on my end."

His eyes shifted away, searching out some far-off point in the space that stretched between the room's walls. "Cordelia's easy to talk to. And she laughs at all my stories." He shrugged a bit as a grin tugged at his mouth. "I was comfortable having her around." His grin faded. "Maybe too comfortable."

J.T.'s gut tightened. "What's that supposed to mean?"

"Nothing untoward," Ike sputtered. "It's just that . . . well . . . she started becoming a pleasant fixture in my day. Talking to her, being with her. I guess I started taking it for granted."

J.T. couldn't be too hard on him for that. He'd been guilty of the same attitude.

"Then she started changing little things about her appearance. Her hairstyle, the cut of her dresses. I didn't say anything about it at first. I figured it was just some notion she'd taken up. But then I overheard some old hens gossiping in the mercantile about how Cordelia must have her sights set on some man to make such efforts. Well, it got me to thinking. And feeling. Things I'd never felt before. I didn't want Cordelia cooking lunches for any other man. Only me."

Ike turned to face J.T., and the earnestness glowing in his eyes erased the last of J.T.'s reservations. "It is my hope to somehow win your sister's affection. And if I am fortunate enough to do so, I plan on making her my wife."

The man had gumption, J.T. would give him that. He wasn't afraid to lay his cards on the table and fight for what he wanted. Had to respect that. But other things spoke even more highly of him. The way his expression softened as he spoke about Delia. The way he cared about earning her affection. He would be a good husband to her.

J.T. stood up and held his hand out to Ike. The other man stared at it a moment before grabbing hold.

"If she'll have you, you're welcome in our family."

He could feel the tension drain out of Ike as he released the man's hand and cuffed him on the shoulder. " 'Course, you might have to share those lunches for a while longer. With me."

Ike grinned. "Deal. Until you find a wife of your own, that is."

They shared a laugh, but as J.T. wandered back out to the street, Ike's parting words climbed under his skin and started itching. A wife of his own. Is that where things were heading with Hannah? He cared about her. A lot. But a wife? He scraped his suddenly damp palms against the sides of his denim trousers. His father had loved his mother, and it destroyed him. J.T. had always blamed his mother for that, but what if his father had been at fault, as well? What if issues other than his mother's dissatisfaction had contributed to the demise of his parents' marriage?

As he neared the livery, Hannah's shop drew J.T.'s attention. An ache settled in his chest. If he let himself love her, would she love him in return? Or would he carry out his father's legacy and disappoint her so often that he drove her away?

CHAPTER 27

Later that week, Hannah sat at her sewing machine, its low-pitched whir blending with the rhythmic drumming that drifted from next door. Jericho had somehow convinced Louisa to let him install new shingles. He'd spent an hour or two on her roof every afternoon for the last four days.

And every afternoon for the last four days, Hannah had found a small token on her staircase as she made her way to her room after closing the shop. Always on the second to last step—the one that had broken and sent her plunging into his arms that first day.

Hannah's foot slowed its pumping of the treadle, and a bemused tingle danced over her skin as she thought about the collection of pint-sized Mason jars decorating the crate near her bed. Monday's jar had held a polished stone, round and smooth. Its deep reddish hue carried a horizontal line of quartz along the top that made her think of a fine lady with diamonds at her neck. A small note was included in the jar. *For the beauty of the earth.*

Tuesday's note had read *For the beauty of the skies.* The jar contained a perfectly formed feather, the color so blue Hannah doubted any jay would have given it up without a fight.

On Wednesday, he'd deviated from the hymn lyrics to compose a verse with a more romantic bent. *For the beauty of your heart.* A cottonwood leaf in that very shape sat in the glass cage, its stunning yellow color singing the glory of autumn.

And yesterday she'd found a blue hair ribbon with a note that said *To match the beauty of your eyes.* She'd woven the ribbon into her braided chignon this morning in hopes that Jericho would see it.

Her chest rose and fell on a dreamy sigh, the seam in Cordelia's skirt only half finished. Jericho Tucker was courting her, truly courting her. At least she assumed it was him. He never signed his name to the notes. But who else could it be? No one else understood the significance of that particular step. No one else had nearly kissed her in the churchyard. Memories of that almost-kiss had distracted her all week. It had to be Jericho leaving the gifts.

And the notes? Well, they gave her heart the biggest thrill of all. The positive references to beauty in each one led her to believe that he might finally see her as more than a stumbling block and consider beauty more than a plague to be avoided.

The door to the shop opened, startling her out of her thoughts. A guilty blush heated her cheeks as Cordelia came in.

"I'm running a little behind schedule," Hannah said, glancing up, "but I'll have this ready for you to try on in a jiffy." She rocked the foot peddle back into motion and zipped to the end of the side seam.

Cordelia ambled behind the counter, perfectly at home in Hannah's shop, and sat on the corner of the worktable. "I'm in no hurry. In fact, I could use some time to think."

"About what?"

"Warren." Cordelia exhaled with enough force that Hannah felt a stirring on the back of her neck.

Hannah repositioned the fabric, folded in a dart, and continued sewing. "He's giving you a hard time again?"

"Yes." The word leaked out of her, slow and miserable. "He was waiting for me when I came out of the telegraph office. I think he might have overheard me asking Ike to join us for the Founders' Day picnic."

Stopping the treadle, Hannah turned around in her chair. "How did that go, by the way?"

A shy smile temporarily erased the worry on Cordelia's face. "Ike said he was too fond of my cooking to turn down the invitation."

Hannah grinned. "I saw the way he was stammering around you at church last Sunday. I think it's more than your cooking that draws him."

"I'm starting to think so, too." Cordelia ducked her head, her cheeks turning a delighted pink.

"I knew he couldn't stay blind to you forever." Hannah laughed, truly happy for her friend. "I can't wait to see you two together at the picnic next Saturday."

"Seeing the two of us together is what got under Warren's skin."

Hannah clipped off the thread ends and flipped the skirt right side out. "I think Warren's sweet on you, Cordelia."

Her friend let out a groan of frustration. "I didn't want to believe you when you suggested that before, but I can't deny it any longer. He proposed to me. Right there on the boardwalk."

Unable to disguise her shock, Hannah sucked in a too-fast breath and started coughing. Cordelia came over and pounded her on the back. Eyes watering from her choking spell, Hannah looked up at Cordelia's grimacing face. "He proposed?"

"Oh, Hannah. It was the most dreadful experience. He insulted Ike and said that he only looked at me because of the change to my appearance. He said Ike didn't care for the true me—not like he did—

and if a man was too ignorant to love me when I was a shy little mouse, he wasn't worth having."

"He actually called you a mouse?" The man had no skill in wooing whatsoever.

Cordelia nodded and started pacing around the table. "I didn't know how to respond, so I asked him why he had never declared himself before."

"What did he say?"

"He claimed he'd been waiting to establish himself in his father's business in order to offer me a secure future. But he's been working there for years and never said a word to me."

"Would you have accepted him if he had?"

Cordelia stopped pacing. "No. At least I don't think so. Oh, I don't know." She crossed her arms over her stomach and hugged her ribs. "I've never had romantic feelings toward Warren, but with no one else knocking at my door, I might have considered it."

"Then I'm glad he never said anything." Hannah laid the skirt aside and went to her friend. "You and Warren would have been a wretched match."

"I know." Her breath quivered as she struggled to contain her emotions. "We were friends in school, though. Two outcasts finding camaraderie with one another—he with his birthmark and me, the shy mouse with the shameful mother everyone gossiped about. We were quite a pair. But having each other eased the loneliness. Whenever he grew too sullen, I would make up silly stories, one more ridiculous than the last, until he smiled. He'd sneak me peppermint sticks and lemon drops from his father's store. There is kindness in him. It's just not as apparent now that he's grown."

Conscience pricked, Hannah closed her lips against the uncharitable comments that had sprung to her tongue. Though sullen and insensitive, Warren deserved a measure of compassion. It couldn't have been easy growing up with such a large mark upon his face. But that wasn't sufficient reason for Cordelia to sacrifice her future by binding herself to a bitter man.

"Did you give him an answer?"

"I tried, but he must have sensed I was working up to a negative response, for he interrupted and said that he would call on me tonight after supper."

Sensing Cordelia's dread over the impending visit, Hannah ushered her into the fitting room. She helped her undress and slipped the new skirt up over her hips. As she made a minor adjustment to the waistline, she met Cordelia's gaze in the mirror.

"You should tell Jericho."

Cordelia looked away. "I know. I just worry that J.T. will toss Warren off the porch or something."

Hannah bit back a laugh as she recalled holding the man back in the churchyard over Ike. "He might at that. But as your brother, he should know of the offer. He can help you decide what to do and be there to back you up should Warren not like your answer."

"You're right. I'll tell him." Cordelia sighed and adopted a woebegone expression that bordered on comic. "I just wish I had a sister to commiserate with after it was all over. Someone like you."

Hannah squirmed a bit as she marked the hem. Had Cordelia guessed her feelings toward Jericho? And if so, what did she think about it? Hannah concentrated on matching up the edges of the skirt's burgundy stripes. "You can commiserate with me anytime you like. You know that."

"Tonight?" Cordelia asked, a touch of genuine pleading blending with the mischief in her tone. "Come to supper. I'd feel so much better with you there. And something tells me J.T. won't mind your company, either."

She *did* know.

Hannah straightened. "Cordelia, I—"

Before she could explain, Cordelia grabbed her in an enthusiastic embrace. "You have no idea how happy having you as a sister will make me. J.T. is a little crusty on the outside, but his heart is true and as big as a mountain. He'd be good to you."

Hannah backed away. "Are my feelings for him so obvious?"

"Only to me. Ever since the day the two of you worked those rings together, I've had a suspicion that something might be brewing, and the way J.T. cared for you after pulling you from the river confirmed it." Cordelia stepped out of the skirt and handed it to Hannah, deliberately holding her gaze. "He may not have fully conceded yet, but I have no doubt that you are infiltrating his defenses."

Hannah's stomach dipped and tickled the way it had when she sledded down Parkman's Hill as a child. Everything within her longed to believe that Cordelia was right. Tentatively, her lips stretched into a smile, and she clasped the hand of the young woman she already loved as a sister. "I'd be honored to join you and your brother for supper tonight."

❦

J.T. answered the knock on his front door, his most intimidating scowl already in place. Delia had warned him of Warren's arrival, and J.T. was none too pleased. He liked and respected the kid's old man, but Warren was immature and so caught up in proving his worth that he rarely looked beyond himself. J.T. had no issue with his marked face or his occupation, certain that a store clerk could adequately provide for a wife. But the kid made that old nag of his drag his sorry hide up the hill to church every Sunday when the animal should have been put out to pasture years ago. If he was selfish in the way he treated his horse, who was to say he'd be any different in the way he treated a wife?

Even if Delia favored such a match, J.T. would have been loath to accept Warren's suit on her behalf. He was thankful his sister's tender heart and girlhood loyalty didn't outweigh her common sense. Ike was a much better choice.

"G-good evening, Mr. Tucker." Warren barely looked him in the eye. Although, to be fair, that was mostly because the kid's long hair dangled in the way. J.T. would've respected him more if he stood up straight, combed his hair back, and took pride in himself. So what if he had a blotch on his face? If he'd stop reminding people that he was ashamed of it by covering it with his hair, folks might actually get used to the thing and forget about it.

J.T. was tempted to educate the fellow, but something told him his advice would not be welcome. Instead, he crossed his arms and stared the young man down. "Warren."

"Is Cordelia at home? I believe she's expecting me." He twitched and flung his hair off his forehead, only to have it fall back in his face.

"She'll be along in a minute," J.T. said. "You planning to visit with her on the porch this evening?"

"Yes, sir."

"Good. I'll keep an eye on you from the kitchen, then."

Warren tugged on his sleeves, looking about as comfortable in his sack suit as a man who had rolled in poison oak the day before.

"Stop terrorizing him, J.T.," Delia said from behind him. "Warren knows how to act the part of a gentleman."

J.T. stepped aside to let his sister pass, his eyes still locked on the man who had come calling. A disturbing flare of insolence crossed Warren's features at Delia's words, as if he were daring J.T. to contradict them. J.T. unfolded his arms and took a step toward him. The insolence vanished. Satisfied, J.T. retreated into the house and closed the door.

He headed for the kitchen and stopped in the doorway. Hannah, a full dishpan between her and the window, was leaning forward, her nose nearly touching the glass.

"I see I'm not the only one interested in what's going on out there."

She jumped, and a plate slid out of her hand, splashing water into her face. "Oh!" She squinted against the unexpected geyser.

J.T. hurried to her side, slid a towel from the bar by the pump, and gently dabbed the droplets from her face. He stroked the cotton cloth over her forehead, cheeks, and chin. Then, just for good measure, he lightly ran it over her lips, as well. Her pink tongue reached out to moisten them again, and heat rose inside him.

"Thank you." Her low voice sent a shiver through him.

He cleared his throat. "You're welcome."

She blinked, and the building fervor in her eyes dispersed, replaced by a teasing twinkle he found almost as alluring. "Now that you've got that towel in hand," she said, "you can dry." Hannah retrieved the sunken plate and handed it to him with a grin.

He raised an eyebrow but accepted the dish. "Just don't tell my sister I know how to do this, or she may put me to work every night."

Hannah extracted her dripping fingers from the water long enough to flick him with a few sprinkles. He frowned, earning him a laugh from the sprite at his side.

"My mama always said dishwater could cure any ailment. It'd be good for you to be close to it more often."

J.T. doubted it could cure what ailed him, but then he wasn't all that sure he wanted to be cured anymore.

They lapsed into a comfortable silence broken only by the clink of crockery and glassware. As he waited for her to pass him another plate, he admired the line of her neck. Slender and pale, with a perfect little hollow near her collar that his lips longed to taste. Veering away from temptation, his gaze roamed up to the braided knot low on her head. A blue thread peeked out at him from between the strands and his heart gave a little leap. She was wearing his ribbon.

A part of him had worried that she'd find his gifts juvenile. Heaven knew he'd felt juvenile leaving them, like a kid in short pants bringing his teacher a fistful of dandelions. After all, what kind of man gave a woman a leaf or a bird feather? Yet after contemplating Ike and Delia's discussion of hymn lyrics, he realized women liked poetry. At least Delia did. His mother would have turned her nose up at a paltry rhyme and objects that cost nothing but patience to acquire. However, he thought Hannah might appreciate them. He'd hoped she would, anyway. A woman who saw beauty in a shiny button and a wooden hummingbird should be able to find it in other small things, too. Right?

He'd stolen the first lines of his poetry from the hymn they'd sung at the close of church last Sunday, only adding a few lines of his own at the end. Each evening, he'd hunted the countryside for the right gift to offer the following day, but he never quite worked up the courage to hand it to her in person. So he'd shoved the things into jars and left them on her step. Not knowing his sister had invited Hannah to dinner, he'd left another gift a mere hour before she showed up at his home. He'd run out of poetic things to say, so he'd simply left the jar, filled with a lopsided bouquet of yellow sunflowers.

Never one to play the coward for long, J.T. steeled himself as Hannah turned to pass him a platter. "So . . . uh . . . did you like the sunflowers?"

Her eyes widened slightly and roses bloomed in her cheeks, but the smile that followed unclenched his gut. "I loved them. And all the other gifts, as well. Thank you."

"You're welcome."

She bent back to her task, rummaging around in the grayish water for something else to wash. "I had hoped they were from you." She spoke in such a quiet tone, he had to strain to hear her. "I would have thanked you earlier, but there was no signature on any of the notes. I didn't want to make a fool of myself if the sender turned out to be someone else."

That's what being a coward got a man—confusion and an

uncomfortable spark of jealousy. Forcing a casual air to his voice he was far from feeling, he asked the question that burned in his belly. "You got someone else courting you?"

"No." The fork she'd been scrubbing slid from her hand, returning to the murky depths. "But then, I wasn't sure I had you courting me, either. I seem to recall you expressing a number of objections to my suitability in the past."

"That's because I was close-minded and couldn't see past my own experiences."

Her head spun toward his and the open vulnerability in her eyes branded his heart. For the first time in his life, he wished he were the kind of man who knew how to woo a woman with pretty words. With his luck, though, he'd mangle the attempt and trample her feelings. He'd have to show her instead.

Slowly, he drew her hands from the water and dried them with his towel, aware that she was watching his movements. He ran his palm up her arm and cupped her shoulder. Then, unable to resist, he traced the shape of that delightful hollow at the base of her neck with his fingertip. A tremor passed through her, and the nearly inaudible sound of her breath catching made his pulse throb.

He slipped his hand around the back of her neck. His fingers toyed with the downy hair at her nape while his thumb caressed her cheek and ear. Hannah's lashes fluttered closed, then languidly lifted to reveal eyes darkened to a midnight blue. Her lips parted slightly, and he extracted his hand just enough to trail his thumb across their softness.

"I was wrong," he murmured. "No one could be more suitable."

Digging his fingers into her hair, he dragged her close and lowered his mouth.

The front door banged closed. Hannah jumped and tried to pull out of his embrace, but he wasn't quite ready to let her go. He might never be.

"Jericho." Hannah's frantic whisper restored his common sense, and he allowed the slender fingers that had been clutching his shirt a moment ago to push him away.

Delia stood in the doorway, looking from him to Hannah and back again. He positioned himself in front of Hannah, trying to absorb the majority of the scrutiny, while mentally listing all the reasons he shouldn't strangle his sister.

"Warren leave?" he groused.

"Not happily, but yes, he accepted my refusal and left." She cocked a hip and planted her fist against it. "You know, he could have been out there compromising my virtue for all the attention you paid. Get distracted, J.T.?"

He snatched the towel from the floor and threw it at her. "Finish up the dishes while I walk Miss Richards home." Taking Hannah's hand, he tugged her toward the door, but after a few faltering steps, she stopped.

"Wait," she said. "Cordelia invited me here tonight in order to have someone to talk to after Mr. Hawkins left." Her face was glowing as red as a radish, yet instead of taking the escape he'd offered, she was holding firm to her promise. "Why don't you finish the dishes while Cordelia and I talk? I'll let you know when I'm ready to go."

"Yeah, big brother. Finish the dishes." The imp tossed the towel in his face and then giggled as she absconded with Hannah, the two disappearing behind the door of her bedroom.

Comforting himself with the fact that he could still look forward to escorting Hannah home, J.T. rolled up his sleeves and plunged his hands into the lukewarm water. He never thought he'd be reduced to doing dishes while the two women he loved talked about him behind closed doors.

The tip of a knife jabbed his finger as that thought took hold. The women he loved. He loved Hannah.

J.T. stuck his pricked finger into his mouth to stem the trickle of blood, then dunked it back in the water.

Father had always warned him that love made a man do crazy things. He'd been right. Two able-bodied women were currently under his roof, yet *he* was the one doing the dishes.

CHAPTER 28

"Did he kiss you?"

Hannah sighed and pressed her shoulder blades into the closed door, wishing she could give an affirmative answer to that question. "We're supposed to be talking about you, remember?"

Cordelia tucked a leg beneath her and sat on the bed. She bounced on the mattress and grinned. "Well, did he?"

Hannah couldn't quite meet Cordelia's eye. "Almost."

Her friend moaned and flopped backward on the bed. "I should have put up with Warren for a few more minutes."

Yes, Hannah's heart cried, but her mind knew better. She moved to the bed and sat on the corner next to her recumbent friend. "Of course not. Now, tell me how things went out there."

Cordelia rolled onto her side to face Hannah. "Some good, some bad. He apologized for waiting so long to tell me of his feelings and then springing them on me without any warning." She fiddled with a button on the front of her dress. "We reminisced a little, which was nice, but then he showed me the ring he'd picked out from his father's store. I panicked."

"Did he propose again?"

"I didn't let him." She finally looked up. "Oh, Hannah, I didn't want to hurt him. I thanked him for being a good friend to me, but he kept shoving that ring in my face as if it would change my mind. I worried that if I didn't escape soon, he would seize my hand and force it onto my finger against my will. I scurried toward the door, said that I was sorry, but I didn't love him the way a wife should love a husband, wished him a good night, and retreated into the house, leaving him out on the porch all by himself." She flopped onto her back and covered her eyes with her arm. "I've never been so rude to anyone in all my life. I feel horrible about it."

"Well, don't." Hannah drew Cordelia's arm away from her face and tugged her up into a sitting position. "Warren was much too forward. He frightened you. You had every right to flee. It would have been foolish not to."

Cordelia laid her head on Hannah's shoulder. "I was so afraid J.T. would storm out and beat Warren to a pulp. When I realized he'd been too hung up on you to even notice what happened, I counted my blessings. I may not want to marry Warren, but I'm not anxious to see him pulverized, either."

A tinge of guilt overshadowed Hannah's joy. What if Cordelia had truly been in trouble? She never would have forgiven herself if she had kept Jericho from intervening.

The thought must have shown on her face, for when Cordelia lifted her head, she gave Hannah a little swat on the arm. "Don't go blaming yourself for anything. If I had needed J.T.'s help, I would have made enough noise to catch his attention. He was distracted, not deaf."

"Just the same, I'm glad you won't have to deal with Warren any longer. He won't continue pursuing you, will he?"

"No. He's not the type to ignore my wishes. He might sulk for a while, and I wouldn't be surprised if he stopped speaking to me, but things will clear up between us eventually. They always do."

"Well, then." Hannah squeezed Cordelia's hand. "Let's put Warren out of our minds for now and focus on Ike, shall we?"

Cordelia grinned and bobbed her head in agreement.

"Founders' Day is only a week away. You and Ike will be together for an entire afternoon. A new dress, a shared picnic, a chance to sneak away from the crowd to talk and possibly even share a kiss."

"If only I could be so lucky."

"We're not going to wait on luck." Hannah arched her brow and gave Cordelia a conspiratorial wink.

"What's dancing around in that mind of yours, Hannah Richards?"

"I might not be able to make Ike kiss you, but I have a plan to ensure he gets a window of opportunity should he wish to try."

༺༻

Founders' Day arrived, and J.T. found himself in the kitchen again, this time fetching and carrying for his sister.

"Place the two covered dishes in the first crate and the stockpot full of fried chicken in the second while I finish up these deviled eggs." Her skirt billowed out behind her as she dashed about the room, turning in circles fast enough to make him dizzy.

"What's in the covered dishes?" He thought of just lifting the lids and seeing for himself, but when Delia was in a tizzy, one didn't touch her food unless he was ready for a smack from a wooden spoon or some other handy utensil. There were too many knives within her reach for him to tempt fate.

"Carrot salad in one, potato in the other." She didn't spare him a glance as she mashed boiled egg yolks with the back of a silver spoon. "You also need to pack two jars of my pickles. One sweet. One dill."

J.T. lugged the heavy dishes to the waiting crates. "You sure you got enough food, sis?"

Delia stopped mashing her yolks for a second and bit her lip. "Maybe not. With Louisa and her brood joining us, as well . . . I thought I had enough, but . . . Better throw in an extra loaf of bread and some apple butter."

"I was kidding." J.T. chuckled and shook his head at her. "You have enough here to feed the entire town. It's a good thing no one rented the General. We'll need that freight wagon to haul all this stuff to the mill pond. Besides, Hannah and Louisa are contributing, too."

She glared at him. "Just the same, add the apple butter. I already have two bread loaves packed in the basket with the pound cake and cookies. Hannah is bringing a batch of biscuits and preserves, so we probably won't need the extra loaf. Louisa said she'd bring sliced ham sandwiches to go with the chicken."

He dug out the jar of apple butter and carried the crates and bread basket out to the wagon. When he returned, Delia had the egg halves back together and skewered with a mess of his toothpicks. She piled them in a small pail and covered them with a checkered cloth. "Don't take this one out until we're ready to go, and then make sure to keep it out of the sun."

"Aye, Captain." J.T. took the pail from her and saluted.

She shoved him. "Stop it, you rascal. I need to get changed." Delia flounced past him, then stopped short. "Oh! I completely forgot about the tin plates, napkins, forks."

J.T. steered her back toward her room. "I'll gather all that stuff. Go get ready. At this rate, the activities are going to be half over before we get there."

With a reluctant nod, she headed off to change. She couldn't let him handle things completely, though, for every few minutes she shouted through the closed door for him to pack something else. A bread knife, the box of tumblers for the lemonade and cider that would be available, two or three old quilts, and on and on until he started to doubt they'd have any room left in the wagon for passengers.

Once everything was finally loaded, J.T. pulled his suit coat from the back of a kitchen chair and slipped his arms into the sleeves. It seemed backward to him to dress up in his Sunday best for a picnic, but women insisted on wearing their finest to these rare social events, and their men were expected to follow suit. He settled the wool coat on his shoulders, gave it a tug, and strode down the hall to rap on Delia's door. "Come on. You've primped enough. Ike's going to think you stood him up if we don't get a move on."

The hinges creaked as she eased the door open. Delia took a tentative step, then bit her lip and ran a hand down the front of her dress. "I feel like I'm a little girl again, dressing up in Mama's clothes. Do I look ridiculous?"

J.T. couldn't speak. He just stared at the lovely woman his sister had become, wondering how he could have missed seeing it until this moment. The dress's green fabric warmed her complexion and brought her face to life. At the same time, the tailored top and striped skirt flattered her figure, nipping in at her newly trim waist and hinting at the curves that remained beneath. She'd even refashioned her bonnet, adding a green ribbon and delicate sprigs of flowers. Hannah had brought the butterfly out of her cocoon. A little color, a sophisticated design, and several weeks of friendship and encouragement had turned a plain Delia into a rare beauty.

He held his hand out to her and led her into the hall so he could make a circle around her. When he faced her again, he leaned in and kissed her cheek. "You look stunning, Delia. Truly. Not even our mother could compare."

"Do you think Ike will approve?"

Offering Delia his arm, J.T. swallowed his guffaw. "Darlin', I doubt he'll be able to take his eyes off of you long enough to do much else."

Seeing her face light up in pleasure warmed J.T.'s heart. He had kept her a prisoner in those drab dresses for too long. Come Christmas, he'd buy her lengths of cloth in sunshine yellow, bluebonnet blue, and prairie grass green to replace her navy, brown, and gray housedresses. Practical could still be pretty.

And wouldn't Hannah laugh her hat off if she ever heard him say such a thing.

They closed up the house and headed to Louisa's place. The three kids whooped and danced about as J.T. turned the wagon and parked in front of the laundry. Louisa scolded them halfheartedly, unable to keep her smile at bay. Their contagious excitement soon infected them all.

J.T. took her basket laden with still more food and packed it away with the rest of the feast while Louisa fussed over Delia's new dress and shared tips on how best to clean the lightweight wool fabric. The kids scrambled into the bed of the wagon, eager to be on their way. As J.T. rearranged things to maximize space, Tessa jumped to her feet and waved vigorously.

"Miss Hannah! Miss Hannah! Are you ready for the picnic?"

A low laugh sounded behind him. "I most certainly am. And I brought something for all of us to play with after the games are through."

J.T. turned to greet her as the kids clamored for her to show them the surprise that her left hand secreted behind her flowing skirts. He didn't recognize the wine-colored dress she wore, but it did a marvelous job of accentuating her slim figure and setting off her pale hair. The design was simple and almost plain in comparison to

Delia's, yet she carried it with such elegance that, to him, she looked like a queen.

Hannah glanced at him as she neared his side and offered a secret smile that immediately set his mind on kisses and long private walks.

"If Mr. Tucker would be so good as to take this pie for me, I'll show you what I brought."

He reached beneath the pie plate in her right hand and grazed her fingers. Making a show of holding the dessert to his nose, he drew whisper-soft circles on the back of her wrist. "Mmmm. Smells like apple." Then he tilted his head to meet her gaze. "I can't wait for a taste."

Fire rose in her cheeks, and she snatched her hand away so fast he nearly dropped the pie. The basket hanging from the crook of her right elbow swung precariously until she steadied it with her hip. She straightened her arm and angled it downward until the handle of the basket slipped into her hand. Then she thrust it at him with a chiding glance that made him laugh.

Throughout it all, she kept her surprise safely out of the children's view with her opposite arm. Stepping away from him, she pulled it out from behind her skirts with a flourish.

"A kite!" Tessa hopped up and down, clapping her hands. The wagon creaked in protest, but no one seemed to care. "And you used the pretty material I like so much. Can I fly it first?"

Danny shot to his feet. "I'm the oldest. I should go first."

"What about me?" Mollie whined.

Hannah grinned at the children. "Everyone will get a turn. I promise." Then her eyes narrowed. "But the next person who asks to go first will wait the longest."

Each little mouth closed, and all three youngsters plopped back down on their bottoms. J.T. was duly impressed.

Reaching around her, he wedged the pie into a protected corner and found a place for the basket, as well. He pivoted back to Hannah and held his palm out. "Your kite, milady?"

She curtsied and handed it to him. "Why, thank you, Sir Tucker. Take care, though. The fabric is wont to snag."

J.T. bowed in return, and the children giggled at their antics. The fabric in question was a rich violet hue that shimmered in the sunlight. He ran his finger across the kite's diamond-shaped body. Its smooth, luxurious texture surprised him.

"Is this silk?" he whispered in her ear.

"Just a small piece." She kept smiling at the children as she spoke to him out of the corner of her mouth. "Tessa has admired that cloth for weeks. This way she can enjoy it."

It had to be one of the most expensive fabrics she carried in her shop, yet she'd made it into a kite to please an eight-year-old girl. "You know it'll probably just get hung up in a tree, right?"

"I certainly hope so." This time she turned her smile on him. "Half the fun of kite flying is rescuing them when they go astray."

Her frolicsome spirit charmed him, heightening his anticipation of spending the day with her.

"All right, everyone," he announced in a loud voice. "Load up. We've got a picnic to go to."

J.T. carefully balanced the kite frame between the bread and sandwich baskets while Louisa seated herself on the tailgate of the wagon, her feet dangling above the road.

"I'll sit back here with my young'uns," she said, waving off J.T.'s offer to ride up front. "That there driver's seat will be crowded enough without me trying to cram in, too."

J.T. tipped his hat to her and made his way to the other ladies waiting patiently for his assistance. He made sure to hand Hannah up first so she could sit next to him. Settling beside her, glad for the tight quarters as his leg pressed against hers, he took up the reins and released the brake. "Everybody ready?"

A chorus of affirmative responses rang out, the women in the front equaling the volume of the kids in the rear. Grinning like a kid himself, J.T. snapped the leather straps and set the vehicle in motion. Something told him this would be a Founders' Day he'd not soon forget.

CHAPTER 29

Thanks to the group's high spirits, Hannah didn't think about their need to cross the river at the ill-fated bridge until it was upon them. She tried to hide her unease beneath a pasted-on smile, but Jericho must have felt her tension, for he took her hand and hooked it under his arm before they reached the wooden structure. Grateful to have something solid to hold on to, and equally grateful that he had the good sense to keep both hands on the reins, Hannah gripped his bicep, comforted by the undeniable strength of the muscle beneath her fingers.

The wheels rolled onto the bridge planks, making a series of hollow thumps. The kids chattered, wind strummed through the river birch leaves, and the horses' hooves clip-clopped in a blend of sound that would have brought a sense of peaceful harmony to any other listener. Yet the roar in Hannah's memory drowned out the gentle song. Her hold on Jericho's arm tightened.

She knew she was being foolish. The river had receded. It was no more threatening than a tub of bathwater. Nevertheless, that logic failed to drive out her fear.

Jericho hugged her hand to his side by squeezing his arm against his ribcage, which helped a bit, but when he started humming, she finally began to relax. The low vibrations calmed and soothed her, and the odd thought that he probably used the same technique on his nervous mares made her lips twitch in genuine amusement. The deep melody of "Rock of Ages" moved through her like hot chocolate, warming her spirit and restoring her equilibrium. Jericho sat solid at her side, but there was another who offered an even greater security, and it was that reminder, more than the soothing hum of the music, that finally banished her fear.

As they returned to the road, Hannah slid her hand out from Jericho's arm. He turned and frowned at her, pointedly looking at her hand as if to chastise it for abandoning its post. She smiled at him and mouthed the words *Thank you*. He winked, then refocused his attention on driving.

They turned north and followed the river until they came upon a glen overflowing with wagons, buggies, and more people than Hannah had ever seen in Coventry at one time. Men tossed horseshoes while women tended babies and visited with neighbors. Girls rolled barrel hoops across the open prairie, and boys chased each other around the grounds while trying to snitch food when their mothers weren't looking. Old folks sat in the shade of the limestone grist mill near the edge of the river and oversaw the distribution of lemonade and cider from the large jugs and kegs available on a sawhorse table sheltered by the east wall.

Hannah struggled to take everything in as the wagon bumped off the road and moved toward an oak tree that would offer the horses and picnickers a touch of shade. "Is the entire county here?" she asked as the General waggled over a particularly uneven stretch of terrain. Stuck in the middle with no handle to grab for balance, she alternated pitching into Jericho and Cordelia until Jericho wrapped his arm around her shoulders and anchored her to his side.

"No, only about a third of the county shows up for Coventry's Founders' Day celebration." Jericho glanced down at her, and Hannah blinked. In the cozy pocket beneath his arm, she'd forgotten she'd even asked the question. "Meridian is the county seat, so most go to their events, but we get farmers and ranchers from within a ten-mile radius or so."

The ground flattened out again as they neared the tree, yet Jericho made no move to release his hold on her. Not that Hannah minded. Well, she minded the amused glances Cordelia kept shooting at her, but she discovered that if she leaned her head slightly into Jericho's chest, she no longer saw them.

All too soon, though, Jericho pulled the rig to a halt. "We're here!"

His announcement was met with squeals of delight and clunking footfalls as the James children scampered out of the wagon bed.

"Stay where I can see you," Louisa warned as the youngsters ran to join their friends.

Jericho got out and circled the wagon to help Cordelia alight, then reached for Hannah. His hands lingered at her waist longer than they had on his sister, and a secret little thrill coursed through her. He graced her with one of his rare, glorious smiles that turned her bones to jelly and then left her in her wobbly state in order to unload the mountain of food Cordelia had packed. It took two large breaths and a stern mental lecture on the fortitude of the Richards women before Hannah's bones stiffened enough to allow her to assist the others.

Louisa spread the quilts out and secured them against the wind with rocks and some of the larger food dishes while Jericho took care of the horses. Cordelia shuffled food back and forth, emptying baskets and organizing everything. Not wanting to interfere with her system, Hannah opted to play it safe and unpack the plates and utensils. As she stacked the forks on top of a pile of bleached linen napkins, she caught a glimpse of Jericho walking toward the group of men congregated at a sandy patch of ground that served as the horseshoe pit.

She admired his confident stride and the way the group eagerly welcomed him into their midst. He was a man a woman would take pride in calling husband. And despite the fact that she had no legal claim to him yet, the possessiveness surging through her veins was undeniable.

Like a cowboy working a herd, Jericho wove in and out of the group until he culled out the steer he wanted. Then with a wave, he and the slightly shorter man departed. She couldn't make out the other fellow's features from this distance, but there was no doubt of his identity.

Pushing aside the box of tumblers she had just opened, Hannah turned to warn Cordelia. In an effort to lay everything out to perfection, she was bent at the waist, painstakingly arranging deviled egg halves in the shape of a daisy on a round platter. The eggs were lovely, but Hannah feared Ike would be too undone by the sight of Cordelia's upended back end to notice. Not exactly the first impression they had envisioned for this all-important day.

Hannah rushed to her friend's side and tried to straighten her posture.

"Just a minute." Cordelia resisted Hannah's efforts, all those exercises lending her an inconvenient amount of strength. "I only have two more—"

"He's coming," Hannah hissed in her ear. "You don't want to greet your beloved with your bum in the air, do you?"

Cordelia popped up so fast, Hannah had to dodge sideways to avoid a mouthful of bonnet. Her friend spun around, and when she spotted the two men closing in, she started wringing her hands in front of her.

"Ike's coming." The dullness of her voice worried Hannah.

"Yes, dear." Hannah smiled and reshaped an uneven pleat in the gathered fabric that draped delicately over Cordelia's hips.

"What do I do? What do I say?" The girl's eyes remained fixed on Ike, but all the color drained from her face. Her fainting into the carrot salad seemed a very real threat.

Hannah stepped in front of her friend and deliberately positioned herself to block Cordelia's view of Ike. "This is just like any other day when you bring him lunch. You will smile and chat as you always do. You will act as if nothing is different, for truly nothing of importance is. The only thing you've changed is your clothes."

"Nothing's different," Cordelia chanted under her breath.

Hearing the men's footsteps behind her, Hannah modeled a bright smile, holding it in place until Cordelia matched it with one of her own. Then swinging wide like a book cover revealing the tantalizing first page of a love story, Hannah moved aside.

No one spoke for several heartbeats. Ike stared at Cordelia, his mouth slightly agape and his brows arched higher than the windows of a London cathedral. Cordelia's smile had slipped to a crooked angle, but she had plenty of color in her cheeks now.

A throat cleared behind them. Louisa sidled past. "I'm gonna go fetch my young'uns."

Ike finally snapped out of his stupor and dragged his hat off his head. "Thank you for inviting me to join you, Miss Tucker. I can't imagine a place I'd rather be."

Cordelia ducked her head for only a moment before bringing her chin back up. Seeing that hard-won confidence at work, Hannah's heart cheered.

"I made several of your favorites," Cordelia said, gesturing toward the blankets. "Fried chicken, potato salad . . . oh, and pound cake."

"My mouth is watering already. May I help you lay out the food?"

Cordelia hesitated. "Well, Hannah has—"

"—been waiting for a chance to scout out a suitable place for kite flying." Hannah gave Cordelia a pointed look before turning her attention to Ike. "If you don't mind taking over for me, Mr. Franklin. I plan to take the James children kite flying after we eat, and knowing which direction to go would save time and hopefully keep any squabbling to a minimum."

Ike chuckled. "I would be more than willing to lend Cori . . . er . . . I mean . . . Miss Tucker a hand."

The poor man's face turned a vivid shade of red, but Hannah could not have been more pleased. A man who gave a woman a pet name, even unintentionally, must surely be smitten.

"Thank you. We'll be back shortly." Hannah tugged on Jericho's arm.

He cocked a brow at her. "We? I'm not going anywhere."

Ike swallowed and reached for the edge of his collar.

"Of course you are," Hannah declared with forced brightness. "I need your expertise. I'm completely unfamiliar with this area. Please?" As unobtrusively as she could, she slid her foot atop his and ground her heel into his toe. His frown held steady as he glared at Ike. Not even a wince. *Drat.* His boots were probably too thick. How was she supposed to signal him to stop his overbearing brother routine if she couldn't get his attention? She was debating whether or not to pinch the back of his arm when he surprised her by capitulating.

"Fifteen minutes," he grumbled, and stalked off toward the river.

"Thank you!" Hannah raised her voice, yet Jericho gave no indication that he heard her. She shrugged. "I guess he's eager to start the search."

"Or eager to get back," Ike mumbled.

Hannah bent close to him. "Well, I bought you fifteen minutes. Make good use of it."

His startled eyes shot to hers, and then a grin stole over his features. "An excellent notion, Miss Richards."

"What's an excellent notion?" Cordelia looked as if she wanted to crawl into a hole. Either that or bury her brother in one.

Hannah winked at her. "I'll let Ike explain." Then she dashed after Jericho.

When she caught up to him, he started limping. Dramatically.

"What were you trying to do back there, woman? Cripple me?"

She would have felt more guilt if the hitch in his step hadn't materialized out of thin air. "What were *you* trying to do? Ruin Cordelia's courtship?"

"I was just setting some boundaries." His limp miraculously disappeared.

"Well, you didn't have to scowl so fiercely while you did it."

A mischievous twinkle lit his eyes. "Nope. That was purely for fun."

"Jericho Tucker." She meant to scold him, but the laughter bubbling out of her throat got in the way. "You're terrible."

"Not always." His eyes changed. Their sparkle melted into a heated glow that made her insides flutter. He drew a line down her arm from her shoulder to her wrist and clasped her hand, weaving his fingers between hers. "Hannah, I—"

"J.T.!" A huffing Tom jogged up to them.

Jericho dropped her hand. A chill passed through her as the wind erased the warmth of his grip.

"I signed us up for the three-legged race. The Harris brothers think they can beat us this year, but I told 'em not to get their hopes up." Tom glanced over at Hannah and grinned. "We ain't been beat in three years, not since my legs grew long enough to keep up with his." He thrust his thumb at Jericho, who was doing an admirable job of hiding his disgruntlement over the untimely interruption.

Hannah tried to do the same, but as Jericho turned the conversation to kite flying and the best location for such sport, she bit her lip in frustration.

Five minutes. If Tom had taken just five minutes longer to find them, Jericho would have told her . . . told her . . . well . . . something important—she was sure of it. She had felt the significance of the moment all the way down to her toes. Now all her toes felt were the pebbles that poked against the soles of her shoes as they made their way back to the picnic.

CHAPTER 30

The day was too fine for Hannah to let regrets weigh her down for long. Food, however, was a different story. She couldn't remember ever having eaten so much. Hoping to walk off the lethargy that tempted her to lie on the quilt and nap in the sunshine, she let Tessa talk her into a game of graces.

Margaret Paxton, the banker's wife, had brought a crate full of supplies for the game, and several pairs of young ladies loitered near the mill testing their skill. Tessa skipped up to the box and selected a set of dowel rods for each of them.

"What color hoop should we use?" she asked when Hannah caught up to her.

Each of the wooden circles, about the size of a large embroidery hoop, had been decorated with different colored ribbons.

Hannah peered into the box. Three hoops remained: red and white, green and yellow, or brown and orange. "You pick. Just not the orange one." She scrunched up her nose and Tessa giggled. They had long ago agreed that orange was only attractive on round fruit, wildflowers, and butterflies.

Opting for the red and white, Tessa held it away from her and ran to her position a couple yards away, letting the ribbon tails stream out behind her. She hung the hoop over the end of one dowel, then brought the tip of the second into the circle, crossing the two sticks to form an X.

"Ready?"

Hannah nodded and stepped out with one leg to broaden her stance. "Ready."

In a quick motion, Tessa flung her arms up and out, uncrossing the dowels. The hoop flew through the air. The object of the game was for Hannah to catch it on both her rods, but Tessa's throw was short and the wind was tugging the hoop to the left. Too much of a competitor to let the hoop fall to the ground, Hannah grabbed a handful of her skirt and dashed forward. Like a fencer brandishing a foil, she stabbed her dowel through the center of the beribboned hoop and snatched it out of the air.

"Yay!" Tessa cried. "Good catch, Miss Hannah. Nine more and you win!"

She was ahead seven to five when Cordelia and Ike strolled by to watch. Her hand tucked securely into the crook of Ike's arm, Cordelia was beaming. Hannah smiled as the couple passed, so caught up in her friend's happiness that Tessa's next shot arched over her head before she even realized it had been launched.

"Ha! You missed. My turn."

Hannah used her rod to retrieve the hoop from the ground. "All right, you little imp. See if you can catch this one." Hannah sailed it a bit higher than usual, but Tessa got under it and made the snag.

"I did it!" She jumped and gave a little whoop of glee, earning a smile from Mrs. Paxton, who had just refilled her lemonade glass.

"A fine catch, Tessa," the banker's wife said. "But remember, this is a game of elegance and poise, not a rough-and-tumble sport."

Hannah couldn't help wondering if the gentle reproof wasn't as much for her as Tessa. None of the other girls were playing with the same degree of zealousness. Of course, none of the others seemed to be having half as much fun, either. Nevertheless, she supposed she ought to set a more decorous example for her young protégée. Especially with a lady like Margaret Paxton looking on. The woman exuded class and sophistication. All without ever making one feel inferior. It was quite a remarkable talent and surely stemmed from a humble spirit. She would be the ideal client for a dressmaker who longed to promote a balance between inner and outer beauty.

The red hoop sailing toward her head snapped Hannah out of her preoccupation. She leapt backward and raised her sticks at the last minute, deflecting it before it collided with her chin. Unfortunately, she was not deft enough to catch it, only knock it to the ground. Tessa laughed as Hannah retrieved the hoop. The sound was so playful and jolly, though, Hannah couldn't help but smile. She flung the hoop back into the air, and the girl caught it easily.

"Better watch out, Miss Hannah. We're all tied up now."

"So you think you can beat me, do you?" Hannah waved her sticks at Tessa. "Give me your best shot."

In her enthusiasm, Tessa lofted the hoop high and dangerously off course. It veered to the right, directly toward the spot where Cordelia had stopped to chat with Mrs. Paxton. Hannah bolted after it, but she knew she'd never get there in time.

"Look out!" she cried.

Mrs. Paxton turned, and with a skill unexpected in one so genteel, caught the hoop with one hand and flicked her wrist to send it back to Tessa in a perfect arc.

Hannah stuttered to a halt and stared.

"Bravo, my dear!" Elliott Paxton called out from his seat near the cider table. "Just like the old days, eh, Maggie?"

Pink streaks appeared across the lady's cheeks as she waved away her husband's comment, but she turned to Hannah with a welcoming smile.

"Don't look so surprised, Miss Richards," she said. "I haven't always been a staid banker's wife."

Hannah grinned.

"I was just complimenting Miss Tucker on her beautiful new dress," Mrs. Paxton said, expertly shifting the subject away from herself. "The change in her is extraordinary, and she tells me that you are the one responsible for it."

Excitement fluttered in Hannah's stomach. The lady admired her work.

"Cordelia's been a lovely client. She has a wonderful eye for fashion, as you can see in the colors she selected."

"And you have a wonderful skill with a needle to craft such a becoming design."

Cordelia nodded, her eyes bright as they slid from Hannah to Mrs. Paxton. "Oh, yes. Miss Richards tailors everything to perfection. I doubt you could find a better dressmaker in all of Texas."

The banker's wife gave Cordelia's polonaise and skirt another perusal, then assessed the one Hannah wore. "I usually have Elliott drive me to Waco when the girls and I need new gowns, but now that Coventry has a qualified seamstress, I may have to forfeit those shopping trips and invest our funds closer to home."

Fireworks of glee exploded inside Hannah's chest, but she forced her features into a serene expression. "I would be glad to assist you, Mrs. Paxton. Please stop by the shop at any time."

"Thank you. I just might do that."

At that moment, Tessa ran up, grabbed Hannah's hand, and started tugging her toward the center of the glen. "Come on, Miss Hannah. The race is about to start. We've got to cheer on Tom and Mr. Tucker!"

"Tessa, it's not polite to interrupt."

The little girl's face looked properly contrite . . . for all of two seconds. "I'm sorry, but this is important. We don't want to miss it."

No, they didn't. Hannah surveyed the grounds, searching for Jericho in the crowd of men and boys who were lining up at the start. Her heart longed to be at the race; however, responsible business practices dictated she not rush off and risk offending an important potential client.

"Oh my. We can't have you miss the excitement." Mrs. Paxton's hand closed over the end of Hannah's dowel rods, graciously solving her dilemma. "Let me put these away for you."

"Thank you, ma'am," Hannah said.

"Hurry on, now. You don't want to miss the start."

Hannah gave Tessa's arm a little shake. "Let's go." The girl took off, dragging Hannah behind her. Hoping that Tessa's enthusiasm would rate as an adequate excuse for her own hurried pace, Hannah did nothing to slow the girl down. The sooner they got there, the better.

J.T. toed the imaginary starting line, one arm behind Tom's back as the partners gripped each other's shoulders for balance. The Harris brothers stood two pairs down, shooting taunting looks J.T.'s way as the judge inspected the bandanna tied around his and Tom's ankles. Will and Archie would be the only real competition. Most teams consisted of kids or young men with their sweethearts. Fellows typically cajoled their gals into participating just to have an excuse to wrap their arms around them. Such pairings always led to a surplus of silly giggling and quick tumbles.

Although J.T. had to admit that he'd much rather be holding on to Hannah right now than his stablehand. It might be worth a loss. Then again, recalling how hard she'd pushed when she'd challenged him to try those clubs and rings of hers, she might prove to be the toughest competitor of the lot. He wondered if being in a fashionable dress would slow her down at all. He grinned. Probably not.

"What's got you smiling, Tucker?" Will Harris called. "You looking forward to the view of my back as Archie and I breeze across the finish line?"

J.T. snorted. "The only way I'll see your back is if you fall flat on your face at the start. Otherwise, Tom and I will be too far ahead to see much of anything except victory."

Will raised his chin a notch. "Not this year."

The starter stepped into position in front of the racers, and the good-natured ribbing died. A blue bandanna fluttered at the end of his hand.

Having removed his coat for the event, J.T. relished the breeze that fluttered his shirt sleeves. But he would not be distracted. He targeted the finish line. Tom's fingers dug into the muscles at his neck. Together they leaned forward, ready for the signal.

The starter's arm shot straight up, brandishing that blue kerchief like a flag on a pole. "On your mark!" he shouted. "Get set . . . Go!"

His arm dropped and the hobbled racers surged onto the course. Several pairs stumbled as soon as they began, but J.T. paid them no mind. He focused on the ground ahead, alert for any dip or hole that could derail his team as they gradually increased their pace to an uneven hop-jog gait.

Cheers rang out from the sidelines, and for a moment, J.T. wished Hannah hadn't been off playing with Tessa when the racers were called to the field. It was a trivial fair game, not a true athletic contest, but even so, a man liked to have the support of his woman when competing against other males. How else did one get the chance to impress her? Hearing tales of his prowess after the fact never inspired the same degree of awe as firsthand experience.

They reached the halfway point, and J.T. glanced to the side. The Harris brothers were running neck-and-neck with them. The crowd's cheers narrowed to the two front teams. Calls for Tom and J.T. mingled with equal enthusiasm for Will and Archie. But then a different name came through, a name only one person of his acquaintance ever used.

"Go, Jericho!"

His head shot up, and he searched the crowd for Hannah's face.

Then his toe struck a rock, nearly sending him and Tom sprawling onto the ground.

"Watch out, J.T. They're gonna pass us."

Tom's strength steadied him as he turned his attention back to the race. A new fire blazed in his belly. There was no way he'd let Will Harris beat him if Hannah was watching.

"Let's take them on the hill."

Tom grunted his agreement.

The last few yards of the course sloped gently upward. It wasn't a hill, really. However, if a team tried to take it too fast, the slight rise could throw them off balance. J.T. had always approached it with caution in the past, but today he planned to attack it like a renegade Apache.

He sped up his metronomic exhalations and their footsteps followed. They pulled a couple steps ahead. Then their balance faltered. They leaned forward, fighting the momentum. They stumbled. The ground rushed up to meet them. With a mighty lunge, they crossed the line and crashed into the earth.

"Tucker and Packard," the announcer shouted. "By a nose."

Hurrahs erupted from the spectators. J.T. rolled onto his back still tethered to Tom. His chest heaved, his knee ached from where he'd landed on it, but he didn't care about the pain. He'd won.

Tom untied the bandanna around their ankles and scrambled to his feet. "We did it, J.T. We did it!"

"Yep" was all J.T. could manage.

Will Harris strode over and extended a hand. "You might've won, Tucker, but at least Archie and I kept our feet. It was worth coming in second just to see you two tripping all over yourselves like that."

J.T. clasped the fellow's wrist and let him help him to his feet. He chuckled ruefully as he dusted the dirt from his trousers. "If you'll promise to put on as good a show next year, I'd consider playing second fiddle myself."

Will grinned. "No promises, Tuck—"

Before the man could finish spitting out his words, a beautiful blonde whirlwind blew past him and launched herself at J.T.

"You won!"

He caught her around the waist and lifted her off her feet, her excitement revitalizing his tired body. She squealed and her smile nearly obliterated the sun as she threw her head back and exulted in the moment, uncaring that others looked on with avid curiosity.

Man, how he loved this woman.

"If I had known this was the prize, I would have fallen on my face to win, too." Will's dry comment brought a blush to Hannah's cheeks, and she straightened her bent legs back toward the ground. J.T. set her down but kept his hand at her waist, staking a claim for all to see.

"Does that mean I get a turn holding her?" Tom asked, and for the first time, J.T. saw him as a man instead of a kid. It was a bit unnerving. Thankfully, Will interrupted.

"I don't think Tucker wants to share, Tom." The men standing around snickered.

"Well, that don't seem fair. I won, too."

"Yes, you did." Hannah stepped away from J.T.'s hold, and he had to grit his teeth to stop himself from grabbing her back. She walked over to Tom and placed a chaste kiss on his cheek. "Congratulations, Tom."

A silly grin spread across his face. "I gotta go tell Ma!" He lumbered off, once again fully the kid his underdeveloped mind dictated that he be.

"So what's the prize for second?" Will asked, looking more at J.T. than Hannah.

J.T. glared at his audacious question, which only made Will grin more. Taking Hannah's hand, J.T. started leading her away. "Sorry, fellas. You'll have to find your own prize. This one's mine."

CHAPTER 31

Hannah followed Jericho, eager to escape the men's teasing. Once they separated themselves from the group, the Harris brothers faded from her mind and she became consumed by the way Jericho's warm hand enveloped hers. Strong, capable, protective. And at that moment, connected. To her.

Jericho slowed his pace to a stroll. His callused palm rubbed against her smoother skin, creating a delicious friction that tingled up her arm. He stroked the back of her hand with his thumb and angled his face toward her, curling his lips in the hint of a smile. Hannah's heart thumped heavy and hard. Conscious of the picnic activity around them, she shied away from the heat of his gaze and focused instead on the dips and ruts of the ground. But she had never been more aware of the man at her side.

"I'm sorry I caused such a scene back there," she said, needing to do something to diffuse her growing restlessness. "I didn't intend to throw myself at you, I promise. It just sort of . . . happened."

Jericho tugged her to a halt. "Darlin', you can throw yourself into my arms anytime you like." His tawny eyes shone with humor . . . and something deeper that made her breath quiver. "I promise I'll always catch you." The soft, husky tone of his voice vibrated through her and left her wanting to hide away with him somewhere and explore the meaning behind his words. But she couldn't. She had a kite to fly and children to entertain.

"We should get back," she said, dipping her chin.

Jericho released her hand and cleared his throat. "Tom showed me a good place for kite flying. It's upriver a little ways but easy to get to." He placed his hand at the small of her back and guided her toward the wagon.

Grateful for the ordinary conversation, she tried to subdue her bucking emotions. "That sounds lovely. I'm sure the children will be pleased."

She and Jericho lapsed into silence as they walked across the glen. Hannah glanced his way and caught him staring, the look in his eyes hinting at things unsaid. Her pulse flittered. Would he finish the conversation he had started earlier that day, before Tom had interrupted them?

Hannah held her breath, aching with the need for him to declare his feelings. His warm regard revealed his attraction, and his possessiveness had been evident as he staked his claim in front of the Harris brothers. Yet she longed for the words, for the assurance that she had, indeed, penetrated his heart as he had penetrated hers. Had Jericho grown to care enough for her that he would be willing to set aside his past hurts and tie himself to a dressmaker for the rest of his days? She stole another peek at him, her chest tight with hope. But he looked to the ground without speaking, and her breath leaked out in disappointment.

Grant me patience, Lord. You have promised that things work together for good for those that love you, and whether that good entails a life with Jericho or not, I will trust in your faithfulness. She tried to stop there, but a desire tugged on her soul that wouldn't be denied. She couldn't let the prayer go without at least presenting the request that burned within her. *I love him, Lord. I love him with all my heart. Please grant me a future with this man. Please.*

With a quiet sigh, Hannah released her worry and welcomed the lightness that followed. The sun glowed in the sky, a cool breeze tickled her cheeks, and children's laughter filled the air. It was a beautiful day, a day made for rejoicing. She wouldn't ruin it with unproductive frets.

As Jericho steered her toward their picnic spot, Tessa spotted the children and grabbed the kite from where it had been propped against the tree. She hopped up and down on her toes and waved at them to hurry.

Hannah's feet slowed. "Oh no."

Jericho turned to her. "What?"

"I have no idea how to choose who goes first. They've all been so good. Any suggestions?"

The question hung between them for a split second, as if Jericho couldn't quite believe she was asking him for advice, but in a flash, the glimmer of surprise on his face disappeared beneath his customary confidence. She even detected a swagger in his step as he urged her forward.

"I think I can come up with something that will work."

And he did. A game of short straws, or toothpicks in this case, determined the order. Ike volunteered to help Cordelia pack up the leftover food and supplies, which allowed Louisa to join the kite-flying expedition. Mother and children ran ahead, but Jericho stalled, taking extra time to fold his coat into a lopsided square and lay it on the blanket.

An exasperated Cordelia shot Hannah a pleading look. Hannah deciphered the hint and dragged Jericho away. As they walked, he glanced over his shoulder more than once and grumbled about the folly of leaving his sister alone with Ike when he couldn't keep an eye on them.

Hannah gave him a little swat on the arm. "Leave them be, Jericho.

Half the town will be chaperoning them while you're gone. Besides, I think you can trust Ike not to take advantage of your sister," she said. "Just as I trust you."

His lips thinned, but he gave a firm nod. "You're right."

They lengthened their stride to catch up to the James family. As they closed the gap, however, Jericho bent close one more time. "I'm still gonna glare and growl at him, though, to keep him on the straight and narrow until he puts a ring on Delia's finger. Maybe even after."

Hannah smiled. "I wouldn't expect anything less."

The wind proved perfect for kite flying. Each child took a turn holding the string, but young Mollie had trouble keeping the purple diamond aloft. After the third crash, Hannah took charge. Running the length of the clearing with the James children chasing after her, she lofted the kite into the air and sent it soaring. Dangerously out of breath, she handed the spool to Mollie and motioned for Tessa to give her sister a hand while she braced her arm against a tree for support. A wave of dizziness assailed her as her chest heaved.

"You should've asked me to do the running," a low voice grumbled at her side. "You're about to pass out."

"I . . . am . . . not." Somehow she managed to spit out the words between gasps.

Jericho took her arm, but she pulled away, mortified by her condition. She should have been able to run twice that distance without getting winded. Of course, she didn't usually exercise while wearing a corset and twenty pounds of fashionable garb.

"Stubborn woman." Jericho glowered. "Once in a while it'd be nice if you actually admitted that you need my help." He left her standing at the base of that tree with a queasy feeling in her stomach.

She'd hurt him. It'd been there in his eyes. He thought she didn't need him, but nothing could be further from the truth. She needed him so much, she ached with it. But how was he to know that?

Slowly, Hannah's lungs regained a calm rhythm and her mind cleared. She hated appearing weak. All the pitying glances she'd endured after her swimming accident as a child were enough to last a lifetime. When her mother had brought home Dr. Lewis's book and started her on his calisthenic regimen, Hannah had vowed to regain her strength no matter the cost. And she had. Never quitting once, not even when her lungs burned as if she had breathed in a thousand tiny embers or when muscle cramps woke her from a sound sleep, sending teary rivulets down her cheeks as she bit on her pillow to contain her cries. She took pride in her hard-won physical strength. Yet that pride had just pushed the man she loved away.

Jericho was right. She *was* stubborn. Foolish, too.

Determined to rejoin the group and find a way to privately apologize to Jericho, Hannah let go of the tree and stepped forward... directly into a prairie dog hole. Her heel caught, her ankle twisted, and she stumbled sideways into the prickly pear cactus plant that she'd been careful to avoid earlier. A pair of pointed spines pierced her skirt and inner layers to stab the tender flesh at the back of her thigh. With a yelp, she jumped forward, only to hear an ominous ripping noise from behind.

Hannah closed her eyes and moaned. Why did it have to be her new dress? Her right ankle throbbed, her thigh stung, and now her skirt was caught on a cactus. The Lord must've decided to help her get rid of that troublesome pride.

"Miss Hannah, come see!" Mollie called from a few yards away. "I'm flying it all by myself."

"You're doing great, sweetheart. I'll be there in just a minute." She waved to the happy gathering, but when Jericho turned to look at her, her hand fell back to her side. "Mr. Tucker? Might I prevail upon you for some assistance?"

He stared at her for what felt like ages without taking a single step in her direction. Then, finally, he trudged across the field, the suspicion lighting his eyes becoming less deniable the closer he came.

Jericho halted a couple feet away and questioned her with a raised eyebrow. Hannah swallowed. Her pride didn't go down easily.

CHAPTER 32

J.T. crossed his arms over his chest and waited. *She better not be patronizing me.* Just because he wanted her to admit that she needed help once in a while didn't mean he would stand for her manufacturing some ridiculous predicament in a half-baked attempt to placate him.

A heavy gust of wind billowed across them and Hannah teetered. She shifted her weight to compensate and winced.

He unlaced his arms and took a step forward. "You hurt?"

"Not badly." She tried to smile, but her lips only curved on one side. "My main problem is that I'm stuck to a cactus."

"Stuck to a—" A chortle escaped, obliterating the rest of his sentence. Reining in his laughter, he cupped her shoulders and pulled her forward a bit to judge the extent of the snare. Sure enough, she was stuck. One of the pleats that used to drape so delicately along the back of her skirt now listed gracelessly to the side, gouged by a wicked-looking spine. Several other spines had snagged the wine-colored fabric closer to the ground, as well.

"How'd you manage to get tangled up with a cactus?" J.T. crouched beside her and started extricating her from the prickly plant.

"Well, believe it or not, I was on my way to apologize to you when a prairie-dog hole jumped up and grabbed my shoe heel."

Her turn of phrase made him smile. But the story explained her wince. Probably sprained her ankle. He tugged the last piece of material free. "Shouldn't a seamstress know enough to avoid the sharp end of needles?"

"Oh, we seamstresses jab ourselves all the time, a hazard of the trade."

J.T. looked up at her then, meaning to tell her she'd been successfully detached, but he got lost in her smile and had to answer with one of his own. They stayed that way for a moment until Hannah blinked and twisted her neck as if trying to see the back of her dress.

"How bad does it look?"

It looked pretty good from where he sat. But J.T. figured she was referring to the dress, not the shapely curves beneath. He placed his hands on his knees and pushed to a stand. "There's a fair-sized hole where one of the flounces tore off. But you can't see your bloomers or nothing."

"Jericho!" Hannah's face flamed and J.T. chuckled. Man, but the woman was fun to tease.

He took her arm, thankful when she made no effort to pull away this time. "How's the ankle?"

"Tender but not too bad," she said as she limped along beside him. "I'm sure it will be fine after I rest a bit."

"I should take you home." J.T. wasn't ready for his day with her to end, but she needed to get that ankle propped up.

They approached a stand of mesquite that offered a bit of shade and slowed. Hannah turned to him, but her gaze moved past his shoulder to follow the children who were playing in the clearing behind him. "I wouldn't mind slipping out early to avoid the embarrassment of displaying a torn skirt, but I don't want the others to have to leave because of my mishap."

"Tom can ride back with us," J.T. said as he grasped her waist and hoisted her up onto a bent mesquite trunk that grew at a nearly horizontal angle. She gave a startled little squeal and grabbed his arms for support as he set her on the improvised bench. Her feet dangled a good eighteen inches above the ground, but at least she wouldn't have to stand. "He can drop us in town and drive the General back out here to pick up the rest of the group later."

"All right."

By this time, the kids had noticed Hannah's return and descended upon them with questions about why she was sitting in a tree.

After assuring everyone that Hannah was fine and leaving them strict orders not to let his prisoner escape while he was gone, J.T. hiked back to the picnic area, located Tom, and explained the situation to Delia. It took a while to hitch up the team and maneuver the General over the rough prairie ground, but he managed to fetch Hannah and the James clan back to the picnic without bumping anyone out or breaking an axle. J.T. dropped Louisa and the kids off with Delia and Ike, picked up Tom, and finally steered the rig toward town.

"You think I got time to get back before the square dancin' starts?" Tom called from the back of the wagon as J.T. pulled the General to a halt in front of Hannah's dress shop.

"I reckon so." He set the brake and climbed down, not surprised when Tom vaulted over the side to meet him and take up the reins. "They had just started setting up the plank floor when we were leaving. The fiddler hadn't even warmed up. You'll have time."

The kid loved a lively tune, and the whole town enjoyed watching his high-kicking antics as he promenaded his ma and any other gals he could get his hands on across the floor. Such vigorous enthusiasm always generated friendly laughter among the spectators, and if Tom got a little mixed up at the caller's instructions from time to time, no one minded. They'd just grin and point him in the right direction. It wouldn't be the same without him there.

J.T. reached up for Hannah and fit his hands to her waist as he lowered her to the street. He held her gaze for a moment. "The ankle holding up?"

She nodded, and he slowly released his grip, making sure she was steady before shifting his attention to Tom.

"Don't be in too big a hurry, son. Hold the team to a moderate pace. You'll get back in plenty of time."

"Yes, sir."

As soon as J.T. stepped away from the wheels, Tom had the General in motion. Shaking his head, J.T. chuckled under his breath. The kid was chomping at the bit more than the horses were.

He turned to share his smile with Hannah, but she wasn't looking at him. Lines marred her forehead as she stared at her shop. Coming alongside her, he linked his arm through hers. "What is it?"

She took a tentative step forward. "I don't know, but something's wrong."

He took a second look, narrowing his eyes to filter out the glare of the sun. He couldn't be sure at this distance, but the door to the shop looked slightly ajar. "Did you lock up before the picnic?"

"Yes."

Hannah pulled away from him and climbed onto the boardwalk. Instinct sent him after her. He clamped a hand on her arm and brought her to a halt.

"Wait. Give me your key."

She obeyed, a question on her face.

"Stay here while I check it out."

Suddenly, she was the one gripping *his* arm. "You don't think someone is in there, do you? I don't want you hurt."

He patted her hand where it lay across his forearm. "I'm sure it's nothing. Probably a flaw in the lock that kept it from latching all the way. I just want to make sure everything's safe before you go in. All right?"

She nodded and let go of his arm.

Senses on alert, J.T. approached the shop door. It was definitely ajar. He flattened his back against the wall, tucked Hannah's key into his trouser pocket, and ran his fingers along the edge of the doorjamb. Splinters where the wood had been damaged jabbed his skin. Someone had pried his way in.

He pressed the toe of his boot against the door and, in a swift move, flung it open. No gunshot or running footsteps broke the quiet, only the squeak of the hinges. Cautiously, J.T. leaned into the doorway. Whoever had intruded was long gone, but he had left an indelible impression behind in his absence. J.T.'s stomach churned, and bile rose in his throat.

Stepping over the threshold, he surveyed the damage. The shelves Hannah had so meticulously hung had been torn down. Bolts of fabric lay unwound and scattered upon the floor. Not only had the miscreant tossed the expensive material on the ground, but he had trod on it, crushing it beneath his heel in several places as evidenced by numerous dusty boot prints and crinkled sections of cloth. Thankfully, the sewing cabinet stood intact, but all of the drawers were missing. J.T. could only assume they'd been dumped somewhere behind the counter.

He balled his hands into fists, longing to mash them into the face of the person or people responsible for this attack.

A tiny tortured cry sounded behind him.

J.T. whirled. Hannah's wounded expression twisted his gut. "Come on," he murmured, forcing her leaden feet back toward the door. "I'll take you home. You don't need to see this right now." Seeing her shiver, he tucked her under his arm and steered her through the doorway. Her neck craned as they went, as if she were unable to pull her gaze away from the destruction. A fierce protectiveness surged within him. He would make this right for her. Somehow, he would fix it.

He grabbed hold of the door and moved to shut it, but Hannah's gasp stopped him. He lifted his head and saw what had distressed her. Tacked to the inside of the door was a note.

You never should have come.

CHAPTER 33

A chill snaked through Hannah as she read the ominous words. She would've felt better believing a group of unruly boys were responsible for this violation. Then the deed would have been random, impersonal. But the note destroyed that hope. Someone wanted her gone. Hannah wrapped her arms around her middle.

Jericho snatched the offending paper from the door, crumpled it into a ball, and hurled it into the depths of the shop. He steered Hannah onto the walkway, then slammed the door hard enough to shake the outer wall. Hannah flinched.

He stood with his back to her, the muscles in his shoulders twitching beneath his suspenders. She wanted him to hold her, to comfort her, to convince her she had nothing to fear, but the anger emanating from him made her pause.

"Jericho?"

His chest expanded as he inhaled, and an audible release of air followed. The tension in his neck dissipated. His fisted hands uncurled.

When he turned, the solicitous expression on his face eradicated the wall between them.

"I'm so sorry, darlin'. I—"

Hannah dove into his arms and burrowed into his chest. She clung to his waist, anchoring herself to his strength. As his arms enfolded her, the tears she had held at bay fell in earnest.

Why? Why would someone do such a thing? It cut her heart to ribbons. It wasn't so much the damage to her property but the hatred burning behind the act. What had she done to inspire such hostility?

She sank further into Jericho's embrace, her energy flagging as despondency took hold. Her knees wobbled, and Jericho scooped her up. He carried her to Ezra's bench and settled her in his lap.

Neither of them spoke, but his presence, his touch soaked into her soul like a balm on an open wound. Gradually her sobs slowed to occasional hiccups, and he fumbled for a handkerchief. While she dried her eyes and blew her nose, he untied her bonnet strings, set the hat aside, and tucked her head under his chin.

Hannah couldn't say how long they stayed that way, but when she finally raised her head, the sun was swimming on the edge of the horizon. Not quite able to meet Jericho's eyes yet, she stared at his chest. Dark blue splotches marred the sky-blue fabric of his shirt, soggy from her blubbering. She covered the largest spot with her hand. The warmth of his skin seeped through the wet cloth, his heart thumping a steady beat. A beat that seemed to accelerate.

"I'm sorry I wept all over you. I made quite a mess of your shirt." She made to remove her hand, but Jericho covered it with his own and held it in place. Hannah slowly tilted her chin to meet his gaze.

"Are you all right?"

She nodded. "Yes. Thank you. I feel much better." Suddenly shy and uncomfortable, Hannah slid off his lap and stood on the boardwalk. Even her ankle felt sturdier. She plucked her bonnet off the bench but didn't put it back on. "I . . . I should change." She forced a false smile onto her face as Jericho rose to his feet. His eyes narrowed slightly, and she knew she hadn't fooled him. "That's why we're here, right?" she said brightly, as she stepped toward the stairs. "I'll just let you get back to your business while I . . ."

Her hand clutched the rail, but her feet refused to budge. Pulse jumping, mouth dry, Hannah eyed the stairs as if they were the teeth of some feral creature that would chomp into her leg the minute she set foot in its territory. She couldn't do it. What if the same person who ransacked her shop had been in her personal rooms, touching her things, violating her privacy?

Jericho came beside her in an instant. "I'll go up with you."

He took the first step and held out his hand. Taking a deep breath, she fit her palm to his and let him lead her all the way to the top.

The door loomed large, but Jericho faced it down, key in hand. He unlatched it, pushed the portal open, and stepped inside. He returned seconds later, a gentle smile curving his lips.

"Everything's still neat and tidy."

Thank you, Lord. Hannah swayed in relief and gripped the railing to her left as she steadied her shaking legs. After a moment, she stepped inside, her eyes scanning the room from wall to wall, searching for anything out of place. Jericho remained behind, giving her the privacy to explore on her own. Moving through the chamber, she fingered the cloth that covered her table, toyed with the spindles of the new chairs, traced the nickel-plated design on the stove, and ruffled the pleats on her ugly orange curtain.

Normal. Everything was blessedly, wonderfully normal.

"Put together a bag of clothes and whatever else you might need. You're staying with Delia tonight." His voice rumbled through her with a comforting authority.

Jericho's arrogant manner had irked her in the past, but hearing the tender concern behind his soft-spoken command made all the difference. He wasn't trying to dictate to her. He was trying to protect her. And she was only too eager to surrender. After all, she truly had no desire to stay in her room tonight. Alone. Vulnerable. Just a thin door standing between her and the person who wanted her gone. Suppressing a shiver, Hannah nodded and ducked behind the curtain to collect her things.

Later that evening after a light supper, J.T. sat at the kitchen table across from Delia and Hannah, drawing circles around the rim of his coffee cup.

"I can't believe it," Delia said once Hannah finished her tale. "We've never had vandals in Coventry. Do you think they were after your money?"

"I made a deposit yesterday, so there wasn't much in the till." Hannah glanced up at him and swallowed. He could sense her lingering unease, and it tore at his heart. More than anything, he wanted to take that from her, absorb it into himself if need be. He held her gaze, as if that limited connection could siphon off some her distress. And perhaps it had, for she sat a little straighter when she turned back to Delia. "I don't think the vandal was after money. I think he wanted to scare me. He left a note saying I should never have come here."

Delia gasped and set aside her tea to squeeze Hannah's hand. "How awful for you." She shook her head. "To think someone we know could do such a horrible thing. . . . Well, it . . . it defies belief." A thoughtful look crossed her face. "Do you have any idea who the culprit could have been?"

J.T. halted his cup halfway to his mouth at his sister's question. He'd been wanting to ask Hannah the very same thing ever since they got back to the house, but he'd not had the chance.

Hannah hesitated, her focus dancing from Delia to him and back again. "I can only think of one person who has ever treated me with any degree of hostility."

His cup clunked against the tabletop. "Who?"

"I . . . I have no proof it was him, of course."

J.T. pressed to his feet and leaned over the table. "Who?"

Hannah glanced back to Delia, then looked down at her cup. "Warren."

Delia made a little choking sound. "Warren Hawkins? Surely not. I've known him since we were kids."

J.T. gritted his teeth and pushed away from the table. He whirled toward the wall and gripped the edge of the cabinet that held Delia's baking supplies. Digging his fingers into the wood until his knuckles whitened, he struggled to master the rage that speared through him.

Warren. First he'd tried to force Delia into a match she didn't want, and now he'd taken out his anger on Hannah. The scoundrel needed someone to pound some sense into him. J.T.'s biceps twitched at the thought of fulfilling that duty.

"I'm sorry, Cordelia, but I can think of no one else." Hannah's quiet regret inflamed his need for justice. She was the last person who needed to apologize for anything.

When Delia finally responded, her voice broke, as if tears were near the surface. "It's because of me, isn't it?"

"No. Of course not," Hannah asserted, but when J.T. turned around, Delia was nodding.

"Yes. Yes it is. He blamed you for the changes he saw in me. He probably thought that if you hadn't come to Coventry, Ike would've never paid me any mind. When I refused his proposal, he struck out at you." Her lip trembled as tears rolled down her cheeks. "Oh, Hannah. Can you ever forgive me?"

Now they both were apologizing! A growl built in his throat, though he pressed his mouth into a thin line to keep it from escaping.

Hannah grabbed both of Delia's hands. "You've done nothing

wrong, Cordelia, and I won't have you thinking you did. We don't know for sure that Warren is the one who broke into my shop. But even if he was, you're not responsible. He made the choice to act shamefully, not you."

J.T.'s jaw ached from clamping it so tight. He hoped the Lord would keep Warren out of his path tonight, because he wasn't sure he would stop himself from pummeling the man. But Hannah was right. They needed proof.

"I don't recall seeing Warren at the picnic today. Did you see him, Delia?" He kept his tone as neutral as he could manage but apparently wasn't too successful, for Hannah's head spun toward him.

Delia sniffed a couple times, then met his eyes. "I don't think so. But he might have been avoiding me since I was with Ike. A conversation between us would have been awkward."

J.T. strode to the door and took his hat down from the peg. He fingered the brim for a moment and then set it on his head. "I'm going out for a while, but I'll be back."

Out of the corner of his eye, he saw Hannah rise and move toward him. "Jericho? What are you—?"

He didn't wait to hear the rest of the question. Without looking back, he stepped into the night and closed the door behind him.

CHAPTER 34

J.T. pounded on the back door of the mercantile. "Open up, Hawkins. I need a word with you." He waited a couple seconds and started pounding again.

"Yeah, yeah. I'm coming. Keep your boots on." The store owner cracked the door and peered out. "This better be an emergency. I don't do business after hours."

"This isn't business."

"Tucker?" Hawkins pulled the door wide. "What in the blue blazes are you doing hammerin' a hole in my door?"

The man had a napkin tucked into his shirt collar, and crumbs speckled his mustache. However, J.T. could summon little regret for disrupting his meal.

"Your boy home?"

"Nope. Took the train down to Temple this afternoon."

The Gulf, Colorado and Santa Fe didn't depart until around three o'clock, which left plenty of time for Warren to sabotage Hannah's shop before leaving town. A convenient arrangement.

"Thinking 'bout opening a second store there now that they're building up the place," Hawkins rambled. "Used to just be a bunch of railroad men thereabouts, but since they sold off town lots back in June, it's really growing. I tried to convince Warren to go several months back, but he weren't interested till recently."

Probably because of his spontaneous plan to marry Delia.

"When do you expect him home?"

The abrupt question put a halt to the storekeeper's chatter. He eyed J.T. with suspicion.

"A couple days. Why? You got a problem with him?"

J.T.'s lips tightened into a grim line. "Yes, sir. I do."

Hawkins yanked the napkin out from under his chin and tossed it aside. "Now, see here, Tucker. Warren told me about his plans to hitch up with your sister, and if you're thinking to try and scare him off with your high-handed ways, you can forget it." He advanced on J.T., poking him in the chest.

J.T. held his ground—and his temper. Barely.

"I thought you were above judging a person by his appearance," the storekeeper spat, "but you can't see past his birthmark, can you? You have no right to come to my house, interrupt my supper, and accuse my son of not being good enough for your sister. Get out of here."

The man's face had gone quite red, and veins popped out of his neck. He backed into the house and would've slammed the door in J.T.'s face had J.T. not shoved his foot into the opening.

Jaw clenched, J.T. grabbed the edge of the door and muscled it open until he could see Hawkins's eye. "I don't give a fig about Warren's face. It's his actions and attitude that I take exception to. Did he tell you that he sprung a proposal on Delia without a single act of courting? Did he mention that Delia turned him down? And did you happen to notice that instead of accepting her answer with gentlemanly grace, he blamed Miss Richards for his troubles, a woman innocent in this whole affair?"

Some of the color faded from the man's cheeks. "Cordelia turned him down? Warren said she wanted some time to consider his offer. I figured he was hoping to win her acceptance with the financial promise of the new store."

J.T. released the door and stepped back. "Look. I don't have any great love for your son, but Delia has considered him a friend since their school days. Out of respect for her, I wouldn't have come about Warren's actions, but the safety of someone I care about may be at stake." He paused a moment, an idea taking root. "Can I show you something? It won't take long."

Hawkins seemed to measure him with his eyes and finally gave a jerky nod. "Let me fetch my coat."

When he returned, J.T. led him to Hannah's shop. He still had her key, having forgotten to return it during the process of getting her settled.

"Why did you bring me here?" Hawkins asked as J.T. fit the key into the lock.

"You'll see." The door swung in, and J.T. entered, his boot heels click-clacking against the floorboards in a hollow rhythm that echoed eerily in the abandoned room. Hawkins followed. Sunset had come and gone, but the twilight of early evening sufficiently revealed the destruction amid the shadows.

J.T. wove through the maze of fabrics and notions, careful not to do any further damage as he made his way to the far wall, intent on collecting the paper ball resting in the corner.

"Was Miss Richards harmed?" Hawkins choked out the question.

J.T. didn't turn. "No. She discovered this mess when I escorted her home from the picnic this afternoon." And it had devastated her. J.T. could still feel the heat of her tears as she'd wept against his chest.

He gently lifted a length of blue cloth from the floor and draped it over the counter to clear a path and noticed Hannah's collection of fashion magazines and pattern books scattered over the counter's surface and the floor behind. Pages had been ripped from the bindings and showered like giant confetti. A cover from *Peterson's* lay beside the blue fabric. The fashionable woman on the cover seemed to glare at him in accusation.

How many times as a child had he wanted to do the same thing? To tear up his mother's magazines, to set them on fire, or sink them in the river? He'd blamed the world of fashion for stealing away his mother in the same way Warren had blamed Hannah for Cordelia's lack of interest. The reality hit him like a blow. It sickened him to think he shared anything in common with that worm. But it couldn't be denied. His hatred of fashion was just as irrational as Warren's hatred of Hannah. Deep down, he knew this. The truth had been growing in him over the last several weeks. Hadn't Christ taught that money itself was not evil, but the choice of men to love it, crave it, and make it their god was the sin that destroyed their souls? So it was with fancy clothes.

Pretty fabric and stylish designs held no innate power to corrupt. It was the sinful desires of the heart that turned one to vanity, condescension, or covetousness. If one could learn to manage his money without greed consuming him, surely a woman could do the same with clothing. Hannah lived out such balance every day, and now that he thought of it, so did many other women of the community.

His mother had been weak, and she'd made destructive choices. Yet with a child's loyalty, he'd been unable to place the responsibility on her shoulders. So he'd blamed the clothes, the man who'd taken her away, and even his father for not fulfilling her needs. He'd thought his growing love for Hannah had erased his prejudice, but with a flash of insight, he realized he'd never be completely free until he let go of the final weight dragging on him.

J.T.'s hand shook as he reached for the magazine cover and smoothed out the bent corner.

Mama, you were wrong and you hurt me. But . . . I forgive you.

His eyes slid closed as a gentle lightness enveloped his soul. For a moment he even forgot where he was and what he was doing. That is, until Hawkins shuffled up behind him.

"My heart goes out to the poor gal," he said. "She's a good customer. Always goes out of her way to be kind and include the mercantile in her business. I'm sorry this happened to her, but I don't see what this has to do with me or my son."

J.T. snapped back to the present. The hunger for justice still growled to be fed, but the anger that had previously accompanied it had cooled considerably. He sidestepped an overturned display dummy and reached for the wad of paper he sought.

"Miss Richards was reluctant to voice her thoughts when we asked her if she had any idea who could have done this. She had no proof of a specific person's involvement, but she did mention one name—a man who had treated her with disdain in recent days." Taking care not to tear the crumpled paper, J.T. opened the ball and pressed it against his thigh to iron out the creases.

Hawkins blew out an impatient breath. "Come on, Tucker. This was probably just a bunch of kids getting into mischief while everyone was away at the picnic. Boys do stuff like this all the time. It's not some personal vendetta."

"That's where you're wrong." J.T. handed him the note. "Do you recognize the handwriting?"

The storekeeper stared at it, and his hand trembled just enough to rustle the paper. "It's . . . uh . . . hard to tell, what with all the wrinkles on the page and the dim lighting." But there was a nervous edge to his voice that confirmed J.T.'s suspicions.

"I think we can safely conclude this wasn't a prank, don't you think?"

Hawkins pushed the paper back at J.T. as if it pained him to touch it. "The note does seem to . . . uh . . . indicate a more personal agenda. But the woman wasn't hurt. No lasting damage done." He looked frantically around the room as if in search of something to validate his desperate words. "The sewing cabinet is intact, the windows unbroken. A true criminal would not have spared those. And really, this is nothing more serious than a large mess. It can be cleaned up, most of the material salvaged. It could have been much worse."

J.T.'s temper sparked anew. "You didn't see her face when she walked through the door. You didn't hold her while she sobbed or feel her tremors as her heart broke. You didn't taste her fear when she faced the staircase, terrified that a similar violation had occurred in her personal quarters. Who's to say the man who did this will stop at one attack? How is she ever to feel safe?"

Hawkins backed away, sputtering excuses.

J.T. trailed him and held the note up in front of his face. "Hannah named Warren as the man who has been acting embittered toward her, blaming her for Delia's rejection of his suit." He set his mouth close to the other man's ear. "Is this your son's writing?"

"I . . . I can't be sure."

J.T. folded the paper into a small rectangle and stuffed it into the man's coat pocket. "Take it home. Examine it in better light. Compare it to an inventory list or something that Warren has written. Take care of this matter with your son, Hawkins. Because if you don't, I will."

CHAPTER 35

Hannah stood in Cordelia's kitchen after church the next day, drying the dishes while her mind wandered to the shop. Although shivers coursed through her at the prospect, she needed to spend the afternoon sorting through the debris to see what she could salvage. As tempting as it was to take refuge among friends and let Jericho watch over her, she couldn't allow fear to dictate her actions. Or lack of action, as the case may be.

"Thank you for letting me stay here last night," Hannah said as she reached for the platter Cordelia held out to her.

Cordelia laid a damp hand on her arm, and the warm moisture soaked through Hannah's sleeve. "You can stay here as long as you like."

Hannah shrugged. "Jericho said that Warren would be out of town until Tuesday, so there's no reason to impose on you any longer."

"You're not an imposition. How could you be? You're practically family."

A little thrill shot through Hannah at Cordelia's words, but she couldn't let them sway her. She needed to move forward.

Founders' Day had been a rousing success in showcasing Cordelia's new style and Hannah's design skills. In fact, several women had spoken to her about dressmaking projects that morning after services. Retreat now would destroy the momentum she had gained yesterday. And worse, it would mean giving Warren or whomever was responsible for vandalizing her shop exactly what he wanted.

Hannah inhaled a fortifying breath and rubbed the dishtowel along the decorated edge of the oval dish. She stared at the tiny blue flowers instead of the sympathetic eyes of her friend, afraid that the warm acceptance in their depths would erode her determination. "I appreciate all you and Jericho have done for me. Truly. But I can't hide here. The longer I stay away, the harder it will be to return." Hannah set the platter on the table and reached for the dripping pan.

Cordelia released the pan, her mouth flattening into a tight line as she shoved a greasy pot into the dishwater. Her elbows wagged as she scoured it with enough vigor to rub a hole through the bottom. "I wish this whole mess with Warren had never started. You've done nothing to deserve such vile treatment."

Guilt lingered behind her friend's frustration, and Hannah rushed to dispel it. "Don't worry about me," she said with a grin and a playful bump to Cordelia's flapping elbow. "I'll be too busy catering to all my new customers to think about anything else. Besides, maybe the vandalism will draw extra attention to the shop, and God will turn something Warren meant for harm into a blessing. All I need is an afternoon to tidy things up a bit, and I'll be back in business. Better than before. You'll see."

An answering smile eased across Cordelia's lips. She lifted the scrubbed pot out of the water and started to extend it to Hannah, but stopped and slipped it back into the dishpan. "Why don't you take J.T. his lunch since he rushed off in such a hurry today? Then, as soon as

I finish cleaning the roasting pan and set my bread dough to rise for Monday's loaves, I'll come lend a hand."

"Perfect." Hannah draped the dishtowel over Cordelia's shoulder and untied the borrowed apron from around her waist. Having help would greatly lighten the work, but more than that, it would give her company. Despite her brave talk, she really didn't want to be alone in the shop. Not if she didn't have to be. She trusted the Lord to answer her prayers for courage, but in the meantime, a friend to share the load would be a blessing indeed.

Hannah collected the basket Cordelia had set aside for her brother and headed for the livery. She'd thought Jericho had been acting strange when he rushed off after seeing them home, but Cordelia had assured her that he often had to tend to his animals and rigs after services since several townspeople rented them for the drive to church.

Still, a little niggle of disquiet picked at her. He'd been so hard to read last night, coming in from his undisclosed outing with no more to say than that he'd talked to Mr. Hawkins and Warren would be out of town until Tuesday. Then he'd urged her to get some sleep, which had been nearly impossible, what with his pacing in the kitchen like a soldier on patrol. By the time his boots finally fell silent, Hannah had been ready to tie him up herself.

He'd been solicitous that morning, though, watching for Ezra at her request and notifying the older man that she would attend services with the Tuckers. Jericho's solid presence beside her held her fears at bay and allowed her to focus more clearly on worship. But then he'd ushered them back to the house only to leave them the minute their feet hit the porch. The abruptness of it all had left her feeling shuffled and dumped and more than a little confused.

Did Jericho regret becoming involved with her? Hannah's stride faltered at the thought. Perhaps all the trouble with the shop reinforced his previous view that her profession was a stumbling block—not only to women, but now to him. After all, he was being dragged into something that undoubtedly put him at odds with men he considered friends and business associates.

What could she do to make it up to him? Close the shop? A swift, stabbing pain speared her side and brought her to a halt at the edge of the livery stable. Could she do that? Sacrifice her dream in order to share a life with the man she loved?

Hannah swallowed hard. She visualized herself in a flourishing dress shop, a full-grown Tessa working by her side. Happy clients. A sizable bank account. Yet she'd go upstairs to an empty room every night. No strong arms to embrace her and soothe away her hurts, no tender kisses to make her heart sing, no one to tease and to be teased by in return. Without Jericho, success would be hollow. Could she give it up? Yes . . . if she knew he loved her in return, she could. But did he?

A moan vibrated in her throat. Why did everything have to be so complicated?

A verse floated through her mind about not taking thought for tomorrow since today carried sufficient trouble unto itself. Her lips twisted into a wry grin. The Lord could not have sent her a more apt reminder. Hannah straightened her spine. She'd deal with today's problems and leave tomorrow in God's hands. That's where it belonged anyway.

Stepping into the dim interior of the stable, Hannah paused as her eyes adjusted to the lack of sunlight. The pungent smells of manure and old hay wrinkled her nose, but she made no effort to block the odor with her handkerchief. She needed to get used to it if she hoped to be a livery owner's wife.

A movement near one of the middle stalls caught her eye. "Jericho?" She started forward.

"Nope. Just me." Tom turned, a grin stretching wide over his teeth. "Oh, and Mr. Culpepper."

"Ezra?"

The older man emerged from inside the stall.

"What are you doing here?"

"That you, Miz Hannah?" He shuffled closer and heaved a sigh. "Old Jackson threw a shoe. With the smithy closed on Sundays, I convinced young Tom to let me stable him here until tomorrow. I'll rent a horse to take me and the buggy home, then return it when I come to the depot in the morning. Don't want Jackson going lame trudging up to my place without a shoe."

"Of course not."

"I am glad I ran into you, though." Ezra winked at her as he moved past, heading for his buggy. "I brung you something."

Hannah followed him, her curiosity piqued. "You did?" A tiny thrill of excitement coursed through her at the prospect until a more logical explanation came to mind. "Do you have more mending that needs to be done?"

Ezra's laugh boomed through the stable, eliciting an answering bray from old Jackson. "Now, why would I bring you mending on the Lord's Day, Miz Hannah?" He shook his head as he reached to retrieve a small paper-wrapped parcel from the seat cushion. "Nah. I brung you a gift." He presented it to her with a gleam in his eye.

"I meant to give it to you when I picked you up for services this mornin', but you'd already made plans to trade in my company for that Tucker fellow."

The parcel sat heavy in her hand, but she ignored it, worried that she had truly hurt the man's feelings. "Oh, Ezra. It wasn't like that at all. I just—"

His chuckle cut short her apology. "No. No. I'm just giving you a hard time. A gal as purty as you deserves to be courted by a young buck. Besides, I seen the way he looks at you. Reminds me of when I was courtin' my Alice."

Warmth crept into Hannah's cheeks, and not knowing what to say, she dipped her head to examine the gift her friend had given her. The brown paper crinkled as she unfolded it. She lifted one side, and a small silver cylinder rolled into her hand. The needle case was delicately tooled with a leaf pattern that flowed up the side and over the pull-off lid.

"This is beautiful." Her hushed voice echoed a reverent tone as she drank in the loveliness of the silver case. "But it's too much. I can't accept it." She tried to hand it back, but Ezra took her hand and folded her fingers back over her palm, trapping the gift inside.

"Alice would want you to have it."

Tears welled in Hannah's eyes. He was giving her something of Alice's?

A wistful look passed over Ezra's face. "I decided to finally go through her things. The day after you paid me a call, as a matter of fact. I figure on giving most of her clothes to the poor box at church . . . since I ain't never gonna wear 'em." He winked at Hannah and she smiled, thanking God for how far this grieving man had come. "And I'll prob'ly send a box of stuff back to her sister in St. Louis. But when I saw this here case, I knew you were the one who had to have it.

"Alice would have liked you, Miz Hannah. And she would've appreciated what you done for me. Maybe having something of hers will help you feel like you know her even though you two never met."

Hannah bent forward and touched a kiss to Ezra's cheek, right above his whiskers. "I feel as if I already know her—through you." She stepped back and held the needle case to her heart. "Thank you, Ezra. I will treasure this."

Tom brought out a horse and started hitching it to the buggy. As he adjusted the collar, he shot a questioning glance at Hannah. "You lookin' for J.T.?"

"Yes," she said, stepping back to give him room to work. "I brought him some lunch. Is he here?"

"Nope. Ain't seen him since church."

"That's odd. He said he had business to take care of." Something twinged in her stomach. Had he manufactured an excuse to get away from her? Surely not. Jericho was an honorable man. But why . . . ?

For heaven's sake. All this negative thinking was getting her nowhere. She'd just received a lovely gift from a dear friend. She had no cause to feel morose. Careful not to drop the precious needle case, Hannah slipped it into her skirt pocket and patted it against her side. Such a thoughtful gift, equally as thoughtful as . . . her chairs.

"Ezra?"

The man had moved away from her to help Tom buckle all the necessary straps. Upon hearing his name, though, he turned.

Hannah smiled to cover her discomfiture over the question she was about to ask. "Did you by chance leave another gift for me on my landing? I only ask because I found a pair of oak dining chairs there with no note or other clue as to who they were from. With all your woodworking, I thought maybe they were from you."

Ezra scratched his beard. "No. Can't say they were. They just showed up?"

"Yes. I'd like to thank whomever is responsible. If I can determine who that person is."

Tom worked his way down the horse's back, checking the harness. "Mighta been J.T."

Hannah's heart gave a little leap. "You think Jericho left me the chairs?"

Tom shrugged. "Don't know fer sure. He bought a couple from the junkman a couple weeks back, though, and I saw him working on 'em in the corner over there a few times." He pointed to a recess hidden by buggies and buckboards. "They aren't there now."

"I knew that boy was smitten," Ezra murmured just loud enough for Hannah to hear.

She stared at the empty corner, a grin breaking free across her face. Cordelia had warned her that Jericho didn't handle gratitude well. That's probably why he hadn't said anything. But he best prepare himself. The next time she saw him, she was going to bombard him with thanks. In fact, she thought as she glanced down at the lunch basket still slung over her arm, maybe she could finagle a meeting in the next hour or so.

"I need to be going, gentlemen." She eased her way toward the livery door. "Tom, if you happen to see Mr. Tucker, tell him I have his lunch. He can stop by the dress shop whenever he wishes to claim it."

Tom yelled an "okay" to her back as she bustled across the street. She smiled, both at Tom's limitless exuberance and at the warmth that radiated through her at the thought of Jericho's painstaking attentions on her behalf.

As she neared her shop, though, her step faltered. Beyond the display window, a dark figure was roaming about inside. Had they been wrong to assume Warren's guilt?

Whoever he was, the person inside had no right to be in her shop. Indignation swept over her like a prairie fire. Hannah jutted out her chin and stalked forward. The vandal had escaped detection last time, but not today. Nothing was going to stop her from uncovering his identity.

Caution kept her boldness in check as she concealed her body behind the wall that stretched between the two shop windows. It wouldn't do to have the villain catch sight of her and flee before she figured out who he was. Balancing one hand on the back of Ezra's bench, she pressed the other to the glass. She squinted against the reflective glare and leaned in until her forehead rested against the curve of her fingers. The shadowy figure finally took shape. Her heart pounded in anticipated victory. Then he turned, and Hannah gasped.

CHAPTER 36

Tears burned the back of Hannah's eyes. Jericho stood in the middle of her shop, flower-sprigged fabric tangled around his torso. Having pivoted too quickly, he teetered while trying to avoid stepping on a coil of lace that lay directly under his raised boot. He managed to regain his footing, but almost took a tumble in the process. A muted laugh puffed out of her at the same time a tear fell from her lashes. Her rugged liveryman was draped in pink calico.

Jericho Tucker, a self-proclaimed despiser of fashion, flounces, and frills, was chin deep in feminine trappings. All for her.

Hannah sank onto the bench, her legs suddenly too weak to support her weight. Jericho's actions had always spoken more eloquently than his words, and at this moment, the message could not be clearer. He loved her.

J.T. lopped off the soiled section of fabric with a pair of Hannah's shears and finally freed himself from the ridiculous pink cocoon that nearly felled him. He folded the cloth over his arm, its raggedly cut end leaving pink strings stuck to his sleeve. He brushed at them, but they held firm. Rolling his eyes, he let them be and continued working. Once he had the material folded into a shape that loosely resembled a square, he slapped it on top of the four others already piled on the counter.

As he reached for the bit of lace near his boot, he glanced over the room. He'd wanted to have most of the mess cleaned up before she arrived, but not knowing where things belonged or even what half of them were had slowed him down. He was tempted to fetch a pitchfork and muck the place out like one of his stalls, but he supposed Hannah wouldn't appreciate that type of efficiency.

The creak of door hinges brought his head up.

"You're a hard man to find." Hannah strode into the shop, letting the door close behind her. She raised an arm toward him and revealed a basket. "I brought you some lunch."

"Thanks." J.T. straightened and tossed the bit of lace in his hand onto the counter. An unexpected awkwardness closed off his throat. She probably expected some kind of explanation for his furtive behavior, but his tongue felt about three feet thick. He doubted anything intelligible would make it out of his mouth even if he tried.

It wasn't like he hadn't expected her to show up at some point, but something about the way she was looking at him made his breath shallow and his pulse accelerated. Beyond affection, beyond desire, a new light glowed in the depths of her eyes, one that seemed to penetrate the core of his soul and lay bare his secrets.

Setting the basket on the counter, she sauntered toward him, the intensity of her gaze unrelenting. He cleared his throat and took a step back, but Hannah didn't let him retreat. Like a mesmerist, she held him enthralled. He couldn't have moved if he wanted to. Which he didn't. She reached up and stroked his jaw, freeing the small muscle beneath her fingers to twitch. Then she braced her hands on his shoulders and rose up on her tiptoes. The lashes framing those fathomless blue eyes fluttered closed, and her lips brushed against his. The feathery caress lingered only an instant, but his insides trembled. Closing his own eyes, he savored the velvety touch.

"I love you, Jericho Tucker."

For a moment he forgot how to breathe.

What miracle had led him to this woman?

He opened his eyes to find hers shining up at him with a love so real even his carefully cultivated cynicism could not deny its existence. At first, he was so humbled by the sight, he could do nothing more than drink it in. Then joy and possessiveness like he'd never known exploded in his chest. Pulling her to him, J.T. claimed her mouth. His hands slid up her back, pressing her close. She leaned into him and raised up on her toes as she returned his kiss. The taste of her lips tantalized him, stirring a craving that begged a lifetime to explore.

After a moment, Hannah slid back down to her flat feet. J.T. followed, caressing her cheek with the pad of his thumb, his forehead bent to hers. She inhaled a shaky breath and then stepped back. Reluctantly, he let her go. She bit her lip and turned toward the counter, pressing her palms into the wood. A long tress of golden hair had fallen from the knot he had thoroughly mussed. Hunkering down, he retrieved two hairpins from the floor, then stood and moved behind her.

"Here," he mumbled, setting the pins on the counter next to her left hand. "Sorry. Your ... uh ... hair ..." He was stammering like an idiot. Yet she smiled at him anyway, a tinge of pink dusting her face.

"Thank you." She gathered the pins and edged around the counter, heading for the dressing room. He watched her until she disappeared behind the wall. Then he leaned against the counter and blew out a harsh breath.

He should have said something. Told her what was in his heart or at least spouted some romantic nonsense that women put such stock in. But no, he'd just stood there, mute as a fence post as she'd spoken the words he'd ached an eternity to hear.

"It looks like the fitting room escaped unscathed." Hannah emerged from the back, her hair once again pinned up properly, although she dropped her bonnet on the worktable as she walked by. She smiled, but her gaze shied away from his as she drew closer. "The mirror's intact and the skirt panels I'd been piecing together on the tailoring dummy are undisturbed."

"That's good." He couldn't seem to look anywhere but her mouth. Her lips were moist, as if she'd just licked them, and all he could think about was tasting them again. Just one kiss. One . . .

J.T. snatched a toothpick out of his shirt pocket and shoved it between his teeth. There. He couldn't kiss her now without impaling her. Surely that would help him hold on to his common sense. All they needed was for someone to walk into the shop and catch them in an embrace like that last one. Not likely with everything closed on Sunday, but he couldn't afford to take that chance. Hannah's reputation would be shredded. J.T. chomped down hard and prayed for restraint.

They set to work, Hannah organizing all the smaller items that had been dumped out of her sewing cabinet, and J.T. continuing his self-assigned task of separating the blemished fabric from the salvageable. Cordelia arrived a short time later, and within a couple of hours, the three of them had the place back in order.

After a cold supper of chopped ham sandwiches at the Tucker house, J.T. and Cordelia tried to convince Hannah to stay at their house another night, but she insisted on returning to her own place. So J.T. escorted her home, carrying her bag as they strolled down the quiet street.

When they passed the livery, Hannah peeked up at him, an impish sparkle in her eye. "Thank you for the chairs."

His brow furrowed. "What chairs?"

She giggled. "The ones you left on my landing."

J.T. halted in the middle of the street. "How did you—"

"Don't worry." She spun around in front of him and he could see laughter in her face. "I won't tell anyone that you're really a sweet, caring man underneath all those frowns."

"Good. A man has his reputation to consider," he grouched, forcing his features into a scowl when what they wanted to do was grin. "That'd be almost as bad as you trying to hang curtains in my livery."

Her eyes danced. "What a lovely idea! Why, that pink calico you wrapped yourself in earlier today would be just the thing."

J.T. growled and lunged for her. With a sound that was half giggle, half squeal, Hannah darted out of his reach. But not for long. He chased her down and captured her waist in the crook of his arm. She pivoted to face him, her joy stealing his breath with its beauty. Unable to help himself, he dropped a quick kiss on her forehead before recalling they were in the middle of the street. Quirking a half grin, he tugged her forward. "Come on. Let's get you home."

When they reached the staircase, she didn't hesitate to make the climb. He took that as a good sign that her fear had receded. When they reached the small landing at the top, she pushed her key into the lock and turned to face him.

"Thank you, Jericho. For being there when I needed you yesterday, for helping with the shop, for everything."

Uncomfortable with her gratitude, he ducked his head so the brim of his hat shielded his face from her, using the excuse of setting her bag down to justify bypassing her earnest expression. He mumbled something that he hoped would pass for a reply, while all the time his heart was pumping faster and faster under his ribs.

He'd intended to tell her how he felt when they got here. To the top of the steps. It was the perfect time. They were alone. The fading light softened the surroundings. He'd even spent the better part of the afternoon rehashing the words he could say. Not that he'd come up with anything good enough, but that didn't matter. She deserved the words. Even if he mangled them in the process.

So sure he could say them this time, he looked into her face. And froze.

She waited.

Nothing came.

A sick sensation swirled in his gut. He wanted to tell her, he just . . . couldn't.

If he spoke of his feelings, there would be no going back. What was left of his defenses would be stripped bare, leaving him completely vulnerable.

Like his father.

J.T. stared at her, willing her to read the apology in his eyes. Her smile never dimmed, but her shoulders dipped slightly—and that tiny show of disappointment knifed through him.

What is wrong with me? He'd fight a rabid cougar with his bare hands to protect this woman but he couldn't spit out a handful of love words. It was pathetic.

Angry at himself, he turned away and coughed to loosen his throat. "I'll be sleeping at the livery until we get things settled with Warren. I don't expect trouble, but I wanted you to know I'd be close at hand should you need anything."

"Thank you."

Out of the corner of his eye, he saw her stoop to collect her bag. Then the sound of the door unlatching clicked loud in his ears.

Panic clawed at him. *Say something!*

He spun around and grabbed her arm. "Hannah, I . . ."

She came to him easily, too easily. Instead of forcing the words he needed to say past his lips, he pulled her into his embrace, tucking her head into the hollow between his shoulder and his chest. A perfect fit.

J.T. tightened his hold, trying to communicate through his arms what his mouth was unable to say. But then Hannah patted his chest near where her head lay, and her quiet voice drizzled over him like honey.

"It's all right, Jericho. I can hear your heart."

And he got the strangest feeling that she could.

CHAPTER 37

Over the next few days, business poured into Hannah's shop, and she gladly welcomed the distraction. Whether the client wanted a simple alteration, an old dress remade into a more current style, or a completely new, custom-designed ensemble, Hannah gave each woman her utmost attention and courtesy. She planned to prove to the women of Coventry that she could be trusted with their fashion needs and exceed their expectations by completing the promised items ahead of schedule and with impeccable quality.

Needless to say, when she finally dragged herself up the stairs each evening, she barely managed to keep her eyes open long enough to eat a cold biscuit and wash her face before collapsing into bed. A soft lantern glow from the livery's office across the street filtered through her window to warm her room and her heart as she eased into slumber. True to his word, Jericho was watching over her.

When she awoke on Thursday morning, her eyelids felt like sandpaper as they scraped open. She'd stayed in the shop until after midnight trying to piece together the perfect bodice for the eldest of Mrs.

Paxton's daughters. This was to be the girl's first dress with long skirts, a gift for her sixteenth birthday.

By angling the pattern pieces in a judicious manner, Hannah recovered enough undamaged material from the length of trampled pink calico to cut several usable panels. However, necessity demanded smaller than normal seam allowances in order to avoid the soiled sections. This made assembly more difficult. She'd had to rip out one seam five times before everything finally lay just right.

Unwilling to quit until she'd accomplished her task last night, Hannah was now paying the price for her obsession. Not even a splash of cold water could enliven her wan complexion or remove the lavender circles from under her eyes. Maybe a brisk walk would add some color to her cheeks. She didn't want to meet her customers, or worse, Jericho, looking as if she belonged in a box at the undertaker's.

Lacing up her low-heeled boots, she thanked the Lord for the blessing of many clients, reminding herself that the added work *was* a blessing, and asked for sufficient energy to meet the demands of the day. Then after a few calisthenic exercises to animate her muscles, she headed outside.

And found Jericho sitting on her steps.

He stood, took one look at her face, and scowled so darkly she would have flinched had she the energy to spare.

"You look terrible."

Hannah sighed. "Just what every girl dreams of hearing from her beau."

Unfortunately the sarcasm bounced right off him without leaving so much as a dent. He took her arm and helped her down the rest of the stairs as if she were an invalid, frowning all the while. "You didn't put out your light until the wee hours last night. You're working too hard."

"I'm fine, Jericho." At the bottom step, Hannah tugged her arm free. "I know my limits. You don't have to worry about me."

"But I do anyway," he muttered, letting her go.

Touched by his concern yet irritated at the same time by his over-bearing manner, Hannah edged away from him. It didn't matter that he was right. She was too tired to guard her words, and if he started lecturing her, she'd probably say something she'd regret. That surely wouldn't aid her in getting him to admit his feelings. No, best to retreat before swords were drawn.

Hannah gave her best imitation of a perky smile, despite the fact that the corners of her mouth seemed to weigh fifty pounds each, and threw some spring into her step as she strode toward the outskirts of town. After a few steps, she turned to wave farewell. "My morning walk will put everything to rights. You'll see."

And it did, for a while. But by midafternoon, she found herself repeatedly snapping her neck up after nodding off at her sewing machine. The first three times, she shook her head and set back to work. The fourth time, she got up and paced the length of her shop. Twice. The fifth time, however, she stopped caring and laid her head in the crook of her arm, willing to let sleep claim the victory.

Thankfully, she wasn't so far gone that she failed to hear the door as it swung open on its unoiled hinges. Bolting upright in her seat, she swiped at her eyes to remove any sleep residue lurking there and fluffed the peacock blue fabric pooled in her lap, hoping she looked industrious instead of like someone who'd just been caught napping.

"I'll be right with you," she called.

"It's just me." Cordelia's familiar voice filled the room.

Hannah sagged in relief.

"I came to invite you to supper." Her friend sauntered behind the counter and leaned against it as Hannah set the blue fabric aside and rose to meet her.

A quiet dinner with friends sounded heavenly, but she really needed to finish this alteration so she could get back to work on the Paxton dress. And with all her little dozes, the chance of finishing by supper-time was rather remote.

"I would love to come, but I've got so much to do here. Perhaps one day next week when things slow down again?"

"J.T. said you'd be stubborn about this."

Hannah bristled. "Did your brother put you up to this? For pity's sake, Cordelia, I'm a grown woman. I don't need someone to tell me when to eat, when to sleep, when to—"

An ill-timed yawn interrupted her diatribe. Hannah hid her gaping mouth behind her hand and glowered at Cordelia as if it were somehow her fault.

Cordelia just smiled. "J.T. did volunteer to forcibly remove you from the shop if you refused to come, but I assured him such tactics wouldn't be necessary. After all, you're a sensible woman who can recognize the signs of having pushed yourself too far. Say . . . falling asleep in the middle of a sewing project?"

The smug look on Cordelia's face was really quite annoying. Hannah crossed her arms over her chest, not yet willing to concede the point.

"The truth is, when J.T. suggested you come for supper, I leapt at the chance. Not just because I enjoy your company, but because I could use your help." Cordelia's smugness disappeared behind a pleading expression, one that was much more difficult for Hannah to dismiss.

Hannah's arms flopped to her sides. "What kind of help?"

"Ike's coming to dinner, too. And I'm afraid J.T. will hound him with questions about his intentions and so forth. The poor man will probably never want to have dinner with me again."

"Nonsense," Hannah declared. "If it means spending time with you, a little verbal sparring won't keep him away."

"But if you were there to distract J.T., our time together could be so much more pleasant. Please?"

Hannah rolled her eyes to the ceiling and sighed. "Oh, all right. I'll come."

Cordelia beamed. "Thank you!" She practically skipped to the door. "Oh, by the way, we're having beef roast with potatoes, carrots, and onions; cornbread; cabbage salad; baked tomatoes; and fresh apple pie. Ike's favorites."

Hannah had always supposed Ike was a man of good taste, and this confirmed it. Her mouth was already watering. She hadn't taken the time to cook a decent meal for herself all week. She'd fried up a little bacon yesterday and nibbled on some boiled eggs at noon, but beyond that, her diet had been sadly lacking. Maybe she did need a break.

When closing time arrived, she set aside the alteration project with two feet of the hem left to sew. Her fingers itched to complete the task before leaving for the day, but thoughts of Cordelia's roast set her stomach to growling, and the sound drowned out the siren call of the unfinished project.

Wanting to make a better impression on Jericho at supper than she had that morning, Hannah closed the shop and rushed upstairs to tidy her appearance. She couldn't do much to disguise the shadowy circles under her eyes, but she could change into the blue dress he liked and twist her hair into a more fashionable chignon than the plain knot at the base of her skull now. After brushing and braiding, pinning and primping, Hannah surveyed the results in the small mirror above her washstand. Not perfect, but hopefully good enough to erase Jericho's scowl and keep the lectures at bay. As a final touch, she pinched her cheeks several times and then headed downstairs.

A cool breeze carrying the smell of rain drifted over her and drew her face toward the overcast sky. She closed her eyes and inhaled deeply. Her spirit absorbed the quiet, replenishing the peace that had been worn threadbare by busyness. In an effort to please her clients, she'd become consumed by work and forgotten the need to be still in the Lord's presence.

Forgive me.

Perhaps Jericho's arrival on her step had a divine purpose as well as a human one. A reminder to keep things in balance. If there was a time to be born and a time to die, a time to kill and a time to heal, surely there must be a time to work and a time to rest. Or better yet, eat.

With a grin, Hannah opened her eyes and set out across the road. An impromptu tune rose inside her, dancing a cheerful jig across the roof of her mouth and buzzing against her lips. Her fingertips tickled the wood siding of the livery as she passed, and her mind drifted to Jericho. Was there something she could do to make it easier for him to declare himself? She saw his love in his eyes and in his actions, yet some unseen barrier blocked the words.

Maybe it would help if she stopped calling him by the name he despised. She'd started calling him Jericho to irritate him, but now she considered it more of an endearment, a name only *she* called him. But what if he still hated it? Kindness would dictate she stop using it and defer to his preference—J.T. She doubted such a small gesture would free his tongue in and of itself, but it couldn't hurt. And tonight at dinner would be the perfect time to try it out. And again when he walked her home. Would he be so pleased that he'd kiss her again outside her door? She bit her lip to keep the tingling sensation in her chest from erupting in an embarrassing giggle. Not that anyone was around to hear. This end of town was quite deserted at suppertime.

She rounded the corner and the Tucker home came into sight. From a distance, she could make out Cordelia and Ike on the porch, laughing and talking. Her hand in his.

Hannah stopped before they could see her and scurried behind an oak tree several feet off the road. Cordelia would no doubt welcome her arrival with a smile, but Hannah suspected her friend would prefer a few more minutes alone with her suitor. She planned to give her just that.

A rustling in the brush to her right drew her attention from the happy couple. Before she had fully turned, though, a man lunged at her.

Hannah shrieked, but the man clamped a bony hand over her mouth and slammed her into the tree. The back of her head crashed against the unforgiving trunk. Pain ricocheted through her skull. Stunned from the blow, she offered little resistance as he pressed his forearm against her collarbone and trapped her legs with his weight. As pain receded, panic surged. She grabbed at the arm that imprisoned her and frantically twisted her head from side to side, wanting freedom, wanting away, wanting to deny that this was happening. Her nails dug into the man's wiry forearm. He hissed but did not lessen his hold.

"Be still or I'll cut you. Understand?"

Hannah stilled. She knew that voice.

The pressure at her neck lessened as her attacker lifted his arm to brandish a pocket-sized knife close to her left cheek. The fading light glimmered off the short silver blade. A frisson of fear slithered down her back. Yet it had more to do with the man than the weapon. Flaring her nostrils to take in as much air as possible above iron fingers that smelled of ink and onions, Hannah shifted her focus from the knife to the hardened face behind it. Small eyes brimmed with accusation. Overlong hair. Blotched skin growing redder and more pronounced as she stared.

Warren.

CHAPTER 38

As J.T. had prepared to leave the livery, one of the horses he'd been stabling for a traveler at the hotel began showing mild signs of colic. After lunging in the paddock for twenty minutes, the animal seemed some improved, and J.T. led him inside to a stall. He offered the sorrel a small handful of grain to see if he would eat, and when the gelding nuzzled it from his palm, J.T.'s spirits lifted. A truly colicky horse would have turned his nose up at the feed.

Stroking the sorrel's side, he backed out of the stall and handed the empty lead line to Tom. "Keep an eye on him till I get back. Don't give him anything to eat. He can have a little water but nothing else. Got it?"

"Yes, sir. No feed. Got it."

"And if he gets restless or tries to roll, come get me at the house, right away."

Tom nodded. "I'll watch him real close. I promise."

J.T. clapped the young man on the shoulder. "I know you will. You're a good liveryman, Tom."

The grin that split the boy's face was a mile wide and brighter than a full moon on a clear night. J.T. thumped him on the arm and left, confident the kid would keep a faithful vigil.

On his way out, he passed through his office to lock up. J.T. glanced at the clock on his desk as he shoved his ledger into the top drawer and frowned. He should've been home ten minutes ago. Cordelia would skin him alive if his tardiness caused Ike's meal to be less than perfect. Although the delay did afford him the opportunity to check on Hannah, kidnap her if necessary. If the woman couldn't see the wisdom in taking time to rest, he had no qualms about forcing a bit on her.

J.T. raised two fingers to his temple in a parting salute to Tom and jogged across the street to Hannah's shop. He peered through the window, checking to see if she was inside. When he didn't find her, he nodded to himself in satisfaction.

Good. The woman possessed some sense after all.

⁂

How could she have been so senseless? Hannah swallowed a moan. She'd been aware of Warren's return to town earlier in the week, but with her nose to the grindstone at the dress shop, she hadn't spared him more than a passing thought. Now she'd practically thrown herself into his path with her silly matchmaking efforts. There was no telling how long he'd been spying on Cordelia, stewing about her burgeoning relationship with Ike. His fuse was already lit, and she'd walked right into the explosion.

Defiance burned in his eyes as he bent his head close to hers. "Father's sending me away, you know." He spoke conversationally, as if they were passing time in the aisles of the mercantile. "Says it's time for me to stand on my own two feet and run a store of my own, but I think there's more to it than that." He pressed the flat edge of the knife against her cheek.

Hannah whimpered and shut her eyes, afraid to move as he trailed the cool metal downward. The pointed tip caught slightly on her skin as it reached the edge of her jaw. She squeezed her eyes tighter.

God, help me!

Warren laughed at her, a quiet little huff, but it was enough to goad her pride. Then, as if the Lord himself were speaking to her, a verse rang in her head. *"God hath not given us the spirit of fear; but of power."* It was time to tap into that power. She'd quivered enough for this little weasel. No more.

Hannah opened her eyes and glared at Warren. The snide grin on his face slipped for a moment, but he recovered quickly. He held the blade before her eyes as if inviting her to examine its sharpness, but when her eyes stayed fixed on him instead of the knife, his lips curled into a snarl.

"Cordelia should have been mine," he spat. "Ever since we were kids together, I knew we would marry. Then you swept into town with your fancy ways and started changing her. Changing everything."

Hannah shook her head, the bark of the tree scraping against her scalp. She mumbled a denial against his hand, but he ignored her.

Warren glanced at a spot beyond the tree—probably the Tuckers' porch—and his eyes softened. Sadness dulled the rage.

"She liked me," he said, an undeniable wistfulness in his voice. "*Me*. People always see the mark on my face, never me. But Cordelia was different. She looked me in the eyes when we talked. She brought me gifts and baked cookies on my birthday. She would've made me the perfect wife."

But you would've made her a terrible husband.

Warren pierced her with a glare as if he'd heard her thoughts. "You stole my future from me," he accused, his face mere inches from hers. "You dressed her up in showy clothes, made her do those ridiculous exercises until she no longer even resembled herself, and started throwing her at every available man in town."

If Hannah could've found a way to open her mouth, she would've bit him for that. How dare he describe Cordelia like some kind of hussy? And her like a madam in a bordello? Hannah scratched at his eyes. The fiend!

Warren jerked his head back and swore.

"Maybe you need to see what it's like to have people stare, to whisper behind their hands when you walk by." He brought the knife back up to her face, this time the sharpened edge pressed against her skin. She froze. Her eyes slid to the corners of her lids as she tried to monitor the threat. Would he really cut her? Hannah's heart throbbed, swollen with fear. She'd pushed him too far.

Her chest heaved, yet she struggled to draw sufficient air into her lungs with her mouth still covered and her nose suddenly too small for the job. Her vision began to blur. Through a sheen of tears, she refocused on Warren, pleading silently.

His wicked smile taunted her. "Just one slice is all it would take. Just a little pressure . . ."

The blade pricked her cheek near the corner of her left eye. Hannah winced. A drop of something warm trickled past her ear.

Warren's eyes rounded in horror. His grip loosened. "I . . . I'm sorry." He yanked the knife away from her face and stepped back, releasing her. "I only meant to scare you. I never intended to actually—"

A growl from behind him cut off his words as Jericho wrenched Warren away from her and flung him to the ground. The knife tumbled into the grass and leaves at Hannah's feet. She braced herself against the tree trunk, sucking in fresh, sweet-smelling air as tremors quivered through her limbs.

"You all right, Hannah?" Jericho called without taking his eyes off Warren.

"Yes." Her first attempt came out in a wisp of breath. She cleared her throat and said it again, stronger. "Yes. I'm fine." When she trusted her legs to support her, she bent to retrieve the knife in case Warren thought to use it on Jericho. With shaky hands, she folded it shut and slipped it into the pocket of her skirt.

"You need someone to take your frustrations out on, Hawkins? Try me." Jericho's low voice rumbled the challenge. Back on his feet, Warren crouched, apparently preparing to take Jericho up on his offer.

The two men paced in a circle, shooting each other wary glances as they moved deeper into the cover of the surrounding mesquite brush. Hannah guessed neither of them wanted to draw Cordelia's attention or Ike's interference. The house was a good fifty yards away, but if the couple happened to look up, the old oak would only block so much of their view. The denser brush would afford a more private place for the men to pummel each other.

Hannah followed, determined to keep an eye on Jericho as well as conceal her position from her friend. Cordelia had a tendency to blame herself for Warren's attacks. She didn't need guilt plaguing her tonight of all nights.

Despite his smaller size, Warren was the first to make a move. He launched himself at Jericho with surprising speed. Hannah bit back a cry as Jericho stood his ground and let the man come. Warren landed a blow to Jericho's midsection an instant before Jericho wrapped a muscled arm around his neck and tossed him aside.

Warren shook it off and charged again. This time Jericho side-stepped the assault and kicked out a leg to trip his opponent. Warren stumbled to a knee but jumped back to his feet. He spun around and made another pass. And met Jericho's fist with his belly. He doubled over with a moan.

"Are you done?" Jericho asked.

Although he was obviously no match for Jericho's strength and skill, Warren shook his head no.

Hannah cringed as the man slowly straightened and turned to face Jericho. Did he actually think he could win? Or was he welcoming the pain as some kind of punishment?

As much as she longed for justice after Warren's foul treatment of her, his repeated humiliation was becoming a torture to watch.

Warren staggered forward again, swinging his arms widely. Jericho struck a clean blow to the man's chin, felling him like a hewn tree. He lay still for a moment, then rolled to his stomach and pushed up to his hands and knees. Jericho gripped him under his arms and put him to his feet. Drooping and bent, he swayed sideways, but still managed to advance once again.

Jericho sighed.

Hannah couldn't take it anymore. Warren hadn't really meant to hurt her. The look of horror on his face when he realized what he'd done had proven that. It was an accident. One brought on by his idiotic refusal to accept that he couldn't have what he wanted, but an accident nonetheless.

"Catch him and hold him, Jericho. He's had enough."

Jericho did as she asked, swiveling the fellow around to trap his arms behind his back. He held him fast, and by the way Warren sagged, Hannah got the impression Jericho was holding him up more than pinning him down.

Hannah walked up to Warren, no longer compelled to demand justice but to offer mercy. "Go home, Warren," she said. "Start your new store. Leave all this bitterness behind and give yourself a fresh start. It's over."

Warren tugged his arms free and, with effort, managed to straighten to his full height. He made no further apology, yet something shone in his eyes she didn't remember seeing before. The seeds of a newfound maturity? She prayed it was so.

Jericho dusted the man's back, sending a shower of dirt and leaves to the ground. Then he moved to Hannah's side. "When do you leave, Warren?"

Warren stretched out his neck and looked Jericho in the eye. "Monday."

"I expect you to keep your distance. If I catch you anywhere near Miss Richards or my sister between now and then," Jericho growled in a voice laced with steel, "I'll wire the county sheriff and have you brought up on charges. Understand?"

"Yes."

"Good." Jericho jerked his chin in the direction of the road. "Now, get out of here."

As Warren trudged back to the road, Hannah nestled into Jericho's side. He wrapped his arm around her and hugged her tight as he watched Warren disappear around the corner. She buried her face in his shirt and breathed deeply, the scent and nearness of him soothing away the last of her agitation.

He pulled back slightly and placed a tender kiss on her forehead. Then he touched his lips to the cut below her eye. He pulled a handkerchief from his trouser pocket and held it to her face. "It doesn't seem too deep. I think it's already clotted. We can wash it up at the house."

"Do you think Cordelia will notice?"

"Probably, but that can't be helped."

Hannah sighed. "Well, let's get going, then. Cordelia's waiting on us." Hannah stepped out of his embrace and tugged on his arm when he didn't move fast enough for her. "Come on, Jer . . . I mean, J.T. I'm starving."

CHAPTER 39

"What did you just call me?" J.T. raised a brow and refused to budge. The words had come out more like an accusation than the simple question he'd intended. But then, that was probably due to the fact that his insides were still churning.

I could have lost her.

The image of that knife slicing into her cheek would haunt him for weeks. Years, maybe. It had taken all the self-control he possessed not to thrash Warren to a bloody pulp for putting his hands on her and accosting her with that blade. The man could have put out her eye or slipped and nicked a vein in her neck. The very idea made his blood run cold.

Hannah looked at the ground and kicked at a fallen acorn, the simple motion a reminder that she was safe. The danger had passed.

"I thought you preferred being called by your initials," she said.

"By everyone else, sure. But not you."

Her head snapped up. "Not me? Why?"

J.T. closed the small distance between them and cupped her jaw in his hand. He brushed his thumb over her lips, delighting in the breathy sigh that whispered past his knuckle. "There's something about the sound of my given name coming from you that makes me proud to own it."

A mist settled over the deep blue of her eyes, and the knot in his chest began to unravel. He slid his hand from her neck to her shoulder and gently massaged the muscles beneath his fingers. "Do you remember telling me that the name Jericho suited me?" He pulled a wry face. "I think you were trying to jab my pride at the time with a rather uncomplimentary comparison, but you were right. It does suit me. Or at least it has since the day I met you."

For once, Hannah seemed to be the one incapable of speech. She just stared at him, a cautious hope shimmering in her eyes. J.T. trailed his hand from her shoulder to her wrist and twined his fingers with hers. He'd not disappoint her. Not this time.

Glancing down at their joined hands, he cleared his throat. "I wanted to protect myself from making the same mistakes my father made. He let a beautiful woman into his heart only to have her tear it to shreds. I couldn't fall into the same trap. So I built a wall—a wall like the one that surrounded the city of Jericho in the Bible."

Her breath caught.

J.T. squeezed her hand and lifted his eyes to meet her love-filled gaze. "You were beautiful, fashionable, and independent—everything I considered a threat. Yet you laid siege to my heart anyway. You walked circles around me, Hannah, and somewhere along the way, that wall of mine crumbled, and you captured my heart."

He brought her hand to his mouth and pressed his lips to her knuckles. Her chest rose and fell between them, her breathing uneven. Slowly, he slipped his fingers free of hers, drawing out the touch as he watched her eyes darken. He cradled the sides of her face, the softness of her skin heaven in his hands.

"I love you, Hannah."

He touched his lips to hers in a delicate kiss, sealing his love chastely upon her. But as he drew back, the feisty, independent woman in his arms clasped his face with both hands and pulled his mouth back down to hers. Willingly surrendering his freedom, J.T. yielded to his captor, claiming victory himself as the taste of her filled him. He wrapped his arms around her and deepened the kiss. His mind, his heart were consumed with her as he gave all of himself, holding nothing back. She answered in equal measure, and a moan rose in Jericho's throat. He pressed her close, marveling at the way her soft curves conformed to the angles of his arms, the way her lips fit so perfectly against his, the way her love erased all his past hurts. She'd been tailor-made for him.

Slowly, he pulled away and watched as her light brown lashes fluttered open. Her mouth curved in a satisfied smile that warmed his blood.

"So you really don't mind if I call you Jericho?"

"Nope." He held up a cautionary hand. "On two conditions."

Hannah blinked up at him.

"First, you have to marry me. I can't let just anyone go around calling me Jericho, after all. Only family gets that privilege. Second—"

"Wait a minute." Hannah pressed her fingers against his lips to silence him. "Was that a proposal? Did Jericho Tucker, the man who disdains fashion and all its trappings, just ask a dressmaker to marry him?"

J.T. gazed into her beloved twilight eyes and shook his head. "No. Jericho Tucker, the man who thanks God every day for bringing beauty back into his life, is asking a dressmaker to marry him." He inhaled a shuddering breath and captured her hands between his own. "Will you, Hannah? Will you marry this grouchy old liveryman who loves you more than life itself?"

A radiant smile burst across her face as she nodded again and again. "Yes, Jericho. Oh, yes!"

Triumph and joy shot through him. With an exultant shout, he lifted her from the ground, her feet kicking back behind her. She laughed, and the sound sprinkled over him like a gentle summer rain, refreshing his soul. She was his. Really and truly his.

J.T. lowered Hannah until her toes touched the earth, and for a moment they just grinned at each other like a pair of empty-headed fools. A pair of very happy empty-headed fools.

"What's the second condition?" Hannah asked, finally breaking the silence.

J.T. squinted in confusion. "What?"

"I agreed to marry you. What else do I have to do in order to call you Jericho?"

Ah, yes. He'd nearly forgotten. Wrestling his smile into a more subdued, serious line, he placed his hand over his heart. "You must vow never to name any of our sons after Canaanite cities. I may have developed a new appreciation for *Jericho* in recent months, but no boy should be saddled with a name like Gezer or Eglon." His body convulsed in an exaggerated shudder.

Hannah's lip protruded in a delicious little mock pout. "Oh. But I had my heart set on naming our firstborn Megiddo."

A chuckle vibrated in J.T.'s chest as he steered Hannah back toward the road and the house he would soon share with her. Life with this vibrant woman was sure to be filled with rich colors, frequent laughter, and bountiful love. What could be more beautiful?

About the Author

KAREN WITEMEYER holds a master's degree in Psychology from Abilene Christian University and is a member of ACFW, RWA, and the Texas Coalition of Authors. She has published fiction in Focus on the Family's children's magazine, and has written several articles for online publications and anthologies. *A Tailor-Made Bride* is her first novel. Karen lives in Abilene, Texas, with her husband and three children.